JUL - - 2019

THE
SNAKES

THE
SNAKES

A NOVEL

Sadie Jones

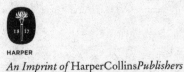

HARPER
An Imprint of HarperCollinsPublishers

THE SNAKES. Copyright © 2019 by Sadie Jones. All rights reserved. Printed in the United States of America. No part of this book may be used or reproduced in any manner whatsoever without written permission except in the case of brief quotations embodied in critical articles and reviews. For information address HarperCollins Publishers, 195 Broadway, New York, NY 10007.

HarperCollins books may be purchased for educational, business, or sales promotional use. For information, please email the Special Markets Department at SPsales@harpercollins.com.

First published in the United Kingdom in 2019 by Chatto & Windus, an imprint of Vintage

FIRST U.S. EDITION

Library of Congress Cataloging-in-Publication Data has been applied for.

ISBN 978-0-06-289702-2

19 20 21 22 23   LSC   10 9 8 7 6 5 4 3 2

For R.A.H.

All sins are attempts to fill voids.
Simone Weil

PART ONE

1

The night they decided to leave London Bea had a dream. Dreams are like silent films; guns are fired without shots, people talk without voices. This dream was deafening. The noise woke Bea up, shocked breathless, and terrified.

She didn't think she'd had the dream because they had decided to go away, it was more likely because of what had happened with the Italian leather holdall and the girl with the knife.

The holdall was made of dark red leather and looked too good for its surroundings. Bea had stopped walking when she saw it, in the window of the charity shop on the Holloway Road. It was lying beneath the long pleats of a nylon skirt on a headless mannequin, which had been styled with a pink jumper in a way that was supposed to be retro but was just old-lady. The red leather holdall was glamorous. It looked as though George Clooney had stopped by on his way to meet Julia Roberts at a little airfield somewhere, and forgotten it. Bea could see its quality but could not see its price. There were plastic-amber beads in the display, and some high heels and an enormous-looking evening dress, drooping on another mannequin. Bea shielded her eyes, her face close to the reflecting glass. Dan would love the holdall. It was stylish and cool. She went to the door. When she pushed, it moved, but didn't open. There were bags of donations piled against it on the inside, and a pair of jeans wedged between the rubber seal and the floor. Looking through the glass she could see a woman and a girl at the back of the shop, talking. The woman was behind the counter and the girl had one hand on a push-chair. It looked like they were arguing. Bea pushed the door harder and put her head through the gap.

'Excuse me,' she said.

Neither of them turned.

'Excuse me?' said Bea again. 'Hi.'

'Fuck off,' said the girl, still not turning.

Bea couldn't see them clearly. The air smelled musty and the street was very loud.

'It's all right!' called the woman at the counter, but she sounded frightened.

Bea looked at the passers-by on the pavement, hurrying, unnoticing, then she put her shoulder against the door and pushed it hard, and squeezed through the gap into the shop. The door closed behind her.

'Fuck off,' said the girl, turning round to face Bea. She was holding a knife.

It wasn't a fighting knife, it looked like a kitchen knife, and she didn't hold it out, just gripped it in her hand. Behind her, the woman opened her eyes wide in a mute distress signal.

'What do you want?' said the girl.

'Are you all right?' Bea asked.

The girl was tall, with long legs in skinny jeans and trainers that seemed too big for the rest of her.

4

'What are you doing? Go away,' she said. Bea thought she looked high. She was speedy and scattered.

The woman behind the counter walked backwards, silently, disappearing into the darkness of a doorway. Bea smiled at the girl to keep her attention. She had been crying. Her make-up was smudged and her skin was very white. She didn't look as if she knew she was holding a knife.

'I just wanted to ask how much that bag in the window is,' said Bea. 'The red one?'

The girl was confused, eyes darting from one place to another. She wiped her face and tucked her hair behind her ear.

'Sorry,' said Bea. 'You don't work here, do you?'

'I had to get out,' said the girl. 'Are you judging me? You don't even know me.'

'Can you put that away?' said Bea. 'It's scary. Do you mind? Can you put it in your bag?'

The girl looked down at the knife in her hand. She jabbed it at the empty air, and laughed. 'I'm sorry,' she said. 'It's not funny.'

Still holding on to the pushchair, she knelt down and shoved the kitchen knife in the clutter of her gaping bag. Bea could see the baby's feet sticking out but she couldn't see the rest of its body. She thought the woman must have called the police. She walked towards the girl.

'I'm on my lunch hour,' she said. 'I was just passing. Are you going to be OK?'

'What?' said the girl.

'Are you OK?'

'What's your name?' said the girl.

'Bea,' said Bea. 'What's yours?'

'Emma,' said the girl, 'and this is Thomas.' She nodded towards the baby.

'Like the Tank Engine,' said Bea.

The girl smiled. 'Yes.'

Bea took a few more steps, and leaned over to look into the pushchair. The baby was very young, very small. He was asleep. His hands were curled up by his head, his tiny fingers were as clean as freshly shelled peas. Then they heard sirens. Emma tensed and stared towards the sound. Then blue light flashed onto the walls as the police cars pulled up at the kerb. Two cars and a van. Doors opened and police got out in what looked like a crowd, dark, heavy clothes, pulling on caps and jackets, talking on their radios.

'Shit, shit, shit, shit, shit –' said Emma, and scrabbled back against the counter, weak-legged, grabbing at her bag and the pushchair pulling them towards her.

'I'm really sorry,' said Bea. 'It's OK.'

A policeman forced the door open, another peered in through the glass.

'I'm sorry,' said Bea again. Emma was backed up, crouching against the counter with the pushchair.

Bea went towards the policeman in the doorway, her hands open in front of her and said, 'I think a lady called you?'

'We had a report of a weapon,' he said, looking past her and seeing Emma.

'It's all right, she's not – dangerous,' said Bea completely sure, suddenly frightened. 'She's just in a mess –'

But then there were six policemen and a policewoman in the shop. Quickly, they closed in on Emma. They asked her where the knife was, and told her to keep still and asked about the knife again. They tried to separate her from the baby but she wouldn't let go of the pushchair. Panicking, surrounded, she seemed to dissolve in front of Bea's eyes, transforming from herself into an object. Bea backed slowly away towards the wall feeling sick with herself, and guilty. After a few minutes, a policeman came over and took her name and asked her what had happened, and then the woman who ran the shop came out from where she had been hiding, somewhere out the back, and gave them her details, while the girl, surrounded, began to fight.

'You bitch, you cunt,' she said, as the police took hold of her arms. They prised her hands off the pushchair. A policewoman bent to look inside.

'What's his name?' she asked

'Get off him,' said Emma, crying.

'I really don't think she was going to do anything,' said Bea to the policemen, but nobody was listening.

They took Emma out into the street, three of them holding her, having to drag her with them.

'Don't worry about it. We know her,' one of the policemen said to Bea, smiling. 'She's always around here.'

'Is there anything I can do?' said Bea. 'I work in psycho-therapy, just down the road.'

She wouldn't normally have said that, like she thought she was important, but she felt embarrassed by her humanity, and interfering, and she wanted him to know she wasn't just a member of the public being sentimental. Even as she thought it she knew that was exactly what she was.

The police stayed around for a few minutes and unstrapped the baby from the pushchair and put him into one of the cars. They couldn't work out how to fold it up, and struggled with it, and with Emma, getting her into the van, demonstrating to the small crowd gathered that they were not taking pleasure in overpowering her. It was easy, they were so much stronger. The matter-of-fact way they dealt with her looked more brutal than if they had been angry. They forced her into the van calmly, and slammed the doors on her, then the van and the two cars drove away, and the people on the pavement carried on and the life of the street was normal again, with nothing to show they had been there except for Bea, standing there, watching, until they had disappeared. A violent criminal would have gained more attention. There was no easier person to discard than a damaged girl. The woman who worked in the shop came out and stood next to her.

'I can't believe how quickly they got here,' she said.

'Only because of the knife,' said Bea.

'You were brilliant,' said the woman.

'No, I wasn't.'

'Do you want a cup of tea? I'm Veena.'

They went inside.

'Bloody donations,' said Veena, stepping over the bags. 'They're the worst part of this job.' She kicked them away, 'You wouldn't believe the rubbish people give us. Bags of dirty clothes, like we're a laundry.'

They stood together in the silent aftermath, the musty air and shadows of the shop.

'Do you need a hand?' said Bea. 'I've still got twenty minutes, and I only work down the road.'

She and Veena drank tea and sorted clothes until it was time for Bea to leave.

'Thank God you came in,' said Veena.

'I was looking at the holdall in the window,' said Bea.

'The red one? That's Italian leather. I'll give you half price.'

Even at half price it was more than she could afford but Bea bought it to cheer Veena up, and because she knew Dan would love it.

In the afternoon there was the safeguarding meeting with the rest of the practice. Safeguarding was always the same: we can't be accused of *this*, because we've done *that*; did you see the letter from the Trust? The guidelines from NICE? Bea took the minutes, and tried not to think about where Emma was or what would happen to her baby. She tried not to remember his defenceless hands. Then, after the meeting, back in her therapy room she waited for her half-past-two clients, a couple with their teenage son. The son gave Bea despairing looks as his father talked. The mother pretended to listen but her hand kept going for her phone, like a gunfighter. Then at four fifteen Bea saw Jill, whose husband had died of cancer, and at five thirty, Lily, who suffered from anorexia and whose family's distress was nothing in the face of her feeble, unbreakable rage. From half past six Bea wrote up her notes and from seven she was alone. Her colleagues went home to cats and dogs and children.

'You won't get a medal,' they said.

'Bless you, love.'

A personality quiz had once told Bea to stop being self-sacrificing. *Don't be a doormat*, it said. It had struck her as a particularly modern assumption that giving diminished the self rather than nourished it. She didn't equate giving with sacrifice. And she wasn't a doormat, she was a psychotherapist. She left her desk with a note for the morning – *Chase up Lily's psych assess. Finish safeguarding mins* – turned off the lights, and shut down the office. She went up the basement steps, the pristine hoarding hanging on the scaffold above, swinging in the wind. *200 Luxury*

Apartments. Rooftop Terrace. Pool. Gym. 24-Hour Porter. 36 Retail Units. 46,000 Sq. Ft. The cold air hit her face like a drink of water and she saw her bus and ran. Foot in a puddle. Banging on the doors. Thanking the driver, tripping on a backpack, looking out at the crowds and wondering about all the lives and thoughts behind the faces. Holding tightly to the rail. Jostled in the crowded bus her thoughts drained away like a wave from the sand. Air between the grains, quiet in her head as the sounds receded. Peace. A voice, a cough, bus stopped, and off. Bus stop. People surging right when she was heading left. Someone banged her shoulder – stranger, not thief. Off the kerb. Cross the street. Reach the house. Bag. Keys. Front door. Inside. And stairs. And she could smell cooking from the ground-floor flat. Cumin and onions. She hadn't been to the shops. Her shoes were wet. She would put them on the radiator. She got to her door, at an angle on the landing, and their neighbour's bicycle next to it, dripping, just home too. Home. She went inside and there was Dan.

He was in jeans and a paint-spattered T-shirt. There was paint all over it. Green and blue from wiping his hands or cleaning brushes, and red, splashed like a Jackson Pollock on the white cotton. She couldn't see if the paint was wet or dry.

'Have you been painting?' she said, happy at the thought and holding his present behind her back.

'No.' He sounded angry she would ask. 'I haven't been painting, I've been at work. I just wanted to get out of that suit. How can I come home and paint, after what I do all day?'

'Oh. OK,' she said. 'How was it?'

'My day? It was the normal shit. Yours?'

'Mine was – interesting,' said Bea. She told him about the girl in the Oxfam shop, and about her clients. 'I've got a present for you.'

She gave him the Italian leather holdall.

'Oh shit,' he said. 'I'm sorry, babe.'

'It's OK.'

'Why do I always end up apologising?'

'You don't need to. It's just hand luggage.'

'Yeah,' he laughed. 'Hand luggage. But we never go anywhere.'

'We might.'

'I love you,' he said. 'You're beautiful.'

'No, I'm not,' said Bea.

Bea and Dan had met at the Bussey Building in Peckham on a warm evening in June, in 2016. She was out for a club night with her girls, going up the crowded concrete stairwell, when she saw the metal doors to one of the galleries were propped open, and the small groups of people standing awkwardly inside. It felt mean to walk past as if it were a market stall.

'Let's have a look,' she said to her friends.

She saw Dan the moment they walked in. She tried not to stare. She hated how obvious it was to notice the most attractive man in the room, but she couldn't help it; he was noticeable. He was standing with his hands in his pockets looking at the floor, not demonstrating himself like beautiful people usually did. He seemed uneasy, and she wondered why.

Bea was right, Dan had been uneasy, more nervous than he'd been at his graduation show, a few weeks before. The night was showcasing a selection of that year's graduate pieces on the theme of 'Father'. His work was hanging on a public wall – not any wall – here. He had lived round the corner from the Bussey his whole life. It had been the first place outside the Tate that he'd seen art, and the first time he'd glimpsed it as a possible life, not for the imaginary Them but for him; not just as personal catharsis but a potential future. He'd also just started sleeping with his tutor, and now her husband and child had come along to the party for the show. She hadn't even told Dan she was married. Caught between her and the other students, who were all younger than he was and seemed so confident of their talent, he found himself staring at the floor. There were painfully bright strip lights hanging from the high-up ceiling, and the art was glaring from plasterboard, eight feet high, both aggressive and vulnerable, waiting to be judged. He saw the five girls stop at his painting with their arms crossed. Despite his nerves, partly just to get away from his tutor's husband, he approached them.

The painting was a fusion of abstract and figurative images of women – women, in swathes and layers of bodies, hair and faces. Bea saw him watching.

'Hey,' he said.

'Is it yours?' she asked.

'Yeah.'

'There's no father in it,' she said. 'Isn't the show about fathers?'

'Yes,' said Dan.

She wanted to say, *You're good at women, you like bodies, I think it's beautiful,* but she would never have said something like that.

'It's good,' she said, with no conviction.

'I don't know,' he said, looking at the painting, blankly.

'Art's not my subject, but I really like it,' said Bea.

'I worked so long at it, I can't see it any more,' said Dan. 'It's not how I wanted it to be.'

'Nothing ever is,' she said, and smiled.

'I guess not,' said Dan, and a silence fell between them, then he got caught up talking to somebody else, but when she and her friends left a few minutes later he felt a gap behind him, and when he turned to check, the door to the stairwell seemed particularly empty because she had gone. Later on, up on the roof, he had a beer and watched her, waiting for her to be alone. She stood out, but he didn't know why. It intrigued him that she had such a presence. Her girlfriends were better dressed than she was and one of them was very nice-looking, but only she stood out – in jeans and boots; not big but definitely not skinny – there wasn't anything he could pinpoint that made her shine to him, except maybe that her hair was fair. But he wasn't into blondes. When he knew her, and looked back, he thought it was her character, her inner heart he'd seen, and somehow known he had to try for her. There was a DJ that night, and the bar was glowing pink and green and you could see across all of the city, the small, distant lights dancing in the warm air. Dan stopped her when she was coming back from the toilets.

'Hey,' he said, approaching sideways so as not to scare her off. 'How was your night?'

'Good, thanks,' said Bea, hoping he didn't think she was there to buy paintings.

They talked. She tried to be particularly forthright, so he wouldn't guess she was attracted to him, but he knew anyway. It was obvious. He bought her a drink and asked her about herself. She told him she had just joined Stamford Hill Psycho-therapy and Counselling, and he told her he had just started working as an estate agent. When he said that she stopped looking into his eyes.

'My father's in property,' she said.

'I'm not *in property*,' said Dan. 'It's just a day job.'

She didn't say anything but her openness had gone.

'Got to earn a living,' he said.

'Yes,' said Bea. 'Sure.'

They talked some more and he bought her another drink, and then she bought him one. He told her he had no future as an artist because he thought conceptual art was bullshit and abstracts were boring and people just got them to go with their furniture. She said he should forget the marketplace and just do the work he loved. He talked about Basquiat and Clemente, and explained his submission for *Father* had been defined by having grown up without one. He asked about hers.

'He's very domineering,' said Bea.

Dan said he hated that. 'My mum's the boss,' he said. And he smiled.

Six months later they were living together. Six months after that, he proposed – old-school, with a rose and a ring. They were married eighteen months from their first meeting, and a year on bought their flat. The deposit was made up from Bea's savings and guilt money Dan's father had sent him on his twenty-fifth birthday. Twenty-five thousand pounds. One for every year he hadn't seen him. They called it the 'adulterer's cash'. Once, Dan asked Bea if she ever borrowed from her parents. He knew they were well off.

'No,' she said. 'Never.'

Their flat was a one-bedroom first-floor conversion with a brand-new IKEA kitchen.

'It's amazing! We're so lucky!' she shouted when they moved in, running up and down to touch the windows like a ricocheting pinball – the front, the back, the front – while Dan stood in the middle of the floor and laughed at her.

He changed his job from Foxtons Peckham to Foundations of Holloway. It was her idea. He was still an estate agent but there was a veneer of morality; Foundations only took 1 per cent, whatever the property value. Ethical or not, Dan hated it, from coffee machine to commute, from suit to traffic stink, to almost every single person he met. A fucking estate agent. *Ethical*. It was just selling houses, or, more often, two rooms above a newsagent, or a basement needing change-of-use. He didn't mind so much when he had what were termed 'traditional' buyers, but London had a dearth of those. Sales were often to overseas investors, or buy-to-let, or developers, wanting to knock everything down and start over. Sometimes Dan closed the deal on a property and closed the door, and pictured it; lights out, and no more human life for months. Nobody to pop out for milk or children on the stairs; a London that was rows and rows of film-set frontages. Selling houses was shit enough, without selling them to people who didn't need homes.

On bad days he missed her. He would sit on the train, desperate to be home, staring at his reflection and the other ghostly doppelgängers of his fellow travellers; their possible selves, and he would think of all the things he wanted, that he might never find. Fulfilment. Success. Money. Money – everything in London felt as if it were made of it. Cars were made of rolls of it, and clothes of flimsy sweatshop notes. It was all right for Bea, she loved her work, she didn't mind she wasn't paid enough for it, but Dan had taken years to get the courage up to study art, and now he didn't know where to begin. His portfolio was gathering dust under the bed. At night, he would lie with her in his arms and feel it beneath him, unseen and reproachful. He pictured its dusty fingers reaching out to him as he slept, reminding him of his failings. His life was slipping from his grasp, days he would never have again.

The night Bea came back from work with the Italian leather holdall had been one of those bad days, not because of all the shit that came with selling houses, but the worse shit that came from not selling them; sitting in the office all day, feeling like he was rotting from the inside out. That night, he'd made some pasta while she had a shower and changed, and then they sat eating and looking at the bag she hadn't meant to buy.

'I'm so worried about Emma,' said Bea.

'Who?'

'The girl today. In the shop.'

'You can't worry about everyone. What about you?'

'I'm fine.'

They cleared the plates and turned out lights and took the leather holdall into the bedroom. They made love with it on the floor nearby and afterwards Dan reached down to pick it up and look at it.

'This is quality,' he said.

'It should be.'

'Was it a lot?'

'No, it wasn't bad.'

'Maybe it's a sign,' said Dan.

'I only bought it to make Veena feel better.'

'Who's Veena?'

'The lady in the shop.'

'Yeah, I think it's a sign, though.'

They sat up late and talked. He tried to say how much he hated his job without sounding like he was just complaining, digging out the worst part of his feelings. She wanted to join in, and admitted her own stress, and that the responsibility for people frightened her. But then she remembered the reward it gave her, and felt like she was pretending. Her own problems felt unimportant when she thought of other people's. She didn't say that, she didn't want to undermine him. He had no reward, he was in deficit to his life, paying out and getting nothing back. It all seemed tied together, his pain, and the pain of others, the mob greed and unhappiness. If they could take themselves out, somehow, get away, then maybe he could start afresh.

'We could travel. Just a couple of months,' she said. 'Or three.'

'Away?' he said. 'Away?'

He switched on the light and it shone straight down onto the red leather bag, making it glow brightly. She had said it without thinking, but looking at his face she realised she could not now take it back. Her words had voiced a need in him. His need not hers, to go back now would take something away from him. She knew she couldn't do it.

Bea had a small tattoo of a flame on the back of her neck, under her hair. She'd got it in Prague on her eighteenth birthday, for Dante's Beatrice. The flame was meant to be a source of inspiration and guidance but she thought it looked like an advertisement for British Gas. Dan loved it. To him, it was a sign they were fated to be together and that she was his guiding light. He would lift her hair and kiss the flame, between the top bump of her spine and the nape of her neck. He did it now.

'I'd follow you anywhere,' he said. He would always be able to say it was her idea. 'Let's go.'

It wasn't as radical as it felt. He would have to resign from Foundations but she could take three months unpaid leave from Stamford Hill Psychotherapy. Her post would still be there when they came home, as would the crisis helpline where she volunteered. He would have to find something different. They could get a short-term tenant for the flat and use the Cushion to pay their way. The Cushion was the £4,370 they had in a savings account. When money was tight they reminded themselves of it. We've got the Cushion. Sometimes it was the Fucking Cushion. The Tiny Cushion. The Shrinking Cushion.

'It'll be perfect, babe,' said Dan. 'We can use the Cushion, and everything good will still be the same when we get back.'

'I know,' said Bea.

'Do you really want to go?'

'Yes, I do.'

'You promise?'

'Yes,' she said.

She was happy to go. She was. She thought of work, and the constant effort of reminding herself that hard as she must try to help people, she must never fall into the trap of believing she could save them. She had tried to help Emma. She had failed. She was gripping the framework of her life, but she was power- less. Perhaps it would be good to let it go. She told herself she must. Dan was asleep beside her. Imagining their travels, she surrendered. Soon afterwards she fell asleep. She slept deeply for a while but later, in the darkest part of the night, she had the dream. There was almost nothing else in it but noise and terror; just her and Dan on a white road and the cacophonous sound of screaming like the sound of Hell. It woke her, and she lay trembling, staring into the dark as the sound faded. She lay in the grateful silence, with the white road still in her eyes and dread slipping away into the corners of the room. She thought how strange it was to have a nightmare when they had such plans, and she was so happy.

2

The service station on the A26 from Calais was sunny and civilised. The day was mild. They sat outside and had a coffee, watching children playing on the manufactured grassy slopes. They'd bought a left-hand drive Peugeot in London, the week before they left. It had seventy thousand miles on the clock and a manual gearbox. Most of the car was blue but the bonnet, for no reason the seller would commit to, was matt-black.

'It looks like shit,' Bea had whispered to Dan, out of earshot.

'It is shit, it's nine hundred quid.'

They'd left London the morning before their tenant, a PhD student from Korea, was due to move in. Her rent would cover the mortgage and give them a little extra and they had the Cushion to pay their way. They had imagined their Peugeot would feel at home in France but all the other cars looked sleek and big and they felt like vagrants.

Bea bought a paper map in the shop and spread it out on the table, trundling a peanut along their route. The A26 to Dijon, and her brother Alex's hotel, then south to Lyons, and west, and pray the Peugeot survived the Alps, and on to Milan. Milan, Parma, Bologna – the peanut wobbled towards Rome.

'I'll get you a toy car,' said Dan. 'They had them in the shop.'

'Can't be worse than the car we've got.'

'True.'

'If it dies, we can get buses and trains.'

'*Buses?*'

'Think of all the people we'd meet.'

'Yeah,' he said, 'I am.'

They finished their coffee and set off again. The road was too loud for conversation. Bea spread out the map in front of her, comparing it to the satnav, dreaming. Lorries swayed above them and Dan gripped the wheel in the slipstream. A sideways wind spattered rain and dirt across the road. Then the country and the weather changed.

They stopped again, and Bea drove, swinging back into the line of traffic. It was hot in the car now so they opened the windows an inch. Bea didn't want to use air conditioning because it made her feel guilty.

'Yes, babe, every time someone uses air con a polar bear dies,' said Dan, sweating.

She was not a person who ever dropped litter. He lovingly endured the bags and boxes of packaging that waited around the flat, and mocked her long scrutiny of the council website for collection days and recycling facilities. *Christ*, he would say, *it's only going to get melted down in China and sent back. I know*, she would answer, *but it's all we've got. We have to try.*

The wind rushed and whistled and hot sun baked the black plastic on the dash.

'It's only two more hours,' said Bea.

'God loves an optimist, my mum always says.'

Bea met Dan's mother long before he met her parents. Jean had tidied and cleaned for her visit and put new antimacassars on the backs of the chairs and sofa, and there was freshly baked banana bread, warm, and spread with butter. Dan had met Bea's parents only once, in a cafe on Marylebone High Street soon after they were engaged.

'I suppose you have to, if we're getting married, but it has to be neutral ground,' Bea said. 'I'm not going to Holford Road.'

Dan thought the meeting went all right, but was glad he didn't have to see more of them. Her skinny little mother had said almost nothing, and looked bored, and it was obvious her father wasn't ecstatic his daughter was going to marry a mixed-race unsuccessful estate agent. He didn't think Griff was racist in the way he might have anticipated, but he guessed he had the pragmatic prejudice Dan considered particularly British; if you were rich colour was an accessory, if you were poor it lowered your stock. In the eyes of his future father-in-law Dan's stock couldn't have been lower. They had all drunk their tea, then Griff and Liv Adamson had picked up their designer sunglasses and headed home. They hadn't seen them since that day. They invited only friends to the wedding – and Dan's mother and aunts and cousins – none of Bea's family, except her brother Alex, who didn't come. Dan didn't much like the sound of Alex, a waster who returned Bea's endless effort and generosity with apparent indifference. She had cried after seeing him once. Anyone who made Bea cry was an arsehole as far as Dan was concerned, it took a lot to rock her equilibrium. But Bea insisted she loved her brother. And she couldn't go to France without stopping by.

'He's always asking,' she said. 'And the hotel is on our way.'

They played music through their portable speaker as the trees flashed past like a beat. A family car overtook, with children staring out, squashed against the back window. The mother, glimpsed, was changing a baby, wipes and hands and the tiny feet waving, shouting at her husband.

Alex was seven years older than Bea. She had last seen him at the Priory, when he'd checked himself in. He'd stayed three months that time. Alex hadn't said in his emails whose idea it was to buy a hotel in Burgundy, his or their father's, or Liv's, but it was bizarre. Neither he nor their parents knew anything about the catering industry, and Alex had only been clean six months when he left London to go and run it. She and Dan had googled the Hotel Paligny, but apart from a fancy logo the website said it was under construction.

'Do you think there'll be an industrial kitchen in Alex's hotel,' she asked, 'like in *The Shining?*'

'I don't know,' said Dan, examining playlists on his phone.

She was sick of managing his mood. He had been like this since they arrived in France, fractious about staying with Alex. *Add up all the times we've visited your mother*, she'd say, *that's how long we'll stay with my brother.* She was trying to over-look it, but it didn't feel romantic, it wasn't like the start of an adventure.

Soon after Dijon they came off the autoroute, and through the tolls again. Dan took over the driving. Brown '*ville historique*' signs instructed them they were somewhere beautiful, but it was still just a motorway. Alex had sent directions but they were different to the satnav.

'Beaune,' said Bea, map-reading, as they shot past signs. 'No, sorry – Dole, no, Le Creusot. Fuck. Autun. Definitely Autun.'

Several miles along a dual carriageway they saw the sign for Autun and Beaune, and turned off. Then, suddenly, there were vineyards. The hills were striped with them, like graph paper.

Dan slowed the car to a calmer eighty kilometres per hour and Bea looked out of the window.

'It's not far now,' she said. 'This is pretty.'

'It's not Milan,' said Dan. 'It's not Rome.'

'A few days, then it's done.'

They came to the outskirts of a village.

'There's a sign,' said Bea. 'Slow down –'

'I am!'

'Arnay-sur-Ouche, three kilometres.' She checked the directions.

They passed flat-fronted stucco houses with shutters and window boxes of red flowers that looked vaguely Tyrolean. Vineyards gave way to pastures, woodlands broke the view, and steep hills and bare rock.

'Satnav?' asked Dan.

'It's in and out. Just carry on.'

She texted Alex to say they were nearly there, but the text turned green and she didn't know if he'd received it. They could see a church spire.

'Here we are,' she said, 'Arnay-sur-Ouche'

They followed the one-way system to an irregular square.

'Café de la Place,' said Bea, peering out.

The cafe was on the sunny side of the square, with a French flag on a pole above the door. She could dimly see two waiters inside, but nobody else.

'Left, left here,' she said.

'Towards Clémency?'

'Yes. Then Alex says it's only six kilometres to Paligny village.'

'Meaning what? In miles?'

She ignored him. Narrow fields sloped up to trees on the brow of the hill, and then, as they rounded a bend, suddenly they saw enormous country, rolling and rolling into the distance, and the hills were an expanse of pale blue and greens and Bea had the sensation of being in the centre of a huge land, and the luxury of space.

'Amazing,' she said. Her heart opened up.

'Yeah,' said Dan. 'That's where we go, after this. That's south.'

They went away from the wide country, down, to flatter ground, and more vineyards, patchy and neat. They passed a farmyard and saw some chickens. On a featureless stretch of road, marooned, they saw the sign *Paligny*. They stopped talking. The village was very small, with no church, and no sign for any hotel. They passed some bungalows and a Parisian-looking town house, boarded up. They were out of the village in moments, accelerating.

'Stop!' said Bea, suddenly. 'Stop here.'

Surprised, Dan pulled over, bumping onto grass.

'What is it?'

'I just wanted to stop,' she said.

They both got out, and left the doors open. The engine gave off heat and the smell of oil. Standing there, out of the car, was strange after the hours and hours of battering noise. They stood with their backs to the road. A big pasture sloped down to a stream. There were tall feathery trees along the water and cream-coloured cows grazing.

'See?' said Bea.

They stood and looked.

'Yeah. Fair enough,' Dan conceded. 'This is nice.'

They looked at the pale creamy cows wandering along the bank on the other side of the water at the bottom of the grassy hill. There was a small island in the widest part of the stream; with trees growing on it, and a mother cow with a calf, grazing in the shade. The sun caught the water just right, so that the sky and the white clouds were floating in a mirror. The light moved across the valley, with the smell of the grass and the sound of birds and nothing else, except the faint tinge of hot-oil from the car behind them.

'That's beautiful,' said Dan. 'It looks like a painting. They told us in college those landscape paintings were idealised.'

One of the cows mooed. Others answered, like distant bassoons. They both smiled at the sound. He took her hand and kissed it.

'Better now,' he said. 'I'm sorry.'

'It's OK. He's not your brother.'

'It's weird – being in France.'

'Is it?' France was as close to home as she could imagine.

'I know it's stupid.'

'It isn't.'

'In Berlin I was with mates.'

'You're with one now.'

'I'm a city boy, aren't I? And I don't speak French.'

'I do. We'll be fine. I'm nervous too.'

He didn't ask her what about. The sun had gone from the field and the river wasn't blue any longer, but colourless. The cows stood out whitely, eating.

'Let's go,' said Dan.

They got back into the car. He pulled out onto the narrow road just as a tractor hurtled round the bend. He braked. The tractor sped by, noisy and bright blue. Dust floated. Dan had stalled the car.

'Forgot to look,' he said. 'Wrong side of the road.'

'He was going way too fast.'

They were very close to Alex's hotel now. The road went on and on, feeling longer than it was because it was unknown.

Then, at last, they saw a pair of tall iron gates and a smart, hand-painted sign: *Hotel Paligny*.

'Turn in,' said Bea.

Dan turned in and drove up the short driveway towards a medium-sized nineteenth-century building, half covered in vines.

'Looks all right,' he said, impressed. 'So, what, your dad just – bought this for him?'

'I've no idea,' said Bea.

'It must make good money.'

'You think?'

There were no other cars. They both got out of the Peugeot. Dan went up the steps to the closed door and peered through the glass.

'Doorbell,' said Bea, pointing.

The bell was nestled in leaves along with an RAC badge: *2 Stars*. Dan pressed it and they heard ringing inside but nothing happened.

'Where is he?' he said. He pressed the bell again, insistently, and knocked. 'Fuck. What do we do now?'

They checked their phones. Signal but no messages.

'He must be out,' said Bea.

'Out,' said Dan. The word was loaded.

The place looked deserted except for an open sash window on the first floor. They separated and walked to the edge of the weedy gravel, looking into the surrounding trees. Dan disappeared round the corner of the building. Bea waited. A plane crossed the sky, so high it made no sound. Dan came back.

'What's there?' she asked.

'Side door. It's locked. And a path, to the road, I think.'

'He'll probably be back any minute.'

'Yeah, but, Bea — a receptionist? *People?*'

'He wouldn't have asked us if it wasn't OK —'

'Then how come it's shut?' Anxiety angered him. 'He could be anywhere.'

'We only spoke yesterday.'

'Then he's forgotten.'

'He's not completely non-functioning.'

'Sometimes he is, Bea, by the sounds of it. From what you tell me, sometimes he is *completely non-functioning.*'

Facing each other, ready for a fight, they heard a car, and a black Renault came quickly through the gates and pulled up, grinding its tyres as it stopped. Alex got out before the brake had completely taken.

'*Shit! Bea!* I'm really sorry!'

Dirty jeans and a faded T-shirt, messy hair, smiling. He wrapped his sinewy arms around her.

'I'm really, really sorry,' he said again, to Dan, over her shoulder.

'It's so fine!' said Bea. 'We literally just got here.'

'Where is everybody?' said Dan.

Alex released Bea.

'*So* good to finally meet you,' he said, smiling, like Dan was uncouth for pointing out the obvious before etiquette was observed.

This from the cokehead, thought Dan, this from the smack addict.

'Hey,' he said.

Alex moved in for a hug, but Dan dodged it and they shook hands, then Dan stepped back and put his hands in his pockets. Alex grinned and bounced in front of them, the picture of white entitlement, in his crappy T-shirt, as if he wasn't everything a hotel proprietor shouldn't be. He looked from one to the other and flung his arms out. He didn't look like Bea at all, tall and skinny, darker hair than hers.

'I was getting the dinner in,' he said proudly, 'but I fucked up the timing. I had a whole plan.'

He ran back to the Renault and pulled Monoprix bags from the back with his keys in his mouth, then went up the steps, unlocked the door and shoved it with his shoulder. They followed him inside. There was a reception desk in a big hall and down a short passageway behind that, was a door to the garden, letting in almost no light. He dropped the shopping.

'Have you got your stuff?'

'Alex,' said Bea calmly, 'where is everyone?'

'Everyone?' he asked innocently.

'Aren't there any guests?' she said. 'Where are the staff?'

'Oh. We're a bit quiet at the moment. Come on, I'll show you upstairs, and then we can look around, yeah?'

He ran up the stairs and Bea and Dan followed, not looking at each other.

'Bea! This is so cool!'

The stairs turned a corner and then there was a corridor off to the left with bedrooms on each side. There were brass numbers screwed to the doors, which was reassuring. With a darting, anxious look, Alex said, 'This is you. Number 1. It's the biggest.'

The bedroom had a reproduction *bateau-lit* with a pink bed-spread. Wardrobe. Flowered wallpaper.

'That's the bathroom.' He nodded towards a closed door. 'It's en suite.' He said it as if defending himself against a challenge.

'It's gorgeous,' said Bea. She went to the window. 'What a view.'

'Is it? It's all right, yeah? Look, I've got to go down and – everything all right? I'll leave you to it, yeah? All right, Dan? Dan? Good?'

'Thanks,' said Dan, not able to look at him.

Alex hurried away. They heard him humming.

'What is he, fifteen years old?' said Dan.

'Stop it.'

'It stinks. What's that smell?'

'It's just damp.'

'He's had this place how long?' said Dan. 'Three years?'

'Less than two. It's nice.'

Small stems snapped as she pushed up the sash window. She leaned out. They were above a long garden with a small stone barn at the end of it. Bumpy treetops surrounded the hotel, stretching away. It felt as though you could walk over them and touch the roofs that poked up. The light was fading. The room was musty, but not as bad as the corridor, which smelled of paint as well, and glue.

She turned back to Dan. 'What do you think he tells our father?'

'How would I know?' He looked into the bathroom. 'It's actually not too bad,' he said. 'Mind you, anything's nicer than our bathroom at the flat.'

'Our bathroom's fine,' said Bea, feeling hurt.

Dan crossed the room and opened a second door to another bedroom, similar to theirs, but with no bed.

'Yay,' he said, 'a suite.'

3

Nothing about the Hotel Paligny was ready for business. Dan walked behind, as Alex showed them round. He seemed both proud and ashamed, and Bea was embarrassed for him. She ran out of things to say.

'Ta-da!' he said, entering the dining room. It had twelve bare tables. The windows had no curtains.

He ran to the back door, rattled the handle, then bent to unlock it with a spider key, fumbling and dropping it on the carpet. They waited, Bea refusing to catch Dan's eye, and at last Alex threw open the double doors. Beyond the narrow terrace a stone path led down through tangled grass, studded with dandelions. At the bottom of the garden was the barn and log pile. The heavy buds of roses lolled over cracked flower beds.

'What do you think of my garden furniture? It was dead cheap,' said Alex.

Several tables and chairs were scattered about, they were brand new, with brash, brown matching sunbeds dotted chaotically between.

'Is he taking the piss?' whispered Dan.

In the kitchen Alex pulled the food from the plastic bags. It was not the kitchen Bea had imagined. Next to a wooden dresser there were two trolleys, like operating theatre trolleys, and a line of broken wicker chairs. There was an industrial-size range, with six gas rings, and a fryer, and three microwaves.

They ate in the dining room as darkness fell, with the other tables grouped jealously around them. He hadn't asked anything about their journey, or themselves; being with him was like watching television, or a play.

'It's been cold at night,' he said. 'It's nicer eating in the garden, obviously.'

'Doesn't that get to you?' asked Dan, pointing to the blank glass. Alex jumped up immediately, dodging between the tables, and pulled all the windows open, with creaks and heaving.

'You don't need to —' started Dan.

The gaping windows were as strange as the reflecting glass had been.

'Not so creepy?' Alex came back to the table dusting paint flakes from his hands.

Gathering the tumblers together, he poured the wine, gazing on it as it flowed from the bottle, shining like blackberries. It was the only thing so far to hold his full attention.

'There you go. Cheers.'

'Cheers.'

They drank. He had raided the charcuterie counter at the supermarket, and bought more than they could possibly eat.

'I'll cook for you tomorrow. Sorry. Sidetracked.'

'Please don't worry,' said Bea. 'Sidetracked by what?'

'Oh, you know, hotel business. I think the building work is putting people off?'

Did he mean the dried-out roller leaning against the wall upstairs, the abandoned box of filler?

'I slowed down over the winter,' he said, 'but I've got loads of ideas. I need to find a contractor. I could make it a private members' club, what do you think?'

'But –' Bea began.

'May last year was seriously busy.'

'Really?'

'Honestly, sis, it was mad. People saw it online and they kept calling and calling. I was the only one here. You should have seen it, it was hilarious.' He poured himself more wine. 'So I changed the name. You'll have to come back, when I have the grand opening.'

'When will it be?'

Alex ignored the question. 'So, tell me, Dan. What's the story?'

Seeing his expression, Bea willed Dan to be kind.

'The story?' said Dan.

'Yes. What's going on? Road trip? Odyssey?'

Dan shrugged. 'Kind of.'

'We thought we'd take a break,' said Bea. 'I told you. Hunt out my emails.'

'It's brilliant having you,' said Alex eagerly.

'Yeah, well, thanks, but we can't stay long,' said Dan.

'Really?' Dismayed, Alex put down his glass.

'We could stop by again, on our way back,' said Bea.

'We've got a load of places to see,' said Dan. 'It's not cheap.'

'Shit, don't worry about *that*,' Alex laughed, dismissing finances, all finances, with contempt.

'Right,' said Dan.

Alex turned to Bea. 'You still holding out against Dad?'

'I think he's given up on me,' Bea said. She smiled at Dan.

'OK, so you're broke,' said Alex. 'Don't worry about it. I don't want your pennies.'

'Thanks,' said Bea.

'Stay as long as you like.'

'We've only got three months before Bea needs to get back to work,' said Dan. 'And I need to find a new job.'

'But you could stay a couple of weeks,' Alex pressed. 'Couldn't you?'

'Let's talk about it tomorrow,' said Bea.

'Don't you want to?' said Alex, looking from one to the other.

'Yes,' said Bea, ignoring Dan's look. 'It's just —'

'You can't afford it — Bea, I keep saying, don't worry.'

'I don't,' said Bea.

'It's because of our father,' he said. He lit a cigarette. 'You don't want to stay because he pays.'

'No,' said Bea. 'Of course it's not.'

She felt herself getting warm, and Dan scrutinising her. She didn't want to talk about her parents in front of him. She didn't want to talk about them at all. And she didn't want Alex to.

'Look, OK,' said Alex, tapping his heel on the ground, rapidly. 'Griff gives me his money, and I give you, what? Fucking — croissants. They're still my fucking croissants, right? I mean, what the hell, right?'

'Al, it's fine,' said Bea. 'It's not that. I'm so happy to see you, and I'm so glad we're here.'

'Fuck principles,' said Alex, blinking like there was something in his eye, either not knowing he was doing it, or not able to stop. 'I mean, fuck it. He owns us anyway, Bea.'

She shook her head. Dan looked down at the table, and did not look up again.

'Yeah,' said Alex, 'he owns us and he *owes* us. Take advantage! Think of it as payment – for services *not* rendered by him, right? Compensation or something. Fuck it, right?' He stopped speaking, staring at the end of his cigarette, still blinking, but trying not to.

Neither Dan nor Bea said a word. There was a long silence. Alex stubbed out his cigarette and turned slowly towards Bea. He leaned forward, his face suddenly bright.

'"Have *you* recently been involved in an accident that wasn't your fault?"' he said, like a cold-call salesman.

Dan just stared at him, but then Bea and her brother started to laugh.

'What is it?' said Dan.

Bea and Alex, laughing, gasped.

'Nothing,' said Bea. 'Just nothing.'

They stopped laughing at the same time and there was silence. Alex tipped back his chair, ruminating.

'Spain,' he said, picking up another cigarette and lighting it. '*Espagne.*'

'We want to visit the Alhambra,' said Bea. 'Neither of us have ever seen it.'

'Art's not your thing.'

'It's Dan's thing. He studied it,' said Bea. 'He can teach me.'

'And what about you?' asked Alex. 'How're the nutters of London treating you? The disenfranchised. The depressed. Will they be all right?'

'I had a lot of clients,' she said. She could feel Dan looking at her. She didn't want him to feel guilty, she felt bad enough already.

'Junkies?' asked Alex.

'Not usually. Some, while I was training, but not since I qualified.'

'Did I know you qualified?' He sifted through the past, trying to remember.

'Five years ago.'

'You've been a qualified psychotherapist for five years?'

'You've had other things to worry about.'

'No, it's shit of me.'

'It doesn't matter,' she said.

'I missed your wedding. I missed your thirtieth.'

'It's fine. Alex. It's fine.'

He stared into her eyes. 'I'm going to my meetings,' he said. 'Just so you know.'

She didn't let him see how much she was feeling. 'NA?'

'Yep.'

'Out here?' She pictured French farmers in church halls, surrendering their various addictions to their Higher Power.

'No, no, online,' said Alex. 'It's great. Especially if you can *parlez* the French, like what you and me can do. I drink a load of wine. But not every day. And that's it.'

'OK,' said Bea.

'All right then, sometimes a bit of weed. These provincial French towns, you've no idea how easy it is to get hold of.'

'I can imagine,' she said.

'My little sister, the expert. So I do my building work round the hotel, and odd jobs and things, and it's —'

He stopped. The word 'fine' would not come and he couldn't think of another.

'All right there, Dan?' he said brightly.

'Yes, thanks,' said Dan.

'Enough to eat?'

'Yes,' said Dan, but then took pity. He indicated the cigarettes. 'Can I nick one of those?'

Alex handed him the packet. Dan only smoked to be friendly. Observing a shred of companionship between them Bea stood up.

'Give me your plates. Then I have to go to bed, I'm so tired.'

'You can use any of the dishwashers,' said Alex airily.

She made a pile of the plates and took them back across the small sitting room and the hall and into the kitchen. The giant fridge hummed. In an annexe by the side door she found two full-sized dishwashers, with clean and dirty china distributed randomly between them. She put everything into one. There was a huge glass bowl of different kinds of dishwasher tablets, like pick 'n' mix. She chose one and started up the machine. When she came back into the hall, Dan was waiting.

'Bedtime,' he said.

Alex waved them off up the stairs, like they were on a departing cruise ship, and went out into the garden, singing to himself.

The doors were closed to all the empty rooms along the corridor. They pulled things from their backpacks, and the giant suitcase, scattering clothes onto the floor. It was too late for order. Exhaustion hit them, and made them cold.

'I can't believe only this morning we were on that ferry,' said Bea.

He didn't answer. The unfamiliar bed smelled of washing powder that was not their own, strong and stale. The duvet was too hot and too cold by turns. The window was open, the curtains half closed. They lay next to one another in the strangeness. The mattress was very soft and deep. They listened to the creaks in the unknown, unseen rooms.

'He's a fucking mess,' said Dan.

'Yes, he is.'

'I guess you're used to messes.'

'Yup.'

They faced each other.

'What's all that about your dad?'

'Alex hates living off him.'

'He could always stop.'

'It's complicated.'

'Has he ever worked? It's like benefit scrounging. It's no different. This place must have cost a ton.'

'Not that much,' she said.

'Not that much?' repeated Dan, mystified. 'It's massive.'

There was silence.

'Dan,' she said. 'Please. Please, try to be nice to him. I know he's – not like anyone we know. I know how difficult he seems. But he's so lovely. He is. And he's my brother. Please try.'

'I will,' said Dan. 'I'm sorry.'

He took her hands. They kissed, to make friends, and to find themselves again.

'It's awful, what they've done to him,' she said.

He didn't listen. Difficult childhoods were not unique, they weren't even unusual. He lifted off her T-shirt, like the unveiling of a piece of art, and pulled her close. They heard a noise.

'What's that?' he said.

Her breasts were pressed against his chest, her arms around his neck. They stopped and listened. Above, in the ceiling, they could hear a slipping sound, like the dragging of something very light. Then scratching. Then the slipping sound again, light as a brush on the boards above.

'What could it be?'

The thing above them moved. Then silence. Uncomfortable. They waited, forgetting kissing, not making love.

They both lay still, listening, and after a few minutes, she heard Dan's breaths fall deeper and deeper, as he went to sleep. Carefully, so as not to wake him she put her T-shirt back on as the rustling in the roof started again. She heard doors shutting below, and the screech and shuffle of the sash windows closing, and then, muffled, the creak of Alex's tread on the stairs. It was as if he were a child, playing at adulthood in that made-up doll's house of a hotel. But he was thirty-seven years old. She thought how old they both were; having jobs, and buying cars and travelling from place to place – owning hotels, however chaotic. She was a professional and a taxpayer. Married. Her mind drifted, lost in chronology, so far from her beginning, and long, unknown years from death. She wondered if when she had a baby she would feel settled and grown-up. She didn't think being a mother would stop her questioning her validity. She couldn't remember if she'd taken her pill that morning. Then she remembered she had. She put her hand across her tummy, sleepily, listening to the sounds around her, and then the silences between the sounds.

When she woke the next morning she was alone in the bed. She checked her phone. Ten thirty. She opened the curtains and looked out on the day. Sun gleamed on the leaves and grass, on the walls and window glass. Everything that had seemed oppressive now felt guileless; even the big hotel, with only the three of them inside. She got dressed and went down, smelling something singed and sugary. Alex leaned into the hall from the kitchen.

'Want a croissant? I'm toasting them, they're amazing.'

'Morning. Yes, please. Where's Dan?'

'He was here a minute ago.'

He ducked back into the kitchen and the fire door swung shut. From the stairs she could see the visitors' book below her, lying open, next to the computer. The pages were filled with entries. She reached the hall and went behind the desk, reading the names and countries. The UK, the States, Australia. '*Great stay! Thanks!*' '*Beautiful country and great wines!*'

At the end of January the entries stopped. Dust lay over the desk, and the stacks of files on the small bookshelf looked untouched. She could smell coffee and hear Alex banging around on the other side of the fire door. Propped up on a table behind her was the board for the keys. They hung on hooks below gold-stencilled numbers, and had big wooden tags. Room 1 was missing, it was on her bedside table. A word was written in the gap, in capitals, with a Sharpie. HUBRIS. Behind Room 2 was the word GREED. She pushed aside the others. LUST, ENVY, GLUTTONY, WRATH and SLOTH. Only those seven keys were on the board, the rest of the hooks were empty. Alex opened the kitchen door.

'Breakfast, you lazy cow,' he said.

'What's with the seven deadly sins?'

He smiled. 'I was bored. It was funny at the time. Instead of grape varieties, or Molière, or whatever.'

'You put us in Hubris.'

'It's not personal. D'you want some coffee?'

'Yes, please. Alex?'

'Yup.'

She felt awkward. 'Why did you make up the guests?'

He narrowed his eyes.

'In the book. All the names. Why did you make them up?'

39

'I didn't.'

He was so brazen she doubted herself. 'Yes, you did.'

'FUCKING HELL!' He kicked the door. It was a petulant kick, like a rock musician, leg flying sideways and the door banged, booming against the wall.

They heard running. Dan came in from the sitting room.

'What the fuck?' he said. 'What's going on? Why are you shouting at Bea?'

'I wasn't,' said Alex. His rage, like a blown light bulb, had gone.

'You were!' Dan came towards him.

'Why would anyone shout at Bea?' said Alex sadly.

Dan looked from one to the other.

'It's fine, Dan,' she said. 'There are fake names in the guest-book. I was just asking about them.'

'What?' said Dan.

'They aren't *all* fake,' said Alex.

'There aren't even that *many*,' she said.

She thought of him getting bored with his game and giving up, and she couldn't help laughing. Alex laughed too, but Dan couldn't see anything funny.

'Wait, you're registering phoney guests?' he said.

'It takes ages,' said Alex.

'Yeah, but *why*?'

Alex shrugged.

'What *for* Alex?' said Dan.

'I don't know, Dan,' said Alex tiredly. 'Seriously, who cares?' He went back into the kitchen.

'Why d'you have to be so aggressive?' said Bea.

'I didn't raise my voice,' said Dan.

'You never do,' she said. 'You don't have to.'

'I was trying to find out what's going on here. This isn't a hotel.'

'It's none of our business,' she said.

'You mean *mine*.'

'No. It's his place –'

'It's your *dad's* place, Bea.'

'What's the difference?'

'I thought you didn't want anything to do with him –'

'It's not me! It's Alex! He can do what he wants.'

'Because he has the choice, doesn't he? It's a sham – this whole thing is a game.'

'So what, though? What's your problem?'

'I mean, what's going on? Is he just pretending about everything – or what?'

'God, Dan, I don't know, ask him!'

'I did!'

'You were really nasty about it!'

'It's all a laugh to both of you, isn't it?'

'It's not –' she said. 'I'm just trying to make him feel better.'

'Yeah, it's harsh, living *in a hotel*, doing nothing.'

He was angry, and jealous. It wasn't her fault. 'OK, whatever,' she said. 'I'm going out.'

'Out? Where?'

It pleased her how shocked he was to be deserted. 'I'm going for a walk,' she said.

'Don't you want breakfast?'

'Oh, fuck off, Dan,' she said, then, at the door, relented. 'I'll see you in a bit. It's fine.' She didn't slam it, she shut it, and he was alone.

When she had gone, he shook his head at himself.

'Nice one,' he said, out loud.

His mother had had a boyfriend once, who yelled at her. He had never forgotten, as a child, seeing the way her head shrank into her shoulders – his big woman of a mother – terrified the guy would smack her. Dan was never anything but ashamed of being angry with Bea and she was right, he had been aggressive to Alex. He would have loved her to be wrong just one time. No, that wasn't it, he'd hate that. He needed her compass. He went into the kitchen to make peace with her brother, who was poking burnt bits out from between the holes in the gas stove.

'Bea gone out?' he said.

'Yeah, for a walk,' said Dan. 'D'you need a hand?'

Alex took the question in the spirit it was intended.

'No thank you very much,' he answered. 'But it's coffee time.'

They took some coffee and more croissants into the garden, and sat at the nearest table.

'*Salut*,' said Alex, raising his cup.

'What?'

'Cheers.'

'Yeah. Cheers,' said Dan.

'Happy holidays,' said Alex. 'Where would you normally be now?'

'In the office,' Dan said. 'Waiting for lunchtime.'

The morning air was soft with dew and full of sunshine. A million miles away Foundations of Holloway were halfway through Thursday morning; cold-calling clients and talking shit. He noticed the coffee was very good. He leaned back slightly in his chair. He noticed the patterns the light made on the grass, how they moved. Out of habit, he practised making them into a flat plane of coloured shapes and lines, to work out how to paint them. Alex was staring at him.

'Bea's husband, Dan,' he said.

'Excuse me?'

Alex dunked his croissant in a pot of jam. 'Estate agent. Wants to be an artist.' He spoke as if he were reciting from a crib sheet. 'No previous spouse, so far as I'm aware. Brought up in Brixton. Married – two years? How was the wedding?'

'Peckham,' said Dan. 'It was nice.'

'Registry office? Party?'

'Yeah. Why?'

'I'm just asking,' said Alex. 'I wasn't there.'

'Bea invited you.'

'I know.'

He didn't appear to have an agenda but Dan was suspicious, Alex was so smug and pleased about everything. The croissant left flakes in the jam, and he was picking them out and eating them. Dan couldn't work him out. Suddenly, Alex stopped and looked up, bringing himself into focus.

'No, you're right,' he said. 'I guess I *do* have a point.'

'What is it?' said Dan quietly.

'It's just that I don't know you. I don't know you! You're my little sister's husband, and I don't even know you. So, I'm just really happy you're here.'

Disarmed, Dan didn't know how to respond.

'Bea is so precious,' said Alex, gazing at him like a child. 'I mean, she's wonderful. If my family were birds she would definitely have been dropped into the nest by – just – another fucking mother-bird, you know? The Good Cuckoo.'

'OK ...'

'She's worth about fifty million times what *any* of the rest of us are, and that's including Ed the Perfect, whatever she says about him.'

'Your brother Ed?' said Dan. He knew the eldest brother Ed was in banking somewhere, he thought Hong Kong. He had almost forgotten he existed. 'She doesn't really talk about him.'

Alex looked pleased. 'Really?'

'No.'

'Well, Ed's very boring. He's just basically –' He acted a crowd cheering, waving both his hands with a breathy sarcastic sound.

'She doesn't talk about him,' said Dan, 'or your parents. She never says that much.'

'Good,' said Alex. 'See, Bea's the One That Got Away.'

'I guess.'

'Obviously, *I'm* the Massive Screw-Up. Which one are you, in your family?'

'The only one,' said Dan. 'Only child.'

'Black sheep of the family doesn't *begin* to cover what I am,' continued Alex, comfortable talking about feelings, like an inverted, random version of Bea who loved to talk about other people's. 'I'm a cellar full of skeletons, me; the rotting portrait in the Adamson attic, fuck knows –' It was as if his family were bigger than other people, assuming a grander footprint. The self-mythologising was alien to Dan.

'She doesn't talk about you like that,' said Dan. 'She just says she loves you or whatever.'

'Really?' Alex said gratefully. 'Does she? Thanks.'

Dan shrugged him off. Alex went back to the mess of jam and croissant. 'Bea,' he said, between mouthfuls, 'is the crème de la crème de la Adamson. You're lucky to have her.'

'I know.'

'I'm sure she's lucky to have you, too,' Alex added hurriedly. He dipped and scooped the dark, sugary jam, licking his fingers. 'Want some?'

'No, you're all right,' said Dan but he smiled at him.

4

Bea walked along the grassy verge feeling very alone. Dew soaked through her canvas shoes. A truck rattled by. Perhaps it was coming back from a market. There was a path to her left, going into the woods, and she took it. Her very first fight with Dan had been on the Victoria line, on the way to meet his cousin Troy. She had resented the way he prepared her for it, like she was Lady Grantham visiting South Side Chicago. The fight started with each of them explaining themselves but by the time they reached Stockwell it was, *What, am I a project to you, white girl?* and, *Fuck you and your cousin Troy!* They didn't fight often. Neither of them liked it. Thick leaves brushed her skirt, and the ground was soft. There were wild flowers and the green smell of shade. She wondered how he was doing with Alex, what the two of them would think of to say. Ahead, the trees were backlit as the path ended and she saw water. She walked out of the woods, to a riverbank.

The river was brown and slow-moving. She heard a distant road and, downriver, saw a stone bridge, its arches holding shadows. She reached for her phone to see if there was another way back and realised she'd left it by the bed.

'Shit,' she said, in disproportionate panic.

She felt vulnerable without her phone. And she needed to know what time it was. Usually it was important to know exactly. She guessed it must be after eleven. Mid-morning on a Thursday, and she was on a French riverbank with no plan for her day. There was a fisherman on the opposite bank. She could see the nose of his car poking out of the bushes. She wondered why he was not at work; if she were home she would have been at Stamford Hill Psych for three hours. Today, she hadn't even been out of bed until her replacement had finished the first session. Her nine fifteen, James. She reached for her phone again before remembering it wasn't there. Her mind scrolled through the Thursday she was missing. James spent his weekends on Es and GHB, having sex with men he didn't know, and every Monday made his resolutions. Clean on Monday, scared by Wednesday, and always a trigger before Friday – a call from his ex or something at work – and Saturday, every week, the fall. The forty-eight-hour party. Blackouts. Bruises. Shame. He wanted to feel love. He would lean forward urgently to tell her. Her ten fifteen was Tara, who was twenty-five. She was on a waiting list to see a psychiatrist, and shouldn't have been living on her own. Tara harmed herself, and had been fired from her internship. Her mother lived in Washington and her father wasn't speaking to her, and her benefits had been suspended. Her suicidal thoughts frightened her, because she didn't feel sad, it just made unarguable sense to kill herself. She wasn't ill enough for inpatient care in an NHS unit, but wasn't well enough to cope. All Bea could do was offer strategies, she couldn't keep her safe. Leaving Tara had been very hard, even with two months' notice. The guilt was sickening. Again, she reached for her phone; ruled by the ingrained habit. Tara needed more help than Bea could give. She needed everything. Every time she thought of her Bea wanted to cry, but she never had the time. Her eleven fifteen might still be going on; if she had her phone, she'd be able to check. They were a mother and daughter who had been having the same conversation for months, blaming one another for their lives. Bea hoped they would move on but hadn't the heart to stop seeing them. She pictured them tormenting her replacement with their shouting. At half past twelve, notes and a sandwich, then at half past one, safeguarding. At three o'clock a client. Another client. Who? She closed her eyes to remember. Three o'clock on a Thursday. Joel. Joel was a sixteen-year-old boy, who came with his stepmother. He hadn't grown into his long, thin limbs. He had red hair. He was being bullied for it. At four fifteen, Karen, who was a full-time carer for her father who had dementia. Bea was her one hour's respite in the week, she called Bea her saviour. At five thirty, Bill, an ex-soldier. Sometimes he would cry, other times he didn't talk at all. Each day different, each day the same. She didn't know how long she had been standing there, so deep in London that she felt the city's air on her skin. She didn't want Dan to think she wasn't talking to him, because she couldn't text. She shouldn't worry so much about his approval. Stamford Hill Psych, cash-starved as they were, had recently opened a service for digital addiction, and had barely set it up when the appointments flooded in. She didn't need a phone. She did not want to identify with a floating blue dot. She could easily find her own way back to the hotel. Not wanting to retrace her steps she started to walk along the river, looking for another route.

Before long she came to an opening in the thick foliage, and a path. If she followed it away from the river, keeping left, she was bound to find the road. She wrapped her cotton skirt round her legs, stepping carefully. There was toilet paper in shreds on the brambles and a faint smell of shit mixed with the trodden mud. Ahead of her was a gate, hanging open like an invitation, and beyond it a pasture. Bea went through the gate onto the thick, rich grass. There were flattened tyre-tracks and she followed the twin lines, feeling conspicuous in the empty field. The hotel must be less than a mile away.

Reaching the brow of the hill, she saw below her a valley and a farm. Between her and the farmhouse was a vineyard and beyond it, on the opposite side, woods; the same woods that surrounded the hotel. The farmhouse below her was a low building of yellow stucco, with small windows. She could make out a chicken pen and some goats and a dozen or so white Bourgogne cows grazing. No fence separated the vineyard, it just began. The reddish earth was heaped and crumbling around the slender stems which went away in rows towards the house. She started down the hill, taking care, but her feet made prints on the soft soil. Her pale shoes were stained with red. If she saw the farmer she would apologise and ask directions. Her French was fluent, she could explain. She made a mental note to count the times her phone came into her mind and she wondered if she could manage being without one for all the time they were away.

The windows of the house, like holes, were just as blank close up. The only movement was the small unthinking steps of the animals as they ate. She reached a barbed-wire fence. The posts looked new and the wire was thick and tightly strung. She demonstrated looking up and down it – in case

49

anyone was watching – then stooped and climbed between the strands. Her skirt got caught and tore and she scratched the inside of her thigh. Bent double, she couldn't see anything but the magnified twists of wire, and the grass, and she concentrated on getting through. When she was clear, the house seemed suddenly nearer. She couldn't get round it without going into the goat pen, or crossing the enclosures with the chickens, which felt presumptuous. Animals lifted their heads. She could feel the thin cut on her thigh, stinging. The chickens' eyes flicked as they pecked at the ground that was patterned with sticky cracks where water had dried. There were upturned plastic water buckets, a flattened hose and manure, and the fermented smell of silage. The cows grazed peacefully, like refugees from a pastoral canvas. She had no right to be there. She tiptoed past the silent farmhouse towards the road, which, she realised too late, was private. She stopped, paralysed by discomfort. The chickens jostled. The field shelters gaped, the earth bald at their openings. Two big, sandy-coloured rats came into the light. One loped away, marsupial-like, but the other paused, with a raised front leg, looking at Bea brightly. Cold seeped into her shoes. Something touched her foot, like a hair on the skin, and she looked down to see a spider. She was standing in a patch of water, green at the edges. She waited as the spider crossed the top of her foot, leg by leg, and climbed down to the safe ground. The smell rose up. She started towards the path again and then she heard the sound of voices, singing. She stopped and looked round. The valley bounced the faint song back and forth. Then the singing ended and there was quiet. The peeling painted walls of the house were behind her as the voices started again, singing in unison, quite soft and monotonous like a hive of bees. They were coming from the barn ahead of her. There was no other way to get to the road. Goats stared with marble eyes. The barn doors were closed. The singing continued. She couldn't tell how many voices. She was, despite her discomfort, intrigued. Compelled, under cover of the sound, she approached the doors of the barn. Stealthy, creeping, she took a breath, held it, and put her eye to the gap between the shrunken boards. Adjusting to the dark she saw the backs of heads, gleaming hair, then, staring straight at her, a tall man with his arms outstretched and pale, naked skin shining. She almost screamed and nearly choked, and put her hand over her mouth. It wasn't a man, but a full-size altarpiece. The voices stopped and the Christ's wooden eyes stared at Bea. She turned and ran, and her feet slapped down on the hard stones of the track, the stagnant smell of the farmyard came up off her shoes, as she went faster and faster down the hill, which was much longer, much steeper than she'd thought.

She reached the road and had to skid to a stop to avoid a car speeding by. It looked unnaturally fast and shiny, as if she'd crossed from one reality to another. She bent over with her hands on her knees, to catch her breath, adrenaline fizzing. She had trespassed. She couldn't wait to tell Dan. She reached for her phone – and then began to laugh.

Alex was in the garden pulling a petrol mower out of the barn. He was incredulous and amused.

'I can't believe you went round the Swiss-Germans'.'

'The who?' said Dan.

Alex shook the mower, bending over it to listen. 'The Swiss-Germans. German-Swiss. Whatever. Our neighbours.'

'Why would they come here, if they were leaving Switzer-land?' asked Bea. 'Why didn't they go to Germany, if they're German-Swiss?'

'I don't know, Bea.' He went to fetch a petrol can from the barn. 'I hardly see them. They're a family. Or a cult.'

'Cult,' said Dan. 'Got to be. Who converts their barn into a chapel?'

'Right,' said Alex. He knelt to unscrew the rusted cap on the mower tank. 'Very weird.'

'It wasn't converted,' said Bea, 'they were just praying in it.'

'Like you do,' said Dan. 'Just "praying in the barn".'

Alex laughed. He couldn't undo the petrol cap. Unable to resist, Dan went to help him. They struggled with it. Alex fetched a rag and a spanner.

'So I was thinking,' Bea said to Dan, 'what if we get rid of our phones?'

'What?' said Dan, not looking up. 'What for?'

'We rely on them.'

'Exactly.'

'No,' she said, 'I mean too much.'

'Babe, we need to make calls and look shit up.'

The cap came loose and he removed it and Alex began to pour the petrol into the hole.

'Do we really need them, though?' said Bea, to his back.

'Yes.'

'Well, what if I got rid of mine?' said Bea.

'That's nuts,' said Dan. 'What if we lose each other? What if we need to get in touch?'

'I can get one that just makes calls and texts. They still make those don't they?'

'Yes, they're made of wool, I think,' said Alex.

'Yeah,' said Dan. 'Like socks, with aerials.'

He tightened the petrol cap and stood back for Alex to start it up.

'Result!' Alex shouted over the roar, and began cutting the grass.

Dan turned to Bea and smiled.

'This is more like it,' he said. The sun was out. He had made something work. It was enough.

There wasn't anything else that needed doing, so they lay down on the grass by a flower bed. They held hands.

'Holiday,' said Dan, but his voice was drowned by the mower storming towards them through the tangled grass.

'What?' said Bea.

He rolled over, his lips brushing her ear. 'What?' he whispered.

She laughed. 'What did you say?' she whispered back.

'Careful! I'll mow you!' shouted Alex, swerving jerkily around the tables.

They lay in the sun holding hands until the insulating roar stopped, and there was quiet.

'I'm bored and hungry now,' said Alex, wiping his face on his arm. He went inside. 'Don't help me!' he shouted, waving his arm above his head.

Dan's phone rang.

'See?' he said. 'Phone.'

He sat up to look and stopped smiling. 'It's Leanne.'

Lying on her back Bea watched him.

'Hey, Leanne, what's happening? What?' He got to his feet. 'That's no good ... Really? When?'

Listening, Bea could piece together what had happened. Their PhD student tenant had not taken occupancy. Leanne was trying to get hold of her, but couldn't. They had her deposit, but the flat was empty. Once Bea realised they had two of the three months' rent, she almost laughed with relief, but Dan was pacing up and down, shaking his head. He ended the call and faced her.

'That's just so fucking typical,' he said.

'Well, it's OK,' said Bea. 'We can still cover the mortgage.'

'We've lost money,' he said.

'But that's all we've lost.'

'What do you mean, *that's all*?'

'It's only fourteen hundred pounds,' she said.

'That's *the mortgage*,' said Dan.

'*I know.*'

'The mortgage and forty quid a week we were going to use.'

'Forty-three. It's not great.'

'Not great?' He was sarcastic.

'We can still pay the third month,' said Bea. 'We can use the Cushion.'

'The Fucking Cushion is paying for us to do this,' said Dan.

She resented having to talk about it when the sun was shining, and they had been having the first nice time since they'd arrived. She hated hearing the words they always said: the Cushion, the mortgage; she didn't want to hear them, or the tone they used to say them. She knew it would be normal to feel anxious like Dan, but she couldn't. To him money was freedom, to her it was a cage. Having less made her feel lighter.

'So we'll have a bit less to spend,' she said. 'It doesn't matter.'

He looked insulted. He shook his head at her.

'Right. It doesn't matter,' he said.

'I mean, I know it *matters*,' said Bea, 'but we can be careful.'

'We've got less than three grand *now*.' He was upset and scared. 'Altogether. In the world. That's all we've got, Bea. When we get back to London I need to find work, we can't fall behind. We could lose the flat. Things were tight already, as it was.'

'You were going to anyway. My job will cover us for a while. Don't let it ruin our day,' she said.

'*Day?* Try *everything*.'

'So we'll have to miss out on some of the things we planned. Maybe it's better, we'll have less choice.'

'Less choice? How is that good? I chose to go to Rome, but now I'm not going to? I chose to see the Alhambra – this is our chance. After this – I don't know, but we had this.'

'We'll go to Rome. We'll do the sums. And Leanne will probably find us another tenant,' said Bea. 'Hey, we can Airbnb the flat. Why didn't we even think of that?'

He shook his head at her again. 'From here?'

'Leanne will help out. Dan, there's no point going crazy over it –'

'I'm sick of doing fucking sums,' he said. 'All right? I'm fucking sick of it. Every single fucking thing we do we count our pennies. What's the point in coming away if we're going to be sweating over every single fucking thing, like we always do?'

'I know. It's annoying.'

Alex came out with a tray piled with plates, a baguette balanced diagonally across the top of it. He stopped when he saw the way they were standing, like boxers in a ring.

'What's happened?'

'We've lost the tenant for our flat,' said Bea.

'Oh. Huh.' He thought about it. 'Is that the end of the world?'

'No,' said Bea.

They ate leftover cheese with stale baguette and some fruit and cut-up cucumber.

'The pâté looked a bit wrong,' said Alex. 'I binned it.' He had brought wine but stuck to water, draining glass after glass. 'I really don't drink that much alcohol,' he said.

Bea drank water with him in solidarity. Dan got a beer from the fridge and ate lunch like a chore he had to get through, using the beer to wash it down, then got up from the table.

'Listen, is it OK if I use the computer in reception? I need to try and sort things out and my laptop is shit.'

'Whatever,' said Alex. '*Mi casa*, etc.'

Dan forced himself to smile. 'Thanks.'

'Airbnb?' she called after him. 'Do you want a hand?' But he didn't answer, just went in, tripping on the sill into the dining room and having to right himself, even more bad-tempered.

Alex giggled.

'Don't,' said Bea.

'Sorry,' he said. 'But he needs to chill.'

'He's worried.'

'You're not.'

'I probably should be.'

'It's different for us,' said Alex.

'Yes,' she said, 'it is.'

Together, they got up from the table, and lay down on the grass, she with her head in the shade of the table, because she was too fair for sun. He gazed up at the bubbling white clouds.

'Is Dan really an artist?' he said.

She was offended. 'He's not an estate agent,' she said.

'What's wrong with being an estate agent?' said Alex.

'Would you do it?'

'Me? No, but I'm a brat.'

'You're not.'

There was a long silence. The clouds moved slowly above.

'Alex,' she said carefully, 'was it true, what you said about going to online meetings?'

He gave her a sidelong glance. 'Why would I *pretend* to go to meetings?'

'It has been known.'

'Fair point. But I swear, Bea, the NA online community is like one big *family*.'

'Alex –'

'I log off before they get to that serenity prayer bullshit.'

'But you're drinking.'

'Yeah but *they* don't know that, do they?'

She gave up.

'All right,' he said, 'I'm sorry. It's a webcam thing, like a poker table, yeah? And everyone talks about their various shit. On the wagon, off the wagon, down the toilet. Or you can do forums. I love a forum. I'm an expert at group.'

'Yes, you are.'

She knew all about his experiences in group and how much it helped him, once he got over his resistance.

'Turns out I'm not any different to the rest of them,' he'd said. 'I'm so arrogant.'

'You're not arrogant,' Bea had answered. 'You felt left out.'

She turned onto her tummy and rested her chin on the back of one hand, tugging the blades of grass, but not breaking them. If she looked close enough the blades went into darkness and she could see the white part, before they turned green, and the soil.

'*Attention, taken to its highest degree, is the same thing as prayer,*' said Alex.

She looked up. The quotation was from a book of Simone Weil's essays and letters that she had taken in to hospital for him, not that last time at the Priory, but the first, when she was still at university. She was twenty, he wasn't thirty yet. She'd helped him check in, and gone every week from Cambridge to south-west London to visit, carrying books and cheap chocolate in a cotton bookshop bag. It had been summer. The bag would bump against her hip, the handles damp with sweat by the end of the journey. She used to cry on the coach on the way back to Cambridge, but never in front of him. They sat in his room, like a room in a Premier Inn, and talked. They talked about religion, travel and philosophy; her set texts, his desired enlightenment. They talked, but never about the thing they both knew best, their family. It was enough they had both been there.

'Simone Weil is way classier than the serenity prayer,' said Alex. 'I mean, fuck sake, that's some horrible writing. *Grant me the serenity to accept the things I cannot change?*'

'Niebuhr's original starts with "God grant me",' she said, 'and it has Jesus in it. And it's a bit better written.'

'No,' said Alex. 'Fuck God. And Fuck Jesus.'

'Simone Weil was a Christian.'

'Yes, I realise that, she was practically a saint,' said Alex, 'but she wasn't an arsehole.'

'*Attention, taken to its highest degree, is the same thing as prayer.*'

'*Attention, taken to its highest degree, is the same thing as prayer.* It's bigger than addiction, and personal power. It's losing the self through being present.'

'It's a beautiful idea,' she said.

'Since we're on the subject of morality. I was thinking I might convert to Catholicism.'

'No you weren't.'

'I'm living in La France!' he said. 'Why not? And it's all in Latin, so you don't notice the silliness. It's ideal for me. Incense. Architecture. Absolution.'

'On the other hand, you're an atheist,' said Bea. 'Potential stumbling block?'

'Well, yes – the Christian God. I mean, it's bullshit, isn't it?'

She rolled over again onto her back, and risked the sun on her face. 'Religion is a bit of a problem. But religion is a Western construct. God isn't.'

'Yeah, I don't know if I'm an *atheist*,' said Alex. 'Atheism is a belief system in itself. And they're such bullies. That Richard Dawkins doesn't like Jesus because he wants his job. I refuse to be saved by anyone who thinks he has the answer.'

The clouds, thickening, moved slowly, very close to the earth compared to the deep blue beyond.

'I sometimes think the problem is the semantics,' she said. 'The moment we name the mystery "God". Once we do that, we start thinking we know what He wants, and who He likes, and who is and isn't acceptable, then we're in trouble. Who am I to say what God is or isn't?'

'That's what I mean.'

'I love ideas. Not good with absolutes. If I have any belief system, it's that I know I don't know anything. Religious people think they know. Catholics particularly.'

'It was the hypocrisy and paedophiles that put me off,' said Alex, 'but now you mention it presuming to know the mind of God is a bit wankerish. Your Simone Weil said something like – the only sin is failing to recognise how powerless we are.'

'"*Miserable*".'

'Wretched, yes.'

'It's a better word,' said Bea, 'but it seems a bit harsh.'

'She says the rich and powerful can't be pure, because they can't accept they are nothing. They can't accept their *wretchedness*. Like our father. The rich man. The big I Am.'

She looked across at him. His eyes were closed.

'Being nothing is *all right*,' he said quietly. '*Absolute attention*. When I'm thinking how fucked I am. I think about that.'

'That sounds good.'

'I try. I try. But I fail. I just fail. I fail.' The word repeated was like a nail he was driving into himself.

She touched his shoulder.

'Yes,' he said. He sat up, reached for his cigarettes and lit one. 'Do you need to go and pacify your husband?'

'He doesn't need pacifying. He's an adult.'

'Cor,' said Alex. 'I wonder what that's like.'

Dan was on their bed when she came in. He had a sketchbook out, but hadn't opened it. He was playing on his phone.

'Any luck?' said Bea, coming in.

'I registered us on Airbnb. No word from the tenant. Leanne thinks she's back in Seoul.'

'OK,' said Bea, 'nothing more we can do, then. Shall we go into town?'

'Town?'

'You know – sightseeing?' She made a comedy face, but it didn't take.

He shrugged. 'If you want.'

5

Being back in the Peugeot was comforting, the smell reminded them of their long drive, ancient fag smoke and an edge of vomit. They rested their arms on the open windows, sunshine on bare skin, pastures roaring by in a stream of warm air, round the bends towards the village. They had come through Arnay the day before and seen almost nobody. Today the square was filled with market stalls which, even as they got there, were being taken down. The meat and fish on the shaded side of the square, the cheese, fruit and vegetables, all the way to the sweets and children's Disney dresses on plastic hangers, all of it packed up, like a circus leaving town.

'A market,' said Bea.

'We missed it,' said Dan.

The *terrasse* of the Café de la Place was crowded. French families organised their shopping and children, and tourists watched like anthropologists. Dan and Bea found a table at the edge, hard up against the plastic awning, the only one free because it was in full sun. They both put on their sunglasses. Bea was uncomfortable in the heat. Other people felt cool and sexy in the sun, but it set her body into opposition with itself. A small shiny truck was picking up rubbish.

'*J'arrive*,' said a waiter, taking money from a man drinking a cognac.

When he came over, Dan asked for two coffees in French and she looked away so he wouldn't feel embarrassed.

'It's good to be out of that hotel,' he said. 'No offence.'

'It's OK.'

The waiter brought their coffees and they drank them. Afterwards, they left the cafe and crossed the road holding hands, like stepping into the frame of a picture. Children ran across their path, and a rack of clothes, with the person pushing it invisible. They reached the top of the square, where a long, narrow *tabac* and bar occupied the corner under the concrete colonnade. They started up a small street, looking for prettiness, but it soon closed in and became an alley and then barely more than a crevice. The pavements disappeared, and there were bricked-in doorways and graffiti on either side and heaps of wipes or tissues, lumping underfoot, and the smell of piss.

'Desirable,' said Dan, in his estate-agent voice, 'well appointed.'

The noise of the square faded. They passed a bicycle with no wheels leaning beneath peeling posters.

'What's that about the beautiful villages of France?' said Dan.

They heard running feet, yells and a clatter, and two teenage boys careered round the corner towards them, jumping into their way, wild-eyed. The boys swerved, one to each side, shoulders bouncing off the walls, and shouted and were gone.

'Shit,' said Dan. 'Thought they were going to rob us.'

The alley ended in a lopsided fan-shape, with a few back doors and guttering, and the only way to carry on would be a footpath that was more like a concrete drain, downhill past a broken fence. There was a cat lying against the wall in the sun, and a plastic mop with a red handle.

'Dead end,' said Dan.

They looked at the closed doors and loose shutters and a balcony above a door open to a vestibule with a lino floor.

'When I was nine,' said Bea, 'my parents went to the Carribean for Easter and forgot me.'

'Nine?'

She nodded. 'We had this Australian au pair called Jo. It wasn't her fault, she didn't know the housekeeper wasn't home either, and went to visit her boyfriend. Anyway, my parents were on a plane so I couldn't call them.'

'Nine?' said Dan again.

'Yes. I went to sleep under the bed, and in the middle of the night I was woken up by a window smashing. It was unbelievably loud. I stayed under the bed, under all my teddies. And I remember seeing blue lights, flashing on the wall, from the police cars.'

'What happened?'

'It was Alex. It was completely fine. He was meant to be somewhere else, and he thought the house was empty. It was one of the best nights of my life.'

'What are you talking about?'

'I remember hearing him talking to the police at the door. You know, I was hiding upstairs, and he was doing the whole posh-boy, *Oh yes, Officer, Alexander Adamson, thank you, Officer*. And the police went away, and I came down – and I thought he was going to be angry, but he was unbelievably sweet. He let me stay up –'

'He *let you stay up?*'

'Yes, and gave me supper, and made all his friends be nice to me. And the next day we had breakfast. It was just amazing. It was just the best.'

'And your parents?'

'What?'

'I don't even know where to start with this,' said Dan. 'What about the window?'

'I told them I broke it – he wasn't meant to be there. But the point is, it wasn't anything bad. It was Alex. And he was lovely. And I felt this . . . joy.'

'That's your take-away, from being dumped by your parents and scared witless in the middle of the night? Joy.'

They faced one another in the awkward, private space.

'I'm trying to explain how nice he is.'

'I see he's nice.'

'We should have gone the other way from the square,' said Bea.

'It doesn't matter,' he said.

A radio above them somewhere was playing French pop, a man's deep voice pronounced *Europe Deux* smoothly to the empty air. They stood close in the asymmetrical suntrap. It wasn't picturesque. It wasn't anything to do with their shared vision. It was just a place they had stumbled upon. He kept hold of her hands but looked at the ground.

'Why is it', he said, 'that you feel lucky, and I feel unlucky? What is that?'

'I don't know,' said Bea.

He touched her hair with his fingertips, where the sun was catching it, then her cheek, like a blessing, then the small blue stone hanging from the silver necklace he had given her for her thirtieth birthday. They were going to kiss. The radio started playing Ed Sheeran. They started laughing.

'Boy. No escape from that,' said Dan.

'Seriously.'

He pulled her head into his chest and pushed her hair aside to kiss the flame tattoo. They walked back the way they had come and in a few moments they were out in the square again. Already there was almost no trace of the market, just bareness, and scraps of litter eaten up by the small truck as it went back and forth. They went back to the cafe, with the feeling it was their cafe, now they were there a second time, and found a table in the shade and ordered ice cream.

'About your art,' she said, pouring the hot chocolate sauce.

'Let's talk about it another time.'

Art. Even the word came more easily to her than it did him. A notion of fulfilment which had expectation at its core.

'I'm thirty,' said Dan. 'The runners are already on the track. They've started and I'm laps behind.'

'It's not impossible,' she said. 'Just *doing* it. Just doing it would make you happier.'

He watched her scooping up the chocolate sauce and melted vanilla ice cream, and licking her fingers.

'Messy girl,' he said.

He made her feel adorable for spilling ice cream on her hand. She didn't know how he did that.

They walked around the village and looked at the shops, but didn't buy anything, then went back to the car. Bea remembered the way to Paligny and Dan remembered to drive on the right. When they got back to the hotel, it was six o'clock.

*

As they came through the gates, they heard the thick thud of a rock bassline. The sun was behind the trees. They parked in the smoky shadows. Dirty guitar and drums soaked the air. Nirvana's 'Love Buzz'. Alex came running out of the hotel. He was barefoot, and he flung his arms wide.

'Just in time!' he shouted.

Bea and Dan exchanged a look.

'What for?' said Dan warily.

'Tea? Booze? Booze? Tea?' His voice was shrill. 'Booze?'

He rushed inside ahead of them and disappeared through the fire door.

'Is he high?' said Dan.

'I don't know.'

The garden was strewn with traces of activity, the mower stood abandoned in a stretch of tattered stalks. There were two empty bottles of wine, half a baguette, a T-shirt, and a five-litre pot of white paint, on its side on the grass, with a skin forming over the puddle.

'Getting some things together!' they heard Alex shout from inside. 'Hold on!'

'Look at all this,' said Dan, setting the paint pot upright, and shaking his head.

Alex came running out, clutching the hotel visitors' book to his chest and a fistful of pens, which he threw down on a table.

'I thought if I paint the tables they won't look so nasty,' he said. 'I should sand them but I don't have a sander. I should sand them. I should've done it before. I haven't done it.'

They tried not to stare. He sat down and rubbed his hands together and opened the visitors' book.

'Robert Robertson!' he said. 'Too obvious? Tom Thomas. Tom. Tim. Andrew. Thomason Anderson. Shit. Can't think.'

Bea walked slowly towards her brother. Her skirt was pale in the dusk. The white paint on the grass glowed and the sky shone like opal.

'Has something happened?' she asked.

Alex looked up at her. 'Kind of.'

'What is it?'

'They're coming out.'

'Who?'

He didn't answer. She was surprised she'd had to ask, she knew who.

'Our parents,' she said.

He nodded, looking up at her as if there was something she could do. There was nothing. She sat down next to him. They didn't speak.

'Your parents are coming here?' said Dan.

Bea and Alex were looking at one another like people clinging to wreckage.

'When?' she asked.

'Tomorrow.'

'It's OK.'

'It isn't.'

'When were they here last?' she asked.

'He comes –' he shook his head, '*they* come – every couple of months.'

'How long for?'

Alex looked down. 'A few days, a couple of days.' He shrugged, blinking. 'She came alone, once.'

Dan was embarrassed. He started to pick up the bottles from the grass.

'What's really *sick*,' said Alex, 'is that it's sort of nice they bother.'

She tried to take his hand but he pulled it away to bite his thumbnail. Dan approached the table.

'We'll help you clear up,' he said.

Alex looked at him as if they'd never met.

'What do they come for?' asked Dan.

'Just normal shit,' said Alex. 'Whatever.'

'What does that *mean*?' said Dan.

'Dad's got stuff to do,' said Alex. 'They just like it.'

'They like the hotel?' pressed Dan.

'Yes,' said Alex.

'They like staying here?'

'Dan,' said Bea, with a look that meant *Stop talking*.

She was blocking him out. They both were, but he wasn't married to Alex. He waited for a moment, then he went inside.

Neither Alex nor Bea reacted to his leaving. They didn't speak. The minutes went by. The evening settled like a gauze, hiding detail. Bea looked up at the blurry sky.

'Remember waiting for the first star?' she said at last.

'I still do sometimes,' said Alex, but he didn't look up.

'What else? What else do you do?' she asked.

'That,' he said. He moved his head towards the open pages of the visitors' book. 'It's stupid. It helps.'

Bea looked down at the pages of the book. She picked up two pens and held one out.

'Anne and Richard Henderson from Stroud,' she said clearly.

There was a pause, and then he took the pen. She straightened the book for him. Slowly, carefully, he wrote the names.

'What did they like?' he said.

'They liked the weather, and the cooking,' said Bea steadily. He wrote.

'Wait, when were they here?' he asked, panicking. 'When did they stay here?'

'April the 14th,' said Bea. 'They were on their way to Paris.'

'April in Paris,' he enunciated.

He wrote the names, and date, then put down that pen and she handed him another.

'Malcolm Elford,' she said. 'From Guildford.'

'Elford-Guildford,' said Alex, and giggled. He wrote the name and dates himself. 'Mr Elford couldn't be arsed to write a comment. He was only here on business.'

He picked up another pen and stretched his arms up. 'Rebecca and Ian Price from Hull!' he declared to the evening air. 'The *Prices* of *Hull*!'

'They *loved* the food,' said Bea.

'They did!'

They put in twenty names, only pausing for Alex to turn on the outside lights.

'That's better,' he said. He closed the book and the only sound was the treetops slightly rustling in the breeze. 'Does Dan know how shit they were to you?'

'Me?' Bea answered. 'Bits and pieces.'

'Listen, you don't have to stay. I'm used to them.'

'Don't be silly,' said Bea.

'Seriously, go. He sends me off to do stuff, she likes to think we're going to turn this place into something – it's fine. You can come back when they're gone.'

'No,' said Bea. 'I'm here.'

She found Dan at the window in their bedroom, in the dark, as if he had been watching them in the garden. She switched on the light.

'Fucking hell,' she said.

'Did you sort him out?'

'Sort of.'

'You OK?' he said. 'We can just leave if you want.'

'No. I'd like to, but I can't. I'm really sorry.'

'Fine,' he said. 'We'll handle it. Why is it so terrible? You haven't seen them in two years. We'll be polite, do the in-law thing, I get to charm them —'

'No, stop it —'

'How bad can it be?'

She sat on the edge of the bed. She covered her face.

'What?' he said. 'What makes you so crazy?'

'I'm not crazy.' Her voice was muffled by her hands. 'I'm just dreading it.'

He couldn't see her face. He couldn't read her.

'Why?' he asked.

'I just am.'

'Because your mum's a bitch?'

She shook her head.

'Why?' he asked again.

'I don't want you to see them,' she said.

'*Me?*'

'I don't want you having anything to do with them.'

'Why not?' he said. 'What are you afraid of?'

She looked up. He took a step back, and crossed his arms.

'Look, whatever it's about,' he said, 'who gives a shit? Let's just go. Before they get here. We've got enough to deal with. Bea, let's go —' He saw her eyes flicker. 'We can pack up in ten minutes,' he said. 'Alex will handle it. Bea —'

He was going to say more but they heard Alex's footsteps, in the corridor running towards them, and then the bedroom door flew open.

'There you are!'

He was carrying a bottle of wine, a shovel, some bamboo sticks and a fire extinguisher. Three red plastic boxes were slung over his shoulder on strings. He held them up and shook them.

'What are you doing up here? It's time to check the snake traps!'

6

They hurried after him along the corridor.

'There are loads of snakes,' he said. 'But mostly they're just grass snakes. They're sort of company —'

'Company?' said Bea.

'They've got nice round eyes. It's the vipers I don't like. Asp vipers. *Vipera aspis.* They're in the roof, and it pisses me off.'

'I think we heard them above our bed last night,' said Bea.

'Little fuckers keep me up nights,' said Alex, 'snacking on mice. I want them out.'

'Fuck sake,' said Dan quietly, running out of patience.

A short ladder was nailed to the wall, by the corner from the older part of the hotel to the extension. From there on the corridor was undecorated. Bare bulbs hung from the ceiling, and through an open door they saw the leavings of a previous occupant. Beer cans. A sleeping bag.

'Don't look in there,' he said, shutting it.

'Did someone sleep there?' asked Bea.

'Me. When I first moved in. I need to finish those rooms, but I'm getting on with the main hotel first. Up we go. Come on,

Dan, you know you want to smash snakes' heads in. Give in to the urge.'

'You do know snakes are protected?' said Bea. 'Nobody's smashing anything.'

'Yes, I know that, Bea. Chill.'

He started up the ladder. Encumbered by the boxes and sticks, his hand swiped at the trapdoor to the ceiling and his body swung wide, like he was on a rope ladder.

'Why don't we do this tomorrow?' said Bea.

Righting himself, he ignored her. 'OK, it's not nice up there. Hold your nose.'

The traps, slung over Alex's skinny shoulder, swung in front of Bea's face. They had printed diagrams and white writing on the sides that could have been Portuguese.

'Are these legal?' asked Bea.

'Pass me up the rest of the gear when I'm in,' said Alex.

He banged the trapdoor with his fist. Dust fell as it popped up, releasing the faint smell of rotting flesh. Dan and Bea exchanged helpless glances and climbed up after him.

Once inside it was impossible to imagine the rooms below. The smell was liquid and familiar, as if the smell of corpses was not new, and had only to be recognised. Bea breathed lightly through her mouth. The roof beams came up steeply, so that it was too low to stand upright, except in the middle of the joists. Alex put down his shovel and the red traps, pulling a bandana from his pocket and tying it round his mouth and nose.

'I put my foot through over there,' he said, like a bandit.

Light came up through the hole, and dust, swirling.

'SHH!' he whispered. 'They're very shy, but they'll protect their young, so look out.'

Dan tried to find the teenager inside himself who would think this was cool and fun but he couldn't identify with Alex whose risks were all in his head. There was nothing in the real world to threaten him, so he had to create things. Going up into a loft with a rotting floor looking for snakes wasn't adventurous, it was dumb. And it was almost completely dark. Outside, night had fallen.

'Torch?' he asked.

'I don't have one,' said Alex.

'You don't have one?'

'Shit, and I should have brought a bin bag up.'

'I'll get it,' said Dan. 'And I'll get my phone. We can use the torch on that.' He went back down quickly, leaving Alex and Bea alone.

'There are three or four traps up here already,' whispered Alex.

'What's that smell?'

'Dead mouse.'

She was aware of the gap between her parted legs as she balanced on the joists, the air moving her skirt slightly. She could hardly make him out in the gloom.

'If you get rid of the rats,' said Alex, 'then the snakes don't bother coming up.'

'You said mice.'

'It's a fucking zoo, Bea.'

'How do they get in?'

'The snakes? They come up through the vines. They can get through tiny, tiny holes, anywhere.'

She thought of her open windows, and the vines growing thickly around the frame.

'What do we need the bin bags for?'

'Dead things. Other shit. Whatever.'

Something was poking up from behind one of the joists, shining faintly, wavy edged, like a fin.

'What's that?' she asked. 'There.'

'Wait for Dan with the torch.'

Bea took a step closer, balancing carefully. Her brother's hand reached out. It was bony, and her own was strong and steady. She felt as if she were holding him, not the other way round.

'Stick?' she said.

He handed her one of the bamboos and she leaned out and poked the thing sticking up behind the joist. She got the tip underneath it and flicked it. It flew up and settled.

'Oh, it's a skin,' said Alex.

She lifted it again. The snakeskin was rigid, like parchment, and crispy. It wavered on the end of the stick, weighing less than a glove, split and dried out. She imagined the small princely snake leaving it behind to make his legless journey, and wondered if he felt the splinters on his tender body, like the green wood of a peeled stick.

'I wonder if it hurts them to shed their skins,' she said. She didn't feel afraid, standing there in the darkness, imagining snakes, even with the smell of death in the air.

They heard Dan in the corridor then he came cautiously up the ladder, shining his phone beam around. Details popped into the light then disappeared.

'I'll stay here,' he said, 'and shine the torch.' His voice was tight. 'That smell is horrible. You should do this in daylight.'

Alex and Bea went about with sticks and bags while Dan watched, wincing in disgust as he pointed the beam into the corners. Tucked away, where the smell was strongest, they found a dead rat. It was big and soft, and fell apart when Alex picked it up.

'The guests wouldn't like this,' he said and Bea laughed, but Dan didn't.

When they had gone away from Paligny, perhaps she'd tell him everything. She pictured them on the bridge at Avignon, saying unsayable things in the safety of a postcard view.

They laid new traps which Alex had honeyed earlier and took the old ones away, except one, tucked right into the join where the roof met the walls.

'We can leave it. It's probably empty anyway,' said Alex.

'You will let them go, won't you?' she asked. 'You do release them?'

'To tell you the truth, I've never caught one.'

Bea picked up the snakeskin to show Dan.

'Christ!' he shouted, recoiling. 'What's that?'

'It's beautiful,' said Alex. 'Don't you think?'

'Here,' Dan held the bin bag open. He didn't believe Alex thought the thing was beautiful, he was just being pretentious.

'No, I want to keep it,' said Alex. 'I collect them.'

Bea took the skin, like a fish from a hook, and gave it to her brother.

'Thanks. I can oil them and make a jacket. Is snake oil a real thing?'

'No, Alex,' said Dan, 'snake oil is not a real thing.'

They went back downstairs, relieved, but Alex's night was only just beginning. He ran back and forth, fetching whisky and trays of food, putting on music, asking them what they wanted then ignoring them, lost in his hyperactivity and seeking oblivion. He found his phone and a speaker and fumblingly set it up. The speaker was small and distorted the music as he forced the volume up. It blared Pink Floyd from the small mesh oval hugged beneath his arm as he ushered them out into the garden again. Pink Floyd changed to the Flaming Lips.

'I love shuffle!' he shouted.

The terrace lights shone harshly onto the remnants in the garden; the puddle of paint on the grass, the various projects begun and abandoned, lying around like some kind of installation. Bea began collecting things and putting them in piles on the garden tables and dining-room sideboard.

'What a night,' Alex shouted over the music. 'So mild!'

He put the speaker down, and stood shoving ham into his mouth.

'It's too fucking ugly out here,' he said. 'Fucking wall lights. Wait.' He drained his whisky and disappeared inside.

'Bea?' said Dan. Feeling miles and miles apart, they smiled at one another. 'It's all right, babe.'

Alex came back, triumphantly holding up a storm lamp with paraffin sloshing in the base.

'Ahoy,' he said.

He flicked the switch inside the dining room and plunged them into darkness. They saw him silhouetted as the music jumped – and dropped – suddenly, to slow and simple; an acoustic guitar and a harmonica, as clear as a funeral bell on a silent day.

'See?' said Alex. 'See how it changes?'

He put the lamp down.

'I'll do it,' said Bea.

She opened it up and found the wick, and adjusted it, and Alex lit it with his Zippo through the tiny gap, burning his thumb. The flame leapt hugely, showing spiderwebs on the dusty glass. He turned it down and the glow was a comfort. The music went on, Johnny Cash and Jeff Buckley; the pain of the cracked old voice, then the pain of the young one. Alex lit a cigarette with shaking hands, spilling them from the box onto the grass. He bent and offered one to Dan.

'What a fucking mess. I know I'm being an arsehole. I'm really, really sorry.'

Dan took the cigarette. Alex poured another whisky, and held it against his chest.

'What am I doing?' he said.

Bea leaned into the lantern's glow. 'I think you're doing OK.'

Alex yelped, like an animal. 'I'm doing brilliantly.'

With Alex quieter, Bea and Dan took their chance to eat, feeling for ham and bread, digging into the butter, cutting the cheese, fuelling themselves. Alex turned to Dan, struggling to focus.

'You wouldn't take money from a man like my father, would you?' He was ghoulish, pale, glistening with a sheen of sweat.

Dan stopped chewing.

'You're not a total cunt,' said Alex. 'I take a salary. Money. To suck on the giant tit. You wouldn't do that, would you?'

Dan shrugged, at a loss, but Alex had forgotten him. He put his arms around Bea, restricting her.

'See? Dan?' he said. 'This girl . . .'

Bea took his hands off her and held them, steadying him. 'It's all right,' she said.

'She looks into my soul,' said Alex. 'Does she look into yours? She's a guiding light. Port in a storm. All that.'

He let go of Bea's hands, drained his glass and weaving, staggered off. His cigarette fell and rolled onto the ground. Dan stamped it out.

'What are we going to do with him?' he said.

'Oh!' Alex cried theatrically, turning round and dashing his forehead with his hand. 'I forgot the wood!'

'Wood?' said Dan.

'We need to chop some wood. Don't look like that! We need a fire, the *guests* like it.'

He lurched towards them, picked up the whisky bottle and the oil lamp and went off up the garden, leaving them in darkness.

'Fuck,' said Dan. 'He's off again.'

They tracked his pale shirt in the gloom.

'Loads of snakes at this end!' they heard him shout. 'Fuckers!'

His blurry shape hovered. They heard him trip. A bright half-moon, small and silver, revealed monochrome grass, and grey leaves. Alex, distant in the earthly pool of lamplight, stumbled towards the wood store.

'Hey!' called Dan. 'We don't need logs!'

Alex set down the lantern. They saw his white arms, and the glint of metal; he was holding an axe.

'Oh, fucking hell,' said Dan.

'Come on,' said Bea, and got up.

Alex swung the axe experimentally as they approached, holding the whisky bottle in his other hand.

'There's already a load of logs,' said Dan diplomatically. 'You've got a stack, and it's almost summer.'

Alex changed his grip on the axe handle like a ninja. 'But we can chop them! It's fun.'

'No, mate,' said Dan, 'it's stupid.'

'Fun,' said Alex. 'Look. See?' He stumbled on the way to the log pile. 'This one – could be smaller.' He put the bottle down near his legs and hauled one from the stack.

On the terrace the music stopped mid-song and left a sudden quiet. The log toppled. Alex set it on its end again and raised the axe with both hands.

'Al —' said Bea. 'Dan?'

Dan shrugged. He wasn't going to argue with a drunk man swinging an axe.

'Good,' said Alex, and brought the axe down fast.

The blade struck the ground with a slice and a clink.

'SHIT, my arm. My arm. Shit. Shit. Shit.' He began to laugh, yapping and gasping. 'You know in cartoons?' he laughed. 'With the juddering — it hit a stone —'

'Alex —' said Dan, 'mate. Seriously —'

'Just let me do this one,' said Alex. 'Please? Please-please-please — hold the lantern.'

'No,' said Dan.

'OK, OK, OK —' said Alex, readying himself. He raised the axe again, high above his head, and put his foot on the top of the log. It went in and out of the shadow of his body as he tried to get a fix on it.

And then all at once, he gave in and dropped the axe, heavy and harmless on the ground. He stood weaving, and staring.

'Take some in.' He started to pull logs from the stack, making small murmuring sounds.

'At least it will distract him,' said Bea, 'and we can get him back.'

They went to help. Loose moss and woodlice dropped from the logs which were dry on top but damp in places.

'Watch out!' He kicked the stack and made some shouting noises and staggered, dropping logs with a clatter, thudding on the grass. 'For the snakes are not content with my hotel — oh no – little fuckers love to hide in a woodpile they do.' He turned to Dan, squinting. 'I used to chase your wife with worms,' he said. 'When she was little.'

'What?' said Dan.

'Yes,' said Bea, 'he used to chase me round the garden at Holford Road, shaking them at me. It was really funny.'

'No, it wasn't.' Alex was affronted, his white face stretching out at her. 'You hated it. Didn't you?'

'You liked it when I screamed.'

'You were *pretending to be scared*?'

'Sort of.'

'To make me *happy*?'

She nodded.

'I was *thirteen*,' he said, 'you were *six* –'

'It was a good game.'

'Fuck,' said Alex. He gaped. 'There's me, feeling guilty all this time.'

His knees buckled and he collapsed to the ground and sat there. He groped for the bottle, then a cigarette. Bea and Dan sat down with him, making a group around the storm lantern as if it were a campfire, not a single flame.

'Shit, Bea, I don't know what to do,' said Alex. 'I don't know what to fucking do.'

Bea spoke carefully. 'What's the main thing you don't know what to do about?'

'You're so sweet,' he said. 'Our girl's an angel.'

'I know,' said Dan.

'But I don't think she'd understand. I don't think even you would understand.'

'Why wouldn't I?' said Bea. 'Maybe I do.'

Alex closed his eyes. 'It's fine. It's always fine.'

'We'll be here,' she said. 'Me and Dan.'

He shrugged. 'Whatever.'

Nearby, a bird started to sing, suddenly, and it sounded strange in the night-time.

'What is that?' said Bea.

'That?' said Alex. 'Is a nightingale, is what that is.'

'I've never heard one. That's not what I imagined.'

Alex flopped down onto the ground. They listened to the short, harsh chirrups. There was silence. Then, like a percussion instrument changing into a flute, the bird sang a short arpeggio. Silence again. Then the short, quick melody. It was wakeful and young. It would not have been beautiful if the bird hadn't been singing in the dark.

'It sounds like morning,' said Bea.

'That's what's so good,' said Alex.

Dan held out his hand and Bea took it. She leaned against him as they sat on the cool, damp grass.

'"And, for many a time I have been half in love with easeful Death,"' said Alex, flat-out on his back beside them.

Because the words were not his own they came out clearly, like he wasn't drunk, as if they were all somewhere else.

'"And, for many a time I have been half in love with easeful Death,"' he said again.

'"Call'd him soft names in many a mused rhyme,
To take into the air my quiet breath;
Now more than ever seems it rich to die,
To cease upon the midnight with no pain,
While thou art pouring forth thy soul abroad,
In such an ecstasy."'

The nightingale sang on.

'*Pouring forth thy soul in ecstasy*,' he said. 'Anyway. There's more. Whatever.'

'Go on,' said Bea.

'No, that's enough,' he said. 'That. Is. Enough. Of. Tonight.' He roused himself, and got up, onto his knees.

'Only half,' said Bea.

'What?' said Alex.

'Only half in love with death,' said Bea, hating even to say the word.

'Yeah, of course,' said Alex. He stood up. 'That Keats, he couldn't commit to anything.'

Bea and Dan lay in bed with the windows open and the curtains hooked back against the wall.

'Alex used to learn poems by heart when he was a child,' she whispered.

'He's still a child,' said Dan.

'He can't help it.'

Above them the snakes or mice or rats slid about the roof space, more active than before. Dan had wanted to keep the window closed. Bea didn't think snakes really would come in, despite what Alex said.

'Do you think they're playing?'

'Playing?' said Dan. 'You're weird.'

'They're only animals,' she said. 'They're not evil.'

They listened to the sounds.

'You'll probably like my parents when you spend time with them,' she said. 'They can be very charming.'

'I don't care,' said Dan.

'They've got a lot of money,' said Bea. 'You know that?'

'I guess,' said Dan. 'So?'

He kissed her. They made love, being careful with one another, and kind. Afterwards, as they drifted towards sleep, they heard Alex stumbling through the building, knocking into things, talking.

'Is someone else here?' she whispered.

'Talking to himself,' said Dan. 'He should sleep.'

'He can't,' she answered.

Then silence. Then morning.

7

Griff and Liv Adamson's huge bright red four-wheel-drive Porsche Cayenne drove through the gates at six o'clock the next evening. Bea and Dan watched from a window as it pulled up between the battered Peugeot and Alex's black Renault. The driver's door opened, trees sliding from the glass.

'*Bonsoir! Bienvenue! Willkommen!*' Alex cried, bounding out to meet them, long legs flailing like a sunset shadow of himself.

'You all right?' said Dan to Bea.

She crossed her arms over her stomach. 'Fine,' she said.

The three of them had cleaned up all the mess, Alex was contrite and hung-over, and Bea was quiet, dread settling like frost.

Striding across the gravel, Griff stuck out his hand to grasp Alex's, and with the other arm pulled him into an embrace. Liv bent to collect her handbag, tugging at her pashmina which fell forward as she reached into the footwell. Griff and Alex went for the suitcases, and Liv came towards the front door with a girlish step; flat shoes and strawberry-blonde hair landing lightly on her collarbones. She was sixty-three years old and five foot five; she often announced these facts as though they were a virtue.

'Yay,' said Bea tightly. 'Let's do this.' And they went out to meet them.

'Dan!' Liv's huge handbag dangled from her bone-thin forearm. 'Bea! What a surprise. I've almost forgotten what you look like.'

Griff kissed his daughter's cheek and grabbed Dan's hand, slapping his back.

'Good to see you,' he said.

Liv stood on tiptoe to air-kiss Dan, first one side, then the other, so just her perfume and fingertips touched him.

'Dan, so thrilled.'

He looked from his mother-in-law to his wife, searching for something to connect them. It was as if they were made of different material. They were both fair but there was no red in Bea's hair, it was just pale, unbrightened blonde; both were small but Bea the taller of the two, and in outline had a mother's shape; her mother had a child's. But, he realised they had the same heart-shaped face. If the flesh were stripped from Bea's face, you'd have Liv's, everything about her was polished to a point.

'We couldn't believe it when Alex said you would be here,' she said. 'Wow! What do you think of our project?'

'It's good,' said Bea, going to Alex's side, but her mother reached him first.

'Darling, I missed you,' she said, putting her arms around him.

He ducked away and smiled.

'We stopped for lunch near Versailles yesterday,' said Griff. 'It was horrific.'

'You know, that five-star awful,' said Liv sorrowfully.

'Total bullshit. I don't know why she booked it. It was disgusting.'

'You drove?' said Bea.

'They always drive,' said Alex proudly, infantilised.

'I sold the jet last year,' said Griff. Bea saw Dan start, and look at Griff with sudden focus. 'It cost an arm and a leg to get it off the ground, and it was always a palaver trying to find a runway long enough anywhere. We'd have had to leave it at Dijon, so what's the point?'

'The crossing is fine,' said Liv. 'And the drive down is so beautiful. We always love it.'

'I can't stand rented cars,' said Griff. 'They're always completely disgusting, and collecting them is a nightmare.'

'Come in, come in. Let's go in,' said Alex, breaking a sweat.

'Dan?' said Bea.

Startled from his thoughts, he smiled at her, but his smile was false. 'Coming,' he said.

She wanted to say something but there was no time.

In the hall Alex was all eagerness. 'What can I get you?'

'Hang on,' said Griff. 'Blimey. We only just walked in.'

'D'you want to go in the garden? Shall we – we could – you'll want to sit down, yeah?'

'You're the boss,' said Griff. 'Fawlty Towers, eh? Where's Manuel?' He laughed. He wore off-white trousers and a peach-coloured linen shirt, untucked, and handmade shoes.

'Your rooms are ready,' said Alex.

'Christ,' said Griff, 'that makes a change.'

They sat in the smaller of the two sitting rooms. Alex smashed a stemmed glass getting the drinks, and kicked the pieces under the sideboard.

'We stayed in a *really* lovely chateau not far from Dijon last night,' said Liv. 'And the first night, Alex, in that place we stayed last time. In Picardy, do you remember?'

'Unbelievably pretentious,' said Griff.

'But fun,' beamed Liv, 'with a *really* lovely *terrasse*.'

'You two enjoying yourselves?' Griff asked, tapping the arm of his chair, eyes darting at Dan and Bea.

'We only just got here,' said Bea.

'What is this, a holiday?'

'Sort of.'

'Alex said six months.'

'No, three.'

Griff stared from her to Dan and back, and moved on. 'Alex, how's the cellar?'

'It sort of flooded, a couple of months ago,' said Alex. 'The temperature's OK, I think.'

'We picked up a case of Chablis on the way,' said Griff. 'And some Corton.' He blinked, ending the exchange.

'I won't be a minute,' said Bea. She got up. Dan started from his chair.

'I'm fine,' she said. 'Don't get up.'

She went to the kitchen and safe behind the fire door finished making supper, not thinking about the conversation in the sitting room, just focusing on that. She even sang to herself. There were open bottles of wine and jugs of water. They had put two tables together to hide the mess from the paint. They had scraped it off the grass and hosed it, but it still showed. She took cloths from the sideboard in the dining room. They smelled of damp wood as she shook them out over the tables. She carried the dishes out into the garden; thin ham rippling on a long white plate, and roasted vegetables from the supermarket.

'Dinner's ready,' she said, putting her head round the sitting-room door.

Liv inclined her head wearily. She took Alex's arm and they went out together, followed by Griff and Dan, Griff talking non-stop, firing questions, and Dan politely at his side.

They all sat down; Bea next to Dan, contained and still, and Liv next to Alex, twisting towards him and smiling constantly. Griff ate and talked and talked and ate. All through the first course he held forth. Football. Nuclear power. Useless wind turbines. The absurdities of recycling. The misguided regulation of the financial sector. Lobbyists. Petrol. Socialist Europe. His voice was a sandpaper baritone with a diesel boom, consistently aggressive, the difference between a joke and an attack not easily felt out. Liv pushed her food about and said how delicious everything was, as if saying it were eating it. Every now and then she would start talking, as if Griff weren't already speaking, knowing it wouldn't interrupt him. She talked about recent holidays or exhibitions she'd seen, decorating, but it was the names connected to them that were the topic, not the things themselves, and Alex, Bea and Dan were a disappointing, irritating audience.

'You *must* know Jasper,' she'd say. 'You *remember*.'

Griff's voice dominated and the others' wove through it, with Alex laughing at his jokes, out of time, like a drunk musician in a string quintet.

'It's so boring, this sanctity of every human life bullshit,' Griff was saying. 'Thousands stranded on the borders of wherever, hundreds drowned – I'm sorry, nobody likes to say it, but none of these people are essential. They're not useful – so what? The planet is horrifically overpopulated. Horrible for them, personally, obviously, but wouldn't any eco-warrior see it the same way?' He looked around, and landed on Bea. 'Bea? We're parasites, aren't we?'

'Don't answer, Bea,' said Alex, 'it's a trick question.'

'The human race are vermin,' said Griff. 'Some need to go, surely the weakest, and most parasitical? We need to approach these things rationally.'

'Like Nazis,' said Bea, falling into his trap.

'Still in love with your student politics?' Griff barked at her. 'Still a lefty?'

'There's no useful answer to that.'

'I can imagine the whining that goes on amongst NHS social workers, nothing but moaning, I should think.'

'I'm not a social worker,' said Bea.

'It's the pen-pushers I blame, more than anyone.' And he was away again, on bureaucracy, and the oppression of free enterprise.

As he talked, Liv reached into her bag beside her chair. She took out her reading glasses and shyly put them on.

Bea stopped listening, transfixed by her mother, who beneath the cover of Griff's voice, took Alex's hand and placed it on the table. She rolled up his sleeve and bent over his bare arm, inspecting it, tracing her fingers, inch by inch along his veins. Griff lost his audience and lost his focus. As the table fell silent Liv looked up and around them all. She was not surprised to be noticed, performing her intimate ritual. Alex sat compliant, like a person sedated.

'Old habits die hard,' said Liv.

She let go of his hand. He tucked it back into his body as she took his other arm gently by the wrist and rolled up that sleeve too, examining his skin from palm to bicep.

'Mum,' he whispered, 'that was *years* ago.'

Her nails were short and glossy.

'You've no idea what I go through, worrying,' she said. She let his shirtsleeve fall, and patted it.

'Bea!' Griff's voice was like a gunshot.

Bea jumped, blood pumped through her chest and up her neck.

'Don't look at your mother like that.'

Liv looked up. 'What have I done? Are we supposed to pretend? I thought you would be all for openness, Bea.'

Bea picked up her empty plate, then Dan's and Alex's, and left the table.

'All right?' she heard Dan say.

She went into the kitchen and put the plates down anywhere, on the counter somewhere. They wouldn't notice. She could take two minutes. She stood in beautiful solitude. She listened attentively to the whir of the fridge motor, and the electric clock ticking, in minuscule, measured steps. She wanted to bolt, like a flight animal from a predator. Her heart raced. She had to grip the countertop. She breathed in, forcing herself to do it slowly. She paid attention to the smell of the chicken, resting in its tin, the grease and salt-smell in the air. She relaxed her fingers, and took air into her lungs and let it out, feet planted, back straight, and she fixed her eyes on the wall ahead of her.

Attention, taken to its highest degree, is the same thing as prayer.

She concentrated on her breathing, measuring it, then the feeling of the counter under her fingers. She heard her mother laughing through the open window. Reaching over the countertop, she closed it. It was quiet now. She imagined shoving things into a bag and going. She pictured getting into the car with Dan. The engine, the tearing gravel.

'Shit,' she whispered. 'Come on.'

She relaxed her eyes. She paid attention. The white wall ahead of her turned insubstantial and disappeared.

It was hard enough for Dan to sit there pretending to be relaxed but when Bea had gone inside Griff turned on him. It felt as if without her he was prey more easily brought down.

'So, Dan, how's married life?'

'Good, yeah, thanks,' said Dan.

'Still an estate agent?'

'I'm taking some time.'

'Alex tells us you decided to quit the rat race.'

'Just until August.'

'Not working out for you?'

Alex got up to collect the rest of the dishes.

'Not now,' said Griff.

He froze.

'Relax,' said Liv.

He sat.

'You should have given me a call, Dan,' Griff said. 'Do you know who I am?'

Dan had never heard anybody actually say that. There was no answer to it.

'Not being funny. Don't take this the wrong way, but what were you both thinking?'

'Pardon?' said Dan. He hadn't said *pardon* since he was about six years old.

'It's not the 1960s,' said Griff. 'Dropping out and tuning in, or whatever the man said. Not that most people were doing that in the sixties, anyway. I certainly wasn't. I was working two jobs. Bought my first property in 1967, famously. I mean, whose idea was it, to go farting off round Europe?'

Across the table, Alex laughed at the word *farting*.

'No,' said Griff, and Alex stopped laughing. Griff turned back to Dan. 'How can you afford it? Have you come into some money? Last I heard, Bea was earning practically nothing, and you were at a high-street estate agent somewhere. Foundations.'

They'd met once, over two years ago, the man was in his seventies and he remembered the name of Dan's office.

'Foundations of Holloway,' said Dan.

'Holloway?' Griff stared at him for a moment and then gave a short laugh, like a depth charge. 'Foundations of Holloway? Priceless.'

'Griff, don't,' said Liv, in a baby voice. She turned from her son, reached across the table and touched Dan's arm. 'Just ignore him,' she said, 'he's a bully. Ignore him.'

'Yes, ignore me,' said Griff.

Inside, when she had recovered herself and could do it, Bea gave her attention to the next thing. She had a task. She could get food onto serving dishes, and take them from one place to another. That was easy. She levered the loose-jointed chicken from the tin and picked up the carving knife. Its blade was slender and very sharp. She put the knife next to the chicken, with some halves of lemon, and carried it out to the garden, her thumb anchoring it, for safety. Someone had turned on the lights. The group at the table were lit on one side only, in darkness on the other. As she approached, she heard her mother say, 'You're an artist, aren't you, Dan?'

Alex jumped up and took the chicken from her and put it in front of his father, like an offering. Bea studied Dan, trying to hear her mother's voice as he heard it, and see what he was thinking.

'You said you'd show me your work. Do you remember?' Liv was saying. Everything she said was banal yet weighted. 'It's such a shame we don't see more of you.'

'Yeah,' said Dan. 'Sorry.'

'Hey, Dan,' said Alex, 'you could work out here if you like. The barn is empty. You could turn it into a studio –'

'Thanks,' said Dan.

Bea thought he looked nothing more than embarrassed. She sat down again. He didn't catch her eye.

Griff picked up the carving knife. 'Greasy,' he said.

'Sorry,' said Alex automatically.

Griff wiped it with his napkin and threw the napkin down.

'First thing tomorrow morning I'm going to get some candles,' said Liv, shuddering. 'This light is awful. When we were here in March it didn't matter, we ate inside.'

'Bea,' said Alex, 'where did we leave the lamp? We've got a lamp.'

'No, no, darling,' said Liv. 'You relax.'

Griff patted Bea's arm. 'Sorry I snapped at you before. Low blood sugar.'

'It doesn't matter,' said Bea.

'A few beautiful things will make so much difference,' said Liv to the table, then turned to Alex. 'We just need to *really* go for it, Alex. This place could be fantastic.'

'I know,' said Alex. 'It could.'

Griff carved the chicken. 'Needn't bother with a knife,' he said, 'could do it with a spoon.'

Chicken and potatoes were doled out. Conversation overlaid the tension, like call-centre hold music. Dan watched Bea's family in action. He had googled his father-in-law. He knew he was rich and seen he had an ego on him when they had met, but nothing prepared him for this. From the moment they got out of the car and started talking about private jets he had begun to lose his bearings. Before, Bea's family money had been notional, he could forget it, but seeing them now, rich was all they were. Everything they did and everything they said radiated it. She had let the facts out gradually, like a trickle of change. Now it was a steady stream. *The jet. New York, the apartment. That gallery I bought you. I said we might see them in Cortina. The cars. Quicker. Easier. Gorgeous. Get.*

'Griff,' said Liv. She had a way of emphasising names and places, that was intimate and drawling. 'Didn't Joe Ka*min*ski start out camping in Marina Foster's *barn*, in *Glouce*stershire?'

The conversation swept over him in an opiate tide. He felt Bea take his hand under the table. He closed his fingers over hers.

'You remember, Griff,' said Liv. 'When he dropped out of *Brist*ol. Now look at him. Such a sweet boy. We had some of his early pieces at my little *gall*ery – you know, to help him out. See, Dan, you could be the next Joe *Kaminski*.'

Completely wrapped in the duvet with just her head showing, Bea watched Dan undress.

'You cold?' he said.

'No.'

'What's all that, with your dad?' said Dan. 'All that *Do you know who I am?*'

'It's just the way he is.'

'I looked him up –'

'When?'

'Long time ago. When we met.'

'Background checks?'

'Like you do.'

'Sure.'

'He's a big-shot developer,' he said. 'Did I miss something?'

'No,' said Bea. 'That's what a big-shot developer looks like.'

He had his T-shirt off, kneeling to undo his trainers, poised like a runner on a track. He did not look tired. She wriggled a little way out of the duvet and sat up.

'What is it?' she said.

'What?'

'Just say it.'

'What's with the private jet?'

'He had a jet.'

'Yeah, I got that,' said Dan. 'You never told me.'

'Why would I tell you? *Ooh, my dad's got a jet.* So what?'

'So what? It's a *jet*,' said Dan.

'Was. He sold it. And?'

'I didn't know he had that kind of cash.'

'Well, he did,' she said. 'Lots of people have jets.'

He was still working on the same lace. It wasn't knotted. 'No, babe,' he said, 'not exactly.'

'I mean lots of rich people,' said Bea. 'What's the difference?'

He shrugged. 'Nothing.' He stood up. He took off both shoes. He went into the bathroom. 'I just didn't realise he had that kind of money.'

He shut the door. She got off the bed and went to the door and opened it. He was bending over the basin.

'Is there a difference, to us?' she said. 'Between well off, and rich, and super-rich?'

He turned. 'No.'

She searched his face. 'I don't take his money. You know that. Is it different, now he *had a private jet*?'

She said it so contemptuously there was only one way to answer.

'No,' he said. 'What's up with you?'

'Why? Nothing.'

'You hate them.'

'I don't *hate* them,' said Bea. 'I'm not twelve.'

'They were terrible parents.'

'I'm over it.'

'I mean, your dad is way worse than she is.'

'He's not worse. He's just greedy. He's ravenous. Nothing is ever enough for him.'

'And her?'

'What do you want me to say?' She almost shouted it.

'Nothing,' he said. 'You want nothing to do with them. I don't either. We're cool.'

She could feel him studying her. She felt plain and clumsy. Her heart was cold and hard.

'Bea.'

'What?'

'I'm on your side.'

'Don't be silly.'

'I said, I'm on your side.'

'I heard.'

'Babe, I just didn't know the guy had a jet.'

She managed a laugh. 'OK.'

In bed, as sleep crept over him, she was wakeful. He was lying behind her. She felt him fall asleep, like he was leaving her alone. His body was there, but he was not.

The hotel was different with her parents in it. She tried to sleep and not listen to the night-time, or think of them there.

At two o'clock she went down to the kitchen for a glass of water; knowing what was up in the roof the kitchen tap seemed safest. She waited as the tap ran cold, filled the glass, and drank, then felt her way back up on tiptoe. Alex's room was at the top of the stairs, to the right, across a landing. There was a glow under the door. Hearing his voice, she stopped. His tone was urgent. She heard a woman's voice gently coaxing. Stock-still, Bea waited, straining her ears, staring at the strip of light beneath his door.

'No, go on,' her brother said.

Bea gripped the banister. The woman's voice sounded unnatural. It wasn't in the room.

'Alex . . .' it said, through the speaker of a computer, '. . . just turning up . . . have to say anything.'

Somebody else said something, a man this time, Bea couldn't hear the words.

'A day at a time,' said the woman.

'Yup,' said Alex.

She heard the miniature slam of the laptop closing, and his chair creaking as he stood up. She ran to her room, shut the door and got back into bed.

'Dan?'

He didn't answer.

She sat against the headboard, looking out through the window at the small, bright moon which seemed to travel as the clouds crossed it. Both her parents were there, just there, right there, in bed, across the hall. How could she not think of it?

The first time she had been seven years old, and it had been winter. Even now, in adulthood, she found something frightening in the short dark days.

That day had been wet, and her fingers red with cold as she dropped her satchel by the coats. Her nanny, Kathryn, was parking the car, and Bea had forgotten to wipe her feet because the Christmas tree had arrived. It stood, unobserved by anyone but her, towering blackly in the hall, fresh from the forest. She remembered staring up at it, and the thrill, then looking down and seeing her shoes were covered with mushy leaves from outside, and that she had made wet prints on the polished marble. She kicked them off and crossed the hallway in her socks.

The kitchen stairs had a glass balustrade. As she went down, she could see the wet grey garden through the windows, and the sofa, and the two of them on the sofa, lying back. She had known immediately. Or maybe she had altered the memory to fit what she knew later. But she remembered clearly that seeing them, she felt fear, and a sense of wrongness so strong it felt alive. She remembered exactly how it was both nothing and everything, the way a nightmare is. Just a normal room, an empty field; terror, long before the axe comes, or the chase. Liv had been on the sofa, and Alex, in his school uniform, was lying back against her breast, and she was holding one of his hands and sucking his fingers. His plate and cup were beside them on the table. She must have been sucking crumbs off him. Then she saw Bea. Bea remembered they had both looked shocked, but she didn't remember what happened immediately afterwards. Kathryn must have come in. There wasn't a scene and it hadn't been dramatic. There was nothing else to remember, except Alex, coming up the stairs past her, to go to his room, and that as he went by she felt his distress like a sickness passing from his body to hers. She had tried to forget it, but she never could.

Her mother had carved him, over time, until he was misshapen. But someone should have helped him. Someone should. It should have been Bea. She thought of him, going to his room after that supper that night, and finding his help online. She had to hope for him. She tried to. But fear was bigger. She didn't know what chance there was that he could save himself.

She imagined waking Dan and telling him. She would probably cry. He would be shocked and disgusted and comfort her. Maybe that would make it worth it. She might feel innocent. Feel innocent and let herself be helped. But she reminded herself it wasn't her damage. It was not she who had been abused – not in that way. It wasn't hers to indulge and suffer over. Liv's motherly crimes against her were vicious, but they were of the common kind. Cruelty was never nice, but it was in the past, and finished, and she'd got over it. She almost had. She was fine. She didn't need looking after. She thought of all the people in the world who did. Almost anyone she could think of needed looking after more than she did. She didn't deserve it.

8

They had breakfast all together in the dining room; Alex running to and from the kitchen, fetching his special scorched croissants and pots of jam. Liv had only green tea. Griff asked for fruit but then didn't like it when it came. He had a small pot of plain yogurt, digging at it as though there were something at the bottom he wanted. In the afternoon the sky lowered over the trees and it began to rain. Griff summoned Bea to speak to him.

'Will you be all right?' said Dan.

'Of course.'

Her father was waiting for her in the bigger of the two sitting rooms, at the far end of the hotel. Alex was at the reception desk. She didn't know where her mother was. She went through the smaller room and past the bare tables in the dining room, and opened the door. Griff was scanning the few pieces of shabby furniture and threadbare rugs as she came in.

'This place is a shithole,' he said. 'I'd have thought Alex would want to make something of it.'

'I think he does. This is the worst room. Why are we in here?'

'It's the biggest.'

She sat at one end of the sofa, with her limbs tucked in, as if she were on a fairground ride in danger of injury. He went to the door.

'Alex!'

In a few moments, Alex appeared.

'A Campari, when you've got a moment, yes?'

'Sure. Bea?'

'No, thanks, I'm good.'

'I'll put a girdle round the Earth in forty minutes,' said Alex.

'Sooner than that, I hope,' said Griff and shut the door.

He jangled his keys in the loose linen of his pocket. Bea switched on the lamp next to her as the rain pattered down outside.

'Where's Liv?' she asked.

'Why?'

She shrugged.

'How much did that awful car outside cost you?' said Griff.

'Our car?' said Bea. 'Why?'

'It's an opener.'

'To what?'

'Indulge me,' said Griff. 'How much?'

'It was under a thousand.'

He stopped prowling the room to stand above her. 'Let me get you a new one.'

She met his eye. 'It's kind of you, but no, thank you.'

'What are you going to do when it breaks down?'

'It might not,' she said. 'It's an adventure.'

'Be a better adventure in a new car.'

'I don't think so.'

'You don't, maybe,' he said, 'what about Dan?'

Bea tried to make him hear her. 'Neither of us wants a new car. Thank you,' she said, steadily.

She started to get up, but Griff sat at the other end of the sofa, facing her. She hadn't been alone in a room with him, she realised, since the day she'd left home. He'd summoned her to talk about money that day, too. Almost all his conversations were about money.

'You're very sure of yourself, aren't you?' he said. He looked pleased with himself, as if he was about to bring her down.

She jumped as Alex opened the door.

'Your drink, sir. Madam, I took the liberty.' He put the Campari in front of Griff and a glass of water for Bea. He winked at her and went, and closed the door behind him.

'So. Dan. An artist, is he?' said her father, eyeing her.

'He'd like to be.'

'You'd like him to be.'

She let it go.

'Quite interesting you've found a husband who's the total opposite of me, isn't it?'

'It might be interesting for you,' said Bea. 'You weren't at the front of my mind.'

'Never heard of Freud?' said Griff, and laughed.

'I can't say I've heard of his "marrying someone different to your father" complex,' said Bea. 'What did you want to talk to me about?'

He leaned towards her. His eyes were pale blue like a baby's eyes, vital in the ageing skin, piercing among the sunspots and the lines.

'Look, darling, I *know* people. I know them well enough to gamble on them. I've built a career around it. Fifty years. Within a few minutes of talking to someone, I know what they want. Knowing what they want, I know how to deal with them.'

'I'm sure that's true,' said Bea. She looked away from his face. She drank some water. The outside of the glass was wet. She put it down.

'He won't forgive you, you know,' said Griff. 'Dan. You're holding him back.'

'No, I'm not.'

'Forcing him to play by your rules.'

'No.'

'Look, assuming he does want to be an artist,' said Griff, 'which, frankly, I doubt, are you seriously kidding yourself that he doesn't think about your money?'

She began to feel sick. Her father pushed the air from the room.

'Not everything is about money,' she said, and felt ridiculous. She seemed to see her words change in the air, from butterflies to caterpillars, and herself reduced, shrink from woman to girl, transformed by his presence.

'I would humbly disagree with you there,' said Griff.

'Dan and I are fine. We're more than fine. We're happy.'

'Look, love,' said her father, 'you do your little counselling job, and I'm sure it must be bloody hard work, I'm not denying that, but you do it for a pittance. And that doesn't bother you. But your bloke out there, he came from *shit* – worse shit than *mine*, apparently, which was no picnic.'

'No, he didn't.'

'You think your childhood was tough?' said Griff.

The question threw her. 'No, of course not.'

'Yes, you do,' said Griff. 'You were a late-mistake baby –'

'I know that –'

'Called you "Oops".' He laughed.

'Yes, I know.'

'*Hello, Oops. Night-night, Oops.* And you and your mother don't get on. You're not her type, basically. And I wasn't around much – so poor you, right?'

'No.' Bea struggled to keep hold of the conversation.

'But that husband of yours –'

'What about him?'

'Well, for a start, he's mixed race – are we still allowed to say that? Whatever. It's not a bonus, anyway. I gather his – what do they call them? His *baby-father*? – from what I gather, his dad did a runner, as per cliché. Care homes. God knows. But *then*, he manages to turn it around, doesn't he? Squeezes enough cash out of the government to get himself educated, gets a job that might actually earn him a decent living, and – blimey! – lands himself a Hampstead Princess. Albeit one dressed like a suburban nanny.'

Bea stared at her wedding ring. When would Griff ever have even seen a suburban nanny, unless he'd screwed one.

'But now,' her father went on, leaning closer, '*now*, because of *you*, his progress has been magically fucking halted, hasn't it?'

'It's not because of me,' she said.

'Look, you've got a tiny fucking flat rented out for pocket change, you've got your husband wandering around France like a gap-year arsehole, talking about being an artist, and the two of you are basically on the road to nowhere, and why? Because of your pride. What are you trying to prove? Use some of your money, set him up in business. If that's too much to ask, at least, if you're going to take time out, be civilised and take a proper holiday!'

He was close enough for her to see the sun damage, the folds in the skin of his neck.

'You don't know anything about Dan,' said Bea. 'You had one conversation with him, two years ago. You don't remember anything about him, because you don't want to remember, because it doesn't fit your stereotype. He put himself through art school, before we met, and his father is white, actually, his mother is black, and he's never been in care – I don't even know where you got that from. And, also, I'm sorry, but there's a difference between a counsellor and a psychotherapist – starting with four years' training.'

She got to her feet.

'Sit down,' he said.

'No. Can I just say, I'm not trying to hurt you, Griff, not taking your money. My choices are not about you. I need to make my own way. And be normal. I would have thought you would respect that.' Griff was smiling up at her, entertained. 'And Dan and me are fine. We're more than fine. We're very, very lucky.'

He checked his watch. 'For a clever girl, you're very stupid.'

'I'm not,' she said. 'I'm not stupid.'

'What makes you so special?'

'Nothing.'

'Sit down.'

'No.'

'Darling.' He smiled, like they were both in on a joke. 'Sit down.'

She sat. She didn't know why. She just found herself doing it.

'Just relax,' he said. 'Have some water. Come on.'

She picked up her glass and had a sip of water, wondering if she was obeying him, or if it was just because her mouth was dry. He seemed to want to connect with her.

'Look at your assets,' he said.

'What assets?'

'Exactly.'

'Excuse me?'

'Not being rude,' said Griff, 'I'd say this to anyone, but you're not the most beautiful girl in the world. Come on, you know that.'

She was both surprised and unsurprised. She had forgotten what it was like to be with her family. Most people weren't cruel like this. Or maybe they just weren't so truthful.

'That's unkind,' she said.

'You're meant to flatter your kids,' he said, 'tell girls they're beautiful. Whatever. I don't care. You were never going to stop traffic. Not like your mum. Fighting them off, she was – still is, for all I know.'

Her legs began to tremble. 'This is not an appropriate conversation,' she said.

Griff laughed. 'Life's not appropriate, love. It's not fair. It's shit. I'm trying to help you out here.'

She steadied her breath. She thought about leaving.

'Money, sex, hunger – these are the drivers,' he said. He held his fingers in front of her face, checking off his list. 'You? You're very smart, apparently, and you've got money. But your husband? He's hungry. Plus, not to put too fine a point on it, he's a very good-looking lad. So what's keeping him?'

Bea's face was burning. It shouldn't be her shame, it was his. She willed herself to be calm, as calm and professional as she was at work. She heard all kinds of things there, and never looked shocked. She had been physically attacked once. She'd handled it. She met his eye again.

'You're being very hurtful,' she said. 'I don't think you realise how hurtful you're being.'

He stared at her for a long moment.

'You're right,' he said.

He sat back and threw up his hands. 'I didn't mean to get into all this. I just want to help you.'

'I know,' said Bea. 'I see that.'

He gazed at his unwanted drink. He looked defeated.

'I can't believe I'm *begging* you to take my money,' he said. 'Grovelling – to help *you*. Bloody hell. Fatherhood.'

'I didn't ask you to,' said Bea. 'I have never asked you for anything. And I never will. If you could –' her mind went blank. Her voice sounded weak. She swallowed. '– be polite. That would be better.'

She left the room. The moment she was away from him, outside the door, tears came painfully into her eyes. They didn't last long.

She didn't tell Dan. She recovered alone. When she saw Griff, later in the day, she met him like a lion tamer and did not show fear.

'You and me flank Alex,' she said to Dan before dinner. 'We'll sit either side of him. There's safety in numbers.'

Alex made the dinner and she and Dan helped.

'Don't let either of them stop you, in the hall, or anywhere, or take you aside. We'll stick together.'

Alex enjoyed the game. 'Thank fuck you're here,' he said. 'It's so different.'

Even at the table, when there was no chance of privacy, she made sure to keep catching Alex's eye, so he wouldn't forget, she sent him fortitude, reminding him of himself.

They'll be gone soon, her look said. *Fuck them.*

It was still raining. They ate in the dining room. Quiches from the freezer. Liv hadn't wanted to let Alex leave her to go to the shops. Pastry, eggs, cheese. Liv's worst foods combined. The quiches were small and circular and slipped about on an oval plate. They made a salad to go with them, the leaves wet from being washed and the dressing sliding off and sugary.

'Christ,' said Griff. 'Tomorrow we eat out.'

He talked about America through most of dinner. 'So Donald Trump is a despicable human being, so what? Look what he's done for America.' Liv talked about the refurbishment of the hotel.

'I need to come down much more often,' she said. 'We didn't realise how much work the old place would need, did we, darling? When we first saw it? We just fell so in love with it. Maybe we should move builders in, and you out and do it properly.'

'No, it's OK,' said Alex. 'I'm doing it. I'm learning.'

Griff boomed on. Brexit. 'Totally incompetent. Government is over. They should have left it to the guys in finance. Clean break.' This led him to Danger. Memories of planes he had flung himself from. Black runs he had conquered. Shark-populated reefs he had perused. Then his thoughts moved on to beauty. Faraway places. Rarity. The difficulty of purchasing truly special things. Acquisitions thwarted by the fetish of conservation.

'Preserve the landscape for the nation. Save the crested newt. Nobody *really* cares about the rare species of fuck-knows-what, they just love obstruction. Meddling –' He stopped. He stared at Bea. 'You look like you've swallowed a lemon,' he barked. 'Come on, Ms Snowflake.'

'What?' said Bea.

'Nothing to say? Won't you lower yourself to debate with me?'

'It's not a debate,' Bea answered. 'You're just talking.'

'All right.' Griff rubbed his hands together. 'Take the floor. Let's have a sermon.'

'You've lost me. Are we on conservation or planning regulations, or Brexit?'

'We're on "Why my father is a capitalist pig, by Bea Adamson". Don't be coy, what's in that expensively educated socialist mind of yours?'

'In Western culture, pigs represent the basest of human urges,' said Bea. 'Greed, obviously –'

'There you go!'

She hated to perform for him.

'You label yourself Capitalist and me Socialist just to put me in opposition,' she said.

'So?'

'You think I blame everything on capitalism.'

'Don't you?'

'Of course not,' she said. 'Alex? Capitalism?'

'A society that runs on the exchange of goods or work for money,' said Alex, eating, not looking up.

'So there's no alternative,' she went on. 'The socialist–capitalist polarity is false and outdated. Friedman v. Marx. It's a twentieth-century obsession. A distraction. Both systems lead to oppression.'

'So your lot are just going to sit around moaning,' said Griff.

'Our lot?' said Bea.

'Liberals. Commies. Whatever.'

Dan laughed at the word. Commies. It sounded so quaint.

'What, you too? Christ,' said Griff, angered. 'Fine.' He pretended to laugh about it. 'You're all commies. Seriously though, you are. The redistribution of wealth? What else would you call it?'

'Just tax, normally,' said Bea. 'Tax, that's all.'

'Tax! Don't start on tax. It's nothing but a witch-hunt. Blah-blah Facebook, blah-blah Starbucks. You'd drive out the businesses – it's all bullshit.' He put on the high, mimicking voice of the whinging lefty. '*It's not fair! Why have they got all the money?*' and snapped back into his normal bass. 'No! Why should I – why should anyone – give away what's mine to incompetent politicians? Where's the justice in that? The vast majority of corporations and companies, and individuals, are acting within the law –'

'I thought you wanted me to speak.'

'Speak then! Bloody hell, do you want a written invitation?'

'Fairness. You accuse people you disagree with of moaning about how unfair things are, but you talk about fairness, too. Fairness and justice. It's the *most* important thing to us all, more than anything else. When you hear someone in pain, or someone unable to accept hardship, or obstacles, it's the unfairness that hurts them most. We're all the same – I can bear any sad story if there's some justice to it. If tragedy is the true consequence of events it hurts, but there's a sort of rigour, there's rightness to it. The thing that is the hardest for people, for *societies* to achieve, is a consensus on what is fair. It's almost impossible. People will often talk with nostalgia about hardships they've endured in the past – wars or poverty – when they have endured them with other people. When we are together, when people are united, there is a sense of rightness that comes out of that, a belief and surrender. Good, healthy societies rely on that feeling to function.

But so do fascist ones. The human need for justice can be exploited so easily, and waves of passion sweep over whole populations – the true belief that they are *right* – and then they're liberated to do terrible things. The collective can turn either way. But one thing is true, always true – I think. I think it's always true.'

She paused, frowning at the word *always,* unsure of her sureness, distrusting her belief. 'If the economic and political basis of our society is the notion of separate, individual people, not responsible for one another, then the justice we look for can only be directed towards ourselves – our needs, our wants, our fighting for what we think is rightfully ours. Human nature is self-serving, surviving, survivalist – we consume by instinct. It's natural to us. And when we're all alone, because of the society we're in, we get frightened, because our greatest need is other people. And in that fear and greed we need to connect, and when we do connect we can only do so badly, we dominate or are dominated.'

She paused again. She felt embarrassed, but it did no good to stay quiet and allow herself the luxury of thinking herself superior, and not take the risk. 'All we have, then, is rational thought; it's everything. The learning of kindness; education, teaching ourselves and others to seek out Good. As individuals, I mean, as individuals we have to force ourselves to give, and to think. When we do that we are strong enough to forget our individual selves. Then – the collective can be good,' she finished quietly.

After dinner, Liv cleared the plates with Alex, and they went to wash up together. Bea followed.

'We're fine,' said Liv. 'We don't need any help.' She un-wedged the kitchen door, and let it close. Bea stayed in the hall, looking at the closed door, unable to move away from it.

Griff was still at the table, playing with his iPad like a child with an abacus.

'Come on, enough now,' said Dan, taking her hand. 'Come up to bed.'

'I'll stay down here a bit,' she said.

'Why?'

'Goodnight.'

'Sure?'

'Yes.'

She kissed him goodnight. He went up, and she stood there, alone in the hall, listening to the muffled clatters behind the baize door. She waited. Her brother's adolescence flicked through her mind in fragments. His sudden absences from home, the expulsions, the useless punishments from Griff. She remembered his padlocked bedroom door which, bro-ken open, revealed such small sins – bottles, Rizla papers, tins of weed.

She remembered how, in the most blameless of situations, it always felt like interrupting, to find him and Liv together. And that he felt trapped.

Bea had always dreaded proof. She rejected what she knew, what she had seen, when she was too young to understand. She almost convinced herself it was a sickness in her, to think up such a thing, until one Easter holiday she saw it. They were at their house in St Barts without Griff, when Alex was seventeen and Bea ten, she had come in from the pool one afternoon and seen, across the courtyard, through Alex's distant, slightly open door, her mother, on her knees, with her head in her son's lap. Both his hands were over his face and his body seemed to be reaching upwards, like a scream – but Bea had turned her head. She remembered distant music from the kitchen and a lizard on the hot wall. Less than a second's glimpse, and she had run away. A few days' sick headache, no appetite, exhaustion – and then back to normal. Years. She had never said a word.

She pushed the door open. They were at the sink. Alex was washing and Liv was wiping baking tins dry. She had a red-and-white-striped tea towel tied around her hips.

'What can I do?' said Bea to their backs.

'Nothing, this is fun,' said Liv. 'It's like being a single girl again. It reminds me of sharing that house in Chelsea, before I met your father.'

'Can I help?' said Bea.

Neither of them turned.

'No,' repeated Liv. 'You go up.'

'Alex?' said Bea.

He didn't answer.

'Alex?'

'Hold on, Mum,' said Alex.

'Really?'

'Just give me a minute. I need to take the rubbish out,' he said.

'I'll wait,' she said, dried her hands and looked around, for-lornly.

Bea followed him through to the annexe. He tied up the bags that were half full, and opened the side door with a key. Bea saw Liv watching them as they went outside. There were boxes of empty bottles and a heap of other rubbish bags stacked against the side wall, some ripped open by foxes, with garbage spilling out.

'Sorry,' he said, cramming what he could into the bag he was carrying and kicking the mess aside. 'I get a bit behind.'

'I don't care,' said Bea. She picked up a crate of bottles, and they went together, down the path, separated from the driveway by a screen of trees and nettles. It was still raining slightly, hard to see but drenching and light.

'God,' she said.

'Yep.'

'We could all run away tomorrow,' she said. 'You, me and Dan? For the day?'

'I can't. I've got a thing Dad needs me to do.'

'What thing?'

'Just an errand.'

They reached the lay-by, and big wheelie bins. Alex flipped up the tops, and flung the bags inside.

'I'll be back in the afternoon.' The rain was fine, like a web on his T-shirt and hair, gathering in droplets. 'She wants to go round the shops with me. Get stuff for the hotel.'

'Maybe the next day?'

'I thought Dan wanted to head off. See the seven wonders and whatever.'

'Not yet.'

He wiped off his hands on his jeans, took a small, flat bottle of brandy from his back pocket and offered it to her.

'*Digestif*?' he said.

She didn't want any but she took a sip for companionship, and handed it back. He drank the rest, sucking the very last of it from the neck. The rain drifted down around them, soundless and soft.

'I'm sorry we can't stay longer,' she said.

He shrugged and threw the small bottle into the bin and wiped his mouth. 'Your husband doesn't like us. Understandable. I don't either.'

'He likes *you.*'

Alex shrugged. 'He thinks I'm an arsehole. He's got a point.'

She shook her head. 'No, he doesn't.'

They started slowly back together, along the road, through the main gate, and up the drive smelling the earth and the fresh leaves, chilled by the wet spring night.

'When you're gone,' said Alex, 'and you look back, this will feel like a dream.'

Bea thought of London, far away, and all the people she'd left behind. She thought of her and Dan and the days ahead, and Alex, left there, stranded. They reached the door.

'Alex –'

He stopped on the front step, mild and unsuspecting. 'Yup?'

She wished she knew what to say.

'Do you think you'll go to an online meeting tonight?' she asked.

'I don't know,' he said. 'Maybe.'

He was sheltered by the porch, and she was in the rain, trying to make him stay with her, outside, where they were free and could talk.

'When you do,' she said, 'you know, at the meetings – are you open with them?'

He became still and closed, withdrawing from her. 'Let's go in,' he said.

Bea didn't move either.

'I need to go,' he said, insistent.

'Why?'

'She wants me to.'

She couldn't let him leave. She stood looking up at him.

'So, if you went online tonight, Alex. To the group you go to —'

'Yes, what?' He was impatient.

'Can you talk about anything?'

He came down the steps towards her, suddenly, and took her arm, pressing himself close to her, cheek to cheek, but looking past her into the darkness, and she sensed the strung-tight heart of him. The rain was heavier now, falling on them, wetting her hair.

'People talk about all kinds of shit,' he whispered, close to her ear. 'You wouldn't believe the fucked-up disgusting shit that people do.'

She was frightened, but felt hopeful, too, closer to truth than she had ever come. Stepping back, to see him clearly, she said, 'I would. I really would.'

He didn't speak. She could not read him.

'There's nothing you can say that would shock me,' she said. 'There's nothing in the world that's unsayable, and I will never, ever think badly of you.'

They looked into each other's eyes, raindrops falling from his hair, trickling down his face.

'Come in,' he said. 'Please, Bea.'

He opened the front door and she followed him in. Her mother was still in the kitchen and the door was closed. She didn't know where her father was. Alex started off, then stopped and turned.

'I'll be back tomorrow night,' he said.

'Where are you going?'

'It's just a thing I do for Dad, I told you. They're going after that. It's fine.'

'And tonight?'

'It's all right.'

Liv opened the kitchen door.

'Darling?' she said, hating to see her children talking.

'Coming,' said Alex.

Liv retreated, and the fire door shut.

'I wish . . .' He smiled. Perhaps he was imagining resolution. A future.

'What?'

The kitchen door opened again. Liv. Hair tucked behind her ears, tea towel in her hand.

'Are you going to leave me to clear all of this up by myself?' she said.

'Sorry, Mum,' said Alex.

He followed on. The door closed with the sound of being sealed. Bea went upstairs. She heard her father's footsteps in the hall.

'ALEX!' he shouted. 'Don't you own a fucking umbrella? It's pissing down! I'm off for my walk.'

There was no answer.

'Never mind! I've got one in the car.'

He left, the front door slammed, and Alex and his mother stayed in the kitchen, cleaning up.

Bea woke in the middle of the night. She didn't know what had woken her. The white noise of the rain had stopped. She realised Dan was not in bed. Silently, she got up and opened the window. She lay and waited for him. The nightingale started to sing, chirps and gaps and trills. She listened to the patterns in the dark. Then Dan was next to her.

'You're dreaming. Go to sleep,' he said.

Alex wasn't there next morning. The hotel felt strange without him. Dan and Bea went to the cafe in Arnay for lunch and her parents went to a hotel.

He wasn't back by four o'clock, and still not back for dinner. Liv sat at his computer in the hall, looking at Pinterest, and calling her friends.

'Lolly! I'm in France. Yes, our project . . .'

Griff tapped out emails on his iPad.

'He said he was going on an errand for you,' said Bea. 'What was it?'

'He went to Mâcon.'

'He should be back, shouldn't he?'

'Alex does this,' Griff said. 'He's always done it.'

That night, Bea and Dan gave up on manners and ate dinner separately from her parents in their room, then watched a movie on Dan's laptop in bed. The image kept freezing and the sound carried on without the picture. Alex's phone was not answering.

'You can't say it's not like him,' said Dan.

Griff's night-time walk was longer than usual, and when he came in they heard him arguing with Liv in their room across the corridor.

Bea fell in and out of sleep, with the sounds of their voices and the shifting noises above her in the roof spilling into her dreams in fragments. She dreamed of people talking, and places she had never been, then woke, then dreamed again, of the familiar and the strange, tainted by fear. And then the night was over, and she saw the beginnings of morning through the curtains and heard the birds. If animals were awake and it was light nothing bad could happen.

Gratefully, she fell into a deep sleep, woken soon afterwards by the doorbell. First, she discarded the sound. It wasn't hers. Then it rang again, and she thought Alex would answer it. It rang again, and she was suddenly awake. She got out of bed fast, pulling on jeans with the white T-shirt she slept in.

'Dan?' she said, but he didn't stir, asleep on his back, oblivious.

She ran down the stairs, holding her hair off her face. Through the window she saw a police car, blue with yellow chevrons, parked at an angle across the gravel. She opened the front door to two gendarmes standing on the steps. One of them spoke to her.

'Do you speak French?'

Her vision expanded, details jumping out. The sun was not yet visible in the clear, pale sky. There was a third officer in the police car, staring straight ahead, like a dummy. Helplessly she wanted to go back.

'Yes,' She nodded. *'I speak French.'*

'What is your name?' he asked.

'Beatrice Adamson,' said Bea. *'What's happened?'* Her hands held the edge of the door, there was grit on the floorboards beneath her bare feet.

'What relation are you to Alexander Adamson?'

'I'm his sister.'

'May we come in?' he said, then, as if as an afterthought, *'I'm sorry to disturb you so early. My name is Blanchard.'*

She had the idea that if she refused she could stop it, that to submit was to invite the Devil. But she had no choice. She opened the door wider. They came into the hall in their army boots and uniforms. She wasn't wearing a bra. She crossed her arms. The younger gendarme, who hadn't spoken, took off his sidecap and looked around.

'*I have bad news,*' said the first man, Blanchard, and waited.

'*What's happened?*' she asked obediently.

'*There has been an accident.*'

She felt very alone. He looked straight into her eyes.

'*Your brother has been involved in a car accident. I'm very sorry to have to tell you, he did not survive. He is dead.*'

She'd heard what he'd said, and half of her felt it was a very small thing, this one fact, and now she knew it, it was done, but the rest of her did not believe him. She watched herself from a distance, standing barefoot in the hall. They were both much taller than she was. She saw herself lean towards them.

'*I'm sorry, could you say that again?*'

'*Your brother, Alexander Adamson, was in a car accident this morning, a few hours ago. I am sorry, madame.*'

'*Where did it happen?*' she asked.

'*Near a town called Oyannax.*'

'*Where is that?*'

He gestured. '*Two hours, from here. Near Bourg-en-Bresse.*'

'*I don't know where that is.*'

There was a silence. She had never heard of those places. She didn't know anything about them.

'*Where?*' she said.

'*Oyannax.*'

'*What did you say your name was?*'

'*My name is Jean Blanchard.*'

She began to shake — not her limbs, but from the inside. She didn't know if she was breathing. He looked concerned. He looked very upset for her, and the other gendarme was staring at her.

'*I'm so sorry you had to do this,*' she said. '*It must be awful telling people these things.*'

'*Why don't you sit down?*' said Blanchard, gesturing his companion to bring a chair.

She heard heavy footsteps on the gravel outside, and they all turned as Griff came into the hall, smart and healthy-looking and full of vitality from his morning walk.

'What's going on?' he demanded, looking from Bea to the two uniformed gendarmes standing beside her, with their holstered guns and heavy boots.

'Bea?'

'Alex is dead,' she said. She shouldn't have just said it. She should have prepared him. She was overwhelmed by remorse. 'I'm sorry, Dad. I'm so sorry.'

Griff didn't say anything, he didn't move at all. She couldn't stop thinking how badly she had done it. She'd been so cruel. She'd done it wrong.

'*Monsieur Adamson?*' said Blanchard. '*You are the father of Alexander Adamson?*'

Griff's eyes didn't leave Bea's face.

'*My father doesn't speak French,*' she said. '*Can you speak to him in English?*'

'Go and wake your mother,' said Griff.

She nodded. She left him with the two gendarmes, and hurried upstairs, but when she saw Alex's bedroom door, she stopped. She was on the landing, out of sight. Dan and her mother didn't know yet. She looked at Alex's bedroom door. She couldn't go past, and not be completely sure that he wasn't inside. He might be in his room. She might have imagined it. It might be a mistake. She heard the men's voices below. She knocked on the door. He was never up so early, she felt mean for waking him. And happy. She clung to the narrow, phantom feeling. She knocked again – and then she opened it. The bed was empty. The small, false feelings dissolved. Alex wasn't in the room but his death was there. She told herself she couldn't believe it, her mind scrabbled to pretend, but loss, whispered and glimpsed, was beginning. And loss believed it. And loss knew death. She stared around the empty room. A whisky bottle on its side. Raw, loose tobacco, scattered in shreds. Ashtrays, mugs, and mugs used as ashtrays. A ceramic Buddha incense holder. Jeans on the floor, and heaps of T-shirts, pants under the bed. Just like Holford Road. He'd hardly changed at all.

Something moved on the wall, just next to her. She thought at first it was a strip of plastic, then she saw it was the snakeskin from the attic, he'd pinned it up beside the bed. Lighter than tissue paper, stiffer, it swayed in the slight breeze. The snakeskin fluttered, lifting from the wall, translucent, silvery. She touched its edge. Then she heard her mother's voice behind her. It was reedy, and weak.

'Who's downstairs?'

Bea heard her footsteps coming closer.

'Bea? What are you doing? Where's Alex?'

Bea turned to face her.

PART TWO

9

Bea didn't remember ever calling her mother *Mummy*. She used her mother's name as little as possible, and they almost never touched. In the last three years she may have felt her mother's lips politely brush her cheek twice, perhaps. Now, half dressed in the corridor between their two rooms Bea took both Liv's hands. It came to her clearly and for the first time there was something greater than her mother's crime. She held her and told her that her son was dead, and felt, despite herself, only pity. Liv's face turned white, as if the skin was pulling back and shrinking. She stared. Gaping, she gripped Bea's hands. Her legs gave way. Her fingers clawed to stop herself falling, but she fell. Bea knelt with her, feeling her mother's spine against her palm, her shoulder blades.

'No, no, no,' Liv moaned.

Bea heard Dan say her name, behind her.

Liv writhed and pulled away. Bea let her go and she went limp. She seemed to disappear, her body lay discarded on the floor like rags. Bea stood up. She turned towards Dan.

'Alex has been in a car accident,' she said. 'He's dead.'

The hard wave hit her. Her face did not feel like hers. Tears fell so fast her eyes hurt and she couldn't see. Dan put his arms around her.

'No, I can't,' she said. She pulled herself back. 'Help me.'

She meant *Help me to not lose control*. He was steady.

'All right, come on,' he said.

He got Liv up from the floor and Bea wiped away her tears with the backs of her hands. Together, they took her downstairs.

In the hall, the gendarme, Blanchard, explained what they knew about the accident, and the timing and what had happened. He had to repeat himself because they couldn't take it in. All the time he was talking, Liv's voice accompanied him, interrupting, full of rage, instructing them. Automatically, Bea tried to comfort her, and Griff held her. When she was helped to sit, she stood, when left alone, she screamed. At times she dropped her head and moaned.

'Tell me again,' said Griff, over her crying. 'Where? Bea? Make him say it.'

Bea obeyed. Dan with his arm firmly around her, said nothing.

At six o'clock that morning, a JCB had hit Alex's Renault on a slip road, not far from Bourg-en-Bresse. The Renault had been parked across the road, with Alex inside it. They thought he must have died quickly, but the officer, Blanchard, didn't like to say too much. He didn't know. The doctor examining at the scene had made a preliminary report, but he couldn't tell them any more than that. He was there to inform the next of kin, and collect them. It was hard to be clear, or to make a plan, Liv needed management, even in her silences.

'Poor woman,' Bea heard the second gendarme saying. *'A mother. My God, poor woman.'*

'It will be necessary for at least one of the family to identify the body,' said Blanchard. 'Would it be possible for you to come with us to Bourg-en-Bresse?'

'They need us to identify him,' Bea said to Griff.

'Fine,' said Griff. 'And tell him I want to see where it happened.'

Bea did as she was told. 'He doesn't know if that's allowed,' she said. 'We need to identify him first.'

'They may have got the wrong person,' said Griff. 'They've probably made a mistake.'

She realised her father was in shock, too, and hadn't taken in what had happened. None of them had. They were at the beginning. They were nothing in the face of it.

'I don't think they've got the wrong person,' she said. 'I think they're sure.'

'Ask him, Bea,' said Griff.

'All right,' she said, but she didn't, she just asked the officers to wait, so they could get dressed properly.

Blanchard wouldn't let Griff drive himself, and Griff wouldn't allow anybody else to drive his car. Nobody wanted to directly contradict him, or tell him he wasn't in his right mind, and there was an awkward, circular argument. In the end, Dan and Bea went in the police car, and Blanchard drove Griff's Porsche, with Griff sitting furiously in the passenger seat and Liv in the back, alone.

It was more than two hours to the Hôpital Centre Fleyriat, which was on the outskirts of Bourg-en-Bresse. Bea and Dan sat in silence and the journey was timeless, just being taken to the next thing, like space travel. Sitting in the back of a French police car was no more strange than anything else. It was as if her brain was deep-frozen. Dan held her hand, and their hands did not change position all the way.

The Centre Fleyriat was surrounded by vast, brand-new-looking car parks in a featureless landscape. The police car and the Porsche parked side by side, with an expanse of tarmac around them. They walked all together in a group to the front entrance, and went inside. There was almost nobody in sight, anywhere in the clean, empty spaces of stone and glass. A woman approached them. She was in her fifties, and had a chignon, an identification badge and highly polished shoes.

'Hélène Guerin,' she said. They all shook hands. 'I am here to help you.' She led them down a corridor and into an immaculate lift. She pressed the button for the basement with a precise movement. *This must be very hard for you,* she said in French, looking up at the numbers as they illuminated. *You and your family have my sympathy.*

Her shoes were patent leather. It seemed odd to meet the family of someone who had died wearing beige patent leather high heels. Bea supposed she hadn't known, getting dressed, what would happen at work. Neither Blanchard nor she looked any of them directly in the eye. They were set apart by crisis.

'After you,' said Hélène Guerin when the lift doors opened. They followed her along a corridor. Griff and Liv were ushered away through an electronic door, and disappeared.

Bea and Dan waited in the low-ceilinged corridor on bright blue plastic chairs, bolted to the floor. Hélène Guerin came back through the electronic doors and sat next to them. She offered them water. When she checked her phone, she did it turned slightly away, out of respect.

'It's all right,' said Bea, 'we don't mind. You must be very busy.'

They sat in silence, still holding hands, with the sound of the circulation of the building beating like life support around them.

'Are you sure you don't want a coffee?' said Dan.

'No thanks,' said Bea.

When Griff and Liv came back they were transformed. Liv was smaller, and weakened. It was as if her insides had been removed and altered, even her clothes didn't sit the same way on her body. At her side, Griff had never looked so powerful, like a man in battle. Liv put both hands over her face. Stumbling, she went towards the desk, where a man was on the phone, but Griff took her arm, and led her away.

'I can't stand it,' she said. 'I want to die.' Her face caved in like melted wax.

Compassion rose in Bea, warm as blood, nauseating.

'All right?' said Dan, seeing how still she was. He held her around the waist. She didn't want to be like her mother. She stood up straighter.

'Come this way, please,' said Hélène Guerin. She took them back into the lift, and through the hospital, to where the gendarmes were waiting.

'Now I want to see where it happened,' said Griff. 'Tell them, Bea.'

'What?'

'Tell them I want to see the place now. I want to see it.'

Bea asked, but nobody would take them.

'Ask him what happens next,' said Griff.

She asked, but Blanchard wasn't sure. The hospital would be in touch, and the police. He advised them to speak to the British Consulate. Hélène Guerin had been assigned by the hospital to help them, but they couldn't see her, she had gone.

'Tell him I want to see the place,' said Griff, again.

'I've told him.'

He made her insist, and to her surprise Blanchard agreed. It seemed there was power in being the victims of a tragedy, nobody seemed to know exactly what to do with them.

'He'll take us later.'

'Find us a hotel,' said Griff. 'I'm not waiting around here.'

'A hotel?'

'Nearby somewhere. Just find the best one and book it. Am I allowed my own car now?'

Blanchard stood under the concrete canopy and watched the family walk back to Griff's red car, marooned in the enormous car park.

Dan googled a hotel as Griff drove, and Bea phoned and booked it. It was near the centre of town, white plaster and balconies and a well-planted square behind looped railings. Bea and Dan sat in the bar while Griff took Liv up. Bea lay down on the banquette in the hotel bar and slept, and Dan sat waiting for her to wake up, then ordered her a cup of tea. The tea came in a tall glass on a saucer, wobbling. His hands hovered over her while she drank.

Later in the afternoon her father came down.

'Bea, come with me.'

She went to his side.

'Dan,' said Griff, 'stay with Liv. The windows open all the way here. Not like in America.'

He handed Dan the key card. 'Up you go.'

'Bea?' said Dan, then did as he was told.

The suite was on the first floor, at the corner of the building. He knocked on the door and said, 'Liv? It's Dan.' When there was no answer he said, 'I'm coming in, if that's OK?' and slipped the key card into the slot. The light flicked green and he opened the door.

The curtains were closed. He was in a vestibule and as his eyes adjusted he saw a sitting room with a sofa and a vast black television, like a black hole in the toile de Jouy wallpaper. Next to the television was a pair of open double doors to the bedroom, and, walking further into the room, he could see the bed and the shape of Liv's body, the upper half covered by the folds of a silk bedspread, also patterned, like the wallpaper.

'Liv?' he said. 'It's Dan.'

She moved her arm to shield her face.

'I'll just — sit in here, if that's OK?' he said. 'Griff and Bea have gone out for a bit, he asked me to come up.'

He went to the double doors and pulled them almost closed, to give her privacy, but open enough so that he would hear if something happened. He didn't know what might happen. Griff had talked about the windows. He pictured her flinging them open, and leaping out, and it being his fault. They were tall, with tiny balconies, too small for standing on. He realised he was placing his trainers soundlessly, like a burglar, and straightened up, glancing around for something to do. It wasn't nice to put the television on, and he wondered if there was a minibar, or if it would be in the bedroom — not that he wanted anything, he just wanted to look inside it, it was what you did in hotel rooms.

An enormous vase of flowers stood on a gilt coffee table in front of the television. He sat on the sofa and stared at it, examining the large pale petals in the gloom, and imagining Bea with Griff, going to where the crash had happened. He hated her going off with her bully of a father. He couldn't think of Alex as dead, it made no sense to him. He felt for Bea, and wanted to be with her, not babysitting her mother, but he felt nothing for Alex. Not yet. No sadness. Nothing. Just anger at being hijacked by a disaster that wasn't his, yet another thing her family had done to her. She didn't even want to know them, and now they were both caught up. There was no point fighting it. He had to do what she wanted, and that meant what Griff wanted. He had to sit and wait in this strange and silent room, with the gaping television screen looming and the waxy petals gleaming. He needed a pee. He couldn't get to the bathroom without going through the bedroom, and he shouldn't do that. He imagined his pee splashing loudly and Liv hearing it. He pictured peeing in the vase of flowers and Liv appearing in the doorway and seeing him.

'Ah –' she said, in the bedroom, on her own. 'Ah, ah, ah.'

It shocked him to hear her, not crying but saying *ah, ah, ah* – over and over. She sounded unaware of the noise she was making. She could do that, if it helped, it wasn't his business. But the wails grew higher and a little louder with every repeated sound. It reminded him of women he'd seen on the news, some Middle Eastern war zone, flattened city, wailing in the rubble of their homes – keening and cawing in animal grief. He sat forward, shaking his head to himself, cornered by the sound. Eventually, he stood up and spoke to her through the gap in the door.

'Liv? It's Dan again. Is there something I can get for you? Are you OK?'

The noise stopped, abruptly. He stood there, listening for her voice, but she didn't say anything. Quietly, he tiptoed back to the sofa and resumed staring at the blank screen and the flowers. He wondered if the room being so expensive made any difference, if it would have been harsher if she'd had to wait in the street, or in the car, or like those other grieving mothers, in the rubble of her home. He felt he should believe distress was the same the world over, wherever it was, but it seemed to him her misery was defined by its luxurious setting, that even the death of a son could be cushioned by wealth. He felt guilty for thinking it. It was probably just his own reaction, to this muffled room, stifled by the scent of room spray and clean carpets. Alex wasn't his brother, but he must be in shock, too.

A knock at the door made him jump and he sprang up and opened it, just a few inches, to see a maid. She looked shocked to see him and took a big step back, her eyes wide in her round and pasty face. Her hair was pinned to her scalp with grips, one hand rested on the push-bar of her trolley, stacked with little decorated bottles for the bathrooms, and the other held her pass key. Dan wanted to explain the room was occupied, and they didn't want to be disturbed, but he didn't know the French words and hesitated over the English ones. The maid's expression hardened. She glanced down the corridor.

'We don't need anything, thank you,' said Dan.

Her mouth was set against him. She hurried off towards the lifts. Dan saw her turn to look at him as she rounded the corner. He shut the door, and went back into the gloomy room, glancing through the gap to where Liv lay. He took out his phone and texted Bea but there was no response.

After a minute or two, there was another knock at the door. He opened it to find a white man in his thirties, with very tidy hair and a dark suit.

'Monsieur,' he said, 'I am Henri Michaud. I am the manager of the hotel.'

Dan saw the maid by the lifts whispering to another maid, both watching.

'May I ask your name?' said the manager.

'Daniel Durrant,' said Dan.

Glancing over his shoulder, he stepped out into the corridor.

'What can I do for you?'

The manager smiled coldly. 'May I ask why you are here? This is Monsieur Adamson's suite.'

'I'm his son-in-law,' said Dan. 'Mrs Adamson is inside. Is there something I can help you with?'

The manager's face flushed, instantly, and it made him look much younger. He was the same age as Dan, and the same height. He darted a look at the maids, standing together at the end of the corridor, exchanging glances.

'Would you bring up some champagne, please?' said Dan. He didn't know why he said it, it just came out.

'Certainly, sir,' said the manager. 'I am very sorry, we didn't know.'

'Forget it.'

'My mistake. The maid.'

'Don't worry about it,' said Dan.

He went back into the suite, and shut the door on him.

When the champagne arrived, he jumped up and closed the gap in the bedroom doors, hastily clearing a space on the table. He overtipped the waiter, and shut him out as fast as he could, then sat there, staring at the dripping silver ice bucket, wondering how it would look to Griff or Bea that he had ordered champagne when Alex had just died, and his mother was prostrate with grief in the room next door. He opened the bottle, deadening the sound with a linen napkin, and poured himself a glass and then he put his feet up on the yellow silk sofa. They had included a small bowl of cashew nuts, which was nice. If Liv came out, he could offer her some.

10

Blanchard drove Griff and Bea to the place, forty minutes away. Bea sat next to Griff in the back of the car. He had his sunglasses on and he wasn't saying anything. Now he had his way he stopped giving instructions. The foreign landscape slipped by, and civilian traffic made way to let them pass. Then there were almost no other cars, just farmland. Blanchard was silent, like her father. She couldn't remember what time it was. In her confusion she couldn't separate all the questions she had, and she looked out at the flat fields and the silence grew heavier and heavier. There was nothing to be said. She would see where it had happened. That was all there was, and dread. They were following in Alex's steps. It had to be done. Seeing where. She took her father's hand.

'I understand,' she said.

He ignored her. She took her hand away. Outside the car, on either side, the farmland was criss-crossed with thin bone-coloured roads. She had never been there but it was familiar, the white road of her nightmare.

'It's from the stone factory,' said Blanchard, as if she'd asked. *'It's stone dust.'*

'Really?' she said, as if she was interested. *Ah, bon?*, like a French phrase book. It was ridiculous of her. In the distance, an industrial-sized agricultural machine moved slowly, spraying something. She didn't know what. She imagined the dust washing from the green leaves. She couldn't picture Alex here. She didn't know why he would have been.

'What is this?' said Griff. 'What was he doing here?'

'I don't know,' she said.

The car swung as Blanchard turned left, at a right angle, and stopped.

'OK,' he said. He got out of the car and opened the door for Griff. Bea got out on her own.

There were young crops growing in neat lines in the fields on either side. Ahead, she could see slack, candy-striped tape cordoning off the road, and yellow '*Route Barrée*' signs. Blanchard's phone rang, loudly, and he answered it. Bea and Griff stood staring at the blowing tape and the accident site beyond it, while he talked. There were jet-black streaks on the road leading to the place where Alex's car was being winched onto a half-trailer. Bea stared at the car, swinging gently on the cables as it rose up. There were several police, or traffic police, in various uniforms, some standing around, others directing the driver of the tow truck lifting Alex's car. Blanchard was arguing with somebody on the phone. Bea couldn't hear the details. She heard him say *Merde*, then *Ça me fait chier* as he walked away, with his back to them.

She and Griff stood side by side behind the blowing tape, staring at the car. It sucked her in, like falling, and she dragged her eyes away, but it drew her back. The small group of traffic police watched too, as the black Renault swung towards the trailer. Everything was in relation to the hanging car, from the far horizon to the nearest figure, feet away. There were two thick troughs gouged through the green shoots in the soft earth of the field by the car, where it had come off the road, and more exposed earth where it had been dragged back. In the middle distance stood a factory, like a cardboard cut-out and on the other side of the car, past the tow truck and trailer, was another line of striped tape and more yellow signs, and she saw two men, who looked like workmen, also watching. They were smoking and talking. Nobody told them not to watch. She heard Blanchard's footsteps as he hung up and came over to them.

'OK, I'm sorry, I need to take you back,' he said.

Griff didn't turn or answer him, he was still staring at Alex's car, hanging on the chains.

'Excuse me? Did you hear? I have to take you back now,' said Blanchard.

'What was Alex doing here?' she asked Griff.

He didn't answer.

'What happens now?' she said.

'They take the car,' said Blanchard. 'They examine it. Look, it's time to go.'

Bea looked at Griff, who still hadn't moved, staring at the crash site from behind his dark glasses.

'Dad?' she said. 'He wants to take us back.' When he didn't answer, she turned to Blanchard. 'Two minutes?' she asked. 'Is that OK?'

He was embarrassed by the situation. 'OK,' he said, sullen in his awkwardness.

She looked from the car to the gouges, and the jet-black skid marks. The static scene animated itself in her mind. She pictured sunrise, and Alex in his car in an early dawn, and the sudden impact as the blue JCB hit. The brakes, the tyres, the car hurled across the road. Blanchard walked back to his car and leaned against it, crossing his booted feet at the ankle. He took out his phone again and lit a cigarette. Sun and shadow moved across the flat land, dotted with houses and, in the distance, the dark green foothills of the Jura. She could hear the brief exchanges of the men, snatches on the breeze, as they loaded the crumpled Renault.

'What was he doing, out here?' she whispered to Griff again.

'He must have been up to something,' he said.

'Up to what?' She imagined Alex driving from the main road at night, and stopping there. 'Why?'

There was a clunk. The Renault stopped in place above the trailer. Abruptly, Griff left her side and ducked under the tape. He strode towards the car.

'*Hey!*' shouted Blanchard. '*Monsieur!*' He shoved his phone into his pocket and started to run after him.

'Dad?' called Bea.

Blanchard ducked under the tape too, and she followed. Griff broke into a run. The three of them ran, their shoes kicking up small storms of dust.

'*Hey, stop!*' called Blanchard.

Ahead, the traffic police waved their arms.

'*Stop!*' they shouted, waving, like people herding an animal, hi-viz armbands glinting in the sun.

'*Monsieur! Stop!*'

Blanchard overtook and barred Griff's way, pulling off his sidecap, out of breath. And holding his arms wide. Griff, thwarted, strained like a dog on a lead.

'*What's he doing?*' Blanchard shouted angrily to Bea.

They were close to it now. It swung above them, violent and torn apart. The driver's door was missing — not hanging, gone — from the crushed side of the car. She could see the leather seats, and cigarette ends tipped out on the carpet. The bonnet was a stub and the buckled wheels thickly caked with earth, but the panels behind the doors were intact, and so was the boot. It was open but undented, just mud-spattered and normal-looking. She stared through the gaping hole at the driver's seat. She could almost see blood. She jammed her hand over her mouth. She had a clear picture of the door being sawed through and pulled off and the ambulance crew dragging out his body. She leaned over her knees to breathe. Blanchard started towards her and seeing him distracted, Griff took his chance. He ran towards the trailer. Bea looked up. Blanchard glared at her and went after him, but it was too late. Griff had sprung up onto the trailer, the powerful jump of a much younger man, and grabbed one of the cables holding the car. The men watched, amazed, as he hooked the fingers of his other hand under the back bumper. The car swung towards him. Thrown back, he hung over the drop, shoulders straining under his linen shirt, then he let go of the bumper, and reached into the open boot, groping for purchase. He clung to the broken car and it moved, swinging on the chains, as he embraced it.

Bea realised that as everyone else was warily closing in on her father, she was walking slowly backwards. Griff put his head against the rim of the boot. It was hard to tell from that distance, but it looked as if his cheek were pressed against it, then he let go, and jumped to the ground. The awkwardness of the jump, half turning in the air, betrayed his age. He twisted his ankle as he landed, and stumbled. Blanchard and two traffic police closed in on him, berating him, and gesturing. Ignoring them, he started back. Limping slightly, he walked towards her. Expressionless, he ducked under the tape, looking down with irritation at the dirt on his hands.

Blanchard stopped in front of her. *'What was he doing?'* He was frightened and angry.

'I don't know, I'm sorry,' said Bea.

'He is not allowed to cross the police tape. This is an official procedure.'

'Yes, I'm sorry,' said Bea.

Blanchard looked over her shoulder at Griff, who stood waiting as if nothing had happened.

'I'm sorry,' said Bea again. *'He just needed to see.'*

His expression changed. *'Are you all right now, madame?'* he asked, like a different man. He put his hand onto her arm, not intimate, but kind.

She nodded.

'It's terrible. I'm sorry for your loss,' he said.

They walked back to the car. Griff was breathing quickly through his nose, his eyes invisible behind his sunglasses. He had taken a red handkerchief from his pocket and was wiping his fingers.

'Come on, then,' he said. 'If we're going.'

Blanchard had nothing more to say to him, he just shook his head and got into the car. Griff got in beside him. Bea looked over her shoulder at Alex's crumpled car for the last time, then she got into the back seat, behind her father, and slammed the door.

'Why did you do that?' she said.

'I had to,' he said.

The car was filled with him. The air was him. She seemed to hear a roaring sound. Her vision blurred and blackened, like paper singeing round the edges. She closed her eyes and concentrated on light. She made a clean space for herself, and when she opened them again the air was back to normal.

Dan came down to the lobby when Bea and Griff got back, checking Bea's face, anxiously. She looked shell-shocked, and very pale.

'Sort out the bill, would you?' said Griff and went upstairs.

Dan asked for it and the receptionist printed it out. When Griff came down with Liv he hardly glanced at it before tossing his credit card onto the leather blotter. Dan thought he saw an expression of surprise, a frown, but couldn't be sure.

Bea thought how strange she and Dan must look next to her parents, as if they weren't together. Her parents had no cheap clothes, and years and years of money made their age powerful, instead of weak. Next to them, she and Dan looked like they'd wandered in off the street – him unshaven, her hair not brushed. He took her hand. He smelled of toothpaste and sweat.

They drove back from Bourg-en-Bresse to Paligny. Bea, infantilised by shock, longed for some humane authority, rules to follow, but they were alone, with nobody to guide them through catastrophe.

On the autoroute, in Griff's red car, hurtling. 160 kilometres an hour. Outside lane. Bearing down on slower cars. Griff demanded she make calls.

'Find out what we need to do.'

Liv sat silently in the passenger seat, like she wasn't there. It was good to have a purpose. Bea called the British Consulate in

Lyons, was directed to Paris, then to Bordeaux, and then back to Lyons.

Stopping at the péage. Liv, fumbling with Griff's credit card.

Bea called their administrator, Hélène Guerin, at the Hôpital Centre Fleyriat, but she wasn't at her desk.

Stopping for petrol. Water. Liv taking painkillers.

At Griff's insistence, Bea called her brother Ed, in Tokyo, and told him. Ed, the first proud son, his father's reflection. After Ed, Alex had been a disappointment before he spoke his first word. Ed, with his smooth passage through prep school, Eton, his East Coast college, Goldman Sachs. It was one o'clock in the morning in Tokyo. She woke him up. She could hear his wife, Elizabeth, in the background.

He immediately exclaimed, *No, no!* – then started to cry, and when he couldn't speak any more Elizabeth came on the phone and Bea told her what had happened, too.

'I'm so sorry, Elizabeth,' she said, stripped back to her compassion for a woman she hardly knew, six thousand miles away. 'I'm sorry to wake you up like this, I'm just so sorry. We thought you should know. Would Ed like to speak again?'

'Tell him I'll call him later,' Griff said.

And when she'd finished with that he had her call the gendarmerie, in Bourg-en-Bresse, to draw from them an estimate of when they would be finished with Alex's car, but they would tell her nothing. She called Hélène Guerin again. She was given reference numbers. Addresses. London numbers.

'My brother Alex was in an accident this morning. He's dead.'

Each time she said it it was new. Dan gripped her hand, he touched her shoulder, but Alex was not his brother. She felt far away from everything.

She imagined Alex driving parallel to their speeding car. She seemed to see him looking, keeping pace. He was only half in love with death, and he had relished the skirmish. He had not wanted it. He can't have meant to die. *Little fuckers keep me up nights, snacking on mice. I want them out.*

It could take until after the weekend to know when his body would be released, then they would bury him. Or burn it.

11

Paligny village and the road back were as empty as ever. Apart from passing a blue car travelling at speed in the opposite direction, they saw nobody. Unlocking the front door and walking into the hotel, it did not feel like there had been a death. It felt like somebody had just left. The four of them who were left made their way through the evening like crash victims themselves. It was strange to eat and walk and talk, and even stranger to go to bed, such a passive, trusting thing to do. They had seen chaos but there was no matching response, only the ordinary, and the flimsy boundaries of time. At eight o'clock, eat. At ten o'clock, go to bed. In the landscape of catastrophe there was the brushing of teeth and toilet paper.

Griff managed Liv like managing a baby, following as she wandered through the hotel, touching things, and went into Alex's room. She lay huddled on his bed and wouldn't let her husband touch her. Angrily, she pushed him off. Bea, crippled by exhaustion, left him to it. She and Dan were practical. They did the minimum. They saved their strength. The talking and coping with her parents was over for the day.

Dan slept, but she did not. She could hear her mother crying through the walls but after a while even that stopped. She sheltered herself in the sweetness of the sound of Dan's breathing as he slept. She welcomed the air from the open window and the outdoor, night-time smells. She listened to the peace. Shock eased like a boot lifting from her chest. The harshness and horror softened. She cried, tears falling, not stopping. The moon rose, slowly, above the line of the trees until, high in the sky, it shone down onto her. It wasn't she who lived a broken life. It was not her body in a hospital basement. Her brother had gone. She had lost him. She was filled with love. But he had gone, and could not feel it.

The next morning, even as she woke, the boot came down on her chest again. It was grey and chilly, the sort of weather that makes skin feel cold to touch, like a reminder of death. She and Dan got up together, taking turns in the bathroom. As they came down the stairs, they saw Griff standing behind the reception desk.

'All right, here's the thing,' he said. 'We're going back to London today, your mother and myself.'

High on sleeplessness, Bea stared.

'*Today?*' said Dan.

'Your mother needs to see Richard.' Richard was their doctor; first-name terms, drugs on tap. 'And you two should move out.'

'Out of the hotel? Why?' said Bea.

'You may as well.'

She thought of Alex's room. Leaving would be like discarding him. Griff looked around the hall.

'It's a shithole.'

'Don't say that.'

'Just move out,' he said. 'I'll pay.'

'No, thanks.'

'Just move.'

'No,' said Bea.

'Fine. Whatever you want. We'll be back in a few days. We can speak on the phone whenever.'

Dan was about to say something.

'You don't mind that we're leaving,' said Griff. It was a statement not a question.

Bea didn't know if she minded or not, she was amazed.

'OK,' said Dan. 'Is there anything else we can do?'

'Funny you should say that. I'll need you to collect the rent from next door.' He came round the desk, looking about for his keys, impatient to go.

'What rent?' said Bea.

'What?' said Griff, distracted or pretending to be.

'Sorry, Griff,' said Dan, 'what rent from next door?'

'Oh. Well. One of Alex's *duties* was to collect the rent from the farm.' He said the word ironically because his dead son had been so inept.

Bea searched his face for grief but saw none. She had the sense he could easily carry on in a world with one less child and never think of it again. That couldn't be. That was mad.

'The German family?' said Dan.

'Oh, you know about them?'

'Just that they're there,' said Bea.

'Right, they rent the place. Paligny used to be the farmhouse for all of this, I suppose.' He gestured to an imaginary estate. 'We inherited them, so to speak. Cash. Once a month.'

'Cash?' said Dan.

'Details all here.' Griff patted a folder on the desk then picked up his laptop, checking his pockets for his wallet. 'Dan, give me a hand with the cases,' he said.

Dan packed up the car with him and Liv came down. They all stood aside for her to pass. Her status had been elevated by grief. It was as if she were a queen. She inhabited the role naturally, it seemed to Bea, as if she had been born to play it. She pulled her pashmina around her shoulders, making a shawl and they processed, with her at their centre, to the car. Dan opened the door of the Porsche for her. She got in, hunched and befuddled, and Bea watched her with a cold heart. All her pity had gone. She was amazed how hard she felt, she scared herself.

'All right?' said Dan to Liv, kindly, as he helped her.

Liv put on her sunglasses. 'I need to go,' she whispered, fingers fluttering around the giant frames. 'I've got to get away.'

'Dan, my briefcase is on the desk,' said Griff. 'Bea?'

Dan went to fetch the briefcase and she went to her father.

'I'm sure the police will need to speak to you,' she said.

He glanced through the windscreen at Liv's shadowy figure. 'They say there's nothing worse than the death of a child,' he said. He gripped Bea's hand, 'I'm so fucking angry,' he hissed. 'Alex kicked us in the teeth all his life. Now he's done it again.'

'Don't feel guilty to be angry,' said Bea, her hand imprisoned by his.

'Why should I feel guilty?' He let go of her and got into the car.

Dan ran out with his briefcase and put it into the back and, as Griff started the engine, he rolled the window down.

'Find a proper hotel,' he said. 'Don't stay here.'

The huge red car slipped between the metal gates, and away.

There was almost no difference between Griff's presence and his absence. He called at every stage of the drive, shouting unnecessarily into the Porsche speaker. The clouds burned off and the chill was gone. The day was sunny. Bea knelt on the swivel chair, elbows on the desk, the receiver slippery in her hand. She made call after call, to the Hôpital Centre Fleyriat, the British Consulate, the police.

My brother has just died, I need advice about how to repatriate his body.

I would like to know when a death certificate will be issued for my brother.

My brother died yesterday, you have his body.

Where do I present my brother's passport and birth certificate?

'For Christ's sake, get yourselves a car,' instructed Griff, from the road.

'We've got a car —'

'A proper car! I won't have you going around in that.'

It occurred to Bea he worried she might have an accident too. She considered the possibility that he feared for her.

'Rent one or buy one, I don't care,' he said. 'Liv's going to read out my credit card number, are you ready?'

It seemed petty to refuse.

'Bea?'

She picked up a pen. 'Yes, go on.'

'Here she is. Just get something new. Whatever. Have it delivered.'

Liv's halting voice read out the numbers. She kept losing track and having to start again. Without speaking, Bea took them down. Her distress and confusion felt so theatrical Bea could not believe they were not a performance. She knew her mother's pain was real but she had no instinct for it, she was no more unseeable on the phone than if she had been standing next to her. Empathy was a sixth sense that Bea relied on; her father's essence was almost tangible. Her mother was like a black fragment in her mind's eye, just a gap. 'Got it?' shouted her father, when Liv had at last stuttered out the numbers. 'Do it now.' Bea hung up. She called Europcar in Beaune and rented a Volkswagen Golf.

'*As soon as possible, please,*' she said. Credit card number, deposit, done. She swivelled the chair to the board behind her, and swung the keys on their hooks to read Alex's black-marker sins. It was just a car. It was just money. She had done it to make her father feel better. The telephone rang. She faced the desk and picked it up.

'Hello.'

'Hello?' said an American man's voice.

'Yes?'

'Is this the Hotel Paligny?'

She had forgotten to say that.

'Sorry, yes, this is the Hotel Paligny, how can I help you?'

Dan, coming into the hall, looked at her enquiringly.

'Do you have a room available June 4th through 9th?' said the voice.

'Yes, we do,' said Bea brightly. 'Would you like to book it?'

Dan was staring at her.

'You know? I'd like something with a view,' said the man. 'But I don't see any of the rooms on your website.'

'I'm sorry about that. The website is under construction.'

Dan waved at her, mouthing something. She turned her back.

'They all have very pretty views,' she said. She seemed to feel Alex smile at her. It was the first time she'd had a sense of his presence. 'They're all en suite.'

'OK, well, I guess I'll just go ahead and book that,' said the American.

'OK, good. Could I have your name?'

'It's Bannam. B, A, double N, A, M – for mother.'

She wrote it down. 'Great.'

He hung up.

'Oh. He's gone,' said Bea.

'What the hell?' said Dan. 'A booking?'

They began to laugh, together. They couldn't stop. The phone rang again. Bea turned away, to answer.

'This is Hélène Guerin, from the Centre Fleuriat.'

She forgot about laughing. *'Thank you for getting back to me,'* she said. *'I've found a funeral director, in London, and they've asked me to find out how long it will be before we have a death certificate.'*

'I can't tell you. You should speak to the British Consulate.'

'I've spoken to the consulate already.'

'Oh, good, you have a contact there,' said Hélène Guerin.

Bea could hear her father, as if he were in the room, shouting about French red tape.

'No,' she said, *'it's not good.'*

'That's all I can do.'

Bea detected impatience in her voice, and was astounded. The woman had been assigned to help them. She was all they had.

'We don't know what's happening,' said Bea. *'Why do you still have my brother's body? How long will you keep it?'*

'I understand, madame, but these things always take time. I told you before, because the circumstances of his death were not clear, there are many things to be done. It's normal.'

'In what way are the circumstances not clear?'

Dan, on the bottom step, watched her, trying to understand.

'I'm sorry, I can't help,' said Hélène Guerin. She was not sorry.

After she put the phone down, Bea called the consulate again, and caught Charlotte Pelham, the vice consul, as she was leaving for the day.

'We don't know what's happening,' said Bea. 'Nobody's telling us anything.'

'Do you remember I mentioned before, it's usual here to hire a lawyer in a situation like this?' said the vice consul.

Bea could hear her packing up her bag. That was what it sounded like. She pictured her rummaging through her make-up.

'But why would we need a lawyer?'

'In any death where the police are involved they, and the authorities, are happier to deal with lawyers. It's the way it's done.'

'The way what's done? I'm sorry. I'm being slow.'

'In a situation like this, when a death is sudden, or unexplained.'

Bea made notes as they talked. She didn't remember Charlotte Pelham mentioning lawyers before. She wasn't sure what she remembered. Her mind was not her normal mind. She thought she had been imagining it, about the make-up. It was Hélène Guerin who was unfeeling, not the vice consul. She corrected herself; nobody was unfeeling. She was oversensitive, because of what had happened. She couldn't expect people to read her mind. She called the funeral director in

London. It was an hour earlier there but even so, the phone went to message. Maybe he was at another funeral. She imagined him walking slowly behind a hearse, in a top hat with a crepe ribbon.

'Hi, it's Beatrice Adamson,' she said, reassured by how cheerful she sounded. 'Just to let you know, we don't have a death certificate for Alex yet? There's a bit of a hold-up here. I'll give you another call in the morning. Thanks very much. Bye.'

She put the phone down. Grief came suddenly, like a kick to the chest. She leaned over the desk to breathe through pain that rolled through her. Her phone rang. Griff.

'Griff.' She was out of breath, like getting up after being knocked over. 'I've spoken to Charlotte Pelham at the embassy. Sorry, the consulate. In Dijon.' She explained what had been said, and the advice to get a lawyer.

'What does she mean, "suspicious"?' he said.

'Not suspicious,' said Bea, staring at her illegible notes. 'She didn't say that. She said unknown, or mysterious.'

He was checking into his hotel at Versailles; she heard footsteps on marble, his and her mother's. He spoke to the bellboy and asked Bea for details, pressing her for facts she did not know yet.

'I don't know why we haven't heard from the police,' she said, pushed as far as she could go. 'I'm telling you everything I know.'

As they got into bed, Dan tried to hug her. 'I'm here for you,' she heard him say.

She turned over to face him, across the pillow.

'When I went with Griff, to see the place where the crash was, he climbed up onto the trailer with Alex's car.'

'What? He did what?'

'He went under the police tape, and climbed up and held it. He sort of – he just hung on to it.'

'Why?'

'It was horrible. He just hugged it.'

She lay staring at his face, not seeing it, just the car hanging over the white road, smelling the inside of it and blood, as if it were she who had embraced the metal.

'I'm here, Bea,' he said, but she couldn't answer.

She fell asleep immediately and slept deeply and woke at seven with her fists clenched. Dan's hand was lying over hers. She left him sleeping, got up and dressed, and her phone rang as she came down, as if Griff sensed she was up. He was on his morning walk. He had spoken to his lawyer and closest associate, Arun Karnad. The name made the past close, present again, all of her childhood, the inside of the house on Holford Road, and Arun, coming by to see Griff.

'Why do we need Arun?' said Bea.

'You aren't getting anywhere, are you?' said Griff.

After they spoke Dan came downstairs rubbing his eyes.

'He says his lawyer is going to find *some people* in London to shift things along,' she told him.

'That's good,' said Dan. 'Are you all right?'

'Yes.'

They ate breakfast.

'Are you all right?' he said again.

'You keep asking,' said Bea.

'I keep wanting to know.'

'I'm fine.'

'It's a lot to deal with.'

'I know. I'm dealing with it.'

'You need some time, Bea.'

'For what? I don't understand why the hospital haven't called. Why hasn't anyone been in touch?'

Her phone rang again. She stood up to answer it. It was her brother, Ed.

'Ed. Are you still in Tokyo?'

'Yup, I'm in the office. Is Mum all right?' he asked.

Ed was the only one of the three of them who could say *Mum* and *Dad* naturally. Not cursed with sensitivity he considered himself above the mass of humanity, who suffered and worried about things they couldn't influence.

'She's very distressed,' said Bea.

His voice, six thousand miles away, was crisp as a City shirt. 'I could kill Alex,' he said 'Ironic, eh? After everything he's put Mum and Dad through already.'

It wouldn't have been kind to talk about what they had put Alex through.

'Handed everything on a plate,' said Ed, 'threw it all away.'

'It was an accident, Ed,' said Bea. 'We don't know the details yet.'

'I meant his life. His *whole life*. Oh Christ, do you think the papers will get hold of it?'

'I don't see why they would.'

'You know what they're like. They keep files.'

He shouted a couple of times and cried once. At the end of their conversation he said, 'See you at the funeral. Whenever that is. Bloody French.'

'Goodbye, Ed.'

He put down the phone and so did she. She pictured the cuts his words had made closing up, leaving her clean and unmarked. He hadn't meant to hurt, he hadn't been thinking about her.

At lunchtime the new VW Golf arrived with a full tank of petrol, and the old Peugeot was removed, as if it had never been.

They went to the vast supermarket and drifted up and down the aisles, eating sandwiches. They opened all the windows on the way home.

'I bet the air con is really good,' said Dan, trying to make her smile.

The seats were hot under their legs. Bea held herself suspended until it was cool enough to sit. He fanned her legs with one hand, with the other on the wheel, and they giggled. It was funny how the mind took breaks where it could. Pulling up in front of the hotel, the atmosphere descended; it felt as though they had been away on holiday.

'Here we are again,' said Dan.

He poured them both big glasses of wine and Griff called from the car again.

'Progress,' she said. 'Arun's found us a lawyer. Philip Roche. The "best French lawyer in London", according to Arun. Has an office in Paris, too.'

Griff and Liv arrived back at Holford Road later that afternoon, and the calls stopped.

Bea tidied the reception desk, at a loss.

'So that's good though, right?' said Dan. 'You don't have to do everything.'

'Maybe I should speak to this lawyer. This Philip Roche,' she said. 'Should I tell him who I've been dealing with?'

'If you want. I don't think you need to.'

'No, you're right,' she said, 'it's good. The hospital might actually speak to him, when he calls.' She straightened the things on the desk. 'There are things we need to know. We have no idea what Alex was doing.'

'Griff said something about wine. I don't know.'

'Did he mention it to you?'

'No,' he said. 'Bea —'

'Do you think he was drunk? He must have been. When will they tell us all this stuff?'

'Bea —'

She sat down. 'Sorry,' she said.

'Don't be sorry.'

He picked up the slim file Griff had left on the desk. It had a white sticker on it. *Orderbrecht.*

'I guess I should look at this,' he said. 'What will you do?'

Bea opened the guestbook. 'I don't know,' she said. 'I can't find Alex's birth certificate. He must have had it here.'

He put down the file, and knelt at her feet. He took her hands. 'Drink up,' he said. He handed her glass to her. 'Have mine, too. Come up with me?'

'I will later. You go.'

When he went upstairs she opened the guestbook and read the list of different coloured names.

Jackie and Helen Brown, from Durban. Fantastic service! Mr and Mrs Avening, from London, had left a brief but friendly *Thanks v. much.* Or rather, they hadn't, Alex had. *Lovely stay. Thanks very much.*

She opened the cupboard in the desk. On the bottom shelf was a navy-blue cloth-backed notebook. She took it out, opened it, and saw Alex's real writing. It was like seeing him, like hearing his voice. Her brother's handwriting was as alive as anything she had ever seen. Shock wasn't short, it didn't end, like being hit. It was as violent as being hit but it went on and on, not stopping. Shock, reaction, shock, reaction. Shock.

Paint for corridor €22 x 8 5-litre tins.

Next to this he had written *8 seems a lot*. In the corner of the page, tiny writing, *shitload*. Her throat and chest shrank up. There was no sound from Dan, upstairs. She rested her hand on the notebook, listening, but she felt nothing. The glass of wine was on the desk. She drank it. Then she drank half of Dan's. She picked up the notebook and went out to the end of the garden, and sat on one of the sunbeds in the glaring heat.

Alex hadn't bothered moving the sunbed to cut the grass. There were long strands around the stubby feet, and mown and unmown swathes in patches all around. The wooden slats were broad beneath her, and slightly sticky from the sun. She wanted to talk to him. She had the feeling if she shouted he would hear. She opened the notebook and looked down at the faintly ruled pages, the biro marks across the small squares.

Call Griff — Go Swiss-Germans! — Abdul 3356738877 — ELECTRICITY!!! Jean (Abdul's mate) 4246543365.

Her tears started again, and through them she saw that next to *Call Griff* were doodles, like worms or curving shells and spirals, one inside the other. The rest of the pages were similarly semi-filled: to-do lists, scribbles; then at the back, at the bottom of the page and in pencil, *Alstrum Lieb*, and a string of numbers. Then some shorter numbers, and another long one, tiny and neat. Bea flicked through the thin pages and saw the name *Florence*, with a love heart next to it like a teenage girl might draw. He had written the name. He had felt something, had drawn hearts. She couldn't ask him about it. Her finger traced the name. She didn't think it was wrong to look, that he'd mind, but she couldn't ask him that, either. She put the book down and lay on the hard sunbed, her eyes still on the pages. She looked up at the sky. She could see the darkness of space beyond the blue.

She wasn't comfortable. She turned onto her side, looking from one empty window of the hotel to another, and then back down to the notebook. The heat was fading. She turned the pages, reading sideways. Her arm fell asleep and she shifted position. Small beetles crawled over the page. The shadows stretched towards her. Deep sleep pulled her down and down. She was aware of distant sounds, then nothing.

When she woke she felt cold. She shivered. She had woken because of the distant telephone and because of the weight of something against her thighs through her cotton skirt, the sense of a movement, that had just stopped. She might have dreamed it, but the weight was real. Her eyes opened. A snake was lying curled between her tummy and her thighs. For a moment she couldn't take it in, then the narrow head stirred in its patterned coils as it nestled, and raised itself. I mustn't move too quickly, she thought. But her body jerked, out of her control. She threw herself backwards onto the grass. Sprawling, she scrambled onto all fours. The snake hadn't moved. She was clear. Bent low, she stared, as the snake reared up, slowly, weightless. She stared into the black discs of its eyes. Its lipless mouth curved up at the sides with strange enthusiasm. Its black tongue flicked. It wasn't very big. Her heart thumped, hugely. The blood pumped through her. Distantly she heard Dan's voice.

'Bea! Griff just rang –' He stopped. She saw him moving towards her, at the edge of her vision. 'Bea ...' he whispered.

He was witnessing the aftermath, not the thing itself.

'Snake on the bed with me!' she cried, gasping. She stood up, shaking vigorously, brushing off her skirt. She rubbed her hair and arms, freshly, warmly human. The small snake, swaying in harmless defence, fixed her with its alien stare. Or perhaps it could not see her. Together they watched it lower its head and flow weightlessly to the ground, then it rippled sideways over the short grass to the longer grass, to the woodpile, and was gone.

'Oh my fucking God,' said Dan.

Bea stood there, out of breath. Appalled. Invigorated.

'Bea?' he said, as she began to walk to the place the snake had disappeared. She felt weightless too, she couldn't feel her legs. 'What are you doing?'

Slowly, she sat on her heels, staring at the log pile, some stacked and some tumbled in a frozen cascade. At the back was a mess of breeze block. She stared into the dark holes. Did snakes reproduce in crevices or need a nest? Did they have eggs, or live young? Reaching out, she touched a log.

'Bea –'

It fell. Ants scattered like a firework. Dan reached her side and took her wrist and pulled her up, his arm around her waist. She pulled away.

'I'm fine,' she said. 'It's fine. It wasn't an adder, it was a grass snake. Alex said the adders have diamond-shaped eyes, do you remember? That was a grass snake. It was harmless.'

'No. Still,' said Dan. 'Fuck sake.'

'I want to tell Alex about it,' she said. 'But I can't.'

They went inside together, but she walked away, and up the stairs.

'I just need to be on my own.'

'Are you sure?' he said from the hall.

'Yes.'

She waited for him to go. Even passing Alex's closed door had been comforting when they were alone at Holford Road. She had liked knowing he was there. Sometimes he'd let her in, and play her music or show her his English essays. It seemed so recent. Now she waited, knocked, and then went in.

She switched on the anglepoise. The LED bulb was ghostly, shining on his unmade bed. She leaned against the closed door and looked slowly around the room. A small desk under the window was covered with handwritten pages. His books were stacked on the desk and floor. Camus and Simone Weil, furry with bookmarks. Henry Miller, Charles Bukowski, *The Way of the Sufi*. She crossed the room and looked down from the window at the top of the new car and the weedy gravel, then back to the unmade bed. She realised her mother had lain there more recently than Alex. She wished she could forget. The books on the desk were worn and soft and solid. They were like promises of freedom. She looked through the pages. Some of them were turned down in the corners, passages underlined, or bordered with strong vertical lines. Simone Weil:

The only way into truth is through one's own annihilation, she read.

He had circled it, in fine black ink, and then in blue. Beneath that book was another, splayed open with a broken spine.

The death before death. Fana. Ego death. Underlined twice.

She looked at the cover. Rumi: *Bridge to the Soul*. Underneath was a writing pad. He had copied the words out and underlined them.

The annihilation of the self. The death of the ego. To lose —

The line ended with a scrawled dash, a breaking-off in pain or boredom, a green biro mark, strong, then fading, then gone. She put the books back, the Simone Weil on the top, as he had left them.

Cocaine, weed, wine, whisky, medication, meditation, philosophy and prayer. Alex had tried to escape himself all his life. Now, he was erased. How had it felt, his death, when the tractor hit the car? Was it only losing consciousness like any other black-out, or did his body see it coming? Had it fought? Help me. Not this. Not now. Distress. Distress. She looked down at the pages; the words and words and words, the small efforts of his pen denting the paper.

Dan knocked on the door and came in.

'It's like a monk's cell,' she said.

Dan looked at all the bottles.

'Probably,' he said.

'Do you think Alex killed himself?' It was amazing the things she heard come out of her mouth. 'Do you think he was dead before the accident?'

It was too big a thing to answer quickly. He left a pause.

'I don't know,' he said. 'I'm sure they'll tell you, when they know.'

'I feel like if I start needing to know everything, I'll go mad.' She looked around the room. 'I don't want to be distracted from him. He's what's important.'

He wanted to take her hand, or hug her, but it would have been like disturbing her.

'But I need to know *something*,' she said.

Downstairs, the telephone rang.

'Bloody hell,' said Dan.

It stopped ringing downstairs, but then her mobile started. It buzzed and sang in the pocket of her skirt. She put down the book and took out the phone. A French number.

'Mrs Adamson?' A man's voice, with a strong French accent.

'No. Yes. I'm Beatrice Durrant,' said Bea. 'Beatrice Adamson. Alex's sister.'

'This is Capitaine Christophe Vincent. The Gendarmerie Nationale. Do you speak French?'

'*Yes, I do.*' The police, she mouthed to Dan.

'*I'm sorry for your loss. I'm on my way to see you, with my colleague.*'

'*Now?*'

'*Yes, I'm on my way.*'

The first thing Dan said when she had put down the phone was, 'Call Griff.' She did.

'You should have Roche with you,' said Griff, from London.

'The lawyer? Why?' said Bea.

'It's his job to liaise.'

'But there's no time, they're coming now.'

12

The unmarked car pulled into the drive and two men got out. They looked up at the hotel, and approached the door just as Bea opened it, with Dan next to her.

'Madame Durrant?' said the first man, holding out his hand. 'Capitaine Christophe Vincent.'

He was about thirty-five, wearing ironed jeans and a cotton shirt with small checks in red and white, and carrying a brown leather jacket that looked brand new. He was tanned, tidy and small-chinned.

'This is my colleague, Detective Perrin.'

Perrin, subordinate, nodded.

'Come in,' said Bea.

She introduced Dan and they came inside. The air was tinged with the lemony smell of Capitaine Vincent's aftershave.

'French is OK?' said Vincent, in English.

'Yes, fine,' said Bea. 'I speak French, but my husband doesn't.'

'French then.'

'Yes,' she answered. *'Do you know how it happened? My parents are in London, but they can come back.'*

Capitaine Vincent didn't answer her. It was strange that he didn't. She had an expectation of what the visit would be like and already this was different. The two policemen looked around at the hall and stairs. Bea and Dan waited, both acutely aware how unlike a hotel Paligny was.

'*May I see your brother's room?*' asked Vincent.

'*Excuse me?*'

'What does he want?' asked Dan.

'To see Alex's room,' said Bea.

'Why?'

She took them up the stairs. *When you're gone, and you look back, this will feel like a dream* Alex had said. She opened his door. They went inside and looked at everything but picked nothing up. Bea watched, with her arms across her body. They bent and read the spines of his books. They looked from the window. They stared at his bed and the snakeskin, fluttering on the wall. Then Vincent turned to her.

'*May we see the rest of the hotel?*'

He was mask-like and incomplete, showing only a part of himself, but she sensed intelligence. And she liked him. She and Dan exchanged a look, and they walked the two detectives through the hotel, from room to room. The four of them stood briefly on the terrace, like prospective housebuyers, then came inside again.

'*Can you tell us what's happening?*' she said.

'*The circumstances of your brother's death are unclear,*' said Capitaine Vincent.

That phrase again. '*What does that* mean?'

He seemed not to hear her. Her phone buzzed. Grateful for the interruption, she took it out.

'Griff.'

'I've had some news from Philip Roche,' said Griff. His booming voice escaped the phone, and both policemen turned to look.

'What is it?' she said.

'Are you there?' said Griff's voice. 'Bea?'

'Yes. Hello?'

'Roche says a judge or a magistrate or something ordered a full post-mortem. Autopsy. Whatever you call it. They moved Alex's body on Wednesday.'

She covered the phone and turned, and walked away to face into the corner. 'Sorry, can you say that again?'

'Roche says they moved Alex's body from Bourg-en-Bresse to a bigger hospital, in Bordeaux, the day before yesterday. They're doing a post-mortem. He says the doctor at the scene of the accident wasn't satisfied, for some reason. Hello?'

'Yes.'

'I thought you were breaking up.'

'No. I'm here,' said Bea. 'What did they find?'

'We don't know.'

'OK.' Her voice shook.

'OK?'

'Yes,' she said more firmly. 'Thanks for letting me know.'

'Good girl. Roche is looking into it. I'll call you if I hear anything.'

'Bye,' she said. She turned back to the room. 'They moved Alex's body to a hospital in Bordeaux on Wednesday,' she said to Dan, forgetting the other two men. 'They did a post-mortem. The doctor who saw him after the accident wasn't satisfied.' She felt sick.

Vincent walked towards her. *'Didn't you know this?'* he said.

She focused on him. *'No. No one has told us anything.'* She thought he looked embarrassed.

'We have only just been brought in,' he said.

'The accident was early Monday morning. Today is Wednesday,' said Bea. She felt irrationally humiliated. 'I've been calling the hospital. Why didn't anybody tell us he wasn't there any more?'

'It happened in a different district,' he said. 'Excuse me.'

He gestured to Perrin and they both went outside. He made a brief phone call, then the two men conferred with one another and then Vincent came back in alone.

'Would you come into the gendarmerie with us now?' He looked from Bea to Dan.

'What did he say?' said Dan.

'Now?' said Bea. 'Both of us?'

'What?' said Dan again.

'Yes, now, you can follow in your car,' said Vincent. 'OK?'

Beaune's medieval centre was distinctive and immaculate, with steep roofs of coloured tiles and cobblestones, but outside the city walls the town could have been anywhere in France. There was nothing medieval about the Gendarmerie Nationale, no touch of the Romanesque; a brutalist concrete barracks in a residential street, facing a row of bourgeois villas. At the end of the road, lollipop trees grew tidily on a roundabout. Two bored-looking young gendarmes armed with assault rifles stood at the gate. Bea and Dan, accompanied by Vincent and Perrin, showed their passports, first to the teenage-looking soldiers, and then a desk sergeant. Bea's bag was searched. They passed through a metal detector and two more soldiers led them across a drill square to another building, upstairs, to an office.

The office was open plan, with cubicles along one side, divided by plastic screens. The air smelled of bitter coffee and cigarettes – not fresh, but smoked outside and carried in on breath and clothing. Perrin and Vincent told them to wait, and they stood by a water cooler. Uniformed gendarmes passed back and forth, some leaving for the day, others working. Bea was the only woman. No one took any notice of them. All around, men talked on phones, officiating over the chaos, as if they could control misfortune. Perrin came back and showed them to a desk, with three chairs and a pot plant. Then he went away. After about five minutes Capitaine Vincent returned and sat down. Clasping his hands together, leaning forward, he said, in English, 'Do you want a glass of water?'

'No, thank you,' said Bea.

'OK.' He began to speak. *'As you know, my name is Capitaine Christophe Vincent –'*

He talked fast. Every so often he would say, *Do you understand?* and Bea would say *Yes*, and translate for Dan. He and his team were officers of the judicial police, he said; OPJs in an SR unit based in Dijon, temporarily operating out of Beaune. SR stood for *section de recherches*. The *procureur* had assigned Alex's case to the Gendarmerie Nationale. *Procureur* translated as *public prosecutor*. It wasn't the same thing, but it was the closest word they could find –

'Wait,' said Dan, 'hold on –'

Caught up in detail, she was frustrated. 'What?' she said.

'Ask him why Alex's death is being investigated.'

She turned back to Capitaine Vincent. *'We don't understand why it's a police matter,'* she said.

Vincent arranged his expression. *'I can't discuss the details of your brother's case with you,'* he said.

'His case?'

All at once, her mind came into focus. She looked into Vincent's light brown eyes, then down, at a yellow block of Post-its on the desk. She noticed the wedding ring on the finger of his tanned and folded hands, and the hum of the strip lights.

'Exactly how did my brother die?' she asked.

Vincent didn't blink. 'We don't have all the results.'

'Why are you questioning us?'

'It's normal,' he said.

'In what way is it normal?'

He shook his head, smiling. Bea thought that she would punch him.

'Madame Durrant, when did you last see Alex?' he asked.

Her mouth was dry. 'On Saturday night, when he left.'

'What time was that?'

'What's going on?' said Dan.

She didn't answer, keeping her eyes on Vincent. 'He left sometime in the night. I spoke to him after dinner, at around half past ten, and then I went to bed.'

'And your husband?' He turned to Dan.

'We all had dinner together,' said Bea. 'Then we went to bed.'

'Where did Alex go?'

'To Mâcon, I think.'

'What was he doing in Mâcon?'

'An errand for my father.'

'What errand?'

'I don't know.'

He put a thin file on top of another file and patted it, as if he had achieved something. He stood up. 'Thank you very much. That's all for now. I can't tell you some things.' He held out his arm, gesturing them to leave. 'I'm sure you understand.'

'No,' said Bea, 'I don't understand.' She stood her ground. 'You haven't helped us at all. Isn't there an organisation we should be speaking to? Don't you have Victim Support?'

'Of course, we have a victim support service in every area of France,' said Vincent.

'Well then —'

'You are not the victim of a crime.'

They left the gendarmerie and Bea called Griff from the car as Dan drove, keeping his eyes on the road, deliberately careful, as he listened.

'Griff, we've just come from the police station,' she said. 'They gave us absolutely no information, and no support.'

Dan had worried for her, but she sounded very strong, her usual calmness combined with Adamson power. He hadn't seen this side of her, he was used to her humility. Even her accent had come up a notch, dropping the everywoman patina she used for work – and, he thought, for the first time, maybe for him. A car honked, and Dan realised he didn't have his lights on. He was shell-shocked from the day, and gripped the wheel of the unfamiliar Golf, double-checking road signs. Keeping right, he thought, tiredly, turning right, staying right.

'Don't worry,' Bea said, on the phone, 'I'm going to write down the details of the whole conversation when we get back to the hotel.'

Griff had the lawyer with him. He put him on.

'Is that Bea? Philip Roche here.'

'Hi, yes. Dan and I have just been interviewed by the police. I think my parents should both come back.'

It wasn't necessary, Vincent had already summoned her parents. They were flying out the next morning. Bea hung up.

'Good,' she said.

There was a silence.

'They must have done the post-mortem,' she said, staring at nothing. 'Don't you think? They must have done it by now. How long does it take?'

'I don't know, babe.'

'An hour? A day?'

'We can ask the lawyer, what's-his-name.'

'Philip Roche.'

For the rest of the journey they talked in circles until she said, 'OK. Enough.'

There was only so much horror she could take. In silence, they approached the Hotel Paligny. They got out of the car looking up at it, against the evening sky.

'Sometimes it feels completely abandoned,' she said, 'and sometimes it's as if he only just left. Do you know what I mean?'

'Yes,' said Dan.

'I don't want to go in.'

'We have to, though, unless you want to go and find some-where else?' said Dan. 'Like your dad said?'

Her face hardened. 'No,' she said. 'We're staying here.'

'We really don't have to.'

'We don't *need* a hotel,' she said stubbornly. 'We've got a hotel.'

'We could go into Arnay for dinner,' said Dan. 'Go to the cafe?'

'I'm not that hungry,' said Bea.

'No, me neither.'

So they went inside.

The hotel felt very empty that night. There was no imprint of its recent visitors, no lingering aftershave smell, nothing different about the things on the desk. It looked undisturbed. It was too big a building to disregard, and they were constantly aware of the rooms around them and the noises that just they were making, with food and plates and clearing up, and their footsteps on the echoing floors. They kept the garden doors locked, and ate in the kitchen, standing up, to avoid the dining room. Bea wondered if Alex had done that when he was alone, or if he'd taken food up to his room. She pictured him eating sandwiches in bed with a book, or by the computer in the hall, watching YouTube, finding friends online.

When they went up to the room, Dan put a chair against the door.

'Why are you doing that?' said Bea.

'Makes me feel better,' said Dan.

She didn't argue, but she wasn't scared. She wasn't sure if anything frightened her, or if everything did. She had been destroyed already.

'I forgot to go and get the rent from the farm for your dad,' said Dan.

'Fuck 'im,' yawned Bea, sleep falling like a fog.

'Don't want to piss him off.'

'Rent,' she murmured with contempt. 'He's got enough money.'

13

To get to the Orderbrecht farm by car they turned left instead of right out of the hotel, and then took another left where the road forked. It narrowed and then doubled back, and they saw the sign *Orderbrecht* on a wooden gate at the start of a track. The track climbed and at the brow of the hill they paused. It was not nearly so strange a place as when Bea had walked through on foot. The herd of white cows grazed among the pens of chickens and goats, and the low yellow farmhouse looked relatively charming in the innocence of the morning sun.

'Is that the barn?' asked Dan, pointing. 'The chapel?'

'Yes, that's it. We shouldn't park outside.'

'In case they're sacrificing something.'

Only six days before, in the garden with Alex, she had told him about spying on the family through the barn door, and they had laughed about it. Time had lost its rational scale. Dan turned the car and left it facing the way they had come, so he wouldn't have to do it when they left, and they walked down to the house, feeling conspicuous. Before they reached the garden gate, a woman opened the front door.

'*Bonjour,*' said Dan.

Her colourless hair was pulled back from a heavy, white face. She had very pale, bare legs and thick socks and a denim skirt. A pair of tattered rubber boots stood on the thread-bare mat outside. Dan put his hand on the gate.

'Bea?' he said. He had exhausted his French with *'bonjour'*.

'Good morning. Are you Madame Orderbrecht?' said Bea.

The woman nodded.

'I'm Bea. Alex Adamson's sister.'

'Hello.' She was expressionless.

'May we?' said Bea.

The woman shrugged. Dan and Bea approached the front door, stepping around a big red tricycle upended on the path.

'I hope it's all right,' said Bea, *'we've come for the rent.'*

Madame Orderbrecht just shrugged, and turned, and went into the kitchen, which was very cluttered and surprisingly dark. Peering in, they could make out two huge dogs, lying under the kitchen table and a baby in a nappy, sitting on the floor nearby. The baby was holding a Barbie doll by the legs, open-mouthed. Madame Orderbrecht opened a drawer in the dresser, and took out an envelope. She came back and put it into Dan's hand. It was thick with banknotes.

'Merci,' said Dan.

Madame Orderbrecht stared at him for a second, then she closed the door on them. They walked back down the path.

'Well, that was easy,' said Dan.

Then there was the choking sound of a diesel engine and a small green tractor appeared from behind one of the out-buildings. An old man was driving, with a teenage boy bal-ancing on the trailer piled with plastic trays of asparagus. There was sand on the sunless white ends of the asparagus, stacked juddering on the trays. The door opened behind them, and Madame Orderbrecht shouted something from the doorway, words that sounded like German spoken backwards, and the old man, seeing her, raised his arm and waved. He and the boy stared at Bea and Dan as the tractor went past. The boy was skinny, with sun-bleached hair, his stick-insect limbs coming out of shorts too big for him and a T-shirt too small. He couldn't have been more than fourteen, but his look was insolent. He had one hand in the gappy pocket of his shorts, so that his sharp hip bone showed, and the other was gripping the bar of the trailer. Through half-closed eyes he stared at Bea's breasts, and twisted his head to keep looking as the tractor bumped on, past them, and out of sight. Dan was looking down at the envelope, and did not notice.

When they were clear, and almost back at the car, he said, 'That's the whitest woman I've ever seen. She made *you* look brown. The kid, too. And the old guy. Jesus, he looked like a duppy.'

'Yes, I saw,' said Bea.

'They looked like freaks.'

He turned his head to try to see through the doors of the barn as they walked past. They got into their car, and drove away along the uneven track.

'This car is so posh and clean,' said Bea. 'It's embarrassing. Rent collecting.'

'Yeah, whatever,' said Dan. 'It's fine.'

The track reached the road. With one hand on the wheel, Dan looked into the soft envelope of cash, flicking his thumb over the notes.

*

Her parents were on their way, there was no time to go back to Paligny, they went straight on to Carrefour, on the ring road outside Dijon.

The supermarket was vast. Eggs. Bread. Fruit. Yogurt. Griff didn't eat breakfast, just coffee and his early-morning walk. Tonic for gin. Washing powder. New, cheap towels, very white with bleach and petrochemicals. Cling film. Toothpaste. Steaks. It was probably more shopping than Bea and Dan had ever done at one time. Bea googled potatoes dauphinoise, standing in the queue to pay. Liv wouldn't eat potatoes, never ate pasta, hated bread. Lights flickered over the line of tills, narrowing away along the row. Dan leaned on the trolley, looking up at her.

'What time do you think they'll be here?' he said.

She was looking at something nearby.

'What room shall we put Philip Roche in?' he asked.

She moved her mouth, but her eyes were fixed on a woman waiting in the queue, at the next till, with a year-old baby on her hip.

'Bea?'

The mother had his small hand, and put it in her mouth, lips cushioning her teeth. His head lolled in paroxyms of silent laughter, completely confident he would not be dropped backwards onto the tiled floor.

'Um-num-num,' the mother said, chewing her baby's fingers.

'Look at her,' said Bea.

'Cute.'

'Do you think that's what it's like? Do you think you want to eat them like that?'

'He is kind of fat and tempting,' said Dan.

Bea's expression was blank. He didn't know what she could have been thinking about, looking at the baby.

'So, what about the bedrooms?' he said.

'Sorry,' she said. 'I can't think.'

They were still making beds when they heard a car and went down to meet it. Griff was driving a black SUV, with another man in the passenger seat. They could just make out Liv in the back seat and, next to her, the shape of another person, another man.

'Four,' said Dan, 'bloody four of them. Who the hell is that?'

Bea bent to look. 'That's Arun. Griff's lawyer.'

Even as Griff got out of the car, he was talking. 'Christ, what a journey. They didn't even have a decent car. You'd think somewhere in Dijon would have a proper range, what do they call them? Prestige cars? Forget it. Not a bit of it, awful.'

'Hello, Griff,' said Bea.

'This is Philip Roche.'

Roche, a small man in a dark suit, came forward. 'How d'you do? I'm sorry for your loss. I hear you had a bit of a shock yesterday. The French system can be quite overwhelming. Your father may have told you, I've applied for the family to have access to the police files.'

'Christ,' said Griff, stretching. 'An hour and a half in a car full of bloody lawyers.'

Next to Arun's chic blandness and Griff's linens and Lobbs, Philip Roche was a study in bourgeois discomfort. Arun smiled, came over, and kissed Bea's cheek.

'Bea. I'm so sorry about Alex.'

'Dan – Arun Karnad. Arun, my husband, Dan.'

Her mother stood a little apart, like a wound-down toy. She wore dark glasses. Her hair was tied back, her thin arms were covered by the sleeves of her black shirt, tucked into jeans. It was easy for Bea to ignore her but the others were satellites to

179

her, as if her tiny body had a gravitational pull, glancing at her, exchanging glances.

'You didn't say Arun was coming,' Bea said.

'Forgot you again, Arun,' Griff laughed, patting him.

'You're a very ill-mannered person.'

Arun was exactly ten years Griff's junior. They'd first worked together as young men, in the early eighties. Arun was elegant, where Griff was not, and, unlike Griff, bald now; his nut-brown, polished head was the most noticeable thing about him. He knew almost everything about Griff, but he wasn't godfather to his children and he hadn't been his best man. Griff had more visible characters for that.

'We don't have enough beds,' said Bea.

'There'll be an IKEA or something, I guess,' said Dan.

'Beds?' said Griff. 'What do we want beds for? We're not staying *here*. After this meeting they've summoned us to, we're on our way to Chateau something or other.' He dropped his voice. 'But something's happened.'

'What's happened?' said Bea. 'What now?'

'Shall we go in, love?' Griff took his wife's arm.

The two of them went ahead. Arun fell into step with Bea, and spoke quietly in her ear. His voice was smooth, well used to undertone.

'Have you seen the paper?'

'What paper?'

'The *Daily Mail*,' said Arun.

'No,' said Bea. 'Why?'

'Your mother feels absolutely awful about it.'

'About what?'

'Don't talk about me! You're talking about me!' said her mother, shrilly with a jerk of her head.

'I'm so sorry.' He pulled a folded copy of the *Mail* from his soft leather briefcase. 'Don't let Liv see,' he whispered. 'She's had a terrible morning. And they were handing them out on the plane. Awful. Page 5.'

Reluctantly, Bea took the newspaper from Arun's hand. He retreated to a tactful distance as Griff shepherded Liv up the stairs. Dan stood awkwardly, near Bea but trying not to interfere. On entering the hotel, Philip Roche stopped and took in its shambolic amateurishness with a mild, observing expression.

'We need to be at the gendarmerie by three,' he said, checking his watch, as Liv and Griff disappeared up the stairs.

Bea opened the newspaper. Page 5. The headline was big; sharp, black letters standing out.

SON OF PROPERTY MOGUL GRIFF ADAMSON DIES IN FRANCE
Alexander Adamson has been found dead in his car in France. Distraught mother, Olivia Adamson, said: 'It's a mystery. Nobody knows what happened to Alex.'

There was a picture, taken years before, of a dishevelled Alex with his arm round the shoulders of someone else's rich kid.

Bea wasn't prepared for the violation, the roof ripped off, and crowds of people looking in, the sudden fresh loss of seeing his face, and he was transformed, by being in the paper.

The 35-year-old was the troubled son of billionaire Bernard 'Griff'
Adamson, who first gained notoriety in the 1970s as one of London's
most ruthless slum landlords —

A picture of Griff shaking hands with a politician.

Griff Adamson, left, ex-director of disgraced property develop-
ment company, Hemisphere, which was the subject of an investi-
gation, came under scrutiny again, recently, when his connection
to —

Another old photograph of Alex, at a charity ball with some
trashed-looking girls. Bea wanted to cover him up, he would
hate it, his nineties hair and the clothes that looked like fancy-
dress for 'the privileged'.

Friends remember Alex as a 'gentle soul', a fun-loving charmer who
lit up a room —

'What was she *doing*, talking to the press?' said Bea, furious.
'They called her at home,' said Arun. 'They took her by sur-
prise.'
'Fucking hell,' Bea said, 'this is disgusting.'
'They did the old trick, "if you talk to us you can give us your
side".'
'How *stupid* can a person be?'
'Bea!' barked Griff, coming back down the stairs. 'Keep your
voice down.'
She shoved the paper back at Arun, and Dan took it from
him.
'Can we get it out of here?' she said. 'Why did you bring it
here? That's my brother.'
'I'm so sorry,' said Arun. 'Forgive me.'
'Throw it out,' said Bea.
'It'll be online,' said Dan, looking up. She saw it was a thrill
to him, that Alex's death had made the papers. He tried to hide
it, but he couldn't.

Arun took the paper, deftly, from his hand. 'I'm so sorry,' he said. 'Your mother feels terrible.'

'No, *I'm* sorry. It's not your fault,' said Bea, then, 'They got his age wrong.'

There was silence.

'It's a quarter past one,' announced Roche, standing alone.

'I don't care,' said Griff. 'Let them wait. And they'd better give us some answers.'

'It really wouldn't do to keep them waiting,' said Roche. His English was stuck somewhere in the twentieth century, the too-perfect grammar of the bilingual.

'Fine,' said Griff. 'Bea, go and get your mother.'

'You get her.'

'Bea!'

'*What?*'

'Please,' said Griff. 'Please would you fetch your mother?'

Bea could never resist a plea for help. She went upstairs for Liv.

Her mother was lying flat on her back, still in her shoes. The curtains were drawn. It was like a room with a body laid out, but it was the wrong body. Her large handbag was open on the corner of the bed. The air smelled strongly of her scent, a single-note essence that clung like the blood of something to everything she touched.

'I'm going to open the window,' said Bea. 'You and Griff have to go to the police station. You need to get up.'

She opened the curtains and lifted the sash. Liv propped herself up on the pillows, slack-faced. Her eyes struggled to focus. Bea wondered if she was unable to speak, rather than choosing not to.

Mother and son overdose within a fortnight of each other. Distraught mother takes own life.

Bea tried to calm down. She did not want to feel this hatred. It turned her stomach.

'Mum —'

'Go-away-I-want-him,' said Liv, blinking like a stroke victim.

Bea clenched and unclenched her fists. 'He's not here,' she said. 'He's dead.'

There was a glass of water by the bed. She handed it to her but Liv shook her head. Anti-anxiety drugs would suppress her respiratory system but they would be unlikely to kill her.

'What have you taken?' said Bea. 'Just Valium?'

Liv focused on Bea. Her face was dead, but behind her eyes, she was all movement inside herself, like a wasp in a glass.

'You hate me,' she said.

'Drink some water,' said Bea. 'We have to go to the police station.'

She helped her mother sit upright. 'Can you stand?' she said.

She got her up, and walked her to the open window. Liv, a graduate of countless yoga classes, breathed deeply in, through her nose, staring without focusing at the trees. Bea watched her. She could easily have pushed her from the window. Everyone was waiting downstairs.

'Have you eaten anything?' she asked. Of course she hadn't. She didn't eat at the best of times. 'You need to eat.'

'I don't want to,' said Liv.

'I don't care.'

'It's impossible for a boy to have a beautiful mother,' said Liv, swaying.

'What?'

Bea stepped back sharply. She was knocked breathless by a pain in her head. She left Liv standing at the window and went into the bathroom. It felt as if two forks were being pressed into the soft skin of her temple. She had to put her hands up to check there was nothing there. She circled her fingers over the jabbing pain. It was alarming. It wasn't like a headache, or any pain she'd ever known. She rubbed at her head. With half-closed eyes, she felt for the tap, and turned it on. *Distraught sister dies of brain haemorrhage*, she thought, as she splashed water on her face. She reached for a towel. The pain had gone. She hung up the towel, and went back to the bedroom. Liv was standing where Bea had left her, crying.

'You can't be late for the police,' said Bea.

'Don't push me around.'

'Come on.'

She told her to undress, and called down to Dan to bring her suitcase up to them.

'You all right up there?' said Dan.

'On our way,' said Bea.

Holding her breath, she helped Liv undress, and into the shower, and turned away while she washed. When Liv came out of the shower she handed her one of the new towels, tugging off the label, which dug into her fingers. Coming back to herself, Liv looked disdainfully at the towel in her hands as if she could smell the supermarket on it.

'What's this?' she said.

'A towel.'

'It's ghastly.' With sudden petulance she threw it to the floor. She began to cry again.

Bea picked it up. She held her mother's tiny wet, naked body in her arms, patting it dry. She thought it was fine, comforting her mother. She must remove herself, like a nurse, and be detached, because it was the right thing to do. Patiently, she dried her soft skin with the new towel, and helped her dress again.

'There's no point taking pills,' slurred Liv, tears dribbling. 'They don't make any difference. Nothing does.'

Philip Roche was waiting by the front door, still in his jacket, and sweating.

'There you are,' said Griff as Liv and Bea came down. 'All right, let's go.'

'We'll see you later,' said Bea. 'Good luck.'

Bea felt strong, but disconnected, still frightened by the pain in her head. She wondered how far she could go, in this new world of compromise with her soul, before she broke.

'Was your mum OK upstairs?' said Dan at her side.

She didn't know how to answer him.

'Bea?'

'She's fine,' she said, knowing he could hear her rage in her voice, unable to contain it.

Griff tucked Liv safely inside the enormous rented SUV, and got in beside her. He switched it on, just as a police car turned, sharply, into the driveway. It crackled to a halt. It was bright blue, with yellow chevrons on the bonnet, which shone garishly against the dark green of the bushes and trees. Griff got out of the car again.

'What's this now?' said Griff. 'Are they coming to get us? I thought we were going in ourselves.'

'That was the plan,' said Roche.

Two uniformed gendarmes got out of the police car and looked around at the faces.

'Madame Durrant?' said one of them.

'Yes. Me,' said Bea, in English.

'What's going on?' said Griff.

The officer consulted a piece of paper. 'Monsieur Durrant? Daniel Durrant?'

Roche trotted briskly over to them. *'Good afternoon. My name is Philip Roche, I represent the family. What can we do for you?'* he said.

The three of them talked, quietly.

'What the bloody hell is going on?' said Griff.

'Just a moment,' said Roche. He left the two policemen, and went over to Dan and Bea.

Arun stood next to Griff, solicitous, as Griff glared, and Liv inside the car stared blankly ahead.

'They want you to go with them,' murmured Roche, bending his head towards them as if he were consulting with a client in the dock.

'They've spoken to us already,' said Dan.

'They should have called first,' said Roche. 'They lack the tea-and-sympathy approach we're used to in Britain.'

'We're not used to anything,' said Bea. 'It's a first for us.'

'Of course.'

'I said, what the hell is going on?' said Griff, with Arun at his side.

'Look, there's nothing sinister about it,' said Roche to Dan and Bea. 'But it's best if you go along.'

'In our car?'

'They want to take you in theirs.'

'Why?' said Dan quickly.

The policemen waited, handcuffs dangling from their belts.

'We can ask questions later,' said Roche.

Bea and Dan got into the police car as the SUV with her parents and the lawyers drove away. One of them said something to her.

'What did you say?'

'I said, could you put your seat belt on?'

Red-faced, she fumbled with it. Dan had already fastened his, subjugated, and betraying nothing.

'Off we go,' said one of the gendarmes cheerily, as if they were off for a trip on a scenic railway. He switched on the car radio and tinny Europop accompanied them out, and onto the road.

14

Being in a room with a gun was disturbing. More so because the gun was in a shoulder holster slung casually on the back of a chair. Bea could see the textured butt poking out, drawing her attention, as if it had a power of its own. It was close enough for her to reach out and touch it if she wanted, because the room was small. Dan was in the cubicle next door. The last she'd seen of him was with his eyebrows raised at her, questioning, as having been to the gendarmerie they were politely separated.

The two detectives had introduced themselves as investigating officers Major Matheo Dufour and Adjutant Nino Luis. It was Nino Luis's gun. He was on the chair with the holster hanging behind him. He was unshaven, in a T-shirt and hoody. She could imagine him in Nice or Marseilles, cornering immigrants on the night-time docks. Dufour was tall and fair, with a wedding ring and white trainers. Beyond the thin partition she could hear blurred sounds of printers and phones ringing, voices.

'OK, *what else?*' said Dufour, as if they had been talking earlier. '*Alex. Was he OK?*'

'*He was — all right,*' she said. '*He was lonely.*'

The curiosity and interest of the detectives was like a distorted copy of her own job. She told them about Alex's drinking, but that he'd said he wasn't using drugs – and she believed him. She told them how playful he had been, and about the snake traps up in the roof. There was a knock on the partition, and Dufour leaned out to talk to someone. Luis looked up from his pad, and Bea smiled politely. He smiled back, but then kept his eyes on her. He didn't look away. She couldn't work out if it was a sexual thing or to gain power, then thought they were the same. Uncomfortable, enduring, she wondered if the British police did the same thing to women, and knew immediately they must. Luis stared at her unselfconsciously, with his legs apart and his gun hanging by his bare arm. Dufour finished his conversation and sat down again. Luis went back to his pad.

'*Was your brother homosexual?*' said Dufour.

'*What?*' said Bea. '*Why?*'

'*Is it a difficult question?*'

He was pushing for answers suddenly, not drawing them out.

'*Do you know something else?*' she said. '*Do you know what happened?*'

'*Tell me about his relationships,*' said Dufour, ignoring her questions. '*Men or women? Did he sleep around?*'

Bea kept silent and counted to ten in her head. It was a tactic she sometimes used in sessions, to shift the balance of power.

'*I hadn't seen my brother for almost two years,*' she said, '*I told you.*'

In the corner, Luis scribbled on.

'*Alex was a fag, wasn't he?*' said Dufour.

He used the word *pédé*. She'd only heard it said in films before, never in real life.

'If you use words like that, I'm leaving,' she said. 'I'm here volun-
tarily.'

There was silence.

'I'm sorry,' he said.

'I don't think Alex was gay,' she said. 'As far as I know he wasn't
very sexually active.'

'Do you know where he went at night?'

'I've told you, we only got here a few days ago.'

'Do you know what methadone is?'

'Yes, of course.'

'Why of course?'

'I work in mental health, in London. I've worked with addicts.'

'Are you an addict?'

'No.'

'Was he prescribed methadone?'

'Not that I know of —'

'Did he have a dealer here?'

'I don't know.'

'Did he have a prescription for diazepam?'

'I don't know.'

'Do you?'

'No. My mother does.'

'Your mother?' That stopped him. 'Why?' The way he asked it
was more gossipy than professional.

'She's neurotic,' said Bea.

'You don't sound sympathetic.'

'I'm not.'

'Did your brother use any of these medications?'

'No.' She corrected herself. 'I don't think so.'

'Did Alex ever mention a bar called Chez Janine?'

'Where is it?'

'Did he mention it to you? Chez Janine.'

'No,' she said.

Then, as if a bell had rung at the end of a lesson the two officers rose from their chairs and politeness returned. Dufour shook out his shoulders.

'OK. Thank you Madame, we'll be in touch.'

Nino Luis opened the door for her, and smiled.

'Goodbye,' she said, in English, looking directly at him.

'It's much more difficult for us, after the first forty-eight hours,' said Dufour. 'We're doing what we can.'

'But why has it taken this long? Why hasn't somebody told us what's happening?'

He smiled ruefully, surrendering all the power he had assumed while questioning her. He became boyish. 'You have to talk to my boss about that,' he said.

'Capitaine Vincent?' she said.

'He's the boss.'

They escorted her to the stairs. She couldn't see Dan, or her parents, or either of the lawyers, anywhere, as she passed through the desks of men. She almost ran down the stairs, and left the gendarmerie alone. On the pavement she texted Dan. *Are you out yet?* But she couldn't wait, she wanted to get away. Walking fast, she passed low, stuccoed garden walls, then wrought-iron gates to courtyards, and narrower streets lined with parked cars, and then the shopping streets and cafes. She stopped and texted Dan again. *Are you still in there? I'm in town. Call me.*

Keeping the phone in her hand, she arrived at a square with a plane tree growing on a raised grass triangle, and the chairs and tables of two different cafes grouped around. She felt like an escapee. She checked her phone again. She decided to get a Coke, for the sugar, and scanned the chairs for a spare seat feeling jittery and strange. The smell of the gendarmerie was still in her nose, the questions, and the closeness of death. A bicycle sped past.

'*Attention!*'

She jumped back. The cafe was busy. There were two young women at the nearest table, laughing. Their voices rose above the hum. Someone put water down for a dog. A man jogged a waiter's elbow and spilled coffee on the tray. Bea walked to an empty table and sat down. She saw the JCB hitting Alex's car as he lay sleeping across the front seats, knocking it, crushed, from the road into the field of young crops. She saw it swinging on chains in the empty afternoon like a hanged man. She ordered a Coke. She got a text from Dan.

Out now, where are you?

In a cafe, she texted back, and told him where. *You OK?*

Yeh. You?

Yes, she answered. *See you in a minute. XXX*

Yeh. He added hearts. Red ones.

He'd bothered with emojis. She pictured him doing it, fresh out of the interview room, on the pavement with the armed soldiers behind him, and she experienced one exquisite moment of joy, and then her father called.

'Bea! Where are you?'

'In a cafe.'

'What? For Christ's sake, this isn't the time to go AWOL.'

'I'm not. I'm waiting for Dan.'

'Isn't he out yet?' He was shouting. She was sure everyone around her could hear every word. 'Come to Chateau — what is it? Hold on,' he yelled. 'Arun?'

She could hear Arun's voice in the background.

'Chateau L'Orée des Vignes,' said Griff. 'I'll send a car.'

'We don't need a car.' The thought of it annoyed her, and then made her want to cry. As if he could make a difference to anything. Ordering cars. Staying in nice places.

'Get a taxi then,' he said. 'It's out towards Meursault. Come right now. Now. L'Orée des Vignes, yes?'

'Got it.'

He hung up.

They left the city in a taxi as the sun was setting, holding hands, quietly delirious with distress and exhaustion. An afternoon in the gendarmerie, and then they were to have a five-star dinner.

'This is so nuts,' said Dan.

'Batshit,' she answered.

'I suppose we have to eat.'

'We've got all that food in the fridge,' she said. 'We did all that shopping. I hate throwing food away.'

'I know, babe.'

The taxi took them up the winding lane to the Chateau L'Orée des Vignes. Flares lit the driveway, leaded turrets gleamed against the blue night sky. They got out, and climbed endless shallow steps.

'What is this, Versailles?' said Dan in awe. He'd taken a module on the Baroque. The scale and grandeur, then and now, were so foreign as to be almost alien.

'It looks like a Disney movie,' said Bea, dismissively, and he felt rebuked.

She plucked at her shirt. 'I think I actually smell.'

'Shh!' said Dan.

They stepped inside. A man in livery approached, exuding disdain.

'I need to go to the loo and sort myself out. I'll see you up there,' said Bea, and deserted him, her Adidas slapping as she ran across the gleaming floor.

'Monsieur?' The waiter could barely be bothered to open his lips. A mile away, from behind a golden desk, the receptionist looked on.

'Mr Adamson?' said Dan. 'Griff Adamson. We're meeting him for dinner?'

Like a magic wand, Griff's name transformed the waiter into a warm and deferential companion.

'Monsieur,' he suggested. 'Come with me.'

They went up a mirrored staircase, across a ballroom to an enormous terrace restaurant, and the waiter bore him proudly to Griff's table, a white linen circle surrounded by other white circles in the dusk, all candlelit. Griff, Arun, Roche and Liv were already seated.

'There you are,' said Griff.

Roche and Arun nodded, and Liv said, 'Hello,' like someone had a gun to her head, and then looked at Griff, as if it was him.

'Bea's — she'll be out in a minute,' said Dan, feeling awkward. He wished he had stopped for a wash, too, and wasn't in a T-shirt.

'No problem,' said Griff. 'Sit there. Drink?'

It was as if they were celebrating something. Dan sat down and reached for a bottle of mineral water but a waiter snatched it up, and poured him a glass, smugly.

'Will you have some wine? A beer?' said Griff.

Nobody else spoke. Before Dan could ask for a beer, red wine was poured into his long-stemmed glass. He thought of Alex sloshing wine into the smeary tumblers at Paligny. He'd been transported from one off-kilter reality to another, from the cops' insinuations in that concrete barracks, to this ancient terrace over a gauzy view, and reflections of candle flames in porcelain and glass.

'So, where's Bea?' asked Griff impatiently.

'Freshening up,' said Dan.

More silence. Arun looked perfectly relaxed, and Roche was studying the menu. Dan wiped his palms on his shorts. People in silk and suits and diamonds were filling up the tables. A string quartet began to play. Lights shone, fan-shaped, up the walls behind him. The sky above was purple-blue, and the distant village glowed with illuminations. It was a rich man's view, but the rich man wasn't interested.

'Arun, order some canapés and whatnot,' said Griff, getting up. 'Dan, come with me.'

'Certainly,' said Arun, picking up the tasselled menu as Griff left the table.

He assumed Dan would follow, and he did, careful not to bump into any chairs as he picked his way. He joined his father-in-law by the balustrade at the terrace edge. It was darker here. There was a sweet smell in the air, drifting up from the valley below.

'That's better,' said Griff, breathing deeply.

'Yes,' said Dan, his anxiety receding under the sedative of comfort. He had been wrong, it wasn't strange to be here after the day they'd had. It was the perfect place to be.

'Funny, what shock does to the brain,' said Griff.

Dan waited for him to elaborate.

'Some things seem important, and then – others.' He gestured, a disappearing into the air. 'D'you know what I mean?'

'I think so.'

'You poor bastard.'

Dan's mind went blank. He couldn't think what Griff meant.

'Are you all right?' Griff asked.

'. . . Yeah?'

'I suppose you're used to it.'

'Excuse me?'

'Police stations,' said Griff.

Dan began to laugh, but stopped himself. He didn't like to offend, Griff meant well. Then he wondered why he was worrying about offending Griff, when he was the one who should be offended.

'No, not really,' he said. 'And we were all in there.'

'Not as long as you.'

'They couldn't find me an interpreter,' said Dan. 'They had to call the university.'

Griff wasn't listening. 'How's she doing?'

'Bea?'

'Obviously.'

It was touching he asked. Fatherly, Dan thought, surprised, feeling a strong need to confide in him.

'A lot of the time she's just, like, normal,' said Dan. 'You can't think about it all the time.'

'It's too much,' said Griff. It didn't usually show that he was in his seventies. It did now, in the visible working of his mind. His face was mobile. He rubbed his eyes. 'Roche says a post-mortem – autopsy, whatever you call it – is a fairly standard thing. He says they wouldn't have the full results yet, but they must know the cause of death.'

'But they haven't told you?'

'No. They haven't. It's bad enough', said Griff tightly, 'without being kept in the dark.'

'I'm sorry.'

'Whatever.'

Bea always said her father's generation didn't have the language to express emotion. Dan put it differently: they were tough old bastards. It was not unenviable.

'What do you think happened?' he asked carefully.

Griff seemed irritated. 'How do I know? But Roche thinks the whole thing could get quite long and drawn out. We won't be able to have a funeral. That's what Liv can't stand. One of the things.'

'I'm sorry,' said Dan again, at a loss to imagine how either of them must feel. He had seen parents grieve the death of children twice before. For something people called 'unthinkable', it seemed to happen a lot. The first was a younger cousin who had drowned, and the second a school friend who had been knifed. Dan knew the best thing was to keep quiet. There was nothing to say.

'Fucking French!' said Griff, out of nowhere. There was rage in his small, gleaming eyes and gathering in his voice. 'Today was outrageous. I recorded everything. I won't stand for it.'

'You recorded it?'

'I record all my meetings.' He tapped his pocket. 'Inappropriate questions. Personal insinuations. Badgering. We're going to sort them out.'

Dan believed him. 'Good.'

'And I just don't want to *get involved*.'

'Involved?'

'Everyone gets into it, don't they? The authorities.' He said the word with contempt. 'This will just bring them all out again, like flies on shit. Government agencies. The fucking press. Whomever. They're all connected. Delving into my affairs. They're like sharks. Vibrations in the water, see?' He held up his hand, fingers shaking to demonstrate. 'And they all come round. I do too well for myself one year – vibration in the water. Alex goes into the

Priory, vibration in the water. Round they come. Circling. See-ing what they can take. You saw it today in the paper. They smell blood or money, and they come after you.'

Dan didn't know what to say.

'Look,' said Griff, 'I'm retired, virtually. I've got about half the money I used to. Less than. I'm downsizing. Sold off a lot of property. I'm old news. What do they want with me?'

'I don't know,' said Dan, transfixed.

'I just want some peace,' said Griff. 'I just want to feel safe, and secure, and have my family feel safe and secure. That's all I want.'

'I understand.'

Griff had relieved himself of a burden. He softened. Tiredly, he looked around, and Dan, looking with him, seemed to see what he saw, feel as he felt; protective of this precious world. Griff turned back to him, and looked directly into his eyes.

'You know I've got nothing to hide,' he said.

'No. Sure,' said Dan uncomfortably.

He looked away from the old man's face across the ter-race, and, like a divine intervention, there was Bea. She was being trailed by the same waiter who'd escorted him. In her shapeless cotton skirt, T-shirt and flat shoes, she was mark-edly worse dressed than anybody else. She looked for him and their eyes met. They were the youngest people there. And the poorest. They were easy to spot. She smiled at him, and it felt as though she were taking his hand. She was an anchor chain, pulling him from the deep, the trail of humble crumbs that would take him home.

'Hurrah,' said Griff, 'there's St Bea. We can eat.'

*

Bea hadn't seen her mother and the two lawyers sitting silently at the big table, she just saw Dan. He came towards her and she kissed him.

'Still smelly?' he said.

'Not so much.' They sat down next to each other, with Roche on her other side. 'I hate him *summoning* us like this,' she whispered, 'it's just medieval, and my mother is completely high.'

'Poor lady,' Dan whispered back. 'Maybe being here will take everyone's minds off things,' he said. 'It's gorgeous.'

'Maybe,' said Bea, because he meant well. The hotel wasn't *gorgeous*, it was probably a Relais & Châteaux. She imagined the upstairs; patterned carpets in the corridors. Pillow menus. Dan wasn't to know it was trying to be something it wasn't, like the recorded string quartet playing classical hits on a loop, and everybody staring at everyone else as if there were movie stars wandering about, instead of just retirees on wine tours. Their waiter came to the table and Bea smiled at him, to make up for her nasty thoughts.

He stood over Liv with his silver pen poised.

'Liv?' said Griff.

'I'm not hungry,' said Liv.

Bea felt hatred. She didn't care about the pretentious hotel, or Griff using his money to swab the blood, it wasn't those things that were making her like this, it was Liv. She turned away to focus on the terrace. Lavender in pots. Shoes. When that didn't work, she looked up, and tried to find a moon.

'Why are you doing this?' said Liv, loudly, to Griff. She gestured wildly and the waiter had to step back to avoid her jerking hands.

'What do you want me to do?' snapped Griff. 'I hate room service, it stinks up the place.'

People turned to look. He and Liv drew attention, a combination of personal power and money; one lent force to the other, the result was magnetism.

'Why don't you order, Liv?'

'No.' Liv's reedy voice was a counterpoint. 'You're incredible. How can you?'

The waiter, caught between them, pretended to be deaf.

'Roche!' barked Griff. 'What will you have?'

The waiter scuttled to Roche's side, but Roche, who had been looking at the menu for half an hour, panicked.

'Bloody hell,' said Griff, 'hasn't anybody made up their minds? Bea? Dan?'

'I'll have a steak,' said Dan promptly. He hadn't understood the menu but he'd had time to think.

'How d'you want it cooked?' prompted Griff before the waiter could ask. 'Come on!'

'I'm going up.' Liv pushed back her chair. 'Griff. Key.'

'Wait!' commanded Griff.

Bea could feel the whole restaurant watching them. It was like her childhood, the awful discomfort of being visible when her natural state was to observe.

'Dan!' barked Griff. 'Your steak?'

'*Just give me the key,*' said Liv, getting up unsteadily, with that blind look she had, demonstrating her pain.

'Medium?' said Dan.

'Right!' boomed Griff. 'Good. Getting somewhere. Does anyone want anything to start?' He looked around the awkward faces.

'Oh my God,' said Liv, holding the back of her chair.

Dan, thinking she was going to fall, jumped up, and pushed past Bea to steady her.

Instantly, she fell into his arms, and pressed her cheek against his chest. She was light and feeble, and he had to hold her up.

Bea stared at the sight of her mother in her husband's arms. Everybody stared, even the waiter. Had there been a photograph taken, the waiter would have been in it, gawping like a single man who had stumbled onto a dance floor full of couples. Griff was the first to turn away.

'Philip?' he said, as if nothing was happening. 'I'm picking up the bill,' he laughed, to cover his fury. 'Can we – just – get on with it? Please.'

'I –' Philip flicked through the menu with quivering fingers. *'I'll have some fish. The bouillabaisse,'* he said.

Tenderly, Dan helped Liv into her chair. She gripped his hand in thanks. He took his seat and turned to check on Bea; her face was still.

'Bea?' said Griff. 'What will you have?'

'I'll have an herb omelette and a salad, please,' she said, automatically.

Dan thought it was the first time he'd ever seen her in these surroundings, and was disturbed how much it felt like her natural habitat. Only a girl born with a silver spoon in her mouth would show her disapproval of luxury by ordering off-menu.

'No hair shirts on the specials?' said Griff.

Dan laughed. He stifled it immediately, but felt Bea's eyes on him.

'Great! How difficult was that?' Griff looked at the waiter. 'And a steak for me. Medium rare, but not too rare. Not bloody. All right? And some chips. And something green for the table. Whatever. Thanks.'

'I'll have the same,' said Arun, unobtrusive.

'Will that be everything?' said the waiter, too scared to leave.

'Yes, thank you,' said Bea, and smiled.

The waiter escaped, gratefully. The strangers at the other tables turned back to their own affairs. Griff looked around at his companions as if he were inspecting disappointing troops.

'If we don't do normal things, it makes it worse,' he said.

'It can't be worse,' said Liv flatly.

'Do you think it's easy for me?' Griff snapped.

'May I say something?' asked Arun, his clean tenor rolling out to reach them, at the perfect pitch. 'If I may?' He smiled.

Arun had lived in England nearly all his life, his Indian origins were barely detectible in his public-school speech, except for the extreme accuracy of his locution, and a certain, particular kindliness.

'I can't imagine what you're going through,' he said, and paused. 'Truly. I can't. My oldest friends. And it would be presumptuous of me to claim I could possibly know how hard this must be. But, if you'll permit me, I would like to say one thing.'

Griff and Liv were captivated, both gazing on him as though he were bringing them a present.

'Despite these difficulties,' he said, 'or perhaps even, if I may, *because* of them, I am honoured you have asked me here. Thank you. And I promise you, I'll do *everything* I can to help you. I cannot apologise enough, if I speak out of turn. And it may seem very strange to raise a glass in these circumstances. But I do. I raise my glass to you all.' He raised his water glass and held it out to Liv, first, and then to Griff. 'As your friend, thank you.'

Liv picked up her glass, her bony wrist flexing. Griff raised his, and so did Dan. Everyone drank. They murmured, a kind of toast. Bea, who had always thought Arun did everything for money, found herself picking up her glass along with them. His kindness shamed her.

'You *should* be bloody grateful, Arun,' barked Griff, 'on the per diem I'm paying you.'

He, Arun and Liv laughed hugely, full of easy emotion. Bea bowed her head. Roche, the newcomer, smiled along, feeling his way.

'We were two *hours* in there,' said Liv. Her tears were flowing again.

'We'll sort them out,' said Griff. 'I said I would.'

'No, we must do everything we can to help them,' said Liv, suddenly determined. 'The captain was really nice, I thought, and rather charming. We need to find out who knows somebody. Philip, do you know the commissioner, or somebody like that?'

She was still slurring her words, and drank more wine, growing more vivacious and imperious. She talked on, demanding responses to disconnected ideas, mentioning diplomats she'd met, and politicians. Then she stopped, as suddenly broken as she had been suddenly commanding.

'Enough,' she said dead-eyed. She stood up.

'Yes, up you go,' said Griff, as meek as a lamb. 'Arun?'

Arun escorted her from the table. Dan half rose, politely, as she left, and so did Roche. They all said goodnight – except Bea. It shocked Dan that she could be so pitiless.

When she had gone, they ate.

'Mission accomplished,' said Griff, as he pushed away his plate. 'Down to business.'

He hailed the waiter, raising his hand like a paddle at an auction.

'Roche, come with us. Fill me in.'

It was half past ten.

*

Escorted by the night manager, Griff, Arun, Roche, Bea and Dan passed the gilded doorways of conference rooms and empty chairs. Tapestry runners crossed the polished floors to doors that opened into empty lifts.

'Let's just go,' said Bea.

'No,' said Dan. He walked ahead, to join Griff.

They arrived at a pair of painted doors. The night manager stepped aside. The tiny private room was airless and highly decorated with plaster and curlicues, like a millefeuille.

'This'll do,' said Griff.

They went inside. Bea sat down on a low, silk sofa, and Dan sat next to her.

'Roche? Let's have it,' said Griff.

'Right,' said Roche. He opened his briefcase. 'As you already know, we have applied for what is known as "access". When the *juge d'instruction* receives the police file from the *section de* —'

'Boring.' Griff raised his voice a notch. 'Speak English. Look. All I want to know is, one: what do the police know? Two: when will we get Alex back?'

'If you'll take a look at this,' said Roche, fiddling with his iPad, 'we at Roche, Crowe, St Johnston —'

'Jesus fucking Christ, put that away!' shouted Griff, his impatience weaponised by grief. 'Tomorrow it will be *four days* since my son's death, and all these gendarmes are doing is harassing his family. Was it an accident? Was it suicide? What happened to him?'

Philip Roche blinked and gaped. He had two successful offices, in Paris and London. He employed fifteen people. A good proportion of his clients were grieving the recent deaths of family members, but was not used to being shouted at. Plucked from his routine at the whim of a noto-rious man, he'd been promised a huge fee but been paid, so far, nothing.

'Come on, come on,' pushed Griff, leaning into his face.

'The French inquisitorial approach can seem personal —'

'No. Shut up. Next. What happens now?'

Roche fumbled with his iPad. 'I don't know.'

'*You don't know?*'

Bea was dry-eyed with exhaustion. The chandelier glared behind her father's head as he towered over Roche, who glanced at his briefcase like it contained a gun he could not reach to defend himself.

'There was definitely a hold-up, immediately after the acci-dent,' he said. 'But —'

'*What now?*'

'Realistically,' said Roche, 'it could be weeks before our application for access comes through.'

'*No,*' said Griff, like training a dog.

'Until then, the SR are not obliged to tell us anything.'

'No. What *now?*'

'I honestly can't tell you.'

'Wrong answer!'

'When we have insight into their thinking —'

'I don't give a rat's arse about their thinking! Are they as incompetent as this in Paris?'

Seeking dignity, Roche got to his feet and walked up and down, clutching his iPad.

'I've put in a request to the *juge* to speed up the process,' he said. 'I can *try* to speak to Capitaine Vincent's superior —'

Griff lost control. 'WHAT HAPPENED TO MY SON? WHAT HAPPENED TO HIM? WHY DON'T YOU FIND

OUT? WHY WON'T ANYONE TALK?' His bass voice broke, and whistled in his throat.

Roche, agape, didn't answer. It was easy to forget Arun was still there. Now, he got up from his chair and touched Roche's arm. Very quickly, he shepherded him out, and closed the door behind them both.

Griff stood rooted, snorting like a bull but with nothing to charge at. Blood tinged with blackness swelled in his face. The door remained closed. The air was stifling. Bea got up from the sofa. She went to him. He grasped her hand, painfully.

'Fuck. Fuck. Fuck,' he said. 'How?'

'I don't know,' she whispered.

'We were a family and now we're not any more. We're the wrong number. It's all wrong. I can't cry. I can't.'

He was almost a foot taller than her. Her hands were lost in the grip of his. Dan stared at the spectacle, the monstrous size of the man, the small, calm quietness of his wife, imprisoned in his hands.

'It's all right,' whispered Bea. 'Whatever you're feeling.'

'Don't try your fucking therapy on me,' Griff hissed, eyes closed.

'Shut up,' she said sweetly, 'I'm not. Here, sit down, now.'

Without exerting any force, she moved him. He sat down, heavily, on a yellow throne-like chair. A waiter knocked and entered.

'Not now,' said Dan automatically.

The waiter left, immediately, and Dan, despite the circumstances, and everything he should have been thinking about, couldn't help but feel a thrill of pride, and that he too belonged.

Sitting now, Griff put his head in his hands. Bea knelt on the floor.

'What makes *you* my confessor?' he rasped. '*You*. This *nobody*.'

'I don't know,' said Bea.

'It's my fault,' said Griff. He opened his eyes. 'It's all my fault.'

'No, it's not.'

'Please – stay here tonight.' He pulled her hands up towards his face. 'Don't go back to that place. Stay here.'

She took her hands away. 'We'll stay until you go up to bed.'

'Stay. I'll pay.'

She smiled. 'We can't.'

'Can't or won't?' said Griff. His eyes gleamed.

'Won't.'

Dan leaned forward. 'If he really wants –'

'No,' said Bea, and meant it.

Griff looked at her coldly. 'St Bea,' he said.

'Bea?' said Dan.

'No,' said Bea, without looking at him.

Dan, ignored and overruled, sat back.

Griff stood up and looked down at his daughter on her knees. 'Whatever. If you change your mind, tell the guy on the desk. I'm sure they can find you something. I'll put you in a taxi. I may as well have my walk now.'

They got into their cab, and he waved them away. Bea turned to see him heading off across the lawn, his long shadow thrown back, up the floodlit facade, fifty feet high.

'We'll pay him back,' said Bea.

'For what?'

'The cab.'

She was staring at the blurred shapes passing the window, eyes flicking in and out of focus. Shock, he thought, there should be more than one word for it. Like all those words for snow in whatever language it was. Hard, ice-like shock. Soft, muffling shock. Brittle, breakable shock. His mind wandered as they turned off the fast road. He was not in shock. Hauled in by the gendarmes and now here he was, after a nice steak dinner, fine. Once, years before, a police van pulled up in front of him on Consort Road. He had been on his way to meet Troy, at the Bussey. They dragged him off the pavement, into the van, and then a cell. He was fourteen at the time. It terrified him so badly he'd cried in front of them, not knowing how far it would go, or what they suspected him of, if anything, and because his mother wouldn't know where he was. His life might have been far from the cliché Griff imagined, but he had every reason to fear the police. And yet, he'd spent half the day in a high-security barracks in the whitest town in the world and not really been bothered. It hadn't touched him. He began to wonder at it, and then realised; it was because he had known Griff was there.

'My father never believed in Alex,' said Bea. 'He didn't help him. Now he's in so much pain.'

Dan tried to care for Alex's memory, or that Griff had failed him.

'So is your mum. Maybe you could be a bit nicer to her.'

She sat up suddenly, so suddenly the driver swerved, checking his mirror.

'It's not *your* family,' she said furiously. 'I'm not interested in *being nice* to her.'

'I'm sorry,' he said. He repressed his outrage at being spoken to like that.

She sat back. 'No. *I'm* sorry.'

They drove up to the hotel, the weeds and stones of the drive-way looked very sharp in the headlights. She paid the cab with money Griff had pressed into her hand, and they let themselves in.

'Home sweet home,' said Dan. The air did smell sweet, and damp.

'We left the back doors open,' she said, feeling the night breeze flowing through the hotel like a river. 'I thought we closed them.'

'I don't remember,' said Dan. 'I'll lock up, you go to bed.'

She went. Some of the doors off the dark corridor were open. She walked into their room, and switched on her bedside lamp.

They lay waiting for sleep. An owl hooted, somewhere in the mass of trees. There was a distant, answering call. Above them, the attic space was still.

'Owls eat snakes, don't they?' said Dan.

'Think so. Mice, definitely.'

'You need to sleep,' he said. 'I'll count you down.'

She settled into the crook of his arm.

'A hundred,' he whispered. 'Ninety-nine, ninety-eight, ninety-seven ... ninety-six ...'

He lost the count at sixty, and stopped.

'He feels so far away tonight,' she said in the darkness, but there was silence. 'Even more far away than dead.'

She lay awake, listening to the owls. She thought of the tiny mice in the imagined safety of the grass, snatched up by beaks bigger than themselves. How alien the air must be, after the solid ground. It must feel like death, even before death came.

15

The next day began quietly. Bea, who had been awake with the sunrise every day since Alex died, slept late. She didn't stir when Dan got up and tiptoed out of the room. He took his clothes, and his laptop, and washed in the bathroom across the corridor, so as not to disturb her. She needed her sleep. Then, down in the hall, he opened up the computer and googled *Alex Adamson, Death*. He wanted to save her from being surprised again. No, not just that. Now that he knew it was in the papers, he felt compelled to look. He wanted to see how other people saw his wife's family, and if there were any pictures of Bea. The other papers had all got hold of what the *Mail* had started, but there was nothing new. The same pictures rehashed the same story, verbatim. But, in the sidebar, old articles about Griff. Dan felt a pornographic shame, clicking through to find the things she'd never told him. He had googled her when they met. He didn't feel bad about that. This was different. He hadn't dug before. He'd checked her out, seen a little bit about Griff, and moved on. Now, hunched over his laptop, in the hall because it was nearest to the router, he delved. Before he'd known Bea well, he had more respect for her privacy. Now her past felt like it was his to plunder, her father's anyway. He saw Griff's other companies, besides Hemisphere, reports of bankruptcies declared and forgotten, and new companies, and a defunct petition against him. He even saw a picture of the private jet. He read the articles, quickly, skimming, listening out for Bea, like he was going through her things behind her back. He hadn't checked so carefully before. He'd seen her father was a businessman, he hadn't looked that far. He had fallen in love with her before he knew about all the money she resolutely would not take. She had stood out, the first time he laid eyes on her, at the Bussey. She wasn't beautiful. He had often wondered exactly what it was that made her shine to him. He assumed it was her soul, that was what he had always believed, that just like in the movies, love had put a spotlight on her. Now it occurred to him that perhaps it was her money that gave her presence in a room, even in its absence. The idea scared him. He realized he had always felt proud of picking her out, as if he had seen a more important beauty. He was glad he hadn't known. It shouldn't make a difference. He told himself it didn't make a difference. As Bea always said, it was her father's money, not hers. They had agreed. It was ironic that the starter money, the guilt money that got them their mortgage on the flat, was from his dad. He'd never thought to question it. She didn't judge him for taking money from his absent, married, lying father, arguably just as dirty as the money from hers, but she wouldn't touch a penny of Griff's riches. Nothing. There was just one picture of Bea that he could see, in Getty Images, with a diagonal stamp across it to keep the copyright. It was a photograph from someone's millennium garden party. *Property developer Griff Adamson, and wife, Olivia, with their three children, Edward (18), Alexander (16) and Beatrice (9).* Griff had one arm around the shoulders of his eldest, Ed, and his other around Liv's waist. She was wearing something Grecian-looking, with long, boho hair. She looked like a perfume commercial. Alex was between Liv and Bea, and holding Bea's hand. Bea was grinning, broadly, like a school photo, her legs planted, sturdily, and Alex was looking off to one side, with his eyes half closed, so you couldn't tell anything about him, except that he was uncomfortable, awkward in himself. Of the five of them, he looked like the marked one, it seemed obvious. Or did he just look tragic, now the worst had happened? It felt strange to see Bea as a child. There was something sick about it. Partly because she wasn't a pretty child. He didn't know if it would have been sicker if she'd been pretty, and thought maybe it would. But he felt bad for her. She just looked plain, and dumpy, and much too keen and cheerful for the surroundings, like she was consciously making the best of it. He didn't know why it made him feel so bad, her sunniness, her cheer. He heard her footsteps on the stairs, and slammed the laptop shut.

'Morning,' she said, as she came down.

She didn't notice how guilty he looked, or the slamming of the computer. She wasn't the kind of girl to notice. She was not suspicious of him.

'You slept ages,' he said. 'That's good. Feel better?'

They had some breakfast then Dan cut the grass and Bea read a book. Stopping, to clear wet, stuck-on grass from the blunt blades, he looked at her while she was reading, unaware of him. She was on her stomach with her knees bent, and her feet crossed at the ankles. The camisole top she had on was not a new one, he couldn't remember when it had been new. One stringy strap had fallen from her shoulder, he could see

213

the side of her breast, full, squashed against her arm. The skirt was almost white, but had been pink, a sort of cotton gathered mid-length thing she wore every summer. She had another like it, he thought. At least one. Her feet were bare. Her hair had a scruffed-up tangled part at the back, where she hadn't bothered brushing it. She had not put on her bra. He thought of her mother's studied chic, the skinny cropped jeans and shirts and simple skirts, which didn't need visible labels to advertise their pedigree. Dan didn't think Liv probably wore the same thing more than five times. Bea's clothes were like family to her, she was nonsensically loyal to them. Everything Liv wore screamed money. Every look she gave or word she spoke, every silence, said *Look at me*. Bea's clothes said as little as was possible to say. Her walk, and manner, the way she spoke, all of it, modestly, quietly assembled, apparently diffident, shouted from the rooftops that she did not care. They were flip sides of the same coin, Liv and Bea, they were both disingenuous. And Bea did care. He knew she did. She looked up.

'Why haven't we heard anything?' she asked. 'Have you checked your phone?'

'Yes, nothing. Try not to think about it.'

'Why were you staring at me?'

'I wasn't,' said Dan. 'I was just thinking you look gorgeous.'

She shrugged him off as if it made her grumpy to be told it, like she always did at compliments, and went back to her book.

She earned all right in her job. She could have bought some new things. He started up the mower. He felt ashamed. He hadn't meant to think that. The dirty engine spat and roared. It wasn't loud enough to block the image of the oil-painting grounds of the Chateau L'Orée from his mind, or the feeling he'd had, standing with Griff on the terrace, like he owned it,

214

or the headlines — *millionaire, billionaire, mogul, playboy* — it was only stubbornness, and phoney, that made Bea wear old clothes.

He paid penance for his thoughts by making lunch with the things in the fridge she had worried would go off. They lay side by side with their plates on the newly cut grass, playing music through Alex's portable speaker and looking at pictures of their lives in London and YouTube, falling through the rabbit hole of connections; cover versions, spinoffs, spoofs. There was nobody there to see them, lying together in the garden, just the tall trees all around and the empty hotel. They even made love, for the first time since it happened. They made love on the grass, as if nobody had recently died, and there was no crisis, and held one another afterwards, resting in the sunshine.

'You'll burn,' he said.

'So will you.'

They roly-polied together into the shade.

'Mind the snakes don't come,' she said.

Their phones shuddered warnings and alerts. Griff would like to see them at the Chateau L'Orée des Vignes later that afternoon.

'Oh God!' shouted Bea in distraction, stretching her arms up to the sky. 'I don't want to go there again!'

He pinned her down and kissed her. 'More luxury. Poor you.'

They heard banging.

'What the hell?' he said.

Banging again. A fist on the door.

'I didn't hear the bell,' said Dan.

'Nor me —'

As they scrambled up, before they had time to go inside, a uniformed gendarme appeared round the corner. He walked straight over the flower bed in his army boots, like an apparition, as if it weren't a flower bed, just earth. They stared at him marching towards them, gun and taser heavily hanging from his belt, with his navy-blue peaked cap pulled down. The banging started again, on the front door.

'They're back here!' the gendarme shouted over his shoulder.

Bea and Dan were dazed; fumbling and scared in their bare feet, clothes in a mess.

'What do you want?' said Bea.

He stood, boots planted wide, staring at them, at a loss.

'I need to go and open the door,' said Bea.

'He stays here,' said the gendarme, pointing at Dan.

'He said "stay here",' Bea told Dan, her voice shaking.

'Why?' said Dan, but he froze.

'I'm going to open the door,' she said in English, then French, holding out her hands to pacify the gendarme.

She ran through the hotel and opened the door to two men, in dark blue bomber jackets and army trousers, with bright white stripes and *Gendarmerie* written on their chests. She didn't recognise either of them.

'What's going on?' she said. She saw a white van and a squad car parked behind them. 'What's he doing?' She pointed at the back garden.

'I'm sorry,' said one of the men. 'We didn't mean to scare you.' He held out a badge. 'TIC.'

The second one set off, round the corner of the hotel.

'I'll sort out Girard,' he said.

'It's OK, I come in?' said the first. 'We speak English?'

Bea didn't want to lose sight of the other man, when Dan was on his own, and the uniformed cop had a gun. She went towards the back door.

'Wait, please,' said the man behind her.

'I need to translate,' said Bea. She heard his boots on the floor behind her, and the nylon rustle of his clothes, and his hand landed on her arm.

'Don't touch me,' she said.

'Wait, please.'

She reached the back door, but it was locked. She turned to go through the sitting room, but he was in her way.

'Please,' he said. 'It's OK.'

She stood there in her cotton skirt, damp from sex with Dan, hair messy, and the imprint of grass on her elbows, loose blades of grass on her feet. He faced her down calmly.

'My name is Officer Lecuyer,' he said.

She could hear men's voices in the garden. She was trapped.

'We are here to search in your brother's room, and my –' his English dried up. 'My friend wants Monsieur Durrant, to ask him questions.'

'Why?'

'Capitaine Vincent is here soon. It's OK.'

The voices in the garden died away, then she saw Dan, accompanied by the two other men, walking past the front window. She read the words *Gendarmerie Identification Criminelle* on the back of the second man's bomber jacket. She wanted to shout Dan's name, but stopped herself.

'Can I speak to him, please?' she said quietly.

Lecuyer stepped aside in a very gentlemanly way, as if he hadn't been intimidating her. Perhaps he hadn't. She had lost her bearings. She didn't know what was normal or if she was safe. She didn't know how scared to be. She went to the front door and opened it. Dan was about to get into the squad car, with the two gendarmes, in a hurry, at his side.

'Call Griff,' he said.

One of them opened the back door for him, and gestured. It wasn't as if he was cuffed or being forced. Perhaps she was overreacting.

'They just want to ask him one or two things,' said the second TIC man, coming close to her. He was young and overweight and his smooth face was shining with sweat.

'Call Griff,' said Dan again.

'What do they want to know?' she said to the TIC man.

'I don't know.' He wiped his clammy face with the flat of his hand and hitched up his elasticated dark blue uniform trousers, which were baggy, and silly looking. 'Nice place,' he said, looking up at the hotel.

'Hey.' The gendarme tapped his watch. 'In the car,' he said to Dan. Dan got in.

'Bea,' he said. 'Fucking call him.'

The gendarme tensed at the word fucking, understood by anybody.

'No trouble, OK?'

'Don't give them any trouble,' she repeated then, realising it sounded as if it came from her. 'He said not −' but the car door slammed shut.

He looked at her through the glass. She smiled, so he wouldn't think she was scared.

The two gendarmes got into the car, and drove him away. He twisted round to look through the back window and then the car disappeared around the corner onto the road.

She was alone with the other two officers. Their van, with Gendarmerie Identification Criminelle printed on the side was parked next to the rented Golf.

'Let's go,' Lecuyer said to her.

They all walked inside together.

'Don't worry,' he said. 'This is, how do you say? Just the beginning.'

'*Do you have authorisation?*' said Bea, fumbling for reason.

'Oh. Yes. *Wait*,' said Lecuyer.

He ran to the van and she and the other one waited, not speaking, until he came back. He held out a clipboard and some sheets of printed paper.

'Here —' Out of breath, he searched for the English word. 'Yes, it's OK. You call my capitaine, if you want. He is here soon.'

Bea took the papers. She couldn't focus on them. Smudged words and photocopies, biro writing in little boxes.

'OK?' he said. 'This is Officer Janssens.'

The fatter one nodded. 'Hi,' he said. '*I'll get the stuff.*'

He went, and Lecuyer stood next her, smiling reassuringly. Ignoring him, she took out her phone and dialled Griffs number and told him what was happening. For once he didn't meet her with demands and rage. He was calm.

'All right,' he said. 'I see. Let me know what happens.'

Janssens came back inside, carrying two white plastic cases.

'OK,' said Lecuyer. 'Your brother's bedroom, please.'

'Up here.'

They jogged up the stairs ahead of her, side by side. She showed them the room and they went in and closed the door.

After a moment, she went back down again and sat at the reception desk, alone. She did not think that she had ever felt so alone. It was like Dan was being torn from her, and the pull from Alex's room held her tight, and the feeling of being torn and pulled got stronger. Dan was further and further away. Panic rose up. She gave herself an order. She ordered her terror to stop and closed the door on it. There was no danger. Dan was innocent and strong. They weren't in America with trigger-happy cowboy cops, or some shadowy uncivilised place; this was Europe. Home from home France. Better than home France. He wasn't going to disappear; there were rules and procedures, and she must trust in that. She put him from her mind.

She could hear the two men moving around in her brother's room above her. She waited, listening, gaining strength, and then she went upstairs. The door was half open now, their shapes moved back and forth. She knocked. Lecuyer poked his head out.

'Would you like some coffee, or some water?' asked Bea.

'Coffee!' he said. 'Thank you very much!'

'What are you looking for?' She made her voice casual.

'Information.' He shrugged. 'It's normal.'

'Normal?'

'With a murder.'

'What?' Bea said.

'A murder,' he said again, and hesitated, thinking she hadn't understood. *'After a murder,'* he said in French.

She didn't respond. It felt as if her mind stopped, as if her pulse had stopped, and she had no need to breathe.

'OK.' He shut the door in her face.

Of course she knew. Of course she had known. She went slowly down the stairs, feet landing slowly, step after step. A murder. She pushed the heavy fire door and went into the kitchen and the door swung closed behind her. It was dark and warm. Murder. Nobody had said it. Alex had died, and for five days, there had been a vacuum. Now it showed itself. Murder. The word rang. It wrote itself on her eyes. Murder. It was a Trojan Horse. Childhood fears and teenage thrills. Red letters, painted backwards on a mirror. Screaming. A newsreader's voice. A man appeared in court today charged with one count of. Charged with. Murder. A man has been found dead. A man was found murdered. A thirty-seven-year-old man has been found dead in his car. Her brother Alex had been murdered. She washed out the aluminium coffee pot under the tap, fingers swiping the ridges on the rim. As she opened the new bag it tore a strip like a cuticle down the side, and spilled coffee grounds onto the floor. She tried to pick it up with kitchen paper, and felt the little dots in the creases of her palms. She rinsed the filter and filled it, and packed down the coffee with the back of a spoon and turned on the gas. With white noise in her mind, she found some biscuits and put them on a tray. Shock, reaction. Shock, reaction. Shock. Murder. Murder. Murder.

She heard a car on the gravel and peered out through the tiny kitchen window, then went to the front door, her phone loose in her hand. The newly arrived car was unmarked, parked neatly next to the white van. Capitaine Vincent, trim and tidy in his ironed jeans and loafers, locked it, with a little *pip*.

'*Bonjour*,' he said, putting on a suit jacket as he came to meet her.

She was beyond politeness, she couldn't find it in herself to pacify or appease. 'I'm sick of speaking French,' she said. 'Can we speak English?'

'*I prefer French*,' said Vincent.

'Fine. Fine,' she said. '*Why have they taken my husband in?*'

'*It's normal*.'

'*It's not! Two men are searching Alex's room. Who is accused of what?*'

'*May I come in?*' he said.

She let him into the hall and followed in the wake of his lemon-smelling aftershave.

'*I'm sorry it looks this way,*' he said.

The rage she felt was dull, like boredom, it had no edge of nerves.

'"Looks"? Can I say, this whole —' she gestured '— thing, it's just —' the only word she could think of was *merde*. 'It's just shit,' she said, in English. 'It's just total fucking shit.'

She smelled scorched coffee from the pot she'd left on the cooker.

'*Something burning?*' said Vincent.

'Hold on.'

She went into the kitchen. It was bubbling around the seam, and the smell mixed with melting rubber.

'Fucking shit,' said Bea. 'Shit.' She switched off the gas and took hold of the black handle with a tea towel, and poured the thick, burnt coffee into the cups.

'*Can I help you?*' asked Vincent, in the doorway behind her.

'No,' said Bea. She stopped fumbling with the slippery coffee cups, and the stupid plates, and turned to face him. Her pain welled up. 'He said *murder*,' she said. '*That one upstairs.*'

'*Yes.*'

'*Why didn't anyone tell us? No one's said anything.*'

He didn't answer. She thought she would begin to scream, but instead, she just shook her head, picked up the tray, and went past him. He held the fire door open for her. She took the coffee and biscuits upstairs, and Vincent followed. At Alex's door he leaned past her shoulder, and knocked.

'*Al-lô?*' he said cheerfully.

Lecuyer opened the door, and took the tray, smiling. '*Thanks a lot!*'

'*Excuse me,*' said Vincent and went inside.

They closed the door on her. She heard them talking. She had the impression Vincent was reprimanding them, but she couldn't be sure. She wouldn't listen at a closed door. She went downstairs again and checked her phone. There were no texts from Dan. Vincent came out of Alex's room and down the stairs.

'It's kind of you, to make them coffee,' he said. 'They're working very hard.'

'I don't care about them. I'm just being civilised,' said Bea.

'I understand,' he said.

She opened the desk drawer and took out Alex's notebook with the blue cloth cover and handed it to him.

'What's this?' he said, taking it.

'You're investigating a murder,' she said.

Above them, they could hear things being moved in Alex's room.

'Alex made notes in there,' she said. 'People's names, and numbers. It might help.'

'Thank you.'

'And what about the farmers, the Orderbrechts?'

He had a knack of appearing deaf. He opened the notebook and looked down at Alex's handwriting.

'Do you know who they are?' she said. 'Or are you just looking at the family?'

He looked up. 'Which family?'

'Mine.'

'You say the family, as if they are not your family. Why is that?'

'I'm trying to be dispassionate,' she said, looking for the French 'impartial' but her mind wouldn't behave, just normal thinking was like trying to talk over a crowd.

'I can't discuss details with you,' he said.

'Do you know who did it?'

She knew it was a stupid question. She felt him staring at her.

'*Do you?*' she said again. Her throat felt narrow, like being choked.

'*Are you all right?*' he said.

'*Who did it?*' Her lungs had gone. She couldn't move to get the air in.

'*Sit down,*' said Capitaine Vincent.

He helped her to the chair behind the desk. She leaned forward, sick to her stomach. She shut her eyes but saw Alex, dead. She smelled blood. She saw the crumpled car.

'*Calm down,*' he said. '*Calm down.*'

She thought there was nothing more upsetting than being told to calm down. She nodded. She bit her lip and breathed through her nose. She forced herself better, and sat up. His hand had briefly touched her shoulder. Now he stood back, separate and respectful.

'OK?' he said.

'*Yes, I'm sorry.*'

'*No, it's OK. It's normal.*'

He looked down at the guestbook, lying on the desk. '*Is this the hotel register?*'

She nodded, wiping tears she hadn't known were there. Vincent spun it round and opened it and flicked through the pages, shaking his head slowly. Bea, leaning back, recovering, began to feel embarrassed. She could see Alex's disguised writing, upside down, and the different names in different colours. She began to blush.

'*No passport details,*' said Vincent.

'*It's not really a register,*' she said.

'*The register is on the computer?*'

'*I don't know the password,*' said Bea. '*Dan might know.*'

'*We can take it?*'

224

'Yes, of course.'

Capitaine Vincent studied the pages silently. Bea stared at the floor, feeling idiotic. *The Prices of Hull!* said Alex's voice loudly and she wanted to smile, her mood soaring, reckless. Vincent closed the book with a snap.

'*So there were no visitors since March?*'

'*There were hardly any visitors,*' she said. '*Ever.*'

'*Why not?*'

'*The hotel needs work.*'

He frowned. '*So who are all these people?*' He waved his hand over the visitors' book, wafting lemon aftershave.

'*We made them up.*'

'*Why?*' said Vincent.

'*I don't know,*' said Bea. '*It was a joke.*'

'*A joke?*'

'*Yes. A prank.*' She used '*blague*' first, then '*farce*', which seemed more appropriate.

'*A practical joke?*' he said.

'*Yes, that's better, a practical joke,*' she said.

'*To trick who?*' asked Vincent.

'*It wasn't a trick,*' she said. '*We weren't trying to fool anybody.*'

He looked at her in silence.

'*Did your brother have his catering hygiene certificates in order?*' asked Vincent.

Bea laughed. It just burst out. She wasn't normal. She needed to control herself.

'*Is that funny?*'

'*No. I'm sorry.*'

He looked slowly around the hall, then behind the desk and swung the room keys with his index finger to read the black letters scrawled on the varnished board.

'Gluttony?' he read. The English lying clumsily on his tongue. 'Lust. Wrath.'

'It was sort of a joke of Alex's,' said Bea, also in English.

'*Another joke?*' He was inscrutable.

'*Yes. How long are they going to keep Dan? What do they want with him?*'

He shrugged. '*Excuse me,*' he said.

He went outside, leaving the front door open, and put Alex's blue notebook in the car, then he made a phone call, standing on the driveway, and then another. Bea sat at the reception desk in the swivel chair, as he talked on the driveway. She texted Dan but got no response. The two detectives came down the stairs, together, with all their equipment. They were as companionable and cheery as before. They didn't say anything to her as they passed, but talked to Vincent for a few moments, outside, then Lecuyer came back in and unplugged the computer.

'Ooph!' he said, lifting it, the cord and plug with its adaptor socket dragging on the floor behind him.

He put it in the van and they all stood talking again. They seemed to be enjoying themselves. Bea got up, and ran to Alex's room.

Everything was different. The air had changed. There was no trace, no feeling of him left. The overhead light was on. A side table stood abandoned on the rug. His clothes were heaped on a chair, T-shirts, jeans, all piled together. Books that had lain about naturally were now in a stack, and the duvet bunched in the middle of the mattress.

She heard Vincent coming up the stairs and wanted to shut the door and sit against it, so he could not come in, but it was too late. He stood in the doorway and watched her pick up the duvet, shake it out, and lay it straight. She went to the window and opened it, then she turned back to the room.

'They've moved everything,' she said in English. 'What do you want?'

In a rage, she kicked the pile of books, noisily, to the floor. Some of them landed open, crushing pages.

'That's not like me,' she said.

She knelt and tidied them again, just for something to do and to get control of herself.

'Madame,' said Vincent, 'I assure you, we are doing everything we can. We are working very hard to discover what happened to your brother.'

He came further into the room.

'*May I?*' He gestured to the chair.

He was waiting for her permission. She got up from the floor and picked up Alex's clothes. Then she sat on the edge of the bed, with them on her lap.

'*Thank you.*' Vincent sat down, crossing his legs and brushing something from his jeans.

The worn cotton T-shirts in her arms were comforting and agonising. It felt too intimate to hold them, empty, and not hers, and losing life every second, but she didn't want to let go of them.

'*Do you know the story about the elephant and the blind men?*' he said.

She looked up at him, too surprised to answer.

'*Do you know it?*' he said.

She did, but he was going to tell it to her.

'*Good,*' he said. '*Three blind men are asked to describe an elephant, yes? The first blind man, he holds out his hand and feels one of the* elephant's long tusks. "You want me to describe it?" he says. "An elephant is long and hard, like a pipe"— or something like that.'

Bea studied him, completely absorbed.

'And the second man, he is holding the elephant's tail. He says, "No, no! An elephant is not like a pipe at all, an elephant has bristles, like a brush."'

He was gesturing and closing his eyes, as if he were discovering an imaginary elephant. She put Alex's clothes down on the bed, next to her.

'And the third man,' said Vincent, 'who is touching the side of the elephant, he says, "You are both wrong, an elephant is definitely big and flat, like a wall." So they can't agree, and they argue, because each one is sure he is right.' He looked at her eagerly. 'OK?'

'Yes,' said Bea.

'I don't remember the end, I think the King comes and explains to them — it doesn't matter, you see, to me, this story is like investigating a crime. We have the witnesses, the evidence — all of these elements. Each one is a small part. My problem is to put them together. That is my job. But for the family, it is different. They are angry. They want to have answers and know everything.'

'Yes.'

'It's hard,' he said. 'People want explanations. For me, when I see the whole story, I find the guilty man, and then it's finished.'

'Justice,' said Bea, looking down.

'Yes,' he said. 'Justice. Peace, maybe.'

She wondered if she ever would feel peace again, or if there could be such a thing as justice for Alex. She didn't think so. Vincent was looking at her. He thought she'd feel better if she talked to him, but he didn't know her.

'Did you study philosophy?' she asked.

'Me?' He smiled, suddenly boyish. 'No. I went to music college. In Bordeaux.'

'Music?'

'Yes, and I am in a rock band with my brother, Félix. We play covers, and some of our own songs, too.'

'Do you write songs?'

'No, no, but Félix does, and he sings.'

'What does Félix do? His work I mean.'

'He's an engineer. Three kids already. I'm just the guitarist. You know—'

He began to play air guitar but stopped, embarrassed to have forgotten himself.

There was an awkward silence.

'That sounds cool,' said Bea, to help him out.

'It's OK,' he said. 'It's not serious.' He brushed off his spotless jeans again.

'But it's good. Your job is very serious,' said Bea.

'Yes,' he answered. 'I am the group leader of an SR. We are the elite in the gendarmerie.'

'There's a version of that story I like,' said Bea, 'where the men aren't blind —'

'But they are blind.'

'No,' said Bea.

'Yes, they are.'

She looked away from him at the invaded room. She had read the Hindu version of the story, the Jain, and the Buddhist. The Christian telling, like his, was a children's story. The one she liked best was the poet Rumi's, and even that had been warped by time and telling, and the Islamic heart of his work altered by western sentiment and soundbites. Rumi's story was a short parable. There was no king and no fight; no wise men, or blind men, just 'a crowd of Hindus' who bring an elephant into a dark room. Nobody in the crowd knows what an elephant is, but each has their opinion.

The sensual eye is like the palm of the hand, she remembered, *it has not the means of covering the whole beast*. She tried to remember the last line. *We are in a clear sea, but we choose only to look at the foam*. She felt the calming pull of it. She looked around the room and thought about the things in it, and how limited they were: herself and Vincent, and then the objects; the bed she sat on, the chair, table, window. She looked harder and seemed to see places where the police had walked, and handprints, the airplane tracks left by their searching eyes. The room felt very small, and she did, too. It was tempting to fall into rage, and easy to cling to the myth of resolution.

'*I'm sorry about before,*' she said. '*You have your job to do.*'

She stood up, and, taking his cue, Capitaine Vincent did too.

'*Don't apologise,*' he said. '*It's very difficult. But we are the* good guys, *yes?*' He said *good guys* in English. She nodded.

'Thank you for talking to me.'

'You're welcome,' said Vincent. 'And thank you, for your courage.'

As they left the room he closed the door behind them quietly, as if a child were sleeping.

As soon as he left, Bea remembered Dan, shocked that she could have forgotten him, and filled with sudden panic, as if she had been dragged from a deep dark place of comfort, guilty in the face of reality. She drove to Chateau L'Orée des Vignes, playing the radio loudly, to block out her thoughts. The calm that she had felt talking to Vincent had gone. She walked from the car, around the outsized giant of a chateau, to the front. Her father had said he'd wait for her in the lobby but he was standing on the forecourt, with the view behind him, in his sunglasses, looking out for her.

'Dad – they're –' She stopped.

'What?'

She wanted to unburden herself of the shock, and share it, but she remembered it would shock him, too.

'What is it?' he said, when he saw her expression.

'Shall we go inside?'

'Tell me now,' he said.

An SUV pulled up very near them and a liveried valet hurried down the steps towards it. All four doors opened and they heard a family, loudly talking.

'Over here,' said Bea. She walked away from the people getting out of the car and her father followed.

She paused, and waited, until she had his attention. She left a silence so he could prepare himself.

'They're calling it murder,' she said.

'Why didn't you tell me?'

'I am telling you.'

He took off his dark glasses and squeezed the bridge of his nose, shutting his eyes. Behind them the noisy family went up the steps. They could hear their rolling cases bumping on the stone.

'When?' said Griff. He meant when did she find out.

'One of the gendarmes just said it, just –' She stopped. 'Like I knew already. While they were looking in Alex's room. But we didn't know, did we?'

'I suspected.'

'They said they were investigating a murder,' she said. 'And then when Capitaine Vincent came, we talked about it.'

'What did he say?'

'He said – I don't know. Nothing. There isn't any detail, or anything. I think they just want to find out everything they can from us.'

'From us? What kind of thing?'

'How we get on – as a family?'

'Are they still searching Paligny, now?'

'No, they left.'

'Where did they look?'

'In his room.'

'What were they looking for?'

'They didn't say. They took a notebook of Alex's and his computer. But they didn't look for fingerprints or anything. I don't know what they were looking for.'

He walked away from her. She watched his back. She saw him take deep breaths and then nod, as if he were listening to himself say something, and responding.

'Is Philip Roche still here?' she asked.

'No. He's gone to Paris.'

'You shouldn't have been so rude to him.'

'He can do whatever he does from his office,' said Griff. 'We've got Arun.'

'Has Arun gone to get Dan?'

'No, but he's on it.'

'What does that mean? What's that? *On it?*'

He raised his hand. 'Leave it alone.'

She went and stood by him. They were both silent, both blind, in the grip of the same paralysis, thinking things too dark to be spoken. Horror was all there was, there wasn't any need to say it.

When Bea spoke, she whispered. 'Why do you think it took so long for them to start investigating?'

'We don't know when they started, do we?'

'We don't know anything,' she said. She thought of Vincent, and their conversation, and a small calm came into her mind. It was coolness and steadiness, and she held on to it.

'Come up to the suite,' said Griff.

She followed him inside. They crossed the lobby and started up the carpeted staircase together, but on the landing she stopped.

'Can Arun come down instead?' she asked. 'I don't want to go to your room.'

They were by the open doors to the high-ceilinged ballroom that led out to the terrace where they had eaten the night before. Her father looked at her for a long moment.

'I know you don't. I'm asking you to,' he said.

'All right, I will.'

'Thank you,' said Griff. 'I don't think we should tell her, do you?'

'It's up to you,' said Bea. 'It might be wrong, not to. There'll never be a good time.'

The ballroom was empty and airy, and through the open doors, waiters could be seen taking down the lunchtime parasols on the terrace, and putting fresh cloths on the tables. A group of Americans came up the stairs.

'Hi!' they grinned, so keen to show the best of themselves. 'How are ya?'

Bea and Griff stepped aside to let them pass.

'I was thinking about Alex's funeral,' he said, when they'd gone. 'If we ever get him back.' Somebody was vacuuming a hallway somewhere in the building. A telephone rang. 'They can't keep him there forever.'

'I know,' said Bea.

It was a very hot day. She could feel the sun's heat on the breeze that came through the open doors, across the polished ballroom.

'It's been almost a week already,' said Griff.

She knew they chilled corpses almost to freezing if they had to store them for any length of time. Alex's body would be no more rotten than when he had been pulled out of his car. She sat down, suddenly, on the bottom step of the staircase behind her. She thought of the decomposing rat in the attic, how loose the body had been. Did they sew Alex's body back together again after the post-mortem, crudely, like Frankenstein's monster, or tidily, as if he'd be using it again?

'I was thinking about what people will say,' said Griff. 'At the funeral. They'll come out of the woodwork, won't they, all his mates. Ex-junkies, his old teachers and what have you, and they'll all yabber on about how *creative* he was, what a *great guy*. I can hear it now. And to be honest with you, your brother was a stranger to me from the day he was born.'

He looked down into her face for a reaction, hoping to shock her.

'I didn't see much of him as a baby,' he said. 'And he was the sort of kid we would have beaten the crap out of at Stratford Grammar. He wouldn't have lasted five minutes. Poetry? I mean, seriously. Who gives a shit?'

Bea looked past him, towards the open doors, trying to feel the fresh air on her face. A butterfly had flown into the ballroom. Luminous and bright blue, it flickered and dipped in the air.

'When was this?' she asked. 'That you were imagining his funeral?'

'Last night. Today.'

234

'Everyone remembering him.'

'Yes.'

'And not being able to appreciate what they said.'

'Yes.'

'That must be horrible,' she said, 'feeling like that.'

'It is,' said Griff. 'Yes, it is. You think you'll have time. To sort stuff out with people.'

'I know.'

'Do you remember Alex's school uniform?'

Her stomach flipped with the acuteness of her memory. 'Yes. At Stowe?'

'No, when he was a little boy.'

He held out his hand, in a rough approximation of Alex's height as a small boy. 'Grey jumper with a red stripe,' he said. 'Red tie. And a cap, like Just William. Always leaving it behind. Always under my feet, in the car. Red blazer.'

'Yes,' said Bea.

She watched the pretty butterfly, and wondered exactly how short its life was, and how far it was through that short life, as it flew about the sterile room, wasting precious seconds. Griff seemed to notice for the first time that she was sitting on the stairs, and that it wasn't normal. He held out his hand.

'Come on,' he said. 'Up you get.'

She took his hand and he pulled her to her feet.

'I sent your brother on an errand,' he said. 'Anybody could have done it for me. Just one of those things, like collecting rent from the farm, just something to make him feel like he had a job, but if I hadn't, he'd still be here. He'd be alive.'

'You couldn't possibly have known.'

He shrugged her off.

'Griff, it was beyond your control.'

'Beyond my control?' He repeated it wonderingly, as if such a thing were unthinkable.

'There was nothing at all you could have done.'

'I shouldn't have sent him.'

'No. That's not true,' said Bea. 'It's easier to blame yourself than to accept your helplessness.'

'Easier?' He sounded offended.

'Yes. Blame. Blaming yourself. Blaming anyone. Raging against it. That's easy. And it will make you mad. You have to try not to.'

He squinted at her, calculating, then gave a sudden, big, barking laugh, like someone who's witnessed a conjuring trick. It made her jump.

'You're actually quite good,' he said. 'You should have been a lawyer.'

16

It wasn't funny any more, Dan thought. It hadn't been before, but he had been able to be cool about it when the cops were talking to the whole family, even the second time. Now this was just him, and he'd been forced to leave Bea, alone with more of them. It was hard not to panic. It wouldn't do any good to fight, but he felt so scared. He pictured losing it in the back of the police car, and trying to escape and when they let him out, inside the compound of the barracks, he could see himself making a run for it, and imagining what would happen then was terrifying. They had guns, they were soldiers, he was in a foreign country and they had no reason to treat him well, and he didn't know what was going on and his wife was alone at Paligny with three men. He didn't need to let his mind go far before it went to very bad places, it didn't take a lot of imagination. So he texted Griff from the back of the car, and texted Bea once, and then concentrated on sitting as quietly and calmly as he could, and not letting them see how scared he was.

They were very courteous. They stood aside for him to go through doors first, and even smiled. He reminded himself of the facts, and that everything else was just his panic talking, and his ingrained, natural distrust of the police. It was all in his mind. He told himself that. He tried to look fine with it all as, just like the afternoon before, he had to wait while they found the interpreter. That's why it had taken longer than Bea's interview. That was the reason, nothing sinister.

Today, he only had to wait twenty minutes. And he was upstairs in an office with people around, and he had his phone, it wasn't like they'd asked him for it. There was nothing to suggest he was doing anything other than helping them with their enquiries. He didn't know where he'd got that phrase. So-and-so was said to be helping the police with their enquiries. So-and-so is not a suspect. He had a feeling so-and-so usually got booked. As far as he could guess, the cops had no more idea what had happened to Alex than he did. They were just digging around. And he was helping them, with their enquiries.

The day before, a detective had asked him basic questions about his whereabouts. And they'd asked about drugs. Today he was interviewed by a tall, fair man with a long neck, who introduced himself as Dufour. From Bea's description, Dan thought it was the same man who'd interviewed her. Dufour, and a smaller man called Luis, with hairy arms and chest, came over and greeted him. Greeted was the wrong word. It was more of a mime. *See you later.* Watch-tapping, thumb jerks. Then they left him on his own. At three o'clock, the interpreter arrived, the same one as the day before, a senior lecturer from the languages department at the University of Bourgogne. She was a skinny little German woman, with short grey hair which would have been pixyish in her youth, but now looked manly. They liked each other, she was out of place too. Her name was Karen

Koch. It had been funny the day before, but it wasn't funny now. When he saw her walking towards him, he felt so lonely it was like seeing his best friend. She was smiling, with pursed lips, inhibited by her role.

'Hello again,' she said, 'what a surprise.'

'Yeah. Hi.'

'How are you today?' Her English came easily and her accent was comforting, he associated it with rational Europe, and bureaucracy.

'I've been better,' said Dan. 'My wife is at home, on her own, with two more of these guys,' he said.

'I wouldn't worry about that,' said Karen.

She was kind. He thought she might be gay. Not that the two were connected. He just thought she might be, because of the hair.

'Thanks,' he said.

They sat waiting together in silent, mismatched companionship. Dufour and Luis came back and all four went into the stairwell, and up the stairs. The two detectives were laughing as they talked, and Dan followed, with Karen Koch.

The second floor had an open-plan low-ceilinged office. It looked like it had been recently dedicated to Alex's case; it wasn't crowded, like downstairs, and the small group of plain-clothes officers seemed to all know one another. They joked around and went out for cigarettes in pairs, looking at Dan as they passed, not trying to hide their interest. It was strange not understanding the language, it sharpened his other senses. Without words, the mood in the air was physical, like prickling on the skin.

At an empty desk, Dufour and Luis shook hands with him, as if he'd only just walked in, and sat down. He didn't like either of them, but they were polite. Dufour was a racist, Luis was not.

Dan didn't ask himself how he knew; he knew, the same way he knew in deceptively polite old England, where these days open hostility was mostly reserved for Muslims. Black had been upgraded recently, now they had found more foreign foreigners to fear, with accents and religion. Karen sat at Dan's side with a notepad. She put on a pair of wire-framed reading glasses.

'OK,' said Dufour, looking down at a file. Then he said something else.

'He says: he's sorry to keep you waiting. They were waiting for me,' Karen smiled.

'Yeah, it's OK,' said Dan. 'But I don't know why I'm here.'

Karen translated this but Dufour looked blank. The other one, Luis, took out a pad and a pencil, and rested the pad on his knee. He held his pencil clumsily. It was not reassuring. Dufour rattled out sentence after sentence, in French that might as well have been Urdu, and Dan, looking at Karen, waiting for her to translate, saw her expression change.

'What is it?' he said.

She turned to him. She was completely different. Not used to doing this job, she couldn't cover her reactions. Dan hadn't realised how much he was counting on her. He smiled, trying to re-establish their tiny bond. He thought of Germany, a country which, in his mind, was a haven of sensible, liberal thought, and hoped with sudden panic that Karen Koch would deliver on his stereotype. He remembered neo-Nazi rallies he had seen, and put them from his mind.

'Detective Dufour says: your wife said you weren't in bed with her the night Mr Adamson died,' she said.

Dan was stunned. He wasn't sure he'd heard her right.

'What?'

'*Quoi?*' said Karen to Dufour.

Dan felt a jolt of adrenaline. He concentrated on not look-ing tense. They mustn't think they were on to something. They weren't on to anything. There had been a mistake. Griff would be working on getting him out, even as he sat there his father-in-law was probably bawling someone out. He thought of Griff's stature, and his money, and held on to the thought. He had connections, he wasn't free-falling, they couldn't hurt him.

'Detective Dufour says: how long were you out?' said Karen.

'I wasn't out. I was in bed, *all night*.'

Suddenly, he remembered Bea's face, her smug calm as he was taken away, and how surprised he'd been that she didn't seem worried. He'd been much more worried about her at the time, but now he couldn't forget it. Usually, she was more likely to jump to conclusions about racism in the police force, and corrupt authorities, and he was the one trying to pacify her. Why had she been so happy to see him go? His thoughts were racing so fast he couldn't focus. Dufour said something else, and Karen turned to him again, her eyes cast down. Two small red patches had appeared on her cheeks.

'He says: your wife woke up in the middle of the night, and you weren't there.'

He remembered. 'OK, yes, I did get up for a — I went to the bathroom, and I went downstairs for some water.'

The other detective, Luis, was writing quickly, leaning the pad on his stocky thigh. It was archaic. The guy could be writ-ing anything. Dan reminded himself he wasn't under suspicion. He was helping them with their enquiries. But he didn't know what they were enquiring about. He felt a vertiginous drop, and held back fear.

'Look, tell him I woke up for, like, five minutes, OK? I got a glass of water, and went back to bed. When I got into bed, Bea said *Where've you been?* I remember it, but it was five minutes. Tops. OK?'

She listened, gravely nodding, then translated, and Dan waited for Dufour's friendly shrug, the *Oh, that explains it then,* but he had moved on to something else.

'He's asking how you felt about Mr Adamson,' said Karen.

'Excuse me?'

'Alex Adamson.'

'Yeah, I know. But "felt about him" – like, in what way?'

Dufour shrugged. Dan thought he'd seen enough of French shrugging.

'I liked him,' said Dan. 'Bea and him were very close.'

Dufour responded immediately. Dan realised he understood. Maybe he just didn't want to speak English, and was only using Karen to translate his questions. He thought maybe they all spoke English, and with the thought, all the men in the room became eavesdroppers. It had been comforting, the sense of being overseen, but now it was the opposite. He needed to relax. He was thirty years old. He was a professional. He went to work in a suit. He wasn't a fourteen-year-old boy, crying for his mother in the Peckham cop shop, the mother he would lie to about it later, so as not to upset her, and get in trouble for staying out.

'How was your childhood?' asked Karen.

'What?' Dan spluttered – it was so weird she asked that.

She looked back at Dufour, for confirmation, and he said something else.

'He says: were you poor, growing up?'

'Poor, like, money?' said Dan stupidly.

Karen nodded gravely. 'Yes, money.'

'I guess, kind of. No. We were good. We were OK.'

Karen made an effort to translate his vagueness.

'What work did she do?'

'My mum? She was a teaching assistant. Now she's a social worker.'

Dufour leaned over the desk, speaking urgently. Dan pretended to be so relaxed that he wasn't even trying to understand, and looked around the office, casually.

'Detective Dufour says: Griff Adamson is a very rich businessman,' said Karen. 'How much did you know about the Adamsons, before you married Beatrice?' She looked sympathetic, like a kindly dentist sticking a probe into his tooth.

'I knew her family did OK,' said Dan guardedly, and the image of Griff and the private jet popped into his head. 'I didn't know any details.'

Dufour said something else, quick-fire, gesturing.

'Yes. OK, Dan,' said Karen. 'He says: will you explain exactly, please, what you knew about your wife's family, and the money they have. Specifically, please.'

Luis looked up, his pencil clutched in his fist. Dan noticed he had a wrist tattoo. What a dick, he thought.

Dufour said, 'Yes?' in English. His eyes were glassy beneath their pale lids, Flemish-looking eyes, Dan thought, like a Dutch portrait. He'd never liked those Dutch artists. He struggled with anything pre-twentieth century. He could do the Italian Renaissance, and get into the Baroque, but those Dutch painters bored him shitless. Except Hieronymus Bosch. Bosch was cool. He took his eyes from Dufour's pallid face, and turned to Karen. Her hands were folded in her lap, and her head was bowed, as if she would hear better if she was not looking at his face. She had lace-up shoes and ankle socks. They looked sort of sweet to him, like she had corns or something.

He wondered if she had children, or grandchildren, even. She could have been anything between thirty-five and sixty. Dufour was waiting.

'What can I tell you?' said Dan. 'When I met Bea, we didn't talk about money. She didn't earn much, and nor did I, but she was middle-class, so I guess –'

'Wait, please,' said Karen.

He stopped. She translated.

'Continue,' she said. She smiled encouragingly. He focused on her lace-up shoes and ankle socks, wondering why they reminded him of Bea – they weren't what she'd wear. Maybe because Karen was guileless, like her.

'I assumed her family had some money. You judge, don't you? I mean, everyone does, right? Except Bea. She doesn't.'

He looked up from Karen's shoes, into her eyes.

'She never asked me the normal questions that people do. Class, money, whatever. She's just not like that.'

Karen kept translating, not looking at Dufour, looking straight at Dan. He could see Bea's face in front of him while he talked, taken back to the night they met, as if under a spell.

'It's almost like she's blind,' he said to Karen. 'Know what I mean? She sees everything and nothing. She didn't describe herself in those terms. Rich, poor, posh – it's not how she thinks.'

'How did you meet?'

'At this place near where I live. I had this art exhibition. She came to see it.'

Dufour laughed and said something.

'An art show?' said Karen coldly. Not coldly to Dan, but because Dufour had been rude.

Dan gave her a smile, to show her it was OK. 'It was a student show.'

'So when did you find out she was an heiress?'

An heiress. It was an archaic word. To be an heiress, Bea would have to inherit, people only inherited on a death. It wasn't the first time it had crossed his mind.

'It wasn't like that,' he said. 'She told me her dad was in property. She said she didn't see her family, and she told me she never borrowed money from them. I respect that. That's it.'

'That's it?'

'Yes.'

Dufour said something. He sounded sarcastic. Dan tried not to look uncomfortable, he didn't mean to lie, but the truth he was telling was not the perfect truth. Karen turned to him.

'He says: it must be exciting for you, to discover your father-in-law is a multimillionaire.'

'Exciting?' Dan's mouth was dry. 'No.'

'Griff Adamson is a property developer,' said Karen. 'You are an estate agent.'

Dan laughed. 'Yeah, but –'

'Were you interested in Beatrice for this reason?'

'No.' Dan looked at Dufour. 'No,' he said again, firmly. He looked back at Karen. 'You can tell him, Bea doesn't even like them. I'd only met them *once*, before coming to France, OK? I didn't know anything about them, and to tell you the truth I'm not all that interested. Can you tell him that?'

Karen nodded briskly, and translated, a long stream of French, while Dan watched Dufour's face for a reaction, and saw none. Then Dufour asked something else.

'He wants to know why Bea doesn't like her family. What have they done to her?'

'Done to her?' Dan felt awkward. 'They haven't done any-thing. She doesn't like their politics.' He shrugged. 'Her mother liked her brothers better.'

'Why?'

'Why? I dunno. Just normal stuff. Bea's very ethical. She's very moral. She just doesn't get on with them, OK?'

Dufour spoke.

'Your mother's home,' said Karen, 'where you grew up. How big is it?'

'Seriously?' said Dan. 'It's a flat.'

'Is it in a bad area?'

'A "bad" area?'

Karen made a face that said *I know, humour him.*

'It's an OK area,' said Dan expressionlessly.

Dufour spoke.

'He says: did you have a rough childhood?'

'No.'

'He says: were you involved with gangs?'

'Has he heard of racial stereotyping?' said Dan. 'You have that expression here, right?'

Karen smiled. Then Dufour spoke and she stopped smiling. 'He says: answer the question.'

'Which one?'

Dufour's glassy eyes examined him, Luis's pencil hovered over his pad. Dan knew what was being assumed, like the ques-tions about drugs the day before; he had to let it roll off. He had to rise above. This guy had probably never been anywhere or seen anything like where Dan grew up. And there wasn't any single word that could describe Dan's first sixteen years, or anybody's. Dufour was speaking, fast.

'He says again: were you involved with gangs?' said Karen.

246

'No.'

'Have you ever stolen anything?'

'No.'

'Do you have a police record?'

'No, I don't have a record. My mum was very strict.'

'He says: where was your father?'

'He didn't live with us.'

'Where did he live?'

'In the country somewhere.'

'What country?'

'No, the country*side*. Surrey or someplace.'

'You didn't see him?'

'No.'

'Were your parents married?'

'None of his business. No, they weren't.'

'Was your mother a good mother?'

'What is this?'

Dufour's words banged out like a military drum. *Did she hate your father? Did she hate white people? Do you hate white people?*

'You're kidding, right?'

'No,' said Karen, 'I'm sorry, he's asking this.'

Dan looked at Dufour, resting his chin on his clasped hands, with his eyebrows raised, acting the big man, as the hairy one scribbled away in the corner.

'This is all irrelevant,' said Dan. 'Can you tell him that?'

Karen nodded, and he could tell she agreed with him. She said something to Dufour. He answered her back, and they had a brief exchange.

'OK,' she said. 'He was explaining to me that this manner of questioning the interested parties, they do this so they can really understand. It's not an interrogation, only –'

Dufour stopped her, sharply. Chastened, she took a sip of water. Dufour spoke again. Very deliberately, Karen replaced her cup on the desk. Without looking at Dan, she translated.

'He wants to know if you had a violent childhood. If your mother was violent, or if you witnessed violence. Domestic violence. Gang violence. Or at school. Violence in your life.'

'My life? My whole life?'

Dufour shrugged.

Dan looked at the telephone on the desk, and the cord, snaking through a hole, out of sight. There had been gangs on the streets and at school, where there had also been a chess club, run by an ancient Hungarian woman, called Mrs Róheim who looked exactly like a man. Of Dan's four closest friends from primary school he lost one to drugs, and one to excessive schoolwork. The third went off the radar, first for the streets, then a girl, then moved to Berlin. The fourth was still Dan's best friend, and worked in TV production, and Dan didn't see enough of him. Ten-year-old Damilola Taylor was murdered fifteen minutes from Dan's home. They were the same age. Dan didn't know Damilola, or any of the African kids, but he knew the gang that killed him by sight. The violence that was in the air most days had been in everything that day. You'd swear you could see it, in the cracks in the pavements and the bricks in the walls; violence and grief. And yes, Dan's mother smacked him, when she was frightened for him, or desperate, for reasons of her own. She also held him close to her heart and kissed his head, and read to him. He'd felt her tears drip from her cheek to his. She had been angry at his father, and described his treatment of her, a woman of Jamaican heritage, as a political act. One of her boyfriends hit Dan in the head once, and when he told her about it she

248

never saw him again. Another had taken them both up in a helicopter for her birthday, high above London. It had been one of the best days of Dan's life. She had quit the boyfriends when she took up the Bible, but her embracing of the notion of sin was a kind of violence in itself. Did Dan have a violent childhood? It had been both playground and minefield, and his home had been his nest as well as his prison. *A rough childhood in a bad area?* Whatever.

He looked from Dufour to Karen, who waited attentively, and back to Dufour.

'Oh look, I don't know,' he said. 'What can I tell you? I told the other guy the same yesterday. I wasn't in gangs, I didn't deal drugs, I finished school. I went to college. That's it.'

Karen translated, with an air of finality. She seemed pleased with his answer, at least. 'How big is your house?'

'Excuse me?'

'Your home, with your wife, is it big, or small?'

'This again? He likes his property, doesn't he? It's small.'

'Why is it so small?'

'It's what we can afford,' said Dan, and felt suddenly humiliated. He could see why Dufour would be suspicious of him. He was related to a multimillionaire, and he was still a failure.

'Is it difficult for you, to live in a small home with your wife, when her family has a lot of money?'

'If he says so. Whatever, right?'

Karen nodded, and smiled, and translated. Dufour shrugged, and then said something with the word *Adamson* in it. That was a relief.

'What did you think of Alex?'

'I've told you. He was OK. A bit weak.'

Dufour sat forward, and said one word.

'Weak?' translated Karen.

Dufour sneered something that Dan didn't like, even before he heard the English.

'He says: is it unfair that you are not weak, and you have nothing, and Alex was a drug addict and had a lot of money?'

Dan sighed and shrugged, again, like he was bored. He was doing all right, but he needed to not look at Dufour's face.

'We don't "have nothing". We're fine.'

'He says: did you resent Alex?'

'No.'

'You weren't jealous?'

'Nope.'

'Do you resent your wife?'

'What?'

'Do you resent her for not being rich, like her family?'

'No,' he said. He rubbed his hands over his face and head. 'Of course not,' he said. 'We agreed, early on, that Bea doesn't ask her parents for money and that's fine by me.' Like a nervous tic, he saw the private jet again, hovering, and blinked it away. Quite deliberately, he pictured Bea, with her arms held out, smiling. He imagined her taking his hand, and her flame tattoo, as if he were lifting her hair to kiss it.

Dufour asked him a question. Karen, drinking water from her plastic cup, put it down impatiently. Her translation was deliberately expressionless and flat, to show what she thought of the question.

'He says: you saw her father's picture in the paper, and how rich he is, and that's why you married her.'

'He said that?' said Dan. 'That's not even a question.'

Karen said something to Dufour, who made an irritated noise, and leaned across the desk. He spoke nastily. Close up, his face was even worse. Dan almost didn't need Karen's translation.

'He says: was that why you married her?'

Dan smiled into Dufour's eyes. 'No, mate, that's not why I married her.' He was amazed how calm he felt, calm and uninhibited. 'I married her because she's matchless,' said Dan. 'The woman is matchless.'

'Matchless?' said Karen.

'Outstanding,' said Dan.

Karen smiled. She blushed. She wasn't gay. Dufour said something else, and she set her mouth, disapprovingly.

'He says: but she is not your type.'

Dan scratched his cheek, to give the impression of being mildly surprised, as if it had never occurred to him that he and Bea weren't an obvious fit in the eyes of the world, and he was mulling it over.

'Huh,' he said, nodding. 'OK.'

'He says: your wife is – what's the right word? Frumpy.'

He hadn't expected that. It was so unusual, and strange-sounding, with the German accent in the 'r'.

'*Frumpy?*'

'Frumpy? Yes, I think so,' said Karen. 'I think this is the word. Frumpy? For instance, not-fashionable?'

'Right,' said Dan, bemused and offended. 'I don't know.'

He thought of Bea, walking in from work in her jeans and green jumper, and telling him what she'd been doing, and that he often thought how brave she must have had to be all day, and how hard-working. She wasn't a beauty until you got her clothes off. She could have made more of herself. She was quiet-looking. That these things were failings in the eyes of this ignorant snake-necked albino-lashed arsehole – Dufour asked him something, but Karen didn't translate, she argued back at him, in rapid French.

'What?' said Dan. 'What's he saying?'

Dufour insisted. She turned back to Dan. Her voice was neutral, but the red spots had come back, like little rashes on her cheeks.

'He says: did your wife go with black men before she met you?' She couldn't meet his eye.

'No,' said Dan, feeling nothing, thinking nothing. 'I was her first.'

Karen translated. He felt sorry for her. She was clearly in a dilemma. Dufour spoke. Dan's eyes were drawn to his face, he tried, but he couldn't look away. Karen snapped something and Dufour hardly acknowledged her. His hair lay flat on his forehead. His hooded eyes held every insult.

'He says: do you *have a thing* for white girls? And I am not happy to ask you this.'

Dan smiled. 'Don't worry about it,' he said evenly. 'You can tell him it depends.'

Karen passed this on, more embarrassed by the second.

'What does it depend on?' she said, quiet as a mouse.

'Whether the white girls are multimillionaires,' said Dan.

Her eyes flew to his face, appalled on his behalf.

'You can tell him,' said Dan. 'The only white girls I go for are minted. My wife has a shit-ton of money. And luckily she likes black cock. Result. Right?'

He was calm, he didn't give a fuck. Dufour got up and left the room. There was a pause.

'Two minutes,' said Luis, from his corner, in heavily accented English.

Dan and Karen sat, not looking at one another. His detachment had evaporated. His heart was pounding. He terrified himself. He'd thought he was fine.

Dufour came back into the room holding an A4 printout. It was a photograph.

'Is this you?' he said in English, holding it out to Dan.

The photograph was very poor quality: a CCTV image from a petrol station. There was a car at the pumps, which could have been Alex's Peugeot, and two men walking across the forecourt. One of them was Alex – or looked like Alex – and the other was taller, and dark, the top half of the body was a smudge, or in shadow.

'Is it you?' said Dufour, pointing.

'No,' said Dan, relieved and frightened at the same time.

'Look again. Is it you?'

'I don't need to look. It's not me,' said Dan.

Dufour put the printout on the desk.

'It isn't me. Karen? You can tell him that's not me.'

'Yes, I'm telling him.'

'What is this? Are they stitching me up? I don't know who that is. That guy has a beard. He looks like he has a beard. It's not me. OK? I wasn't there. I mean, I don't even know where that is, or when that was taken. How would I know? I wouldn't.'

Dufour's telephone rang. He held up his hand for silence, and Dan immediately stopped talking.

17

As Griff opened the door to his suite, Bea heard music. Arun was seated at a grand piano on the far side of the room, tinkling out some Chopin, with an ease that made it sound like a cocktail lounge. He stopped playing as she came in. The room was as chilled and sealed as a fridge. Her mother, in black, lay on a velvet sofa, facing the windows, with her laptop at her side.

'Don't stop,' she said to Arun, then she saw Bea.

'Hi, Arun,' said Bea. 'Dan is still at the police station.'

He got up from the piano, crossed the room, and kissed her cheek. 'You're not to worry.'

'What's she talking about?' said Liv.

'Dan. He's being questioned again,' said Griff.

'Why?' said Liv. 'What's he done?'

'Nothing,' said Bea, thinking how stupid her mother was, and how slow.

'Well, why is he there? What can we do?' said Liv, half rising.

'It's all right, calm down, it's fine,' said Bea.

Her mother swung her legs over the side of the chaise and put her feet on the floor, her hand groping for her water glass.

'I'm trying to help,' she slurred. 'You don't need any help, obviously. You're *fine*.'

'I'm going outside,' said Bea.

Arun followed her to the door. 'I'm expecting to hear back from a number of people, at any moment,' he said. 'There's nothing to worry about, truly.'

'I'll be downstairs.'

'Try to be kind to your mother,' he whispered. 'She's so fragile.'

Bea thought how innocent he was, this shark from the same cold waters as her father.

'Arun!' Her father summoned him from the bedroom.

'Coming –'

He smiled and went. He must make over a million pounds a year, he had a family, and yet he tiptoed around her father like a lackey. Bea stepped out and began to pull the door to. She was almost out of earshot when her mother spoke.

'Bea. Come here.'

Bea considered closing the door and leaving her, but she couldn't do it. She went back inside. Arun and Griff were in the bedroom, and the doors were closed. Her mother held her hand out, and shuffled along the chaise. Reluctantly, Bea crossed the room, and sat with her.

'Look,' said Liv. 'What I found.'

She picked up her laptop, clumsily, and touched the track-pad. Photos came up from the tool bar like a genie from a bottle. There was Alex's face. Bea braced herself. It looked like life. It felt to her like life. The backlit screen was as bright as Liv could make it. She began to swipe. Alex's different faces from different times looked out, uncurated, blurred and clear, caught in movement, unknowing, or smiling, careful sometimes, and deliberately cheerful, and at other times caught in secret, contemplative. She kept expecting to see his car, hanging in the still morning air, or his autopsy, that she had to keep not picturing. Her mother, weeping, sagged, and leaned her torso against Bea's breast and ribs, flicking through the pictures, her finger tap-tapping through the photographs, sometimes so fast it was as if he were transforming from child to adult, and back to child. From teenager in black, to tall and tanned on his gap year, to a small, round-faced boy, then twenty-five, then five, then thirty. She thought of someone harming him. She saw his face split open. Liv stared and flicked through the pictures, murmuring words and little moans, indistinguishable cries and laughs. 'Here. Look. And. See? Ah. See?'

Bea, with one arm around her mother, jammed her other hand over her own mouth. The pain came back, forks stabbing at her temples. She wouldn't have been surprised if blood had trickled down her face.

'Liv,' she said, 'put that down for a second, I need to talk to you.'

She took the laptop from her mother, and moved so that she could see her face.

'The police told us something,' she said. 'Not very much, but you need to be prepared.'

Liv closed her eyes.

'Are you ready?'

Liv didn't speak. Bea was holding her shoulders, partly to be kind and partly to make sure she didn't slump or fall.

'Alex was murdered,' said Bea. 'They don't know who, or why, that's all they said.'

Liv didn't react.

'They're saying that, now, for sure. Do you understand?' said Bea.

Liv began to moan, and then to wail; as she raised her voice Griff came out of the bedroom.

'I told her,' said Bea.

Liv pulled away, and knelt on the ground, wailing and crying. Bea, unmoved, watched her.

'I'm sorry,' she said, pain stabbing her temples.

'Liv. You should rest,' said Griff.

Her mother grabbed the laptop and started to look at the pictures again. Griff touched Bea's shoulder, a two-finger tap, like a signal. Bea got her mother up from the floor. 'Take her in there,' said Griff.

Liv went with her to the bedroom, hanging on to the laptop, but when they got to the bed she let it slide from her hands. She sobbed against Bea's breast, and the laptop fell on its side, half closed, Alex's face illuminating the keyboard. Her tears soaked and spread on Bea's T-shirt. Bea's head hurt so much her eyes were burning.

'Try to sleep,' she said.

She covered her with her pashmina, which was lying on the bed, then straightened the laptop, and put away the pictures, so Alex's face, discarded, wouldn't stare at nothing. She put the laptop on a table as she left the room.

'Don't leave me,' said Liv.

Nothing was enough. Not if they all bled out for her. Griff was standing where Bea had left him, by the sofa, bleak and old and powerless. They looked at one another, but there was nothing to say.

*

Bea left the suite, and went downstairs, across the terrace, and, from there, down the steps into the garden. She needed nothingness to clear her mind. She could still feel her mother's body. Chateau L'Orée des Vignes was the perfect place for nothingness. Fingerposts directed her to *la piscine*, in curly writing. Past an avenue of box hedges, brown with blight, across a rose garden and an arboretum, was a large circular swimming pool set into an unnatural-looking lawn. About forty white plastic sunloungers were ranked around the pool. It was like a waiting room between worlds. She would sit and wait for Dan to be released, and try not to think. Two waiters, carrying trays, crossed paths. A pair of middle-aged women, very darkly tanned, looked up as Bea approached; one said something to the other and they looked down at their magazines again.

'Madame?'

The waiter looked Algerian or Moroccan. Bea ordered an iced coffee and put it on her father's bill without a second thought. She pulled a bed into the shade, and sat down.

Across the pool, a French family had put three sunbeds together, like a camp, and the mother was blowing up bright green frog armbands on the skinny arms of her tiny, naked daughter, a baby, of one or two years old. Bea watched how the woman moved. The sun came out in flashes. The tanning women bent their legs like slalom skiers, and their sunflower faces tracked the light. Bea tucked her skirt around her. She felt insubstantial, her headache had gone. She was hollowed out. These moments without thinking were like holidays. With lonely happiness, she watched the ladies sunbathing, and the French family putting on their suncream. The mother of the small naked girl, finished blowing up the armbands and patted her.

'*Bon.*'

The tiny child, released, euphoric, ran straight towards the swimming pool.

'*Arrête!*' the mother shouted, but the naked baby laughed.

Quick as a leaping fish, she was off the edge, as if she thought she could run across the water, instead, of course, she dropped, and disappeared. Mouth open, she went under, then bobbed, and down again, and out of sight. The mother was on her feet before Bea had time to even sit up. Fully clothed, she jumped in. There was splashing, consternation from all around, and, a moment later, she carried her baby out, wading through the shallows and up the steps, with the child screaming in her arms. Less than five seconds had passed. The father, laughing now, reached for his phone to take a picture, as the mother carried her daughter back, clothes sticking, water pouring from her like a sea creature. She started laughing along with her husband, but the little girl screamed and screamed. The tanning women, disturbed again, raised their heads and stared.

'*There there,*' soothed the mother. '*Chouchou* —'

She covered the angry baby with kisses, and wrapped her in a striped towel, pulling her arm out to dry it, and buried her face in the wishbone groove at the back of her daughter's soft neck, and kissed her.

Longingly, Bea watched them, entranced. She wrapped her arms around herself. She imagined making love with Dan and the feeling of life beginning. She knew her friends' stories of motherhood. They talked as if the thing was mundane, awful even, and moaned about sleeplessness and boredom, but they were keeping heroes' secrets. They were mothers. They had crossed into a place of mortal danger and beauty. They knew they had, they just didn't want to boast. When she was a mother, and Dan was a father, how happy they would be. They would give so much love it was terrifying. The French mother across the pool had ordered something from the waiter. She'd saved a life, now she was having a sandwich. The two waiters were setting up a trestle table for afternoon tea, taking great care with the corners of the cloth, but a wind had come up, and whatever they did, the cloth kept blowing, and showing the scarred wood underneath. Bea's phone buzzed. Griff.

You can get Dan now.

She jumped up and left, apologising to the waiter, and nearly tripping on the steps, then on a sprinkler sticking out of the grass.

Arun was waiting by a long black Mercedes limousine, with *Chateau L'Orée des Vignes* written in gold on the side. When he saw her, he opened the door and she scrambled into the back seat. The engine was already running.

'Jolly good,' he said.

Dan's legs were shaking as he was escorted out of the gendarmerie. He couldn't remember anything that had been asked of him, or a word of what he'd answered, it was a blank. He crossed the drill square courtyard, flanked by Dufour and Luis, and saw Arun through the glass, beyond the metal detector, with the desk sergeant. He stopped himself from waving enthusiastically. Even from a distance, behind reflecting toughened glass, Arun looked immaculate and very rich-looking.

'This way,' said Dufour. 'OK, good.'

He saw Dan through into the security lobby, and then he and Luis went back out across the courtyard again. The soldier on the desk released the second door, and Dan went through it, to the public side, the civilian side. Safety.

'There you are,' said Arun. He was wearing a perfectly cut lightweight navy-blue suit, pale pink shirt and a silk tie. Even his glasses looked shiny, and his head, as if he'd just polished himself. He held out his hand to shake Dan's, and his cuffs slipped a perfect inch and showed his large watch. They shook hands.

'I'm so sorry you've been inconvenienced. I've been try-ing to have a chat with the sergeant here, but my French is not all it should be. He took some convincing I'm not from Syria.'

Dan mumbled something, feeling dazed. Two other soldiers, hanging around behind the desk were talking about them, and staring. Arun placed a thick, sealed white envelope on the desk, addressed in ink to Capitaine Christophe Vincent. He said something in French to the soldier on the desk, then opened the door for Dan. When they reached the gate he stood aside again, to let him through first.

'Ghastly,' he said.

Dan smiled for the first time. *Ghastly.* They passed the last of the soldiers, and they were on the pavement.

'Have you noticed', said Arun, 'how even these days, one can't afford to dress down?'

By *one* he meant *people of colour*. Dan had on a pair of old shorts and a T-shirt, and he hadn't shaved. 'Where's your car?' he said.

'Just round the corner.'

'They've got a CCTV image of Alex with someone,' said Dan. 'It could be anyone, but the cops in there wanted it to be me.'

'Where was it taken?'

'I dunno, a gas station somewhere.'

Arun shook his head. 'Alex was reckless. He was a trusting, tragic character in many ways.'

Dan didn't care about that. 'Yeah, but why are they so interested in me?'

'Don't concern yourself. Their behaviour towards you is a combination of what we might call their *house style* and a certain endemic racism. In any case, they'll certainly hesitate before bothering you again.'

Even in Griff's absence, Dan felt the sedative power of his wealth.

'Thanks.'

'Don't mention it.'

At the little roundabout they crossed the road.

'There we are,' said Arun.

Dan saw a black Mercedes with shaded windows waiting by the kerb.

'We thought it best not to park too close,' smiled Arun. 'It looks rather Russian mafia, don't you think? Very ostentatious.'

The back door opened and Bea clambered out. She threw herself at him and hugged him.

'Oh my God. Are you OK?'

'Just about.'

They all got into the limousine, Arun in the front.

'*Bonjour*,' said the driver, smiling.

'Hey,' said Dan.

The car pulled away. Bea, subdued by his reaction to her, sat back into the corner.

'What did they ask you?' she said.

He didn't answer. He couldn't remember. She looked awkward in the big rich car, and the sight of her was complicated. He thought of Dufour, probing him, and how he had defended her, and felt the need to punish her. He remembered her expression as he was taken away, so calm, implacable. He knew he blamed her but his reasons were obscure, even to himself.

'Did you call Griff?' he said. 'When they took me in?'

'Of course I did.'

The air conditioning made the black leather interior cold and crisp. She had goose pimples on her arms. He leaned back in the deep seat and shut his eyes.

'Why did you tell them I wasn't in bed with you, the night Alex died? Why?' he said quietly. He opened his eyes and looked at her without turning his head. 'Huh?'

'I didn't, did I? I was telling them everything. Every minute. I didn't mean you weren't *there*.'

'OK, never mind.'

'What were they like? How did they treat you?'

He shrugged and looked away. They left the city. Blunted by present comforts, the last two hours blurred. He thought of Karen Koch, and smiled. He took Bea's hand. He felt her relief. He squeezed her hand, and she squeezed back.

'What have you been doing, anyway?' he said.

'I was at the chateau, with my parents.'

She looked exhausted.

'Sorry, Arun,' he said, 'd'you think you could ask the guy to turn the air con down? Or off? My wife's got this weird idea we should save the planet or something.'

He leaned across her, and rolled down her window, and kissed her on his way back. She smiled.

'What else happened?' she said.

'Oh, you know, just the usual shit that happens down the gendarmerie,' he said. 'Not much.'

The open windows brought the smell of warm grass into the car. Arun twisted round to speak to them over his reading glasses.

'Now,' he said, 'what would you like to do?'

'What time is it?' Dan took out his phone, disorientated.

'Griff would love you to come back to the chateau. Yes?'

'Yeah, why not?' said Dan.

'Righty-ho,' said Arun.

'Why?' said Bea.

'To debrief your dad, and thank him,' said Dan.

'He didn't do anything.'

'How do you know?'

'They weren't going to keep you in there,' said Bea.

'I'm happy you're so chilled about it.'

'I'm not.'

'They were writing in notebooks, Bea – with *pencils*. It was scary. No wonder Griff records all his meetings.'

'But it's impossible. It's ridiculous.'

'You weren't there.'

'It must have been horrible,' she said.

'Luckily, your dad isn't just sitting around while some *Frenchman* decides the only black man in the village is a drug-dealing murderer. He has contacts.'

'It doesn't make him God.'

'Your car is up at the chateau, isn't it?' interjected Arun. 'And there's something Griff needs to hear about.'

'What is it?' Bea asked.

'I'll tell you when we get there,' said Dan.

'Dan. Tell me now.'

He didn't want to. 'They've got a CCTV picture,' he said gently. 'A photograph of Alex at a petrol station somewhere, with a guy.'

'What guy?'

'I don't know.'

'Where?'

'I don't know. And it wasn't clear at all. It could have been anyone.'

She stared at him. Her eyes looked particularly clear when she heard things that hurt her, he noticed. He had seen it enough times recently to have learned the look; clear, a little wider, very steady.

'Is that it?' she said.

'Yes.'

'OK.' She turned away from him, absorbing the information. 'They're calling it murder now,' she said. 'Officially.'

They were out of the city, on the dual carriageway now, and the air beat like helicopter blades through the open windows.

'Do you mind?' said Arun, and both back windows rolled slowly up. 'So what's the decision?'

Dan didn't want to be back at Paligny, just the two of them. He needed Griff's context, and his reaction. He needed his company.

'I should be the one to tell him about the CCTV,' he said.

'The chateau it is, then,' said Arun. He took out his handkerchief and dabbed his forehead.

'Sorry, Arun,' said Bea, 'do put on the air conditioning, if you like, I don't want everyone being miserable. It's fine.'

Without speaking, the driver adjusted the dials. Bea took Dan's hand. She kissed it. She whispered, so Arun wouldn't hear.

Do you mind if I wait downstairs?'

'No, sure.'

'It's just – I've just – had enough of my mother for today.'

18

Bea waited in the bar and Dan went upstairs with Arun. The Adamsons' suite occupied the corner of the first floor. A brass plate on the door proclaimed *Suite Présidentielle*.

'Good, you're here,' said Griff, talking before Dan had even closed the door. 'Presidential suite. Christ. The only president to set foot in this place is the president of the West Minge Montrachet Appreciation Society.' He strode away across the room. 'The chief morris dancer of Little Squirtingdon, celebrating being twinned with – what's the village called, Arun? The one just there?'

Arun had melted away into the shadowy expanses of the suite, without actually leaving.

'Sainte –' came his voice from somewhere, but Griff had moved on.

'Anyway, she's in there.' He meant Liv. He went to a faraway sofa.

Dan followed him, stifling his desire to exclaim at the panelling, and the view, framed like a procession of oil paintings along the room. Griff sat, and gestured Dan to join him.

'Ordeal, was it?'

'No, it was all right,' said Dan.

'Fucking outrage,' said Griff.

'More a question of style than substance,' said Arun's voice. Dan still couldn't work out exactly where he was.

'No real trouble?' said Griff, eyes narrowed, ready for the facts.

'No. But – there was something I thought you should know. I told Bea.'

He saw Griff prepare himself; it reminded him of Bea, brave and direct.

'Go on,' said Griff.

'They showed me a CCTV photo.'

'Where from?'

'A petrol station somewhere.'

'What do you mean, somewhere?'

'They didn't tell me.'

'What was it?'

'Alex's car, and Alex, going into the shop, like, to pay, maybe. And another man.'

'Another man? What man?'

'I don't know.'

'Why did they show it to you?'

'They wanted to know if it was me.' He kept eye contact. 'Which was stupid.'

'Obviously. Arun?'

'Don't worry, they have my letter.'

Dan thought of Arun's letter, the white envelope on the front desk at the gendarmerie, and imagined impressive legal threats, and Capitaine Vincent, quaking in his brogues.

'Good. So what did this – *person* look like?' said Griff.

'It was totally out of focus. Dark, maybe, black, maybe – but he could have been anyone. They didn't tell me anything else. Nothing. But I thought you should know about it.'

There was a silence.

'Thank you,' said Griff. 'I appreciate it.'

'Well, thanks for getting me out of there.'

Griff shrugged, but didn't deny it. He stared into space for a moment. 'I'm glad they're moving along,' he said, restrained and calm. 'Arun, give Roche a call.'

'Certainly,' said Arun's voice.

'You know he left?' said Griff to Dan. 'Released him back into the wild, didn't we, Arun?' Griff got up. 'Excuse me.' He crossed the room and went through a door.

Dan breathed again. His mouth was dry.

'Would you like a drink?' said Arun, appearing.

'That would be great.'

Arun went to a cabinet. 'Oops, television.' He opened another. 'There we are. It's beer for you, isn't it?'

He opened the bottled beer and poured it into a tall glass, and put it onto the coffee table in front of Dan.

'I should think you'll be needing that,' he said, like Dan had had a tough week at Foundations of Holloway.

'Thanks.' Dan picked up his glass.

The first sip of beer was icy, and the room smelled of vanilla.

'There's a cloakroom just there, if you like,' said Arun. 'You needn't go through the bedroom.'

Dan took the hint. The tiny cloakroom was entirely pan-elled. His face in the mirror looked like another oil painting, in the dimness, framed by dark wood, like the view from the windows, absorbed into this new world. He washed the parts of himself he could get to easily, and went back out and sat down again, and drank his beer. The gendarmerie, and everything associated with it had almost gone. After a few moments, Griff came out of the bedroom and closed the door.

'She scares me,' he said. 'I don't know if I should say that, about my own wife. But she does.'

'Would you like me to do anything?' said Arun.

'What could you do? Don't be stupid. I don't know if it's the medication, or shock – I've no idea. To be honest, we don't usually spend so much time together.'

Arun handed Griff a gin and tonic, and patted him, once, on the shoulder.

'Thanks,' said Griff, taking a sip. 'Lovely.' He turned to Dan, and smiled. 'My daughter is sulking again, I take it?'

'No, no,' Dan faltered. 'She's downstairs.'

'I was hoping to talk to her.'

'I think she's tired,' said Dan, but there wasn't really any excuse and he felt embarrassed. 'I'm sorry.'

'It's just business,' said Griff. 'You're better qualified, obviously, but I should probably talk to her.'

He came and sat down on the sofa. Dan's curiosity was awakened, like a dog at the smell of meat.

'What kind of thing was it?'

'What? Oh, just some financial business.'

'About the farm? We collected the rent.'

'No, nothing to do with that.'

He put his drink down and sighed and rubbed his face. He looked very tired. 'I just thought I'd have another go. In the circumstances.'

'Why don't you tell me? I could talk to her.'

Griff laughed. 'That's a terrible idea. Why would I talk to you? Your wife wears the trousers.'

'Sorry?' said Dan.

'I'm not being rude, but come on. What's the expression?' He paused. 'Pussy-whipped. That's you.' The words were shocking coming out of his mouth.

'Excuse me?'

'You know, pussy-whipped. My daughter has the upper hand?'

'Yeah, I know what it means.'

'I'm not being funny. I'm the last person to judge anybody's marital arrangements.'

Dan said nothing. Griff watched his face.

'I've offended your pride.'

'No,' said Dan evenly. He wasn't going to fall into Griff's stereotype.

Griff leaned forward and put his big hand on Dan's shoulder. 'Forgive me. Seriously. I'm not myself.'

He looked sad, and Dan believed him. 'It's all right. Forget it.'

He picked up his beer, and finished it. But it was no good. He couldn't leave it alone.

'Bea and I agree about pretty much everything,' he said. 'We've got the same values.'

'And?'

'No *and*.'

'A *but*, then.'

'No,' said Dan. 'I mean, I don't want her to think badly of me.'

Griff smiled.

'Listen, that's not the same as being whipped,' said Dan.

270

'Isn't it? Well, she couldn't have a lower opinion of *me*, and I survive.'

'We're honest with each other.'

'Really?' said Griff. 'Well, that's mistake number one, in a marriage.'

They both laughed at that, and there was peace for a moment, except for Dan's curiosity, snapping at his heels.

'So what was it you wanted to talk to her about? I'll pass it on,' he said.

'Fine.' Griff nodded. 'Arun?'

Arun stepped out of the shadows. Plucking his trousers at the knee, he sat down on a squat, gilded armchair. Griff lay back, almost horizontal, to rest.

'Go ahead,' he said.

'Hotel Paligny, the farm and the surrounding land are owned by a company,' said Arun. 'The land extends to about fifteen hectares –'

'Sorry, which company?' asked Dan.

'Griff's company.'

'LCF?'

'No. A different one.'

'Hemisphere?'

'Done your homework,' Griff murmured, dozing.

Dan was embarrassed. He thought of scrolling through the pictures of Griff's family, hunting down the articles, the records at Companies House.

'No, no, no,' said Arun, 'neither of those. It's offshore.'

'Switzerland?'

Griff snorted. 'Not these days. That's over.'

'I thought Paligny belonged to Alex,' said Dan.

'No,' said Arun.

'No,' said Griff.

'The company is based in Cayman.'

'The company that owns the hotel?' asked Dan.

'Yes,' Arun answered.

'What's it called?'

'The details aren't important.'

'So why are you telling me?'

'Well, you see,' said Arun, 'Griff's initial thought was to sell the property, which he has no use for.'

'Yeah, I know.'

'However, it's becoming clear that the police will require access to all aspects of Alex's life. And that means the hotel, and of course the family, will be under scrutiny.'

'Yeah, OK.'

'And,' said Griff, waking from his doze, 'the French are bastards when it comes to property. Total bastards. Especially since we're reverting to pre-1973 rules. I never would have bought the place if Alex and Liv hadn't had one of their whims. Bad move. Stupid.'

'Never mind, never mind, on we go,' said Arun, his eyes twinkling at Dan. 'So, here we are. It is really so simple, and not clandestine at all.'

'I've got nothing to hide,' said Griff, eyes closed once more.

'The company I mentioned owns Paligny, and – with one or two steps along the way – Griff is the CEO of the company. Ergo, Griff owns the hotel. You see?'

'Yes, of course,' said Dan. 'So?'

'So we thought we might transfer the company into your name.'

'Sorry, mine?'

'The company that owns Paligny.'

'The company in the Cayman Islands?'

'It's based in Cayman, yes,' said Arun. 'It's not as big a thing as you might imagine.'

'Oh, really?' said Dan, amused. He was beginning to get the feeling he was out of his depth. Arun wasn't an idiot. He was the lawyer who'd helped Griff make his millions, not to mention keeping him out of court for forty-five years which, if Dan's recent investigations were accurate, hadn't always been easy. 'How is it *not a big thing*?' he asked.

'Well, for one thing, the company's assets are very, very safe. All very steady, very low-volatility investments,' said Arun.

'Yes, but what's it called?'

'It doesn't matter.'

'I think it does. If you're talking about a company, some off-shore company, you want me to — what? — front up? And you don't want to disclose its name. I should probably know something about it. Some fucking thing.'

'Calm down, dear,' said Griff.

'Hey!'

'Why don't we take a walk outside?' said Arun. 'There's no need to get excited. I promise you, these things take place every day.' He sounded like a surgeon getting out the scalpel.

Dan's phone chirped in his pocket.

Don't make me come up! Car park 15 mins? Love you xxxB

'That's my girl,' he said. *Give me 25*, he texted back.

Dan and Arun strolled the gravelled paths of the parterre, past statuary and urns, like characters in a TV costume drama, except neither he nor Arun fitted the profile of that bleached and fetishised past. Quietly, Arun laid out the terms of Griff's proposed agreement, in all its watertight safety. Paligny would stay in the company name – which was Elven, as it turned out.

'Elven? That's kind of cute,' said Dan.

'Yes, isn't it? Whimsical.'

Elven owned the Hotel Paligny. It would be months before anyone followed the paper trail to Cayman, and, when it was, 'So what?' said Dan.

'Exactly,' said Arun. 'You would own Paligny, it's hardly a crime.'

'So it's all just to keep Griff's finances from being investigated?' said Dan.

'Griff has nothing to hide,' said Arun.

'So he always says.'

'It's very boring and expensive to be audited.'

'What does it involve, anyway? Changing names on the deed, overwriting details?'

'It's not your problem.'

Dan stopped walking, and looked out at the hills and vineyards, and then up at the hotel, then back to Arun's expectant face.

'Sorry, no. Bea wouldn't like this. Thanks and everything, but that's it.'

'That's good,' said Arun.

'Good?'

'I'm always wary of involving family members,' said Arun. 'I've told him before.'

'So, you don't need me?' said Dan.

Arun gave a laugh at the idea. 'No, no, we're fine, thank you.'

'So, why ask?'

'Why? Isn't it obvious to you? Griff worries about Bea. He hoped she might enjoy the money. She's such a stubborn girl.'

'Wait,' said Dan, 'the money?'

'It is all by the by, now.' Arun checked his watch. 'She's waiting for you, I think.'

He held out his hand, but Dan didn't shake it. He tried, but couldn't think of another way to phrase it. 'What kind of money?' he asked.

'As nominal CEO of Elven?' said Arun.

'Yes.'

'There'd be a token salary, obviously.'

'So, what is a nominal CEO's token salary? Out of interest.'

'Oh, gosh, maybe a hundred and fifty a year. Something in that area.'

Just the sound of it – just hearing the numbers – it was humiliating, but it made Dan want to cry. He stood before Arun, dirty, exhausted and unshaven, having spent the day in a concrete barracks, his status as a nobody reinforced, yet again, as if he needed his nose rubbed in it; made to look back at his dingy childhood, have the notion of himself as a student of art sneered at, judging his marriage through the tainted lens of circumstance. The chance to change everything was close enough to touch. Arun stood quietly, waiting, the sleeves of his pale pink shirt were turned up crisply, to the elbow. His wristwatch sparkled.

'His daughter means a great deal to him,' he said at last. 'You understand? He wants to see her financially secure. Sadly, every time, she turns him down.'

There was silence.

'It's a shame,' said Arun.

Dan, impotent, nodded. 'Yes,' he said. 'Shame.'

He shook Arun's hand and walked back through the parterre; along the gravel paths, past a vast mass of tall white lilies, bright white in the sun, down, round the chateau, to the back entrance, and the car park, to meet his wife.

19

A hundred and fifty thousand pounds. A hundred and fifty thousand pounds a year. In the middle of the night, Dan lay in bed and watched Bea sleeping, and hated her. A hundred and fifty thousand. Her rounded cheek was resting on her open hand. She looked about twelve years old. Innocent. This didn't need to have happened, this wasn't where they had to be. He thought of their rain-soaked, stupid honeymoon in Yorkshire, his two cheap M&S suits, the slip-on shoes he hated. He thought of the smell of their old clothes, drying by the radiators, and the twisting in his stomach every time Bea sat down to do the sums for the month. He thought of how she pretended to worry about paying each bill, and made him feel guilty for every takeaway coffee, and sick with himself for going along with her lie. For three years he had hardly let himself think of it; her money, like coins that stacked and heaped and shuffled in an arcade coin-pusher, but never fell. Bea had the key. She could open up the back of the machine, at any time. They could be holding fistfuls of gold, and she knew it, but she kept pretending, fixing broken soles onto her shoes, and telling him how lucky she felt. Lucky. He had thrown away his dreams to spend his days showing strangers around stinking flats vacated by the corpses of threadbare old men; hoping for his reduced, only fair, non-exploitative 1 per cent commission to drag them into the next month, and the next mortgage payment, never having any choices, never doing anything they wanted with the one precious life they had. Because of her. Because of her, his future was in cold storage, and had dried up, and gone. She talked about believing in him, but all the time she held him back.

'Bea, wake up.' He pushed her shoulder. 'Wake up.'

He pushed her again, and she jumped.

'Where's Alex?' she said.

He switched on the light, and she screwed up her eyes in the glare.

'What's happened?' She groped for her phone. It was three o'clock in the morning.

'Nothing,' said Dan. 'Sorry, babe, I didn't mean to scare you, but we need to talk.'

'What about?'

It was wrong to discuss it in bed. 'Get up,' he said. 'You need to.'

'What is it?'

He pulled on his jeans, and, stumbling, she followed him downstairs to the first, small, sitting room.

'Dan?'

The moonlight coming through the window made squares on the floor. Dan felt his way along the wall, to a standard lamp, and switched it on. It was reflected, misshapen, in the black windows.

'Sit down,' he said.

She sat at one end of the sofa and tucked her feet up, pulling her T-shirt over her knees. He sat at the other end, in his jeans, but no shirt, his legs pulled up too, facing her, as he embarked on his bloodless revolution. He began with her father and Arun, and the offer of the company, the ownership of Paligny.

'Why didn't you tell me?' she said.

'It's not a *confession*, Bea.'

'But why didn't you tell me?'

'I needed to think. And you've got enough on your mind. I didn't want to get into it.'

'Think about what?' she asked.

'Just wait. Give me a chance.'

The things he needed to say were pushed out by everything he mustn't, three years of laws she'd laid down for him, without saying a word. Never mention her money. Never even acknowledge its existence. Riches hung above their heads like a golden sky he had to pretend not to see. She waited, her eyes steadily on his.

'Go on,' she prompted.

He couldn't think straight. 'He only offered, because he wants to help.'

She was studying him. He could see her thinking.

'Bea, basically, he loves you. He might be doing it for tax reasons or whatever, but he loves you.'

'It's not love, it's money.'

'So what's wrong with money?'

'Not money. His money. He gets it from turning London into a shopfront.'

'There's no such thing as dirty money or clean money.'

'No, fine then, it's all dirty, but my mother lives off his, and that makes it untouchable.'

'And that's it?'

'Yes. We've talked about this.'

'Not really, babe.'

'Dan, it's so late, I'm –'

'You talked about it, and you never told me how much he had. I mean, you haven't been exactly straight with me. You made a decision about our future, about our security, without ever really discussing it.'

'There's nothing to discuss.'

'Why not? He makes his money selling luxury flats as futures trading. It's not people trafficking.'

'Money he made in the sixties, keeping the Windrush generation in his slums –'

'Yeah, don't lecture me about my history –'

'It's my history, too.'

'I'm not talking about that – ' he said.

She wasn't listening. 'He hardly pays tax! He has no scruples!'

'Shut up!' he shouted.

Now she was quiet, but her hollow-eyed silence was worse judgement than her lecturing.

'I'm sorry. I didn't mean to yell.'

'I don't want his help,' she said stubbornly. 'I don't want his *little offshore company*, or *anything* of his. I'm happy how we are. I love who we are. What's wrong with it?'

'You've got your career,' he said. 'You've got a vocation. It's all right for you.'

'We came away, didn't we?'

'So it's *my* fault now?'

'No, I was happy to come, I didn't mean that. I just want you to find your path.'

'So you say.'

'I'm not the one stopping you, Dan. You could do your own work if you wanted to.'

'You think I don't want to?'

'I think you don't believe in yourself. I think *that* stops you.'

'Oh, right, it's not because I'm already working sixty hours a week to pay the fucking mortgage?'

'Artists do have day jobs. People find a way.'

'Do they?'

'Most people don't make a living out of their art.'

'Oh, really?'

'They work weekends,' she said. 'They do.'

'Yeah? How many? How many of them don't have any financial help? These "people", Bea, are the entitled middle class – how many of these "people finding a way" are like me? How many are black? How many are working five, six days a week, in a fucking estate agent's, and still – Jesus, what are you like? You're a – how high are your standards? What do you expect from me?'

'I don't have the answers, Dan. All I know is that whatever we do, or whatever money we *make*, it must be just ours. It's good, how we live. It's *good*. It's ours and it's clean. I need that, don't you?'

'That's right, hit me with that.'

'With what?' she said.

'Morality. Knockout punch.'

'It's not a fight.'

'Oh yeah? You got me. I'm down.'

'I don't want to bring you down.'

'Forget it,' he said. 'You're totally uncompromising.'

She was surprised. It was almost funny to him how surprised she was. 'Am I?'

'I can't speak to you,' he said.

'You can't speak to me?'

'No.'

She shook her head and rubbed her face. 'You got me out of bed at three in the morning,' she said. 'You'd better try.'

'Then stop staring at me. Come on. You mess up my head. I can't think with you looking at me like that.'

'Really?'

'Really.' He shook his head.

'I don't want to be uncompromising,' she said. She thought for a moment. 'What about if I cover my face?'

'What?' said Dan.

'Like this.' She put her hands over her eyes. 'Better?'

He could only see her nose and mouth.

His anger went away. He had dragged her out of bed to fight with her and she was still trying to help him. And she looked so vulnerable, waiting, blind and hopeful, for him to say his piece. He looked at her mouth, beneath her hands.

'That's kind of hot,' he said.

'Shut up,' she said. 'Maybe you can say it now, how you feel.'

She was right – wasn't she always? – it was easier not to see her eyes. He took a breath and said it. 'When your parents die, you'll inherit their money.'

He looked for a reaction but could not see one. It was perfect. He was released.

'Griff's in his seventies,' he said. 'When he goes, you'll get something like – I don't know, millions, right?'

He noticed she was breathing more quickly. Her lips were parted.

'I've heard about this stuff. I bet he's got money in trust for you already. Is there money I don't know about?'

She nodded.

'OK. So am I meant to not think about it? How can I?'

She didn't say anything, or move.

'When we were first together,' he said, 'you told me about your family, you were like, *They're pretty well off* – yeah, I think *well off* was the word you used. You didn't say *My dad has a few hundred million in the bank –*'

She trapped her lips between her teeth to stop herself correcting him. It made him smile.

'Just stay blind a little longer, babe.'

Free from her gaze, he moved towards her. She waited, silently, for what he would do next, what he would say, breathing through her nose, her T-shirt rising and falling with her breath. Blind and dumb, she had made herself voiceless, just for him. It shouldn't have excited him, but it did.

'OK,' he said. 'Listen. Every day, every time I, like, get a text I've gone overdrawn, or when I don't hit my target at work, there's this thing I get – in my head – I think, Bea's dad has money. Then I feel guilty. And I stop myself. But I wonder, What is it, really, that's stopping us getting some help? You didn't kick up about my dad's money for us, not at all. And he wasn't even a father to me. I met the guy, like, five times in my life, and I don't even remember. You know how that's messed me up, but you were happy to take that twenty-five grand of adulterer's cash, we even laughed about it.'

'Maybe I should do blindfolded sessions,' she said, behind her hands. 'It works.'

Holding up her arms had raised her T-shirt from her legs. He touched her knee and she jumped.

'Sorry,' he said.

'I didn't see you coming.'

'It's OK.'

'Go on,' she said. 'Before. About my parents dying.'

'I shouldn't have said that.'

'It's fine.'

'I'm going to touch you,' he said, to warn her.

He put his hands on her shoulders, and pushed her back-wards, slowly, until he was kneeling between her legs. He low-ered himself onto her, his face tucked between her cheek and the sofa. Her hair touched his lips.

'When they're dead, you'll have it anyway,' he said in her ear. 'So can you tell me – *what are we doing?*'

Her voice was constrained by his weight. 'What do you mean?'

'I fucking hate it. Pretending we don't have a choice.'

'I won't take their money, now or when they're dead,' she said. 'I'm not pretending.'

'What *for? Why?*' he said into her neck. 'It's bullshit.'

She wriggled, grinding herself back, into the cushions, to get away. She got her hands between them, and pushed him off. Now he could see her.

'What is? What's bullshit?' she said through tears. '*Us?*'

'No. No –' He looked down at his hands. 'Don't cry.'

'I'm not crying.'

'I can't do it any more, Bea.'

She untangled herself from him and pulled the T-shirt down over her knees again. 'What can't you do?'

Head down, he stared at his clenched fists pressed together, knuckles straining. 'I can't pretend I see only what you want me to see. It's not about loving you or not loving you. D'you not get it?' He looked up at her.

'I thought we were happy,' she said.

'I hadn't realised how much it was fucking up my head,' he said. 'But I guess it was. I'm sorry.'

'It's not your fault,' she said.

There was silence. They stood outside their marriage, looking in. She got up from the sofa.

'I'm going to bed. I'm tired.'

'Yes. We can talk about it tomorrow.'

She didn't turn. 'Yup.'

'I'm sorry it came up like this.'

He switched off the light, and followed her. In their room, she went to the bathroom and did her teeth again, and avoided herself in the mirror. She got into bed in the dark. They were two new people; the ugly rich girl, and her good-looking husband.

'Goodnight,' she whispered.

'Night, babe.'

She had always known she wasn't strong enough to fight wealth. It was bigger and more beautiful, and it was fierce. Bea wasn't beautiful or fierce. She was easily overshadowed. She felt his body move behind her, and he stretched. The birds began to sing. The sun would soon be up. She closed her eyes.

20

Half asleep, Dan felt Bea get out of bed, and heard her dressing, and then she tiptoed out. When she was gone, the room felt light and easy. He sat up and looked around. It was a heady feeling, opening a vein, and letting out the truth. He'd challenged her and the world still spun. All he asked was that she acknowledged reality, but he was sorry he had made her cry, his timing had been horrible. He picked up his phone and texted her.

Babe, where did you go? Love you.

He added kisses, then got up and made himself some coffee.

Back soon, Bea texted, as she left the driveway, and then turned off her phone. She hadn't slept enough. Her dreams had bled into the light of day, she couldn't rid herself of them. She needed space to think. It wasn't enough to turn the phone off, she'd be tempted. She looked around for somewhere to hide it, to collect on the way back. There was a log, behind the flip-top bins in the lay-by. She propped the phone against it and paused, to mark the place in her mind. She and Alex had stood exactly there, the night he went. In a few warm days, the bushes had grown thicker and higher along the small path that led back to the hotel. She remembered the light rain falling, and them walking together, and the small burning taste of brandy from the bottle he handed to her. She went back across the entrance to the drive, and along the roadside, as the hot sun dried the last of the dew, then left the road and went into the woods.

How angry Dan must be, to fight with her, after what had happened to Alex. He must have lain there, watching her, getting so angry he had to wake her. He had watched her sleeping, and thought about her money, while she hadn't known. It made her ashamed. Leaving Griff's money, she hadn't sacrificed anything, it had only been a release. Every day had been a day of celebration. Not for Dan. How smug of her, not to know, like a princess leaving the palace without her jewels and robes to do good among the villagers. Love me as I am. I'm virtuous. Her father was right. She wasn't perfect. She wasn't even good enough. She was boring. Puritanical. Ugly. Vain. She reached the towpath and the river's edge, but the calmness of the view felt far away. The water wasn't clear, but silty and slow moving. She had hardly any reflection. She didn't need one. Round face, round eyes, fair hair, nothing. Her father had said it, and her mother had, too. It wasn't a new thought, she'd been fighting it for years. She wasn't stupid. She knew about the influence of childhood experiences on a person, she'd had the therapy and done the work. She'd read the books. She did not self-harm. She was not anorexic. She was not an addict. She'd taught herself. She was right to be proud. She had built herself from scratch, piece by piece, and it had taken years. In her mind's eye, she saw Alex's handwriting, circling and underlining words. *The only way into truth is through one's own annihilation.* His broken car hung like a corpse from a noose. Annihilation was not in her armoury. She felt for another weapon.

Attention, taken to its highest degree, is the same thing as prayer.

She grabbed at that, and said it to herself. But there was nothing good to pay attention to.

Attention, taken to its highest degree, is the same thing as prayer.

She knew she looked stupid, standing there. She tried again.

Attention, taken to its highest degree, is the same thing as prayer.

She tried again. She breathed.

Attention, taken to its highest degree, is the same thing as prayer.

Attention, taken to its highest degree, is the same thing as prayer.

She looked down at the grass, and the earth, and the river pulsing at the edge of her vision. The sun beat down on her head, like the light was shining straight into her brain. She looked up and down the riverbank. Not a soul. She pulled off her shoes and went some way along the path. Quickly, she took off her skirt and T-shirt, and dropped them, and then, without putting a toe in to test it, launched herself out into the river. It was freezing, cold that stabbed like spikes. She took a gasping breath.

'God!' she shouted. 'Shit!' more quietly.

She pulled up her legs, thought of parasites, worms and frogs, and kept her chin up.

'Fuck it,' she said, breathless from the cold. 'Fuck that fucking shit. Bastard.'

She took a breath and dived, and opened her eyes, and saw clouds of light, and her own hands, then came back up, water streaming from her hair and gave a yell of a laugh, then dared herself and put her feet down to touch the slimy bottom. She pulled her feet back up, triumphant. Disgusted, delighted, she scrambled back towards the bank. But then, looking up, she saw someone.

A teenage boy was standing by her pile of clothes. Her foot slipped, and scraped against something sharp. She righted herself. The boy looked at her. Stopping, she crouched, feeling the deep water of the big river at her back, and the current, pulling. Bracing her legs, she wiped her eyes. She and the boy looked at one another; she low in the water, he, quite relaxed, on the bank. She felt the weight of her breasts in the saturated cotton of her bra. He was wearing a red-and-white striped T-shirt, like a blond, hatless Waldo. His hands were shoved into the pockets of his shorts, pulling them down below the bony channel of his hips. She recognised him, the boy from the tractor, at the Orderbrechts' farm. Water lapped her collarbones.

'*Va-t-en*,' she said. 'Can you go away?'

His expression didn't change. She remembered how he'd stared from the tractor as it passed.

'Go away. *Va-t-en!*'

Her thighs ached but if she knelt her nose would be underwater. The boy began to move his hand, up and down inside his shorts. He watched her, rubbing himself, smiling as she registered the unmistakable movement.

'*Va-t-en* now!' she said loudly. 'Go away!'

He didn't move, except the hand, inside his shorts. His mouth was slightly open. She thought of screaming, and then that she might laugh, but it really wasn't funny at all.

'*I mean it!*' she shouted. 'Fuck off!'

Abruptly, he squatted down. He stared into her eyes, then pulled his hand out, spat on it, wiped it on his thigh, and reached out to her. His narrow face had a scattering of unsqueezed spots around the edges of his mouth. The sunlight reflected up off the water into his slanting eyes, which were mossy green and quite beautiful. There was something lacking in him. He gestured, as if she would walk towards him through the water and take his hand. She felt slow and calm. She took a big breath.

'DAN!' she shouted, confidently.

The boy stopped smiling and looked over his shoulder.

'DAN!' she shouted again.

He looked back at her.

'DAN!'

He glanced quickly behind again, then stooped, and picked up her clothes, laughing.

'DAN!'

Hopping with excitement, he bundled them into a ball and tossed them into the undergrowth, then sprinted off down the path, and out of sight.

She tottered out of the water on crab legs, blue with cold, and fell onto the ground.

Once she had got her clothes, and dressed, still shivering, she went back to the hotel.

The warm air dried her skin and made it itch. She walked round the back, to go in behind the reception desk, but the seldom-used door was locked, and as she tried the handle, Dan came down the stairs and saw her. He walked towards the door and unlocked it, top and bottom and tugged it open.

'Hey. Where have you been?'

She couldn't think what to say.

'Nowhere.' She started past him.

He saw her hair was wet. He frowned. Her skirt was sticking to her legs, and ripped from where she had pulled it from the bushes, and there was blood on her arm.

'What's that?'

'Scratches.'

'Why?'

'I had to get my skirt out of a bush.'

'What?'

She didn't want his concern, or for him to know she had used his name to save herself.

'What's going on?' he said. 'What's happened?'

'I went swimming.'

'Where? Why?'

'Why shouldn't I?'

'Bea? What the hell?'

'You woke me up at three in the morning to tell me *how you felt*.'

'I thought that was what we're supposed to do. Be honest.'

'I'm going to have a shower.'

'Are you all right?'

'No.'

'We should talk about this.'

'I don't want to talk to you.'

He went to take her arm.

She pulled away, but then halfway up the stairs she turned. 'How could you? You fucking bastard.'

When she was out of sight, round the corner, by Alex's room, he called up after her.

'You could at least talk about it!'

'Why don't I wait until something terrible happens?' she shouted back, staring straight ahead at Alex's door. 'Then wake you up in the middle of the night to tell you I can't stand living with you.'

She went to their room and slammed the door. She cried in the shower, and washed the blood and mud off herself, then watched herself in the mirror as she dried her podgy, dimpled body. She should forgive him but forgiveness wasn't going to help. He didn't want her without her money. She dabbed antiseptic on her grazes, thinking of the boy staring at her, and jerking himself off, and wondering distantly how much danger she had been in, and, if he hadn't run away, how long she would have had to stay in the water. She made herself smile, thinking he couldn't have had much of a look at her to get so excited. She should be relieved not to be hurt, but she didn't care. She noted coolly that she wasn't able to value herself, and she felt sad, because it was something she had worked on being able to do, but it didn't really matter.

She got dressed again, and went out into the heat, and down the drive, to get her phone back. As she approached the gates, a blue car backed into the drive. It looked like a police car, and she began to prepare herself, but it wasn't a police car, it was a different blue, much denser. It idled in the gateway as if the driver was deciding which way to go. She tried, but couldn't see inside, past the reflections of the trees. The car drove off, and when it had gone she went out onto the road, to the lay-by, and got her phone from behind the log. There were a dozen missed calls from Griff, but no messages, nothing from Capitaine Vincent, no numbers she didn't recognise.

'Where were you?' said Dan, when she came back in.

She ignored him, and started up the stairs.

'I heard a car.'

'It was just turning.' She wanted to lie down.

'Look, I'm sorry,' he said. 'Are you OK?'

'I'm tired,' said Bea. 'I was up half the night, remember?'

'I said I'm sorry,' he said again, to her retreating back. Then he added, 'Griff called.'

'So what?'

She felt dread again. 'Has he heard something?'

'No. It was nothing like that. It's OK. He just wants us to go and see them. Spend the day.'

'Why?'

'To be together?' He said it sarcastically.

'No.'

'Bea, come on, what are we going to do here?' He was exasperated. 'Let's just go up to Chateau Whatever –'

'God. It's called Chateau *L'Orée des Vignes*, Dan,' she said. 'It's not that hard.'

'Hey! You're not better than me.'

'I didn't say I was –'

'You didn't need to.'

They went their different ways without another word.

They stopped trying to speak, or act as if things were normal. It was easy not to meet, with the hotel to themselves. She didn't want to eat with him, or be with him, she didn't want to talk, she just wanted to lie down, she tried it, but it was too warm to stay in bed, and the Wi-Fi was weak. She came downstairs.

She curled up on the swivel chair in the hall, and looked at YouTube kittens, and US politics on her phone, while Dan took up residence in the sitting room, with a beer, and played Skyrim. Hours and hours could be lost like that. They were.

*

The afternoon faded quickly and night fell. The fifth day. It was the fifth day since Alex died. She scrolled through videos of empty things, brightly coloured, comforting things, and stared at them with great attention. The view of the drive dimmed, and then it was completely dark. The windows showed the ghostly mirrored desk, and stairs going up to nothingness. The swivel chair kept swivelling. She had to put her foot on the floor to stop it. Her other leg went to sleep. She released it, shaking it out to get the blood flowing.

She heard an engine. Bright white headlights swept across the windows.

'Shit,' she said, jolted from her digital anaesthetic. 'What now?'

Rubbing her dry eyes, she went to the window and peered out. A big black minivan was parking in front of the hotel. It stopped, and the doors opened, and two men got out, dressed in black, intent on something, signalling to one another. Then, like an apparition, her mother, steadying herself on one of the men's arms. Like Cinderella, she had been transformed. She wore a silk dress, in bold rose colours, like moth wings. Griff climbed out too, and Liv went to him on tiptoe, and took his hand. The two men were dressed as waiters. No, they *were* waiters. One of them opened the back of the van, and started rummaging inside. Dan came into the hall.

'What the hell?' he said.

Griff looked in her direction and Bea ducked out of sight, but there was no avoiding them. They heard footsteps on the gravel, and the doorbell rang loudly.

'Did they tell you?' he said.

She shook her head.

He shrugged. 'Can't ignore them.'

'We could.'

He opened the door.

'Can't you put the bloody outside light on?' boomed Griff. 'We can't see a thing out here.'

'It doesn't work,' said Dan.

'The mountain has come to Mohammed. Are we allowed to say that these days?' Griff strode inside, slapping his shoulder.

Liv came in behind him, light-footed; a different person.

'Oh, there you are!' she said, spotting Bea in the shadows. 'My Bea-Bea.'

'There you are!' repeated Griff.

'Yup,' said Bea. 'What's going on?'

In the light from the open door, they could see the elaborate crest on the side of the van, *Chateau L'Orée des Vignes*. The waiters were taking things from the back and assembling them on the gravel, shining a wide-beamed torch, like soldiers deployed on an aid operation.

'We all need cheering up,' said Liv, with shining eyes.

'Cheering up?' said Bea, incredulous.

'We had a talk with Arun,' said Griff.

'*Lovely* Arun had a talk with *us*,' corrected Liv. 'He said we must let go of the expectation of answers.' She spoke as though she were reciting. 'We can't live in limbo.'

'The police investigation is ongoing,' Griff said. 'It's a process. Likely to be a long one.'

'So, we're going to eat in the garden!'

'Your mother organised it,' said Griff, subservient.

'We're going to celebrate life,' said Liv, her voice strident and brittle. 'Alex loved life.'

They had even brought a table. No cheap hexagonals for them. Linen cloths, candlelight, stemmed glasses and a hostess trolley.

'Delightful,' said Bea flatly.

The waiters hurried back and forth from the van.

'We're going to have a party at home,' said Liv. 'I've decided.'

'In London?' said Dan. 'When?'

'Roche cleared it with Vincent,' said Griff.

'As soon as we can,' said Liv.

Dan glanced at Bea to see her reaction. She was blank. One of the waiters was very young; the other, lantern-jawed, was his boss. When Bea showed them the kitchen, they barely hid their disgust. Dan unlocked all the garden doors. They hadn't bothered to open up the back of the hotel all day.

'I don't even need my pashmina,' said Liv. 'Isn't it a beautiful night?'

The question was, where to hold the party? She talked as the waiters trekked across the stringy grass, setting up the table, laying out dinner.

'I thought Stowe would be lovely — what do you think? Because it's so gorgeous, and Alex was so happy there.'

'He was expelled,' said Bea.

But Liv had risen to an altitude too high to be brought down. Bea and Dan, opposite, not beside one another, barely spoke.

'Then I thought, we could go more traditional, and do the Brompton Oratory? But it's not a wedding. Or a funeral.'

Her energy was electric. She thanked the waiters repeatedly, and jumped up to help, running back to the table when they shook her off. Polystyrene trays produced a feast. Lobster, salads and cheeses, on china, linen and silver, a heaped still life against the tattered canvas of Paligny.

'Alex would love this,' said Liv, commanding them to obey. 'It's like an enchanted garden.'

'Yes, it's very nice.' Griff seemed cowed by her, and tentative, like a man handling a bomb.

'We *could* have the party at home.' Liv pushed the chives and dressing from her salad leaves with the back of her knife. 'Or the Chelsea Physic Garden! I can't wait to get out of here. I can't wait to *go*.' She gestured her neck as though she were choking, or overwhelmed by heat.

Dan smiled at Bea but she didn't notice. The waiters put new plates in front of them, the lobster, and silver bowls of sauce. Together, they stirred it and, with a synchronised nod, went inside.

'Liv,' said Griff, 'tell them your idea for the music.'

'Yes, do you remember Alex's friend Will?' she asked. 'Who was in that band?'

Bea, startled by her memory, nodded.

'He lives near us. Tony and Erica's son? We still see them, they're lovely. We saw Will the other day. He's married, and he has two little children! His wife is Billy Henderson's daughter. Anyway, he's working with Tony now, but he still has the band! They play pubs and things. You know, people from that old crowd. He was such a talented boy.'

Bea put down her knife and fork, smelling blood again, the mangled car.

'I wondered if I should ask him to play, at Alex's party,' said Liv.

'He visited him at the Priory,' said Bea.

Liv reached to pat her arm, but Bea pulled away, knocking over a tall glass of water.

'Christ,' said her father. 'What's wrong with you?'

The water pooled and spread. Bea let it run from the table, calmly.

'Liv,' said Dan, 'maybe you should have it at home. More personal, right?'

'Yes, you're right, Dan!' said Liv. 'Griff? Don't you think Dan's right?'

Bea left the table. She went inside. The two waiters were smoking by the open door. The older one threw away his cigarette, and asked her if she needed anything.

'No, thank you. It's all amazing, thanks. I'm just not feeling very well.'

She went upstairs to her room. Dan stayed downstairs. She had known he would. He wasn't doing it because he loved them. He was doing it for the money. She closed her eyes. She paid attention to the silence. She tried to.

The four of them flew back to London, like a family. Bea and Dan brought only a few things, they weren't planning to stay long. The memorial would be in two days. Bea surrendered. She gave up trying to travel separately, then gave up trying to go economy. She didn't have the strength for battle. Liv emailed caterers from the first-class lounge. Eight seats on the plane, because Griff always had his assistant Solange book the row if he was forced to fly a commercial airline. Dan had brought the Italian leather holdall Bea had given him from the Oxfam shop.

'You were right, babe,' he said, as he put it in the overhead locker. 'Turns out I did need hand luggage.'

In the air, after the seat belt sign had been switched off, when the drinks trolley had been and gone, up in the nowhere, high-up place before the descent, the cabin was filled with thin, brilliant sunlight. It seemed to dissolve the sides of the plane, the air was suffused with sky. Bea leaned across the empty seat and took Dan's hand.

'So,' she said briskly. 'How much?'

'I'm sorry?'

'How much money will it take, to stop you thinking I'm a hypocrite?'

'I don't get it.'

'We should put a number on it, shouldn't we?'

'Bea, that's messed up. Seriously?'

He studied her face. Her eyes were as clear and true as ever.

'Think about it, and decide,' she said.

The plane plunged to the right. The wing below them disappeared from view. They put their seat belts on.

'I suppose it's a pretty good problem to have,' she said.

'What is?'

'Too much money.'

'Yeah,' he smiled. 'It is.'

'Better than death and dying. Better than lots of problems.'

They landed at Heathrow around lunchtime.

'This way. This way —' Griff barged ahead.

VIP. Platinum. Ropes unclipped. Smiles.

'You're staying with us presumably?' said Griff, as they skipped the queues. 'Bea? You are coming home?'

PART THREE

21

Griff had bought the house in Holford Road for £2 million in 1994, at the end of five years' regeneration after the losses of '89. He'd recently had it valued at £15.5 million. He wasn't planning to sell, it held sentimental value. When he bought it, Bea was five years old, Alex twelve, and Ed was at Eton. They had done a lot of work to it before moving in, and then again when Ed's eighteenth birthday party got out of hand. Rampaging sixth-formers had smashed chandeliers and crystal vases, and pissed on the sofas and carpets. They had ripped up the oak floorboards and thrown them onto a bonfire of garden furniture, lit with lighter fuel. The neighbours had called the police and the fire brigade. It had made the papers. Griff had been enraged by the high moral tone of the press. Teenage parties often turned into riots. Kids smashed stuff when they were drunk and stoned. Just because these kids went to schools with Latin mottos journalists indulged in end-is-nigh grandstanding. Griff took legal vengeance on the parents of the boys Ed didn't like, and overlooked the others. The only thing that really upset him had been the large turd on his pillow.

They bought another house nearby, and lived there while they redecorated Holford Road; they put in the garaging, pool, gym, and a glass-box extension, increasing the size by almost two thousand square feet. When they moved back in, he made a profit on selling the second house, so there was no harm done, but when it came to Alex's eighteenth birthday, having learned a lesson, they hired a club for the night. Bea spent hers in a bar in Prague, InterRailing, so there was no need to bother about hers.

Holford Road was Griff's favourite house. The duplex on Central Park West, the chalet in Cortina, the manor house in Hampshire, and the house on St Barts were for investment, or entertaining. Holford Road grounded him. Here, he had been through scandal and public disgrace and still hung on to his money. He had reached his fortieth year of marriage in Holford Road; had four fucks serious enough to be called mistresses, and proved himself a gentleman by bringing none of them home — literally, if not figuratively. Griff saw property like any other investment, and cities were only differing markets to him, but Holford Road was more than property. It was a family house. It was English. He was sure his parents had felt the same way about their seven hundred square feet in Whitechapel as he felt about his eight thousand in Holford Road.

Griff's driver Ashir had collected them from Heathrow in an outsized SUV that could hardly squeeze into the driveway, and started getting the luggage from the back before they had all climbed out. Dan squinted up at the house, adjusting from the darkness behind the tinted windows.

'Fuck,' he whispered.

'It's just a house,' said Bea.

Griff, first up the steps, opened the front door. 'Porsche sweet Porsche,' he said, as the four of them came into the hall, then he was off down the spiral stairs. 'I tell you, I never want to see another rented car. That was a nightmare.'

'Kiss the Merc for me,' said Liv.

Blessica came up from the kitchen.

'Oh, Mrs Liv. Oh, Mrs Liv. Home now.'

Overcome with emotion, she ran forward to take the suitcases, her eyes brimming on Liv's behalf.

'Miss Bea!'

'Hi, Blessica, how are you?'

'I'm so sorry. So sorry.'

'Thank you. This is Dan.'

Bea and Dan went up to Bea's room. He didn't say anything as they went up, but his silence spoke. She heard every exclamation of awe as if she could read his mind.

Her window on the second floor, overlooked the street. Dan put down his bag and went through the dressing room, to explore.

'Mind if I take a bath?'

'No, sure.'

Who walks into a house and has a bath? she thought. It was like he had arrived at a hotel. She heard the water rushing from the taps as she turned off the air conditioning and opened the windows. Up in the eaves the ceilings sloped. Liv had redone the room more than once in the ten years since Bea left home, and nothing of her childhood remained. The walls were walnut-panelled now. It was no more strange or painful to be in this familiar-unfamiliar room than anywhere else.

She went into the bathroom. Dan had taken off his T-shirt and was very slowly tipping bath foam into the water, and watching it as it poured. He stirred the water intently with his other hand, then put the glass stopper back in the bottle, wiped it and returned it reverently to the shelf with the others. He watched the bath running for a few more moments, stirred it again, then turned off the taps. In the quiet, he undid his jeans and pulled them off, and then his pants and socks. He kicked them out of sight, so they wouldn't disturb his view, and lowered himself into the hot water. Consciously, gracefully, he went under, with the wordless sounds of a man in heaven. Coming back up with bubbles on his head he sluiced them from front to back, and rubbed his face, luxuriating.

'*Nice*,' he said.

'I'll leave you to it,' said Bea. She turned to go.

'Babe.'

She stopped.

'We should talk. About the money. Get it out of the way.'

She nodded. 'Whenever you like.' She left the room.

They didn't talk that day. He was waiting for her to broach the subject. She meant to, but found she couldn't speak. It was enough managing being home, and spending as little time in the evening with her parents as she could. It wasn't hard to avoid Liv, who was on the phone constantly, enlisting party planners and friends, and Griff retreated to his study. They all went to bed early.

'Are you sad, babe?' said Dan, in the face of her quietness.

It was wrong to use grief as an excuse for the distance between them. 'Yes,' she said. 'Goodnight.'

At five o'clock in the morning she snapped awake. The dawn light made the bedroom dreamlike, with no shadows, an umber rendering of a room that she was not part of, as if she were observing it from another place. She knew why she had woken like that. Like someone had pushed her. It was Monday; seven days exactly since Alex had died. The police had come to Paligny a week ago to tell them. They must have found Alex's body at about the time she had woken. She lay wakefully, staring, and seeing only the white road, and the car wreck, and thinking it was as if a new life had started then, in a new landscape. She turned to look at Dan. She didn't want to risk waking him by getting up, and have to speak, if only to say, *Go back to sleep*, so she lay still. She felt each second of each minute of the three hours until he woke, at eight o'clock. It was a meditation on loss, marking it. Seven days to the moment. There was no possibility of company in that feeling; it wasn't her choice to be alone with it.

She pretended to be asleep when Dan got up. She didn't think he believed her. When he had gone downstairs she sat up, and found Capitaine Vincent's card in her bag, and called him. He did not answer, and she left a message.

'Capitaine Vincent, it's Beatrice Adamson. Please call me, if you need anything.'

She said something else, about wanting to help, but that wasn't really why she'd called him. Her thoughts weren't clear and she knew she sounded emotional. She wished she could delete the message. He wasn't her friend, but he felt like an ally, and she couldn't separate herself. She would have liked to see him.

Later that day, her brother Ed and his wife Elizabeth arrived from Tokyo. They were staying in a hotel, and came by Holford Road to say hello. Elizabeth was a cool, correct person, whose expression became intent whenever she looked at her husband. Efficiently affectionate in public, their private lives were unguessable. They had left their children in Tokyo, but showed pictures on their phones. Ed's feelings were put aside in his mother's presence, as they had always been. He shadowed her politely. He looked very like his father; as tall, but not so broad, and wore a handmade suit. He and Bea hugged. They had never known one another well.

'We still can't believe it's happened,' said Elizabeth. 'Are the papers still snooping around?'

'Not that I know of,' said Griff. 'Arun told them to fuck off, but I don't know if it made any difference. They might not know we're here.'

They sat in the sitting room, drinking coffee, except Liv, who opened a bottle of champagne and walked in and out with her glass, on the phone, busy making plans. Her voice rang out from room to room.

In the afternoon, Alex's friend Will came over for band practice. There was something of Alex about him. They'd been at school together, and both loved art and music, and had been rebels. He brought his daughter, Nell, who was four. She sat on one of the stools at the island unit and watched from a distance as he tuned his guitar. Like his father, he worked at Merrill Lynch now. The other guys in the band walked about the garden with Liv, deciding where the stage should go. Across the room, Dan was making a sandwich with Blessica, pretending he couldn't find the fridge behind the spring-loaded cupboard doors. She was giggling. Will was sitting on the leather sofa near the garden, and Bea was holding his iPad, where he could see the tuning app.

'Your daughter's lovely,' she said.

'Thanks,' said Will. 'You have kids? I guess you're way younger than us.'

'Not *way*. But not yet.'

'Daddy! Play,' said Nell, swinging her feet.

He played a Beatles song, 'Blackbird', halfway through, with a few false starts.

'Are you all right?' he asked when he stopped. 'I'm sorry.'

Bea nodded. 'It's OK, I cry a lot.'

'Look, I'm sorry about Alex. It's just shit. It's such a *shit* thing to happen.'

She appreciated his nerve in not letting it be too huge and terrible to name.

'Thank you,' she said.

'Do the police know anything yet?'

'I don't think so.'

'Your mum is being amazing. I don't know how she does it.'

He paused for her to agree, but she didn't.

'She's given me a whole specific set list,' said Will. '"Blackbird" we always play, but most Beatles songs not so much. She's got loads of those, and loads of Oasis, but I'm pretty sure Alex hated everything after "Definitely Maybe" – pretended to, anyway. We thought we were *so cool*.'

'You were,' Bea smiled. 'So cool. Just play what you want to play. You were his friend.'

'She's his mother. They were so close, weren't they?'

When she didn't answer he said, 'She was always the mother all the guys – I mean,' he corrected himself, 'she was so good-looking, we were all totally in awe of her.'

Bea made some sound, she didn't know, something non-committal.

'It's got to be tough for a girl to have a mum like that,' he said. 'She looked about fifteen.'

'Daddy!' shouted Nell from her stool. 'I'm bored.'

Gratefully, Bea left him, and went over to her. 'Bored?' she said. 'Oh no, that's awful!'

Nell giggled. 'Please may you spin me?' she said.

Standing nearby, Dan watched Bea spin the stool. The little girl tipped her head back. Will played some more chords and sequences, and then sang 'The Man Who Sold the World', from start to finish, perfectly.

'We didn't know it was David Bowie's song,' he said, as the kitchen clapped. 'We thought it was Kurt Cobain.'

Liv came from the terrace to the threshold of the garden door, commanding attention.

'Oh, Will! That was gorgeous. Thank you so much. We're going to have the tables in the garden, if the weather holds. Would you rather play on the terrace, or shall we put the stage at the end?'

'Hey, whatever suits you, Liv,' said Will.

She sat next to him, and touched the neck of his guitar. 'Isn't it lovely? Could you bear to show me a chord? Do you mind?'

'No, sure,' he said. 'Here, like this.'

When the caterers and decorators came and started to lay the dust sheets to protect the floors, Will left. Griff withdrew to his study, and Bea to her room. Dan stayed downstairs, at the island unit with a cup of tea and a croissant, watching Liv and the party planner talking to the workmen in the garden. Blessica had put a slice of butter on a saucer in case he wanted it, and a glass dish of honey. Now she was wiping inside a cupboard. Dan wondered if her apparent adoration for the family was genuine, or if it was like a salaried form of Stockolm syndrome; her own family were in the Philippines. His phone buzzed with a text from Bea.

Come up?

She was summoning him. She was ready to talk. Blessica wouldn't let him clear his plate, she took it from him, and thanked him like he was doing her a favour. He went upstairs.

'So ... shall we sort this out?' said Bea, when he came into the bedroom. She was on the floor, with her back against the bed.

'You want to?' said Dan.

She nodded. He sat down beside her on the floor.

'OK,' she said.

'OK?' His forearms rested on his knees, his hands were clasped, his head bowed, waiting.

'This *thing*,' she said, then stalled.

'What thing?'

'The money.'

'Yes.' His heart beat fast, quickening at the mention of it, along with a kick of shame.

'We have to control it,' she said. 'We have to be distant enough from it. It's very important.'

'OK.'

'We have to decide what we want, and stick to it.'

'Sure.'

'The rest can be put into a trust, and not accessible.'

He felt the thrill, the danger of the taboo. Her trust, her fortune, in all this talk of death, like treasure in a fairy tale.

'I don't want to suddenly find I'm sharing stuff with Ed.'

'What do you mean?'

'Like this house. Deciding whether to sell, what to do with it and all the other places.'

He'd never heard her voice shake. 'What other places?' he said.

'The apartment in New York. Hampshire. The house on St Barts.'

He had been tantalised by these words before, but hearing her say them now made him breathless.

'Ed can have all that stuff,' she said, 'and worry about what to do with it all – he likes it.'

He put his hand on her knee, to steady himself. He felt almost dizzy.

'I just want it *clean*,' she was saying. 'So whatever comes to me is controllable. Otherwise it's our whole lives. It's a recipe for madness.'

'We don't need to be rich,' he said. 'You'll never be like them.'

He kept his hand on her knee and waited.

'So,' she said. 'Have you thought?'

'Yes.' It was time to put a number on it. He tried not to sound as though he'd planned it. 'If we sell our flat, we won't walk away with much.'

'True.'

'So, what if we get a better flat?'

'With a mortgage,' said Bea.

'Why?'

'Who doesn't have a mortgage?' She was scandalised.

'Who, Bea? Very lucky people, that's who,' he said. 'All right. A mortgage. But small.'

'OK,' she said. 'Agreed.'

He tried not to rush. 'And, like you said, I need to take some time out. I've only got my foundation, I was thinking I could do a degree, maybe. But then, that's three years. I'll be thirty-three. So maybe not. Maybe I could just take a few months to think about it.'

'Good idea.'

'And that will cost money.'

'How much money?' she said.

'Like ... twenty-five grand?'

'Twenty-five, OK.' She sounded relieved.

'Or thirty,' he said. 'Thirty – say, thirty-five grand for a year. That's a salary, right?'

'It's more than mine.'

'Which is not much, living in London. So. Thirty-five, to live for a year. And not go back to fucking Foundations of fucking Holloway ever again.' He gave her a flash of a smile.

'A year, from September,' she confirmed.

'Yes.'

She relaxed, a little. She smiled.

'Oh.' His face fell. 'Shit.'

'What?'

'We won't get a mortgage, will we? If I'm not working.' He put his other hand onto her knee, for emphasis, talking straight into her face. 'We should buy the new flat without one.'

As she felt the walls close in, he felt them dissolve – the ceiling, blown clear off, to open sky.

'Go on,' she said, looking into his eyes.

His pupils were dilated, his hands were warm. 'OK, well, *say* ... we get a flat with no mortgage.'

'Everybody wants a home,' she said. 'Everybody needs to own something. Simone Weil calls ownership one of the "needs of the soul". You're right, I'm sorry.'

'No mortgage, then?'

'No.'

'Great,' said Dan. 'Then we should get a house.'

'A *house*?'

'Then we don't have to move, when we have a baby.'

He said it easily, but the silence that followed was like the hush after a bomb blast. She lost her bearings.

'I saw you with that little girl,' said Dan.

'Nell?'

'You want one. A baby. We want one.'

'I know –'

'So, let's get a house.'

'But I don't –'

'Just that, OK? Bea, a house, come on. Nothing massive. Three bedrooms.' His voice sounded restricted, his fingers stroking the sensitive skin behind her knee. 'So the house, and the money for the year. This is good, but what about now?'

'Now?' she asked quietly.

'For travelling. We don't have a tenant now.'

'No, but we've got the Cushion.'

'The Cushion.' He laughed, dismissing it.

'What? It's fine. We worked it out. We've got nearly four grand.'

He made a noise, derisive. 'Right,' he said. 'Be a lot less stressful if we top it up. We could put a few grand in there – maybe, ten?'

'We're only away three months.'

'We could stay in places with, like, clean bathrooms?'

'No, we've decided on a house.'

'Babe –'

'A *house!*' she said.

'Puritan.' He smiled, his hand moving on her thigh.

'So is that it?'

'We'll need to work it out properly,' he said.

'But that's enough?'

'Sure.'

'Really?'

'It's not extreme,' he said.

'No. You're right. It's a house.'

'And a baby.'

'A baby,' she said.

He kissed her again. She loved the taste of him. She had missed it. He was kissing her. He wanted her. His need was urgent. It caught like touchpaper. His fingers pressed into her thighs. A house. And money. A three-bedroom house and a year to breathe. Thirty-five thousand pounds, in a house without a mortgage. He fucked her on the floor while caterers and electricians passed through the rooms below, and afterwards lay sweating by her side.

'Christ, it's hot up here,' he said.

He got up and put on the air conditioning. He flicked the temperature arrow down; twenty-one, twenty, nineteen.

'D'you mind?' he said. 'It's all over the house, one more room isn't going to make any difference.'

Linen beanbags, mismatched chairs; lavender, cornflowers, roses. Decorations filled the house. Tea lights in silver glass hanging from the trees. Fattoush, baba ganoush, labneh, samboussek, batata harra. Food for North Africa because Alex had loved it. Broderie anglaise cloths for France, because he had loved it there, too. A stage for his friends' band, draped with white, and a white backdrop. White amps and speakers.

'I love it,' said Liv. 'It looks like that John Lennon video. It's gorgeous. No black, anywhere. I don't want black.'

And that night, Bea dreamed she was holding Dan's hand, leading him. She saw an enormous snake ahead of them. She looked at it and thought how funny it was to dream something so obvious and Freudian as a snake. Commenting on it she felt safe, but the snake was in front of them on the road. It was standing upright, as tall as a tree, with many body parts, but it was still a snake. It's like a tree but not like a tree, she thought. She looked down, for Dan's hand, but it wasn't in hers. Her hand was severed at the wrist. The paralysis of a nightmare crept over her body. She tried to search for Dan, holding the stump of her wrist in front of her. The snake was huge and tall above her. There was bark on its body, which clicked and creaked as it swayed. Dan was looking down at her from the branches now, saying, *Stop*, and she was hanging from the tree, choking. She felt the weight of her body, swinging.

'Stop it!' said Dan.

She opened her eyes. The snake was towering behind him. He couldn't see it. She woke up. His hand was clamped over her mouth like a kidnapping. She struggled, crushed under his body. He took his hand away.

'You were yelling,' he said. 'I'm sorry.'

22

Bea tiptoed out of the house while the sun was still hidden by haze and walked to the station, the streets she'd walked every day in childhood. The morning was chilly. She was sore from the sex the day before, she felt it when she walked. She remembered the feel of him in her arms, and how soft his neck was against her face, the velvet roughness of the back of his head, where his hair started, and his lips pressed softly on her collarbone. She thought of throwing away her birth control pills, and what it would be like to feel him come inside her, knowing they could make a baby. They could have a baby in a house. It was miraculous. They'd be a family. She tried to believe that he loved her, but she couldn't believe it. She could only think he'd wanted her so badly because of the money, that he'd been fucking her money, and doing it quickly, feeling passionately about her body because of that. She remembered she'd read somewhere you shouldn't flush your birth control pills away, because of the hormones in the water. She wondered what they would call their child. She would like a girl, so she could give a girl unending, easy love, and never have her daughter feel like she had felt. A boy might make her think of her mother. She mustn't be frightened of that. Her mother was nothing to do with her. And Dan might want a son. She didn't care if it was a boy or a girl. A baby was a baby. A baby and Dan. She pushed the other thoughts away. It was vain to worry about how much she was loved all the time. She must try not to be so vain.

She took the train to Holloway, as if she were starting a good working day. Dust-spattered windows, chimneystacks, as if the last two weeks had not happened. For a moment, on the train, Alex wasn't dead, and she and Dan were like they had been. No death. No Griff and Liv. No greed, forcing itself into the cracks. Just coming home from work, eating dinner, going out. Normal. She changed at King's Cross, immensely relieved to be back in crowds where each person looked different, away from the tasteful narrowness of France. Joining the fast-moving people, she caught the Piccadilly line to Holloway Road, and went out into the exhaust-fume, take-away smell of home. She felt like a ghost, or that Paligny was the ghost. *When you're gone, and you look back, this will feel like a dream,* Now he had gone, everything was; life caught between a dream and a nightmare.

The building works above the practice had hardly moved on; the scaffolding was sunbaked now, not dripping. She ran down the basement steps.

'Bea! Oh my God! What the hell are you doing here?'

'I'm just back for a few days,' she said.

'OK, but what are you doing *here*?'

'Can't stay away,' said Bea.

Jen, Gita, Helen, Jeff. Their routine was interrupted, they loved it.

'Do you mind if I just sit for a bit?'

'Whatever you like. It's brilliant to see you.'

It was all exactly as she'd left it. She sat in the office, and watched the start of their day, and then the clients arriving. She felt like a ghost. If she could have joined the living, she would have done. She deflected their questions with questions of her own, and didn't tell them about Alex. There was respite in being in a world where nobody knew.

'I wish I could work,' she said. 'Anything for me to do?'

'You're mad.'

At nine fifteen sessions started and she left. There was no excuse to stay.

'See you in September –'

'Goodbye, have fun –'

She watched the bus that would take her home go by, and almost ran to catch it, so that she could let herself into the empty, unlet flat and hide there. She thought of going to the charity offices where she volunteered, but the team on the helpline might not appreciate her dropping by for no reason. If she called a friend, she would have to talk about herself. She walked north, up Holloway Road, to the Oxfam shop. She was in luck, Veena was there, and the tiny storeroom was in chaos.

Veena was ridiculously happy to be helped. She made them both tea, and then Bea went into the back, with the donations.

'I haven't seen that crazy knife girl again,' said Veena. 'But I do wonder what happened to her.'

'Me too.'

'So, how have you been?'

'Yes, fine,' said Bea. 'Fine.'

Dan dressed and went downstairs. It was half past nine. Electricians were laying cables in the garden. Blessica made him breakfast. He ate it looking up at the chandelier, which was a

319

cluster of long geometric lights, suspended from the hall ceiling hanging down through the void of the double-height space. Dan thought he knew his style, he considered himself someone with a developed aesthetic, but this house threw him off; he couldn't tell how he felt about any of it. He'd studied Murano glass. Were the lights modern Murano? Were they resin? Could they be shell?

'How do you clean those?' he asked Blessica as she ran back down the stairs from answering the door. She just laughed.

He googled three-bedroom houses in London, and marvelled that one of them would be his. One thousand eight hundred square feet, south-facing garden. Add to basket, he thought. Checkout. He heard a door slam, and footsteps, and Griff came down into the kitchen.

'Dan,' he said, 'where's St Beatrice?'

'Gone to see her mates,' said Dan.

'The house is going to be overrun today. I'm going out.'

The doorbell rang again. They heard Liv greet somebody in the hall.

'Why don't you come along?' said Griff. 'Take your son-in-law-to-work day.'

'Work?' said Dan, surprised.

'Takes my mind off things,' said Griff. 'Coming?'

'Do I need to change?' asked Dan.

'Would there be any point?'

Ashir was out front in a Mercedes. Dan had never seen anything like the inside of it, a strange quilted world of headrests and armrests and footwell lighting. Fuck, he thought, as they pulled away. Griff didn't bother speaking, bashing away at his iPad on the other side of the car.

'Where are we going?' asked Dan.

'Wait and see.'

It was quiet in the car, and Dan didn't notice the traffic. They drove through Camden Town and past the British Museum, then crossed the river at Waterloo. Elephant and Castle, the Old Kent Road, and gradually, the streets became familiar.

'Where are we going?' he asked again.

Griff smiled. 'Your manor,' he said.

Dan peered out, through the tinted glass. Peckham High Street. Consort Road. The car felt more and more conspicuous, and it was surreal to glide through the streets of his childhood in the back of it, with people checking them as they went by. Ashir frowned at his satnav, lost in a maze of railway arches and dead ends.

'Where you trying to get to, mate?' asked Dan.

'He's all right,' said Griff. 'Aren't you, Ash?'

'All good,' said Ashir.

They cut around the back of the Peckham bus garage, made a big loop and turned onto Rye Lane.

'Blimey, it is rough,' said Griff. 'Where is the damn place?'

'Which place?' asked Dan, but really, in his heart, he knew.

'Copeland Park,' said Griff. 'The Bussey Building. It should be here. Ash?'

Ashir shrugged.

'It's down there,' said Dan. 'You need to walk.'

'Down that alley?' said Griff. 'Ash?'

'I'll stay here.' Ashir stopped on a zigzag, putting on his hazard lights.

They got out of the Mercedes.

'Lead on,' said Griff.

There was no point asking questions. They passed Khan's Bargains, as a train thundered across the railway bridge. Griff gazed about him like Captain Kirk after teleporting.

'KFC,' he said wonderingly, as he followed Dan into the covered walkway.

'See it there?' said Dan.

The Bussey towered above them, huge and unadorned, and beyond it the cracked concrete and other buildings of Copeland Park; painted letters on the battered walls: *CLF Art Cafe. Block A. Block B. Stairs.* Rusted doors and spray paint, warehouse windows and distant beats.

'I've only seen plans and pictures,' said Griff. He peered into a stairwell. 'I don't particularly get what everyone sees in it, to be honest.'

He was standing in front of a graffiti mural, the bright yellows and blues outshone and shrank him down to size. It was early in the day, still, but the weather was mild, and the food stalls were setting up. People were coming from their offices and shops on Rye Lane to eat, and there was a steady stream going in and out of the various spaces, and even some tourists. Nearby, a girl was stirring a sloppy curry in a huge wok over a gas flame, and the chargrill smoke of jerk pork drifted on the air from a barbecue across the cracked and weedy concrete.

'They can't do much business,' said Griff, squinting into the darkness of the building. 'You can't see inside.'

Dan shrugged. 'Why are we here?' he asked.

'It's a project I'm involved with. I thought it might interest you.'

They walked to a zinc trailer with an awning, serving coffee, and Dan bought them one each. Griff didn't take the lid off his, it was just a prop. He continued to stare, like a Victorian explorer.

'My degree show was here,' said Dan. 'Gallery over there.'

'A gallery,' repeated Griff.

'Where I met Bea,' said Dan.

'Here?' Griff looked at him, full in the face. 'I didn't know that.'

'Bought her a drink up on the roof,' said Dan, pointing.

'Sentimental attachment,' said Griff. 'That's nice.' He put his untouched coffee on the ground, and flicked his fingertips together, to dust them off. 'Here's the thing –'

'You're developing the Bussey,' said Dan quietly.

It had to be said quietly, it was like swearing in church. Even whispering he had the feeling every head would turn, and people would stop in their business, and stare, in shock. It had been a twenty-year battle to save the Bussey from people like Griff. The place was an icon. It was untouchable.

'You can't,' he said. 'It's protected.'

Saving the Bussey was a story Dan had grown up with. Scheduled for demolition more than once, its preservation had been an unlikely triumph; south-east London's haven for the cultural underground, constantly under threat, devotedly defended. Propped up by the EU and the GLA, the Bussey had artists' spaces, club nights, movies on the roof and vinyl in the basement. Even when the EU money disappeared, preserved by law when Dan was still in his teens, it carried on. It never occurred to him it was vulnerable. He should have known. Preservation laws were no more than paper promises. London needed cash.

'Let's walk,' said Griff.

They moved away from the people, towards parked cars and lock-ups, and Griff talked. Still in its early stages, the Bussey Development Project would soon reach consultation, and then it would be public knowledge. The residents would fight.

'Fight? They'll go mental,' said Dan.

'It's a two-billion-pound development,' said Griff. 'It will happen. This whole area will be transformed.'

'Into what?'

'Luxury residential, retail and leisure park,' said Griff. 'The money's Malaysian, but a British company will be the face of it. Nobody wants to see a row of Malaysians in all the pictures. They want British companies, British businessmen. You know, shaking hands over a cement mixer or whatever.'

'You?'

'No, obviously not *me*. That would be a disaster, with my profile. No, no, no, it'll be a *local* developer.'

'Who?'

'They're putting one together now. And they'll need grass-roots support. PR, basically. Persuade the shopkeepers and whoever that they'll be better off.'

Dan stopped looking at him. He watched the people going about, setting up stalls, carrying materials in and out of the warehouse doors. A guy was unloading paintings from the back of his car. Griff was still talking.

'Obviously they'll be better off. It'll bring the whole area up. But people are arseholes. We'll need to draw them in. Sponsored events. Street parties. Give them the feeling the development is part of the community.'

'The feeling?'

'Kids. Balloons and what have you,' said Griff. 'Someone like you could be invaluable.'

'Me?'

'Get the locals onside, take my point?'

Dan took his point completely. Like Muslims on the beat in Bradford, like a black cop at Carnival.

'I've got no experience in PR,' he said.

'Not an issue,' said Griff. 'It's my call, I'm a significant stakeholder. Anyway, it's a doddle. Any moron can do PR. Not that you're a moron. Half my friends' posh-totty daughters go into PR.'

'I don't get it.'

'Maybe you *are* a moron. Do I have to explain?' said Griff. 'You're married to Bea.'

'Is that it?'

'Look, what are you, an artist? That's a rumour so far unproved. I've got no idea if you have any talent whatsoever, and frankly, it doesn't matter. It's time to grow up.'

'What would I tell Bea?'

'You won't be working for me,' said Griff, 'you'll be working for Copeland Park Development Project. CPDP. Catchy.'

Dan looked down at the ground. 'Listen, it's nice of you,' he said.

'I'm not nice.'

There was silence. Silence from Griff was unusual enough to get Dan's attention. He looked up at him.

'I had two boys,' said Griff. 'I've lost one of them. My daughter doesn't want to know me. Ed is fine, I don't worry about him, but Alex was –' He stopped, words stopped by pain. 'My daughter has told me many times she won't take my money. Told me outright. Even when I'm dead. Did you know that? Not the trust I've made for her. Nothing. Do you know what that's like? The world is drowning in shit and my daughter won't get on the lifeboat.'

Dan's pity was laced with excitement, his excitement dignified by sympathy. 'You don't need to worry,' he said. 'She's changed her mind.'

Suddenly, he had Griff's attention. He shouldn't have said it. He should have waited.

'Changed her mind?'

Dan tried to think of a way to say it and not sound greedy. *Don't worry, old man, when you're dead I'll have your riches.*

'Bea's decided – I mean – she wants to ask you about her trust fund.'

'Oh yes?'

'She wants access, to –' He couldn't say *money*. 'Some capital.'

'Bea?' said Griff. 'Are you joking? You are absolutely fucking joking. How on earth did you manage that?'

Dan gave an awkward laugh. 'It wasn't like that.'

'Of course not,' said Griff. His look held both respect and insult. 'What has St Beatrice agreed to?'

'We're going to buy a house.'

'Where?'

'We're not sure yet. There are nice houses in Dalston,' said Dan.

'Why Dalston? We've got a dozen standing empty much more central.'

'We can get three or four beds in Dalston for under two million,' said Dan.

'That's nothing,' said Griff. 'Dalston is still a shithole, but it's coming up.'

'I shouldn't talk about it, without her,' said Dan. 'It's not my – I mean, it's not my money.'

'No, it isn't,' said Griff. 'You don't have any, do you? Perhaps if she's agreed to that, she won't kick up about this.'

'Maybe,' said Dan, who very much doubted Bea's flexibility would stretch to his doing public relations for a property developer.

'Well,' said Griff again. 'What a turn-up. I didn't think any-thing could surprise me. St Beatrice of the Trust Fund –' He laughed.

Dan didn't respond.

'Right then,' said Griff. 'Is there anything more to see?'

'Like what?'

'You tell me.'

'No,' said Dan.

'You're right. I've seen it,' said Griff. 'I just wanted to get out of the house. I often think the British Empire was built by men just getting out of the fucking house. Shall we go? Couple of stops to make.'

'No, you go on,' said Dan.

Griff frowned. 'Do you understand what I'm offering you? I'm offering you a career.'

'Yes,' said Dan. 'I know. I need some time to think.'

'All right. Walk back to the car with me,' said Griff.

His father-in-law was scared to walk through Peckham alone, in the middle of the day. Taking a smug pleasure in his discomfort, Dan walked him back across Copeland Park, past the Bussey, and through the covered alley, to Ashir, waiting in the Mercedes.

When the car had gone he felt relieved, as if, like a costume, the heaviness of disguise was lifted from his shoulders. He was home. He hadn't felt at home when Griff was there. It had been like seeing it through glass. Now it struck him. He walked back to the place where the alley ended, and stood for a while, with the sounds of the streets and planes overhead, and the distant trains, and metal doors, the levels all mixed into the specific soundtrack of his past. Inside the huge brick building some-body banged a snare drum and a fast beat started, then stopped with a kick-boom to the bass. He watched some people going into the basement, to find the vinyl and comic books. He must have spent months of his life down there, sifting through boxes – when he was younger, trying to nick stuff; when he was older, helping out. He felt a helpless, disarmed love, and sadness. He walked out into the sunshine, looking at the scrappy random reality of it, being itself. It was a little breathing space for small endeavours. Of course it would go. Everything went. Like Battersea Power Station before it, a place like that was marked for destruction. If not now, sometime. There would always be someone waiting to take anywhere that had been left behind, and turn it into money. There was no point in being sentimental. He leaned against a wall and watched the people going by, and the girl cooking the curry in the wok. She'd been joined by a friend who had propped up a sign saying 'vegan'. She smiled at Dan. He didn't like white girls with braids. It was just a place, like any place; people buying and selling stuff, it wasn't holy, it wasn't pure, just shrunken, weaker versions of Griff. Small-time commercialism or big-time, there wasn't a difference. It was all bullshit. Vegan food. Yoga studios and craft beer. Galleries for *local artists* who couldn't get their work shown in the real world. The Bussey had given him that, but it had not been a beginning, just a spotlight on his insignificance. Jesus. Luxury flats were too good for it. Luxury flats and that flagrant market-stall holder's call: *30 per cent affordable housing!* That would never get built, for a start. They'd swap it out to another development, trade it or delay it, or cry poor when it came to building. It didn't make any difference which side you were on, it was all just bullshit. But he had met Bea there.

He put his hands in his pockets and walked away, out into the noise of Rye Lane, towards the station. He was very aware of the way he was walking, as he went across the road. He couldn't help noticing how much he'd adapted his walk over the years, and wondering when it had happened. These days, he walked like an estate agent. He could feel it. A commuter's walk. His legs trundling along while his body stayed stiff above the hip, with his arms and hands disconnected, ready to take out his phone, not checking the street for the faces of friends. He walked his commuter's walk down the street that had been home, but wasn't now. He tried to close his heart to it, but his memory was triggered by the smells of fresh meat and fridges coming out of the mini-markets, and the stacks of breadfruit, scarred and leathery, and mop heads, and shelves of hairdressing. The past struck him hard, like being catapulted back through his life. He was nearly crying when he got to the station and he didn't even know why.

By the time he got back to Holford Road he felt better. He sat on one of the tall white stools in the kitchen, and looked at property online, and wondered why he'd got so worked up. Through the glass, the fairy lights were tested – on-off, on-off – like regimented fireflies. Liv had disappeared to her room to get ready, and he didn't know where Griff was. There was a readiness about the house, the calm before the party. He was separated as completely from the confused feelings of his day as a space station from the Earth. He could prepare himself for Bea's reaction. Where her family was involved she was uncharacteristically irrational. It was tempting not to tell her. If he turned Griff down, she need never know. He thought of all the husbands and boyfriends who routinely lied to their women. He had grown up around men to whom secrecy bordered on a belief system. They made every trip to the pub a victory against the matriarchy, and smoking weed or a lunchtime lap dance not just dicking about, but an assertion of the self. As a child, his friends' fathers were mostly of the lie-to-the-wife, betting-shop variety, or, like his, not there. On film, men were either reluctant husbands and fathers, or violently avenging their conveniently murdered wives or children. Extreme violence was justified to save the wife. At college he'd caught on that Hollywood's expedient morality was more a tool of political propaganda than intended role model. His mother dismissed his indignation. *Dan, you think too much!* His mother, the constant worrier, with her late-onset godliness, her stultifying belief. *It's just a movie,* she'd say, followed by, *Go outside! Kick a ball around!* – like they were living in the 1970s. He didn't condemn her. She was all right. She had pinned up his drawings on the fridge door when he was small. She had kept him safe. She was a good mother, on her day. But she was not a father. Negotiating maleness had been, as Bea would put it, *complicated* for Dan. Thou shalt not kill, unless provoked. Thou shalt not commit adultery, except, like Dan's own father, fucking off back to whiter-than-white Surrey. There was no commandment about being in league with thy father-in-law, but Dan knew a sin when he saw it. He did not have a god, but he had Bea. He wasn't going to lie to her. She would understand. She always understood.

On her knees, Bea sorted through the stripy holdalls and bin bags, with the smell of strangers' cupboards getting into her nose and hair, poking and rummaging and folding. There was one expensive coat with a cleaning ticket pinned to it that went straight onto the rail. There were a lot of baby clothes. Meticulous and gentle, Bea sorted them by size, from very tiny to small. But Veena said people were fussy about baby clothes, and would not buy them. She put them aside. Occasionally the bell on the door would ring.

'Morning,' she heard Veena say.

She could not see but she heard, and pictured the people from their voices. Shoppers with children. The old and the unwell. The lonely. Bea, kneeling among limp mountains of clothes, listened. The weather. Their pets. The news. And her mind travelled to the unknown of their lives.

When the floor of the back room at the Oxfam shop was clean and clear, and she had put everything in its proper place, it was closing time. She felt embarrassed to be thanked so effusively, when it had saved her sanity to do it. She said goodbye to Veena, then caught the bus, and then a train. She could have got the Tube, but she didn't want to get out so close to her parents' house. It felt like a sin, to ease without discomfort into so much plenty. She wanted to delay the night. It was after six when she came out of Hampstead Heath station. It had been warm but there was a cool edge to the day's end. She walked onto the Heath, looking out from the heights over the far view of the city. The sun was a dark gold circle in the polluted haze. Dog walkers and commuters strode over the rough grass, the conceit of its scruffiness, as if every blade of grass didn't reek of privilege. She stopped, and watched the view; the sunlight on the distant buildings, and, then she went back to Holford Road. Unable to face entering the house by its front door, she went in by the basement. Coming home to Dan and their flat, she never felt guilty, only lucky. It was just home. She wondered what precise financial distance between richest and poorest made the contrast wicked. She supposed it was a different scale for everybody. And for people like her father, limitless. The lights flicked on as she stepped underground. She could smell chlorine from the pool, and the petrol-and-oil smell from the cars. The huge red Porsche was in there, on the turntable, gleaming in the standby light, and her mother's white Mercedes, and her father's bigger one. She put the combination into the keypad for the inner gate. 010482. Alex's birthday. It hadn't changed. It wouldn't. As she went up, the smell changed from basement to ground floor; room fragrance and glass cleaner. Her feet sank into the rugs laid over the tiles.

Dan was at the island unit. She could tell he had been waiting for her. Something was on his mind. He wasn't waiting with love, he was waiting anxiously, defended. He looked like a person about to try and sell her something. He got down from the stool.

'So, listen,' he said.

'What is it?'

But her father's voice broke the quiet, carrying from the floor above. 'BEA! Are you home?'

They heard his footsteps, quick and urgent, coming down the stairs.

'Bea, I need to talk to you. Can you come to my study? Do you mind?'

'No, sure,' she said, and saw fear in Dan's eyes.

'Alone,' said Griff, stopping Dan in his tracks. 'When you're ready.'

'I'm ready now,' said Bea, making it true.

23

Bea followed her father up the stairs and across the hall to his study. He had to haul the sliding door to open it.

'That needs oiling,' he said.

The room inside was dim. She saw Philip Roche, immediately, sitting on one of the leather sofas, then Arun, over by the bar – but not her mother.

'Hello, Bea,' said Arun.

'What's happened?' she said.

Griff closed the door, and there was a hush in the panelled room.

'Our access came through,' he said. 'Philip has the police file, from the judge.'

'Oh,' said Bea, her stomach dropping like she had fallen, suddenly, from a height.

'Your mother's getting ready for this – party,' said Griff. 'I don't want her to know. I only tell her when she asks. She doesn't ask.'

'I understand,' said Bea.

'Sit down.'

She sat on the sofa opposite Roche, and Griff sat next to her.

Roche took a buff file from the briefcase at his side. He put it on the coffee table. 'I think it's fairly comprehensive,' he said, 'but there are frustrating omissions.'

Arun joined them. They were all around the table, with the pale file on the smoked glass. Bea looked at her father.

'Are you all right?' she asked.

He nodded. She felt her eyes drawn to the file. Trying to comprehend the enormity of her brother's death, she didn't want to know the details. She feared the smallness of horror, and of rage. Roche slipped the elastic from the corners of the file. Griff leaned forward, and took her hand. It was a surprise, but comforting.

'We have to see it, Bea. We have to keep up.'

'Do we?'

'I do.' He was still holding her hand. 'All right. Let's do this,' he said.

'The full autopsy isn't here,' said Roche, 'or the pathologist's report. That's likely to take weeks.'

'Weeks?' asked Griff. 'How can it take weeks?'

'Because of very detailed lab work. But we have the pathologist's preliminary findings, and some of the evidence Capitaine Vincent's *section de recherches* have gathered, thus far. It's very unusual to have access this early.'

'Just get on with it,' said Griff.

'All right,' said Roche, separating one paper from the sheaf in his hands. 'So. The definitive cause of death is not stated.'

'Why not?' said Griff, gripping Bea's hand.

'I'm looking into it,' said Arun. 'Let's deal with what we have. Prepare yourselves, I'm afraid it's quite violent.'

334

A pulse beat in her ears and her mouth was dry. She looked at her father. He was focusing on getting from each second to the next, just like her.

'There is evidence of significant blunt instrument trauma,' said Roche.

Tears came to Bea's eyes but she didn't feel anything yet, she was dislocated.

'We thought it was prescription drugs,' she heard herself say.

'Yes, it mentions "acute toxicity", but the primary cause of death is not recorded.'

She repeated the words *blunt instrument trauma*.

'Yes. To the head and neck. I'm so sorry.'

Griff let go of her hand. He shielded his face. 'We didn't see any injuries, when we – saw him.'

'It was the back of the head,' said Roche. 'Back of head, side of neck. Back and side.'

He separated a piece of paper, a blurred inked diagram of a human body, marked, but Griff didn't move. Bea reached forward and took it from him. The body diagram looked like a crude *Vitruvian Man*, the same pose, duplicated, front and back. There were shaded sections. The back of the skull, shaded. The right side, shaded. The back of the neck, blocked out. She watched her hand give the paper back to Roche, then reach for her water glass. She felt her mouth on the rim, then water. Her hand put the glass down. She saw that her father couldn't speak. He needed her to do it.

'That's what killed him?' she asked.

'It doesn't say, specifically.' Roche took another piece of paper.

'Do they know how long it took?' she asked. 'To die.'

'The report is incomplete.'

'Why?' she asked.

'I don't know.'

'Does it say how much pain he would have been in?'

'No.'

'Does it say how long it took?'

'No.'

'Was he drugged, and then beaten?'

'There are no conclusions, I'm afraid.'

'Why not?'

'I'm looking into it.'

'What killed him?'

She thought she heard Griff make a noise. He might only have flinched.

'I can't say,' said Roche.

'What else?' she said. 'What about the CCTV images?'

Roche laid out the papers; Arun took notes, in pen, on a yellow pad. Most of the documents were in the folder; technical French, full of acronyms. For so much paper it was precious little information, like a planning notification, spattered with killing. There were a number of people's DNA in Alex's car. He had been to several places. There was a report of his being seen in the town of Oyonnax. His credit card receipt from a bar, Chez Janine.

'They asked us about that bar,' said Bea.

There were no conclusions, no shape, only disjointed moments in the progress of many lives.

'There must be something else,' she said.

'There is an absence of some of the evidence that one might expect to see.'

'Why?'

Griff's phone rang, on the sofa next to him. He picked up.

'Yes, I'll be there in a minute.' He put the phone down. 'My wife.'

Roche handed Bea a piece of paper. 'I took the liberty of synopsing the basic timeline Vincent's team are working with, in my simple language. My own words. It may help.'

Bea took the page, and read it.

Saturday, 23:00 — AA left the Hotel Paligny.
Saturday / Sunday, 23:56–00:08, AA bought petrol at the Avia service station, A39, Toulouse-le-Chateau. (Possibly in the company of an unknown man.)
Sunday, AA unaccounted for, up until 20:30.
Sunday, 20:30, AA drinks at a bar, Chez Janine, in Oyannax, in the company of (the same?) man.
Sunday, 23:00, AA and companion leave Chez Janine.
Monday, 06:10, AA's body discovered.

She handed it to Griff. Arun poured more water for her.

'The French use CCTV a great deal less than we do in this country,' said Roche.

'Who was Alex with, in this bar?' she said.

'There's nothing to indicate they know who it was. Or if it's the same person he may have been with at the petrol station.'

'They don't know anything,' said Griff.

'I'm not convinced they're sharing everything with us.'

'Don't they have to?' said Bea.

Roche shrugged. He shuffled through the papers again, and held out several, clipped together. 'These pages detail the interviews with the family.'

'We don't need that,' said Griff. 'We were there.'

'There are photographs, taken at the scene of the accident, and at the mortuary.'

'I don't want to see those,' said Bea. 'Dad?'

'No,' said Griff.

'Do they want us to go back?'

'Not for the moment. I'm sure they'll let us know.'

The conversation died. There was silence for several minutes. Griff asked Arun and Roche to leave them, and when they had both gone, he and Bea sat alone, with the file in front of them, on the coffee table.

Griff got up and poured brandy into two glasses. The doorbell rang, muffled by the thickness of the doors, and the panelled room.

'Knock it back,' he said.

She did. The curtains were drawn, and the lamplight pooled onto the dark walls, soft, like the smell of leather and cigars.

'Your mother's doing better, since you ask,' he said.

She didn't say anything. He pushed the file away.

'Arseholes,' he said.

She nodded. 'You'd think they'd know more.'

'They've got nothing,' said Griff. 'Or if they have they're not telling.'

'I'd rather know nothing,' said Bea. 'I don't understand why we need to see it all.'

'To know what happened.'

'It's happened. It can't un-happen.'

'We'll feel better when we know everything.' He got up and poured himself another brandy, holding up the decanter to her.

'No, thanks,' she said. Then, 'Yes, please.'

He gave it to her, sat down again, checked his phone, and put his feet up on the coffee table. Bea tried not to go over the things that Roche had told them. She didn't want them in her mind. She tried to imagine Alex alive, but she couldn't. She finished her brandy, and traced her finger along the pyramids of the cuts in the glass, watching the light in lines along the edges, tasting the brandy that had been in her mouth. The doorbell rang again.

'Christ,' he said. 'Do you know how many parties I've hidden from, in this room?'

'You love parties.'

'Mostly.'

He got up and poured himself another drink, and some for her, too. Bea poured water from her water glass into her brandy.

'Lightweight,' said Griff. He sat, put his glass down, and stared at his feet. 'When were you born again?'

'Nineteen-eighty-nine.'

'Of course. Worst year of my life.'

She didn't take it personally, he'd lost a lot of money that year.

'Regret is the worst thing,' he said. 'Worse than anything. I hope you won't have regrets, when you're my age.'

They sat staring at the file on the table again. She seemed to see Griff looking down at Alex's peaceful face when he was dead in the hospital in Bourg, not knowing his skull was crushed. She brought her mind back.

'What are your regrets?' she asked.

'Oh, Christ, let me see ... I should probably regret not being around more for you kids, but to be honest, I don't, particularly. There's a modern belief fathers should be, you know, pestering their kids with footballs, fuck knows, doing all that stuff. Was I that bad? To you?'

'You turned up, you went away again. You were who you were.'

'So why all this?'

'All what?'

'Darling, you do a very good impression of hating me.'

'I don't hate you,' she said. 'I just hate what you do, and what you stand for.'

He laughed, a sudden, huge laugh. She laughed, too.

'Not as much as you did, apparently,' he said.

'What do you mean?'

He didn't answer. She wasn't sure he'd heard.

'What's the difference between guilt and shame?' he asked.

'I think guilt is about something you've done,' she said. 'Shame is for what you are.'

He thought about it. 'Right,' he said. 'Guilt is negotiable.' He reviewed his past, the years descending on his face.

'I do feel a bit guilty, probably,' he said. 'I regret causing your mother pain.'

'Do you?'

'Of course. We've never really been mates, Liv and I. Don't know how much she likes me, frankly.'

'Do you like her?' she asked.

'What a question.'

'I don't know how you could.'

He stared at her.

'Do you know what she did?' she said, as if it were a normal question. But then it was hard to speak. 'I've always wondered and never asked. Did you know about her?'

He jolted and flickered, like a machine with a momentary loss of power. She saw the enormity of his denial.

'She's suffering,' he said. 'She can't get out of bed one minute. The next she's talking to thirty friends on the phone.'

'She doesn't exist unless she has an audience.'

'Don't be a bitch.'

'Don't tell me how to talk about her. I can say what I want.'

'Well, I don't want to hear it.'

She looked away.

'I should have been nicer to Alex,' he said.

'. . . Nicer?' she said.

'The damage was done.'

'Yes,' she said, 'it was.'

'I shouldn't have –' He stopped.

'Shouldn't what?' she said, quietly. 'Expected him to get over it?'

'Maybe that's it,' said Griff.

Bea nodded, but could not speak, thinking of Alex, unable to *get over it*. And how alone he must have felt.

'And I wouldn't have sent him to France,' said Griff. 'We were always running from one crisis to another. It was stupid, looking back.'

'I think he loved Paligny, in a way.'

They sat in silence.

'You'll feel better, when you're away from your mother,' he said.

'Why didn't you leave her?'

'Alimony.'

'That's not it.'

'I could never leave her,' he said. He didn't say any more.

There was silence.

'I suppose we should get ready for this circus she's put together.'

'I don't know if I can.'

'Whatever you think best.' He finished his drink and got up. 'All right?'

They reached the door and he opened it for her.

'You were quite brilliant, with Philip Roche, just now – very brave,' he said.

'Thank you.'

'You're welcome.'

24

Bea came out of the study with Griff and they both crossed the hall to the stairs. Somebody had dimmed the lights, and there were voices coming from below, and more, outside the front door.

'Quick, up you go,' said Griff.

On the first floor, he left her, and she went up to her room. She felt dizzy, and had to hold on to the banister. Her empty stomach was acid from the brandy and from feeling too much, and knowing. She saw the diagrams, the shading, marking crushed bone. Her legs gave way. She sat on the stairs and shivered. Nobody could see her. She held herself. She smeared her tears with the heel of her hands, eyes shut tight, and pushing her forehead against her hands.

She could smell Dan's shaving foam as she went into the bedroom. He had just finished dressing.

'Is everything OK?' he said. 'What did Griff want?' But he wasn't looking at her.

'Yes, I'm fine,' she said.

He was doing his hair. She passed him to go into the bathroom.

'Are you sure?' he said. 'What did he say about today? I don't know what he told you,' he said.

She turned. 'What?'

He looked at her, wrong-footed. She didn't know what he was talking about. She shouldn't have drunk the brandy.

'The party?' she said.

'What?' He turned away quickly. 'Can you be quick? It's really late.'

'I don't want to.'

'I'll see you down there.'

He went down the three flights of stairs, towards the party, down and down again, hurrying, embarrassed how relieved he was Griff hadn't told her. Pussy-whipped. He needed not to be so weak. He didn't have to live his life as a nothing. He had the right to change, if he wanted to. He rounded the top of the stairs and saw below him the big hall, and, beneath that, through the glass balustrade, the lower-ground floor. Guests were scattered in small groups in the various spaces of the house. He had the sense of coming upon a cavern under a mountain, and at the end of it was the garden, like another, deeper, cave, with lights like jewels illuminating it, and the people in it. More people were coming into the hall to go down. Waiters crossed the floor. The very long hanging lights, like stalactites, were amber. Even they looked different, glowing with welcome, now.

'Excuse me,' he said, and a girl with a tray of cocktails stopped.

'Good evening, sir,' she said.

'Any chance of a beer?' He thought how he must look; a guest, but still an ordinary person, just like her.

'Of course. I'll come and find you,' she said.

'Thanks.'

The guests had taken Liv's direction, and worn bright colours. Only a few wore black. There was a lively, edgy energy to the sound of their voices, and the laughter. Liv was in white linen. Surrounded by people, she looked plain to the point of sacrificial, except for a huge pair of sunglasses, which gave an impression of almost brutish blindness. Her apricot-coloured hair was loose. With a woman holding her arm, and a man on the other side, patting her shoulder, she went out into the garden, as the candles on the tables were lit and the band set up. Blessica came hurrying past, with a tray of clean glasses, and paused.

'Mr Dan!' she said. 'Hello!'

He wondered if it was phonier to greet staff and ask how they were the whole time, or not to pretend. Bea did, but she was the same to everyone. It was like she was missing a status-awareness gene.

'Hey,' he said, and turned away.

The waitress brought his beer. He took it, and stood looking out through the glass back of the house. In the heart of London, here, the horizon was all treetops and chimney pots, and, above, the fuzzy lilac glow of the city sky.

Bea drank water from the tap and showered and washed her hair, dressing without drying it, and then went down. She felt light-headed, she had to eat something. Even knowing how her mother operated, she was surprised at the size of the crowd. She looked for Dan, from group to group, in the fairground of a garden. It had everything but bunting. A waiter stopped and smiled and held out a tray.

'No, thank you.'

345

She looked, but she could not see Dan. Ed's wife Elizabeth passed, conveying appropriate sympathy, but busy, on her way elsewhere. Bea was largely ignored, invisible. The atmosphere was charged. The guests were alert, their heads and eyes turning and seeking, like periscopes. She saw her brother Ed, talking intently to Arun who, obedient to the Adamson edicts, wore a pale pink linen jacket. His wife, holding his arm, was draped in crimson silk.

'Bea!' Someone shouted her name. 'Hey! Bea!'

It was Will, on the lawn below. His wife was with him, and other friends of Alex's. They all looked up. She made the last descent, into the garden, and Will hugged her. He didn't have to ask why she looked as if she had been crying. He had been crying himself. They were all upset.

'This is so weird,' said Bea.

'I know. But it's good, right? Your mum is amazing. It must be hard for you, too. I'm sorry.'

'It's not your fault.' Her towel-dried hair dripped onto her neck and she squeezed it out.

'Sit with us.'

'OK. Thanks. Have you seen Dan?'

'Look, he's here.'

Dan came out of the crowd. He looked – happy.

'Hey,' he said. 'What took you so long?'

Her mother's voice, as loud as a bell through the speakers, brought the party to a momentary halt.

'Dinner, everyone! Sit down! Wherever you like.'

It took some time for people to seat themselves at the long tables, decorated with flowers and cloths. Supper was brought out. The younger people stuck together, like tourists. Many of them wore black, ignorant of or ignoring Liv's instruction. They were emotional and kind to each other. Bea could see most of them were a little drunk, or maybe high; coke, or MDMA. All the old crowd, come to celebrate Alex's life, able to play with the things that had helped destroy him. Some of them had children, and the children played on the grass, or sat on the steps with their phones, where the waiters were trying to walk, taking selfies and giggling. The weather wasn't warm or settled. The sky was overcast. A breeze snatched at the garden and terrace heaters were switched on. Among the older people, Bea recognised a few faces, and others, probably photographed often enough that they were absorbed into the consciousness, looked as if she should recognise them. It was a rich crowd; not the clothes or face work, or the tone of their voices, or the excess of the feast. The richness was far stronger than that. It was in the people themselves. She wondered what level of wealth it took, to rearrange the molecules. *Too rich* and *too poor* were slippery creatures, they were always out of reach. But she knew, in every part of herself, how sick it was to live with such disparity, when beyond the garden wall, just there, was poverty. Not even a mile away, not another country, but hers. It wasn't an effort to think of it, she had only to stop trying not to. It took constant vigilance to live blinkered, so the rich wouldn't lose their minds with terror, under the eyes of the poor, and the poor lose hope. She wasn't hungry but she ate, to steady herself, and get rid of the brandy feeling, then she drank wine to blunt her senses. She needed not to see too clearly. Beside her, Dan was excitable and staring, like he'd had a line of coke. Maybe he had. There must be enough of it around. She was astounded at the carnival atmosphere, as if death and disaster fed her mother and her mother fed the house. Apart from Will, and one or two others, near her, she could not see one shred of honest feeling in the crowd. She caught Griff's eye, occasionally, knowing what they knew, having heard what they had just heard, but he was as loud and ebullient as ever. He was used to pretending. It was second nature to him.

'Remember at Westminster,' Will was saying, 'down the Two Chairmen? So long as we took our ties off, we always got served. Alex could charm the birds from the trees.'

'Remember that time in Tuscany?'

'Remember Alex's parka, in the nineties?'

'Oh my *God*!'

'Remember – '

She wasn't ready for this. She didn't know how they could have such fun with it, so soon. He was hardly cold. Or rather, said her shock, he was almost frozen. His corpse was shrouded in a plastic bag. Locked in a metal drawer. She hoped they would not bury him. She could imagine the purifying annihilation of cremation, the bright blaze, releasing him. She couldn't bear the thought of his body in the ground. Then Griff was standing on the stage, with a microphone. The background music died.

'Good evening, everybody.'

His amplified voice was right next to her, deep and clear. The people stopped and watched him quietly.

'You may have noticed there were one or two reporters outside the house. What happened to Alex is seen as fodder by certain newspapers in this country. I don't have to ask you not to speak to them. It's pretty disgusting they should come here, trying to get at us now, if you ask me.'

A few people said, 'Hear hear.' He nodded his thanks.

'For those of you who don't know, the investigation into my son's death is ongoing. Just now the –' He stopped.

His eyes were closed as he stood before the hushed guests. He opened them.

'I don't know when my son is coming home. I don't know when we can have a funeral. Thank you for coming tonight.'

He left the stage to subdued clapping. The music started again.

'At least it's not fucking Ed Sheeran,' said Bea, and laughed.

She saw how shocked the people nearest her looked, and that Dan wasn't laughing with her. Her heart hardened and defended itself. The conversation started up around them. She was going to lose herself. She needed to tell him about Roche's visit.

'Let's go in,' she said.

'I was in Peckham today,' said Dan.

The word was out of place, ridiculous. She thought she'd misheard.

'Peckham? Oh, did you go to see your mum?'

'No. I was there with Griff.'

'With Griff? Why?'

'He offered me a job.'

The music got louder. The speaker near her blared.

'Did you hear me?' said Dan. 'Your dad offered me a job today.'

Waiters leaned between them, and cleared, and others stood ready, with trays of dessert.

'Yes, I heard,' she said. 'I don't know what to say.'

'Are you OK?' he asked.

'No. Can we talk about this later?'

'Yeah, sure, if you want.'

Dessert was a syllabub, served in sherry glasses, sprinkled with purple petals. Bea saw her mother getting up from the table to cry, and be comforted, standing. Recovering, she laughed, and sat down again.

'I just can't believe your mum managed to do all this,' someone said. 'It's gorgeous.'

'Is Liv all right?' said Will's wife. 'She looks so beautiful.'

'She's fine,' said Bea. 'She's loving it.'

She got up and left, and went through the tables to the front, to join her father, who was with his own small group of favoured men. He introduced her, king-like.

'This is my daughter – you all know her. Bea.'

They greeted her, and made space.

'She hates me,' said Griff. 'Don't you, darling?' He was slightly drunk.

'I can't bear you,' said Bea.

'Surely not,' said one man. Alex's godfather, Rupert somebody. In shipping, she remembered.

'I'm sure you set a good example,' said another, who owned a private bank, laughing.

'Bea doesn't think so. She's a truth-teller. Or a-sayer, or a-seer, whichever word it is.'

'I'm a psychotherapist,' said Bea.

'Oh, marvellous,' said the godfather.

'Well done you,' said the banker.

'What job did you offer Dan?' she asked him. 'Why?'

As one, the men turned away, to give them privacy, but Griff addressed them.

'She's angry with me.'

The men gave the impression they were part of the conversation, waiting to see what Griff wanted them to say, and if his daughter was going to make a scene they could talk about, later on.

'I told him,' Griff said, 'I said: the world is drowning, and I'm offering you a place on the lifeboat.'

'Your analogy is paranoid,' said Bea. 'You're confusing survival with greed.'

'Here we go, lecture me,' said Griff.

'Why aren't your opinions lectures, only mine?' said Bea. 'Your "survival" has turned London into a super-condo.'

'Oh yes, I'm Godzilla, aren't I?'

'That wasn't me, Dad, that was the *Daily Mirror*.'

'I don't make the rules. Nurses and teachers are never going to live in Belgravia, Bea – get over it. Vast amounts of revenue flow through this city, from the banks and property. Vast.'

'What does it do for anyone? You and this lot are the only ones who benefit.'

'Not just me, love,' he said. 'You too, Trust Fund Beatrice. I hear you want to *access your capital*, as Dan put it. You'll have to drop the bleeding-heart socialist crap now, won't you?'

He saw how shocked she was. He looked away from her face, and stared up to the sky, terrace heaters reflected in his eyes, tawny orange, chimney red.

'That boy must have you on the ropes,' he said. 'You must be terrified, to abandon your principles after all this time.'

The music stopped. Lights came up on the stage. Everyone turned to look.

'Good evening,' said Will into the microphone. 'I'm Will, Alex's friend, and this is my band. Liv asked us to play a few songs.'

Whoops. Clapping. He adjusted the microphone, and looked down at his hands on his guitar, but Liv, below him, waved for attention. She came up the steps, her white shift shining gold. She took off her dark glasses and smiled. The party was hushed

351

and waiting. He handed her the microphone, and she took it in both hands, her mouth close to it.

'We would've liked to be doing all this for Alex's wedding day,' she said. There was a feedback whine. 'Sorry! Hello.'

'Hello!' said many voices.

She beamed. 'I can't see you very well.' She searched the crowd and pointed. 'Johnny – darling Johnny.' The man next to Bea waved. 'Christine and Mike – thank you.'

Quietly, Bea got up. She kept to the side of the lawn, trying not to run. Liv's voice swelled and filled the garden.

'Lolly and Marco,' said Liv, amplified, behind her. 'And Lee, *darling.* I'm so glad you could make it. Thank you, darling, thank you. I loved my beautiful son. If I could trade places with him, I would. I called him my little prince.' Her voice rose. 'He was so sweet, so gentle. He was too gentle for this world.'

Bea had reached the terrace. She ran into the kitchen, up the next flight of stairs to the ground floor, up again, and up again until she reached her room. She remembered Alex, in the garden at Paligny, swinging the axe as he gazed at the sky. She remembered the nightingale's song.

25

Dan didn't follow Bea. He watched the band with everyone else. The party guests bobbed about near the stage, like a mini music festival for old rich people, while the waiters cleared the tables under the cover of the music. Bea didn't reappear. The band played 'Blackbird', last, and everyone cried and clapped. It said something about Dan's life that he was having the best time he'd had in weeks, watching middle-aged white men play to a crowd of millionaires at a memorial for a guy he hadn't even liked.

Liv was constantly in a crowd, but when there was time, she sought him out, and came up to him. She was like a wood sprite, thought Dan, who was quite drunk. Her pupils were dilated in the dark.

'How are you, Dan?' she asked.

He wondered how Bea could hate her mother like she did. His own mother had messed up a lot, but he could still be in the same room with her. It was Bea who had helped heal him. Bea, who was still hung up on hating her own mother, like a teenager.

'Yeah, I'm all right, Liv, you doing OK?'

'I'm – doing – OK,' she said slowly, nodding, repeating the words as if they were profound. 'Doing OK, thank you.'

She held his arm, with two hands, gazing around, smiling at the people drifting back towards the house, each of them pausing to squeeze her hand, or blow her kisses.

'What a beautiful night,' she said flatly.

'It was. I'm so sorry.'

'God,' she said. She put on her dark glasses.

'Cool look,' said Dan, with stilted levity.

It worked. She was laughing again. 'Come on inside with me,' she said.

'I'll walk you in.'

'Your generation of men are so good at feelings. So kind. So lovely.'

'I was brought up by my mother. Had to be.'

They started in, arm in arm.

'Just a moment,' said Liv.

Gripping his hand, for balance, she took off her dark glasses again, and looked up at the sky.

'You can't see stars in London,' she said mournfully. 'Even here. What's that line, in the poem about the stars? *Doubt the stars are made of fire? Doubt* something-something, *But never doubt I love.* I don't know.'

'Sorry,' said Dan, 'can't help you.'

'I can't remember it. Alex would. It was one of the first poems he learned. I loved him, Dan. And he loved me.'

Someone passed, and squeezed her hand. 'See you inside,' said Liv.

'I'm sure he knew, how much you loved him,' said Dan.

'He did,' she said. She brought her gaze from the sky above, down, to his face. 'People don't understand purity. They want to destroy it.'

She was looking at him fiercely. Her grief was monstrous.

A very short man with a bow tie and a bald head stepped in front of her. He had a cigar and was in his seventies, his deeply tanned face was frozen-looking, smooth and plump, and fixed in a grin, with ice-white tombstone teeth and liver spots.

'My darling girl!' he shouted in an accent – Italian, possibly. The neck beneath his stiff face hung in folds and wrinkles, with a last little flap above his tight collar.

He and Liv clasped one another's hands, and Dan, gratefully, said goodnight.

He saw Bea's packed things the moment he came into the bedroom. She was sitting up in bed, and her backpack and bulging cloth shoulder bag were leaning against the wall.

'What's going on?' he said.

'What job did my father offer you?'

'Just a job. In PR. Not for him. Another company.'

'PR? Dan. What did you say?'

'I didn't.' He gestured at her packed things, against the wall. 'You didn't think to, maybe, run this by me?'

'I can't stay in this house,' she said. 'I've booked the Eurostar. We can take the train to Beaune, and get a cab to Paligny. If the police say we can go, let's just go.'

He took off his T-shirt and went into the bathroom. She heard him showering. She didn't move. He came back in, in one of the towelling robes from the bathroom.

'Your mum,' he said, 'she's grieving. And you won't even give her the time of day. It's shit. Do you not see that?'

'No,' she said quietly.

'No?'

355

'You're wrong about her.'

'I'm wrong,' he said. 'That's it. I'm wrong?'

'Yes.'

'It's terrible, what happened to Alex. It's terrible. Obviously. And I'm sorry. But I tell you, it's put you in a different light for me, girl. They've lost their son. We should be standing by them.'

'Really? We?'

'Yes.'

'Your family loyalty is touching,' she said. 'And I can see you really need to stay on their good side, now you've named your price.'

'Hey –'

'But you haven't got it in writing yet. All this money you think we need. So you should probably stay on my good side, too.'

The house was silent the next morning when Dan and Bea came down with their bags. The caterers had cleared away a lot, but not everything, and Liv had told them to come at noon to do the rest. Stacked boxes and washed cutlery lay waiting. Blessica was polishing a vase in the kitchen.

'Good morning, Mr Dan. Morning, Miss Beatrice,' she said.

'Good morning, Blessica,' said Bea. 'How are you?'

'Very well. Coffee machine hot for you. Early bird!'

'Thank you,' said Bea.

'You go today, shame!'

Dan wasn't in the mood for her. 'Let's just go and talk to Griff,' he said. 'Sort this out.'

Bea looked at him coldly. 'Blessica, do you know where my father is?'

'In the study. Very messy. I can't clean in there.' She laughed.

Bea knocked on the door.

'Come!' said Griff.

Dan pushed it open and let her through ahead of him. There were dirty glasses littering the coffee table, and the smell of the stale brandy, transporting her to the night before. The buff police file was where they had left it. Bea tried not to look. Griff was at his desk, with the curtains open behind him.

'You're up early,' she said.

'Been for my walk. Kick-starter.'

'We're going to go today,' said Bea. 'We're just off.'

'Back to Paligny?'

'Yes. I'll speak to the police when we get there, and see if there's anything else we can do. Then if they say we can go, we'll head off.'

'Fine.' He came round the desk, to hug her goodbye.

'Before we go —' said Dan. He looked at Bea, prompting her. 'Bea?'

Griff looked from one to the other. 'What's afoot?' he asked.

'Shall we sit down?' said Bea.

'I don't know,' said Griff, 'shall you?'

'I know Dan told you yesterday, we want to buy a house,' she said. 'And I wanted to let you know, whatever we find, I want to match what we spend with donations to charity.'

Griff seemed unperturbed. 'Bit extreme. Not as stupid as it sounds, probably,' he said, 'from a tax point of view. Arun can sort you out.'

'We won't be looking until we get back,' said Bea.

'Dan mentioned Dalston,' said Griff.

'Did he?' Bea looked at Dan.

'Where was that flat we offered you, when you got married?' said Griff.

'What flat?' said Dan quickly. 'What?'

'Didn't you tell him?' Griff looked from Dan to Bea. 'Wedding present. I sent you the details. Notting Hill, wasn't it?'

'I don't remember,' said Bea. She had thrown the details away, unread. But she remembered the glossy brochure going into the bin, and how happy that had made her.

'I never saw it,' said Dan tightly.

'Fine,' said Griff. 'Let's not get into it.'

'Let's not,' she said. 'We should go.'

'Bea?' said Dan.

Bea looked him in the eye. 'You ask,' she said. 'If you want to.'

'Ask me what?' said Griff, amused.

'Did you know our tenant fell through?' said Dan.

'What tenant?'

'We had a tenant for our flat. It was our travelling money, and she never turned up.'

'No, I didn't know,' said Griff, 'but go on.'

'It's left us a bit short,' said Dan.

Bea went red, and stood looking at her feet.

'So, use your money,' Griff said to her. 'What's the problem?'

'I don't have any of the bank details,' she said quietly.

'What? Christ, I don't know,' said Griff impatiently. 'Talk to Arun.'

'OK,' said Dan hastily. 'We'll do that. Thanks.'

Bea looked up. 'OK, we should go. We need to get to St Pancras. Our train's at eleven.' She went to her father. 'Goodbye, Dad.' She kissed his cheek. 'I love you.'

Dan held out his hand. 'Thanks a lot. Thanks very much. I'm sorry to bother you with all of this. Thanks.'

Griff did not speak. He was thinking. She touched Dan's arm.

'Dan?'

They both turned to go. They reached the door, and she tugged at it, but it stuck.

'If it's cash you need,' said Griff, behind her, 'it's not a problem, there's some at the hotel.'

She stopped pulling at the door.

'What?' said Dan.

'There's money at Paligny,' said Griff. 'You can take some of that.'

'What money?' said Dan.

Bea stared at Griff, examining him.

'What do you need?' said Griff. 'A few thousand?'

'Sorry,' said Dan, 'I don't get it.'

'I've just told you.'

'What money is it?' said Bea slowly.

'It's just a bit of cash,' said Griff.

'How much cash?'

Griff gazed into space and blew out his cheeks.

'A few hundred thousand?' he said. 'If you two wouldn't mind dropping it off somewhere safe, you can skim off whatever you need. It's in euros. Arun will give you James Florence's number. Bea, you remember James Florence?'

'No.' She didn't, but she remembered his name in Alex's notebook. She had thought it was a girlfriend. She felt over-whelmed by sadness. Florence hadn't been a girl, just another contact of Griff's.

'You can meet James, and hand it over. Wherever you like.'

She looked steadily at her father, and didn't speak for a moment. Then she said, 'Did you tell the police about this?'

'Tell them what?'

'That there's money in the hotel.'

'Why would I tell the police?'

'*Why?*' She walked away and stood with her back to the room.

Dan watched her. He looked from Griff to Bea, waiting. She turned to face her father.

'Did Alex know?' she said.

'Just forget it,' said Griff, suddenly uncomfortable, regretting having spoken. Dan had never seen him look like that.

'Did he know?' she repeated.

'Of course he did.'

'What money is it?'

'For God's sake, Bea, calm down.'

'I am calm. Answer me.'

'It's just some money. We were clearing some cash out of a defunct company. Tiny company I set up ages ago. Alex used to pop over and get bits of it, when we visited.'

'Pop over?'

'To Switzerland.'

'You sent Alex to Switzerland, to pick up cases of cash?'

'It's really not that big a deal.'

'Did you do this whenever you came? Is that why you went to see him? Was that all it was?'

'Don't be silly.'

'You made Alex go to Switzerland, and bring money back into France? Illegally?'

'Christ,' said Griff, 'you make it sound like gun-running. I'm trying to do you a favour.'

'Me?'

'You say you need cash –'

She went to the bar and poured a glass of water from a jug. Dan saw her hands were shaking. He thought of Griff's boundless possessions. The houses. The villas. The cars. He saw the private jet in his mind, soaring into a blue sky.

'Sorry,' he said, 'you keep euros, in cash, at Paligny? How do you bring it back?'

'None of your business.'

Bea's back was still turned to them. She was drinking the water, not looking at either of them, but Dan didn't need to try, to know what she was thinking.

'That kind of money is peanuts to you,' he said.

Griff shrugged. 'Only people like you think there's small money and big money. How do you think the big money gets that way?'

'But it's illegal to move cash. Why would you do that?' Dan said.

'Fun,' said Bea, still turned away from them both. 'He does it for fun.'

'Is that it?' said Dan. 'Seriously?'

'Alex got a kick out of it,' said Griff.

'A kick?'

'We both did.'

'Yeah, some guys take their sons to the football,' said Dan. 'They get lap dances. So that was the "errand". Did you tell the police you knew where he'd gone?'

'Of course I told them,' said Griff. 'What do you think I am? Obviously I told them. I said he'd gone to Switzerland, for a meeting.'

'Not Mâcon? You told us Mâcon before.'

'No, I straightened that out.'

Slowly, Bea turned back towards the room.

'So,' said Dan, 'Alex had an envelope – or what – a briefcase? Full of money, in the car?'

Dan was aware of Bea's anger.

'And you didn't tell the police,' he said, 'when they interviewed you? You just said he was in Switzerland? If he had it with him, whoever attacked him took it.'

Bea's hand was over her mouth.

'Some French copper could've pinched it,' said Griff quickly. 'Or the ambulance crew. Or he may not even have collected it. Whatever.'

'*Whatever?*' said Bea, finding her voice at last.

'What's the difference?'

'You were looking for it, in the car,' said Bea. 'That's what you were doing.'

He shrugged but he could not meet her eye.

'You let us stay there,' she said. 'At Paligny.'

'I tried to make you leave,' said Griff.

'Anything could have happened.'

'But nothing did,' he said.

'It could've done!' said Dan.

'I *asked* you to get out of there.' Griff was stony-faced, unrepentant. 'I repeatedly invited you, didn't I? To come and stay with us. I practically begged *her*.' He gestured at Bea furiously. 'She refused me.'

'We didn't know we were in danger,' said Bea.

'Oh, grow up, you weren't *in danger*. This is unbelievable. What's wrong with you both?' said Griff. 'I'm doing you a huge favour. There is money at Paligny. I am asking you, as a courtesy to me –'

'Where is it?' said Bea. 'Where in the hotel is it?'

'If I knew, I would have got it myself.'

'You don't know?'

'No.'

'You have no idea?' said Dan.

'You know what Alex was like,' said Griff. 'He'd hide it around the place, and make a game of it. He put it under the floorboards once.'

'Maybe he was scared,' said Bea. 'To be alone with it.'

'He wasn't *scared*. It was a game, that's all.'

'He was just trying to please you,' said Bea. 'All he ever did – '

'All right! It was stupid.'

'It was *wrong*.'

'It was stupid of us. I grant you. I see that now, but it's done. If I could undo it, I would. I would never have sent him off that night – is that what you want me to say? I've said it before. Obviously I regret it. Maybe he got drunk and blabbed about it, he was completely out of control. It was a mistake, all right? But if he'd told anyone there was more at the hotel, then someone would have robbed the place, and they didn't. They haven't, have they?'

Bea looked at her father, for a long moment. Dan went and stood next to her.

'This money is a completely separate issue,' said Griff. 'It has nothing to do with the police investigation. Nothing. If they do search the hotel, or if someone finds it when I sell the place, it will just muddy the waters. It's not going to do Alex any good, is it? It's not helpful for the authorities to get involved with me, and my tax situation, when they should be trying to find out what happened to your brother. Just take the money out of the building. Help me. Help yourself. Help Alex. Isn't that what matters? Will you do it, please?'

Dan took her hand.

'No,' said Bea. 'We won't.'

26

They both turned off their phones as they left the house. They got to St Pancras and caught the eleven o'clock Eurostar, almost without speaking. They took their seats and waited. The air in the carriage was stuffy and still, not circulating yet, and the train idled, and clicked. They didn't talk. Eventually they set off, and the tracks below them swerved and slowly crossed, and the ropes of wire and blackish brick buildings sped, and blurred, outside. As they neared the coast, the train slowed, as if it was storing energy for the tunnel, then it sank into the deep cutting. The wire fences on either side rose, then disappeared from sight. They dipped and rushed through darkness, with a hundred feet of rock above them, and a hundred more of water. She didn't have her laptop, but she had a notebook. She found a pen.

Liv,

I'd call you nothing at all, but I want you to know this letter is for you, and that I know what you did to my brother. You are not a mother. You think you loved him, but you didn't. Whatever sick fantasy you have, that what you did was natural, or special, it wasn't. It was

~~disgusting~~ abuse. The regret of my life is that I didn't stop you, and I didn't help Alex. I was a coward. And Griff was too. If there was a God, you would be punished for what you did to him. I carry rage and hatred all the time. I lie to Dan ~~because I feel~~. Why am I ashamed? I look at you and feel ashamed. ~~I see~~ I have ~~seen~~ worked with paedophiles. Murderers. Drink drivers who killed people. Abusers. I can't think about ~~you~~ what you did ~~to Alex who. I can't put his name in the same~~ None compare to you. <u>None.</u> I wish there was a Hell and I could see you in it. Paedophiles are nearly always the victims of abuse. Some of them think they are above the law, and morality does not apply to them. I've felt pity for them but I don't feel it for you. I don't care what ~~happened~~ might have happened ~~in your childhood~~ to you, when you were a child, or waste time wondering if it made you this way. ~~I hope it was very bad~~. I believe you were born corrupt. You destroyed Alex. He was a child and you had no right to hurt him. If you had even a moment of conscience I would try my hardest to forgive you. I'm happy you hate me and I don't have to bear the insult of your ~~approval~~ so-called love. There are no words to condemn you. ~~But~~ <u>I saw you abuse your son</u>. ~~I want to not have it in my~~ You Killed Him. I need to cut this pain from myself. Not for you but for Me. ~~I'm~~ Sometimes I'm glad he's dead. At least he's free from you.

Beatrice

She finished writing. It felt like poison filled her stomach and her blood. She tore out the page, and folded it, and put it in her pocket, and the train rose up out of the tunnel into France.

PART FOUR

27

Inside Paligny at five o'clock that afternoon it was dark. They felt tired and strange from travelling, and being there again. The hotel was exactly the same, and the sameness made it feel more empty, and sinister. In the few days they had been away, the weeds had grown taller and the vines thicker on the windows. Capitaine Vincent's card had the grenade symbol of the gendarmerie centred above his name and number. It was dusty from the seams in the bottom of her cotton bag and the corners were bent.

'Do you trust him?' asked Dan.

'Yes. Completely.'

'OK.'

She called the number, staring at the card. The phone rang out.

'Capitaine Vincent, this is Beatrice Adamson, could you call me?'

Then she called the gendarmerie, in Beaune, and left a message for his team. They packed up the last of their things. It was muggy; everything felt damp.

'It's weird being here, knowing there's all that money somewhere,' he said.

'It's frightening,' she said.

'Yes. Let's just go.'

'But if Alex did tell – somebody – it was here, Griff's probably right, they would have been here by now.'

'I don't much want to take the chance.'

'No. I know. I wish the police would call back.'

'It doesn't matter, Bea. Let's go,' said Dan. 'If they call, they call. We can stay somewhere nearby.'

She was looking down at her hands. She didn't answer.

'What?' he said.

She got up and walked away from him.

'I want to look for this money,' she said.

'What for?'

'I need to see it.'

'Why?'

'I want to see what's so important to everybody.'

He could not dissuade her. He tried, but he wanted to see it too.

They looked in cupboards and drawers; the wardrobes, and chests of drawers in the bedrooms, and the sideboard in the dining room. The act of searching made the need to find it stronger.

'We need to be thorough,' she said. 'I'll start at the top, and you start at the bottom.'

The wine cellar was not as big as the ground floor itself. It was accessed by an outside door, down small stone steps, or from the annexe by the kitchen. Outside, in the dusk, Dan pushed the door open. The handle was loose in the soft wood and the lock was broken. He went inside, stooping, and hunching his shoulders, scared of vermin. It was too damp for snakes. Part of the floor was dirt and most of the rest was stone, except for in one place, where there were boards. It looked to Dan as though there might be another cellar, deeper, underneath.

A ladder leaned against the wall, but it didn't look as if it had been used recently, the rungs dripped with rags of spiderweb. The ceiling was part beamed, too low to stand upright. He switched on his phone for the torch. Immediately, texts from Griff came flooding in. He didn't read them. He shone the torch about the cellar. In the arches of the foundations there were wine racks with twists of newspaper propping up their wooden feet. One of the racks had been tipped over, and there was smashed glass, and cracked bottles lying on the ground, and small, muddy puddles in patches. Crates were stacked against the walls. He saw an enormous rat disappear between them. He went looking for the money. Griff had said Alex had hidden the money under the floorboards. The drama and stupidity sounded like him. If he'd valued it as he should have done, and valued himself, he wouldn't have been playing games to please his father, he would have used it to make a life, not the mess he did. But then, thinking of Bea, Dan pitied him.

With an unlit candle in one hand and the matches and saucer in the pocket of her skirt, Bea went along the corridor to the ladder on the wall and climbed up, into the roof space. She had to bang the trapdoor with the heel of her hand, like Alex had done. Wiping dust from her cheek onto her arm, she looked up through the hole into the velvet black. The rotting smell touched her, but it was fainter than it had been. She remembered clearing up the mess and the small floppy corpse of the rat, disintegrating as Alex picked it up.

371

She listened, then clambered up onto her knees, and then her feet, shaking off her skirt. She took the saucer from her pocket, and the matches, and lit the candle, squashing it into the drops as they cooled. She looked around. The flickering flame made shadows move, the angles tilted and jumped. Things seemed to be alive on the beams because of the small shadows wriggling on their bumpy surfaces. As her eyes adjusted she looked up into the apex of the roof. She felt Alex's presence there, up in the attic, more than in his plundered room below, as if he'd left a smudge of himself. Perhaps because his memory was still new, his death still fresh. It was strange how strong the feeling was; that without a funeral, he did not rest. The instinct was medieval.

She bent forward, feeling the heat of the candle flame. There was no movement nearby, not of snakes or anything else, just occasional shifting in the sound of the wood. Balancing, so as not to step onto plasterboard, she examined the empty sections between the joists. No bag. No case. No backpack. That store of surfeit, unnecessary money. Cash. Gold. Treasure. That kick, that drug, that habit. It was a need, hollow and hungry, and never filled up. Above, she heard the tiny steps of a bird on the roof.

She'd reached the end of the first long side. She couldn't see the red plastic snake traps except one, near her foot. She put the saucer down, and lifted it, testing the weight. It moved easily. There didn't seem to be anything there. She picked it up, with both hands, and shook it. Empty. She put the trap down and bent double, legs braced, holding out the candle, looking around. She could see the white lettering and red edges of another trap in the flickering light. Between her and the trap was a rolled-up carpet, a cardboard box and a rubbish bag, with dust on its plastic folds. The shadows loomed over the little group, like a time-lapse sunrise. Leaning close, she touched the roll of carpet; spiky coir and a rubber underlay, in squares, like French notebooks. She poked her finger into the carpet tunnel, circling the gap. She felt only air. She tried to lift it, but with one hand it was too heavy, and she lost her balance, arms splaying as she teetered on the beam. The candle fell. It hit the joist and went out, rolling into the darkness with little thuds.

'Shit,' said her voice.

She bent down and felt around the joists and plasterboard methodically, patting back and forth. Her fingers touched the candle and she picked it up and struck a match. The sulphurous burn-off stung her nose.

Illuminated, Bea organised herself. A dirty old rubbish bag seemed a good place to hide something valuable. She pictured Alex smiling, as he dropped the money in. Gingerly, she lifted the edge. The sides whispered on her hand. Between the damp and rigid folds of paper, groping, she touched something soft, and pulled her hand back. Firmly, she grabbed it again, and dragged the bag and pushed it open with her toe. The mouth gaped. She saw a mop head, not an animal, nothing dead. She carried on.

Her back was aching from bending. The hand with the candle shook. She swapped it to the other hand as she reached the second red box, and pushed it with her foot. It was hollow-light, too, like the first. She saw a mouse-trap with a tiny, long-dead mouse, the bar clamped across its back, like a staple. In the far part of the roof, she saw another trap. Seeing it there, tucked away, she remembered Alex had said to leave it. She'd have to go down on her knees to get into the corner. She put the candle down, and crawled. As the roof and floor met, she reached for the trap. She touched the sharp rim of the hole. She hooked her index finger inside it. It was heavy. The other traps had slid easily. If there was a snake inside it was a big one. She took her hand away. She listened. Nothing. She reached out again. It wasn't going to move – not with one finger. She needed to lie flat. She didn't want to lie down along the joist. Slowly, she lowered herself. The splintery wood cut into her body and between her legs, and her skirt fell into the gaps. She hoped a spider wouldn't run up inside it, or a mouse. Straining, she put a hand on each side of the trap and pulled. Scraping and bumping, it slid towards her. She got up on one knee, and pulled it out, triumphant. She crawled backwards with it and got to her feet. It was as heavy as a small suitcase.

Balancing the candle on top of the trap, she wobbled back to the ladder, where the electric light shone, clean and modern, from the corridor below. She put the trap down, blew out the candle, and manoeuvred herself onto the ladder. Halfway down, she reached for it, unbalanced by the sudden weight. It was hard to climb down, holding the snake trap. She should find another way, or call for Dan, but he was in the cellar. The carpet of the corridor below her was tantalisingly close. She held the heavy trap with one hand, trying to hook her elbow round the back of the ladder, but there wasn't enough of a gap for her arm to fit – hardly room for a hand. Helpless, she fell backwards, paddling. The trap fell too, crashing to the ground.

She fell onto her side, banging her hip and head. The corridor was sideways. The trap was broken open by the fall. It was full of banknotes; blocks of them, in rows, wrapped in plastic.

Bea sat up and dusted off her arms, looking down at the money. The plastic sleeves were wrinkled and reflecting. The money looked dreamlike. She knelt in front of it and eased a block from the top layer. Hundred-euro notes. There was another layer the same underneath. She pulled at the corner of the plastic envelope. It came off easily, and the slab of money slid out onto her palm. She sat there, holding it. It was about five centimetres thick, with a white paper band around the green banknotes. They were stacked so perfectly it was almost smooth-sided. She lifted it and smelled the metallic, inky smell, a cleaner smell than money usually had. She traced the silver strip with her fingertip and tilted it to the light, watching the rainbow colours of the hologram glint and change, like scales. She slipped the stack back into its sleeve and pressed it into place. She stared at it as her bruises came into focus, her sweat cooled, and the dirt on her skin began to itch.

Bea wiped the snake trap so the duvet wouldn't get dirty, and sat on the bed with the money. There were three blocks lengthways, and four across, in three layers. Thirty-six blocks of hundred-euro notes. She couldn't count how many notes were in a stack without breaking one of the paper seals but she guessed maybe two hundred. Two or three. So, each block was about twenty thousand euros. There was around eight hundred thousand euros on her bed. It was roughly equivalent to twenty years of her salary, or, for her father, petty cash. She should go and tell Dan. He was searching for nothing.

She put the flat of her hand on top of the money. She felt warmth and static coming off the plastic. It was as if it were alive. One banknote had value, you could buy things with it — food, clothes — but a box-full felt different. It had power. She should tell Dan. But she didn't get up or call for him, she sat, looking at the money.

Once, when she was a child, her nanny had left her looking at the comics in the supermarket for a moment, to go outside and chat to a friend. She remembered standing there, as people walked past, happily waiting, and looking at Sylvester the Cat. Her eyes had drifted to the shelf above, to a newspaper, and a photograph of dozens of drowned cattle, lying in a heap. The dead cows were stacked, limp and bony, like unlit bonfires. The picture next to it was worse. She saw people wading through water, with a landslide of debris behind them that had been their homes. Shocked beyond words, Bea stared at the people, waist-deep in water, and at the dead cattle, and then looked around for help, thinking everyone walking past must be stop-ping and staring too.

'What happened?' she said. 'Look.'

She pointed, but nobody looked. No one was interested in the cows or the crying people but somebody asked where her mummy was, and then someone else stopped to see what was happening. Bea started to cry as well, hating it because these people were worried about the wrong thing. Kathryn always left her on her own, and she always came back.

Bea had known what news was, and that there were other countries, away from Britain, where people went on hol-iday and foreigners lived. She'd been to some of them. In the weeks and months that followed she nurtured compli-cated fantasies involving Griff's plane, and money, and packed lunches. She was astounded to learn that even Griff wasn't rich enough to save Peru. But her fantasies persisted. Like any well-fed child, seeing poverty around them, in people on the pavements, on the way to school, she would imagine what a hundred pounds might do to help. Or a thousand. In her dreams, money transformed misery to joy. But she grew up and realised that it was embarrassing to scatter largesse, like the heroine of a Victorian book; it stank of elitism. She learned that generosity must appear detached if it wasn't to be judged phoney or sentimental, and saw the instinct to give, that was in almost everyone, when consistently condemned, faded. She had often thought how it was expedient to those on the winning side to characterise kindness as humiliating.

She had been embarrassed out of her childhood hopes, if not their political successors, but now, with the hard-shelled red plastic treasure chest in front of her, she backslid, helplessly, into fantasy. Hungrily, she pictured stuffing envelopes of cash through letter boxes, running rampant on a spree of altruism. And in that moment, for the first time in her life, she understood how rich she was, and how very much richer she had yet to be. The small box of money in front of her was a fraction of the wealth she had at her disposal. It wasn't the love of money that was the root of all evil, only the love of it above other things. Like fire, it could be a good servant. If she could be disciplined, not be seduced, or let it master her. If she were strong enough not to be corrupted. If she were vigilant, and did not let it rule her. She was elated, she found she was quivering with it. She asked herself if what she was feeling was temptation and decided it was not. Why should the corrupt have a monopoly on wealth when the world needed it so badly? She looked down at the money and placed her hand on it again, and felt its promise. She had trained and worked to give something to the world, but she made so little difference. She was a good person. She knew she was good. She could help. She didn't believe it *could* be wrong. She dared imagine justice.

28

The money sat between them on the bed. They both looked down at it.

'Do you think it's stolen?' he said. 'Like, maybe your father is into something serious we don't even know about?'

'No. It was just him and Alex, playing with matches. He's like the boss of a drug cartel slipping a gram of coke into his sock at the airport. He loves risk. He's always loved it.'

'But Alex couldn't pay the bills in cash, they couldn't spend it, so — what? Does he launder it? Bea, that's not like tax avoidance schemes you hear about, that's criminal.'

'Did you think he was just hard-working and lucky? Do you know the people he associates with?'

Dan felt Griff diminishing before his eyes. 'I don't get it,' he said. 'He's got everything.'

They both looked down at the box again. It was like sharing a bed with live explosives. It had a character, as if they weren't alone.

'We need to put it back,' he said. 'Where's the top of this thing?'

She reached for it and handed it to him. He held it, poised, and looked at the money beneath the plastic.

'Didn't think much of me, did he?' he said. 'Thought I was greedy enough to clean up his mess.' He was still staring at the money. 'Sort of makes you want to pull it out, tear off the seals and throw it round the room, you know? Make a heap of it and, like, roll around on the bed. Light it up like a cigar.'

'Best not.'

'Yeah.'

He put the lid on. His fingers fumbled the catches. They snapped shut with loud, strong clicks.

'What shall we do with it?' he said.

All at once the hotel seemed very big and empty. They realised night had almost fallen.

'I don't want to stay here with it,' said Bea.

'We won't.'

'I don't even want to be nearby. Or anywhere quiet. I want to be in Beaune for the night.'

'Yeah, OK,' said Dan. 'But don't worry, it'll be fine. Nobody knows it's here.'

They both looked at the money again. Then they heard a car door slam. They hadn't even heard a car approaching. They stared at each other.

'Shit. Fuck. Shit,' said Dan.

'What shall we do?'

The doorbell rang.

'*Bonjour?*' shouted a male voice. '*Il y a quelqu'un?*'

They went into the sitting room with Capitaine Vincent. There was something different about him – something missing.

'*I didn't get a call from you,*' said Bea.

'*I called you back immediately,*' said Vincent.

She checked her phone. She'd had it on silent.

'*What is it?*' he said.

Bea twisted her fingers together, searching for words. 'Dan?'

'Yep?'

'I'm going to try and explain it all to him. I can't keep translating.'

'It's all right. I can wait. Tell me after.'

He sat down and so did the detective, looking from Dan's to Bea's face expectantly.

'*Alex went to Switzerland the night he died – did my father tell you?*'

Vincent, poker-faced, didn't answer. She must not expect the whole picture. She must describe her part to him, the piece that she could see.

'*Just after the accident Griff insisted we went to see where it happened. They were still clearing the road. He looked in the boot of Alex's car – there was an officer from Bresse with us, but I don't remember what he was called. Something beginning with B? Did anyone tell you?*'

He carried on looking at her coolly.

'*Alex would have had lots of cash, in the car with him. My father told me, this morning. He would have had thousands of euros. He brought it from Switzerland, for my father. He's closing an account there, I think.*'

She waited for him to speak, but he didn't, so she carried on.

'*We think it must have been stolen from Alex. The night he was killed.*'

'*Anything else?*'

'*Yes. There's more money, here in the hotel.*'

'*Here?*'

'*Yes. Money that Alex brought in from, I guess, a Swiss account, or company, of my father's. It's quite a lot of money.*'

It was impossible to tell if Vincent was surprised, or even interested.

'*Have you seen anybody unusual in the area?*' he asked.

'*I don't know. Dan, have we seen anyone unusual in the area?*'

Dan shrugged. 'I don't know. We don't see anyone out here.'

'*Has anybody been here, to the hotel?*' asked Vincent.

'*No.*'

Then she remembered the blue car, turning in, after she'd been in the river, when she went to get her phone.

'*A car turned in, a few days ago. It was probably just lost.*'

'*What kind of car?*'

'*I don't know. It was blue.*'

He looked at his watch. '*What are your plans?*'

'*We're going to spend the night in Beaune, and then head off. Away.*'

'*Out of France?*'

'*Yes.*'

He pursed his lips, considering. '*It would be better if you stayed nearby. We'll need you to come into the gendarmerie on Monday.*'

'He wants us to stay,' Bea told Dan.

'How long for?'

'A few days, only,' said Vincent, in English.

'Can you take the money with you now?' she said.

He laughed. 'No.'

'We don't want it here.'

Dan went to get it and Bea and Vincent sat in silence. He was not as closely shaved as usual, and he was wearing trainers with his jeans, not loafers. He had come alone. She wondered if he had been going away for the weekend when they interrupted his plans, and realised what was different; there was no smell of aftershave. It was like he was missing an item of his uniform.

Dan came back in, carrying the red snake trap. He put it down on the coffee table where it sat, crude and ugly, with the smearing grime and the white lettering on the side. Seeing it, Vincent stood up, suspiciously. Dan undid the catches and took off the lid, revealing the money, shining like guts.

'*We really don't want it here,*' said Bea. '*Isn't it evidence, or something?*'

Vincent got to his feet. He stood over the table, looking down at it. He whistled.

'I know,' said Dan.

Vincent shook his head. '*I can't take it.*'

'*Why not?*' said Bea, then to Dan, 'He won't take it.'

'That's reasonable,' said Dan.

'*I need paperwork. I must follow procedure. This is serious. You don't understand. You think you know where this has come from, but there's more to it. I can't touch it.*'

'*Please?*'

'*Madame, I can't just take your money in my car.*'

'*But it's not ours.*'

He took out his phone and went over to the window, speaking rapidly in a quiet voice. He finished the call and turned back to the room. '*There's nothing to worry about. You might have to come back, to meet my colleagues. Is that acceptable?*'

'He wants us to come back tomorrow, and let someone in, to collect it.'

'We can do that.'

'OK.' She turned to Vincent. '*Yes, that's fine.*'

'*One of my team will call, very soon. OK?*' he said.

They showed him out. The clean smell of a clear night came in as she opened the door, and he stood on the steps with his keys, and the quiet dark behind him.

'When I asked my father why he searched Alex's car after the accident he lied to me. He probably lied to you, too. I want you to know that I am not loyal to my parents.'

'I understand,' he said, in English.

She did not want him to leave. She felt very close to him, his formality was comforting. She imagined him driving away from them, his car disappearing along the empty road, and she and Dan alone again, and unprotected. Her instinct longed for him to stay and she listened to her fear.

'Do you think we're in danger?' she asked.

He did not answer immediately. She thought of the elephant, and what she was allowed to know, and not know.

'Your brother's wallet and identity card were not taken. Or tampered with,' he said. 'There is no way of knowing if he gave away his address before that. But it's been a week now —' He shook his head. 'I'm sorry I have no answers for you. But I think it's better you are leaving, just in case.'

'It's all right,' she said. 'Have a good weekend.'

He shook Dan's hand, and then hers.

'We have a lot of information we are analysing. We won't give up.'

He got into his car, and they watched as he reversed, then turned his car towards the gate. Dan put his arms around her waist as he drove away.

'OK, let's get out of here,' he said.

They took the money upstairs and put it back up in the attic near the top of the ladder and bolted the trapdoor. Bea got their things and put them in the hall, and Dan went round the hotel, checking the windows and doors were locked. They tidied the kitchen together, throwing away the food in the fridge and wiping down the surfaces. They put the rubbish bags outside the side door.

Nobody from Vincent's team called. They both kept checking their phones. Bea found a small hotel in Beaune for them to spend the night. It was a little like Paligny, but in the town, by the medieval walls. The woman offered them a room on the first floor, or a bigger one in an annexe in the garden. Bea took the one in the main hotel. She didn't want to be isolated. She wanted people. She imagined a dining room, with busy waiters and the companionable voices of strangers.

She went upstairs to say goodbye to Alex's room, and heard Dan's voice in the hall.

'Bea! Let's go!'

She heard a car go by.

'Hold on,' she called.

She stood in the bedroom doorway. Her mother would strip it for keepsakes, fetishise and fawn over them. She wanted to take just one thing for herself, something he would want her to have. She switched on the bedside light, looking around the room, and questioning the air. The seconds passed, but she had no sense of his presence at all. She heard the growl of a car and saw headlights approaching, shining straight onto the hotel, then the scrunch of the gravel. Quickly, she turned off the bedside light and went to the window. She couldn't see Dan down there. The car stopped below her and the engine was switched off. The door opened and a man got out. She could see the top of his head, hair buzz-cut almost to the scalp, and balding. He looked up – and she dodged behind the curtain. She heard him walking to the door. She left the room just as the doorbell rang.

She didn't know where Dan was. She stood very still at the top of the stairs, waiting.

'HELLO?' called the man, American. 'Hel-lo?'

She didn't move. She heard Dan's voice, and talking, muffled, and then receding. She pulled her phone from her pocket but dropped it, thudding, onto the floor. Scrabbling to pick it up she heard footsteps coming into the hall. She gripped her phone, panic in her blood and brain, quick and slow, trying to listen, trying to think.

'Through here,' said Dan.

'Oh, great.'

She couldn't hide and leave Dan on his own. She went downstairs.

The stranger had his back to her, with one hand in his pocket and a large black backpack at his feet. He turned.

'Hi,' he said, and smiled.

He was in his late thirties, tanned and unshaven, with a high, bony forehead and a wide smile, as if his small teeth ran straight across his mouth. He wore a brown leather jacket and a red T-shirt with a faded symbol on the front.

'I have some stuff, but it's in the car,' he said.

She couldn't see Dan's face behind him.

'I'm Russ. Is Alex here?'

Bea's mind was blank.

'Are you a friend?' said Dan.

The man turned to look at him. 'Yeah, like I said. Is he around?'

'No,' said Dan.

'I booked a room. Russ Bannam?' He looked at Bea again. 'Was it you I spoke with, a while back, on the phone?'

Bea remembered. She had taken his name. At first she felt relief, but then she realized he'd called just after Alex died.

'Beatrice? You're Beatrice, right?'

'Look, we're not really open,' said Dan.

'You're not —?'

'The hotel isn't open,' said Dan. 'I'm sorry. Alex was in an accident. He died.'

'He died?' said the man. 'He's dead? What kind of an accident?'

'In his car.'

He frowned. He nodded, gazing into the middle distance. Then he looked at Bea directly. 'That's awful. My God. I am so sorry for your loss.'

'Thank you.'

'My God,' he said again.

'I shouldn't have taken your booking. It was just after it happened. I wasn't thinking.'

'Sure.'

He looked around the hall, and up the stairs, and ran his hand over his shaved head, back and forth, nodding slowly.

'Shit,' he said. 'Shit. I can't believe it.'

Neither Dan nor Bea spoke.

'Huh.' He rolled his head and stretched his neck. 'Could I get a drink?'

Neither of them answered. He looked from one to the other.

'I can get a drink, right? Is that OK?'

There was a pause. It felt impossible to refuse him.

'Sure,' said Dan. 'Come through.'

The man picked up his backpack and followed Dan into the sitting room.

Bea stayed exactly where she was. She found Vincent's number on her phone, and called it, staring at the shiny blue BMW through the window. The phone went to voicemail.

'*This is Beatrice. A man has come to the hotel. He says he knew Alex. His name is Russ Bannam.*'

Walking to the window she read out the number plate on the car, then hung up and went to join them.

29

They sat on the terrace at one of the hexagonal tables. Moths gathered around the three lamps on the back wall. Russ sat with his foot hitched up on his knee, his whisky glass resting in his palm.

'I'm not surprised this place isn't exactly *as advertised*. But it's a nice place, right? Kind of how I pictured it, give or take.'

'Alex never mentioned you,' said Dan.

'He didn't even mention my name? Russ? No?'

'No,' said Dan.

Russ looked at Bea.

'No,' she said.

'Huh,' he shrugged, and went back to his whisky.

'How did you know him?' asked Dan.

'We met in Paris, a few months back.'

'How?'

'Listen, can I get another drink?'

Dan pushed the bottle towards him.

'Thanks. Join me?'

'No, thanks. So how did you meet Alex?'

Russ rolled tobacco in Rizla paper, slipping the tight cigarette quickly in and out of his mouth.

'Some bar, near Bastille.' He pronounced the double L. 'You know Paris?' He lit his cigarette.

'What was he doing in Paris?' asked Dan.

'Hey, we were both pretty drunk. Anyway, he told me about this place, and he said I should come visit. He said it was pretty lonely, living out here, so I was kind of surprised when a woman answered the phone. But that was you, right?' He smiled at Bea, pleased to make the connection. 'Yeah – he said his sister was coming to stay.'

'Did he?'

'Let you in on a secret,' he said. 'I only made the booking because I thought Alex would want me to.'

'How do you mean?' said Dan.

'You know, to *make it look good* for Dad.' He winked. There was a hint of country in his voice, a South-Western twang.

'Did he say that?'

'Sure,' Russ laughed, showing his teeth in a wide grin. 'Alex isn't – I'm sorry – *wasn't* exactly the secretive type.' He stared into his drink. 'Listen, it's too bad.'

Bea and Dan exchanged a glance, but he looked up and caught them at it.

'Are you both on duty or something? I hate to drink alone.'

Again, refusing him seemed too big a statement, and a risk. Bea fetched glasses from the sideboard in the dining room. Dan poured whisky for himself and for her.

'There you go,' said Russ approvingly. He raised his glass. 'Cheers! Or whatever you guys say.'

Bea checked her phone. Everything about him seemed both natural and constructed, there was no trace of tension, no hint of anything but pleasantness. His unmixed friendliness was compelling, chivvying them, like cows into a pen, with only one direction to go.

'So, what are you doing in France?' asked Dan.

Russ talked and talked and said nothing. They were only sipping their whisky but drinking with him changed things. It turned them into his friends, credulous and weak.

'Listen, sometimes I hate the States,' he said, as if they'd asked. 'And I've lived all over. I was born in Minnesota, went to college on the East Coast, worked my way over to the West, and lived pretty much everywhere in between. I *like* Europe.' He said it generously. 'I *always* like coming to Europe. And I know some people in London, and I spent a little time there, but I guess it got tired, so –' he sighed the words out, a long-story-short – '*any*way, I've been on the move since Christmas, just taking it easy, meeting different people, travelling around. And Alex was one of those, you know, a guy I met one night. I *like* meeting new people when I travel.'

They watched him talk, rolling his cigarettes without looking, the tiny filter in his lips, either oblivious to being watched, or loving it. It was tempting to believe there was something innocuous about a person who could talk like that.

'I mean, this could be a hell of a nice place, couldn't it?' he said. 'I know Alex had all kinds of plans for it.'

'So,' said Dan abruptly, putting down his glass, 'where are you planning to stay tonight?'

Russ looked taken aback. 'I can't stay here?'

'I need to talk to Bea. Excuse us,' said Dan, and they both stood up. It didn't make a dent in his cheerfulness.

'Yeah, sure, go ahead,' he said.

They both went inside. They could see Russ through the window, lighting his roll-up and nodding his head, as if he was listening to music, or somebody talking.

'I called Vincent,' she said, not taking her eyes from him.

'Did he answer?'

'Voicemail.'

'Everything he's saying he could have got from Alex in one night,' said Dan.

'I know.'

They were both very calm and measured, each of them waiting for the other to say the unsayable.

'I'll call Vincent again,' said Bea.

'I'll tell this guy he has to go.'

'Maybe we should just leave him here?'

'No, I'll tell him.'

'Why?'

But Dan had gone back outside.

Bea went into the hall. Vincent's number didn't even ring, just two short beeps. She went through the calls on the tiny grey screen, trying to find the gendarmerie number. She heard a noise behind her. Russ was in the room.

'Hey! Do you have a speaker, or something like that?' He was ebullient, making it ridiculous to fear him. But still, she feared him.

'A speaker?'

Dan caught up behind.

'I'm going to go get mine from the car,' said Russ.

He went to the front door, quickly.

'Hold on!' he said. 'Just be a tick!'

He went out, leaving the door open.

'I told him,' said Dan. He laughed, not like a real laugh, panic. 'He wants us to hear some band. He says he'll go after that.'

'This is so mad,' said Bea.

'Yeah.'

'I don't know what to do.'

They heard the pip of the central lock as Russ opened his car. Dan looked outside.

'Nice car.'

'BMW.' Russ was rummaging inside.

'That's an M4,' said Dan. 'That's got to be sixty grand's worth of car.'

Russ looked over his shoulder at them, grinning, and held something up.

'Got it!'

He ran back in, flat-footed and clownish, opening his arms as if he were welcoming them. 'Listen, I feel bad I busted in on you like this. Seriously.'

'It's OK,' said Dan automatically, he didn't know why he said it, locked in by an unspoken rule, politeness, or the need for normality.

Russ was all performance, busying himself with his phone and the Bluetooth. It struck Bea that he was just the sort of person Alex would have liked. He could never see what was clear to her, that only very damaged people could perform like that. He looked up, and directly into her eyes, as if he were reading her mind.

'I am going to leave. I understand you're closing the place up and everything. And it's a bad time. I totally get it.'

Bea nodded.

'So let's have one more drink, OK?' he grinned. 'I have this band I recorded on my phone, when I was in Marseille? They're so cool, I mean it. They're from the south – not like the south of the States, the south of Europe – seriously, someplace like *Albania* or something, and they have *kind* of like a gypsy sound, but more like gypsy meets Hendrix meets like a nineties House vibe. Alex loved them.'

It was dizzying, impossible, to hear Alex's name.

'I really wanted to play it for him, because he saw them in Paris last year? And he was pissed I was going to see them, they don't have any quality live recordings. They're called Les Nine Idiots, or Neuf Diables, or some shit like that, and I swear Alex is going to –' He tripped over Alex's death like a body, then continued, more subdued. 'I swear Alex would have loved it.' He held up his phone and the speaker. 'I have it right here. Les Neuf Cercles, recorded live, man, gold dust. D'you have someplace I can plug this in? It's out of juice.'

'Sure,' said Dan. 'In here.'

He turned his back, and Russ followed him into the sitting room. Their voices shrank away, then Gypsy-Hendrix-House blasted out.

'Hey, Beatrice!' shouted Russ.

Her hands were shaking. She found the gendarmerie number. She looked back towards the front door. Their car keys were on the reception desk. The phone was answered immediately, and she asked for anyone on Vincent's team.

'*Try again tomorrow,*' said a voice, bored and faraway.

'*Please ask somebody from the SR to call me, it's urgent,*' she said.

'*If it's an emergency, call 112 or 17.*'

She hung up and went back outside. Dan and Russ were sitting again. The music screaming from the overloaded speaker on the sideboard.

'Scare those snakes away, Bea,' said Dan, drinking whisky with Russ.

She couldn't gauge him. They were being separated.

'What snakes?' said Russ. 'There are snakes?'

She sat down, tucking her skirt under her thighs.

'Snakes?' he said. He leaned forward and his scalp reflected the light, his eyes creased in the glare. 'So tell me.'

She had to raise her voice over the music.

'There are snakes here.'

'Bea woke up with one next to her, on a sunbed,' said Dan.

She looked at him quickly, trying to catch his eye.

'No kidding?' said Russ. 'Did you lose your shit? What did it do?'

'No. Nothing, it just looked at me.'

'I heard of a guy, woke up one time with a snake *in* his sleeping bag,' said Russ.

Bea got up. When she was behind Russ's head, gave Dan a look – a nod – then went inside to the speaker, and turned it off.

'You didn't like it?' said Russ.

'OK,' said Dan, beginning to stand up.

Russ didn't follow, and didn't stop talking, and Dan stayed in his seat.

'I love reptiles,' he said, as if there had been no interruption.

Bea stood, half in, half out of the house. He sloshed whisky in his glass and then in Dan's.

'I used to keep them when I was a kid. Yeah, I had those little, you know, what do you call them, terrapins, and for a while I kept a frog, but I really loved my snakes. I loved my fucking snakes, they were awesome. I know, right? *Paging Dr Freud!* my sister used to say. But oh, man, they're insane! They don't obey the rules *whatsoever*. The way they move, or reproduce – I mean, snakes have two dicks. Excuse me, I apologise, we just met, I know, but it's true. Come *on!* Two dicks, man!'

Dan laughed, a reflex, and Bea's hand tightened on her phone.

'Plus,' said Russ, 'you have no fucking idea what they're thinking. They freak *everyone* the fuck out. I used to take them into my sister's room and scare the crap out of her. I had heated tanks for them and shit, and you gotta feed them mice, right? Frozen mice.' He laughed, and reached for the bottle again.

'OK, it's time to go,' said Dan. He stood up and Russ's expression changed. It went as blank as a stone.

He looked from one to the other, the smile wiped from his face. There was a silence.

'OK,' he said.

Very slowly, he picked up his backpack. He put his tobacco and papers into the side pocket. He got up and turned towards the hotel. In silence, they followed him through the sitting room and into the hall. They were almost at the door. He stopped.

'Forgot my speaker,' he said.

He went back past them and they waited.

'Why don't you go into the kitchen?' said Dan quietly. 'I can handle this.'

He looked at her steadily. She felt the change in the air. It made her feel better and worse that he was ready to fight, both shielded and helpless, like holding a knife and fearing an axe. She shook her head. They heard Russ's footsteps and he came into the hall.

'Got it,' he said.

As he passed her she could smell him, and see the worn seams of his jacket, and the bristles on his head. Dan opened the door. With a sudden movement Russ threw back his arm and flung his backpack towards the car. It landed against the wheel. He rubbed both hands over his head. He flexed his neck with a small jerk of his head.

'Did I do something to piss you off?' he said quietly.

'It's just time to go, mate,' said Dan.

Bea held her phone up, letting him know she was ready. Russ was tall, but Dan was younger and fitter than he was.

'I don't know what you both *think* about me.'

Dan said nothing, holding the door open. Russ made a short, ironic sound.

'Hey. I get it.'

Dan nodded. Russ moved his head in Bea's direction.

'I guess I should apologise. And I'm sorry about Alex. He was a – he was a good guy. He was a friend of mine.'

Bea felt unaccountably guilty, as if he had pressed a button in her, marked *Sympathy*. He went out to his car. Dan waited for him to get into it, and until he had started the engine, before he closed the front door.

Neither of them moved. They didn't even look at one another. They heard the vibration of heavy bass inside the car, and watched through the glass as he reversed the BMW, idled for a moment, and drove out through the gates.

Bea's phone vibrated in her hand and the feeble screen glowed. It was Capitaine Vincent. He had just come out of the cinema.

They met a Detective Jean Clement, at the gendarmerie. It was shut for the night. The buildings were silent, and the parade square was invisible, hidden in the dark. The two soldiers on the gate looked tired beneath the bright white security lights. The glass-walled reception was a luminous box, floating in space, with a solitary officer at the desk inside. Detective Clement took them through the powered-down metal detector, across the square, up into the office, where he switched on all the lights, and took down Russ's description. They had coffee.

Clement was scruffy and polite, wearing a gun in a shoulder holster and wrinkled jeans. They hadn't met him before. They liked him more than either Dufour or Luis. He asked after her father.

'It's a tragedy,' he said. 'I'm sorry about your brother. The English newspapers telephoned here.' He sounded incredulous at the idea of journalists pursuing information from the police, and didn't say anything else about it.

They left the gendarmerie after midnight and said goodbye to Clement on the pavement.

'OK, take care, yeah?' he said, in English, as he walked away.

Bea shivered with cold and lonely fear as she fumbled with the keys to open the car again.

'Here, let me,' said Dan, taking the keys. 'Nearly there.'

They had to ring the doorbell at the hotel. Inside, the owner took their names, tapping them into her computer with long varnished nails. There was an overweight little dog with ears like small wings, staring at them from the stairs, and leaflets on a table and fans and birdcages in corners by tiny polished tables. The hotelier had blonde hair with the dark roots showing.

'May I show you to your room?' she said. 'If you want something just ask, there's always someone here.'

They could hear laughing and talking from behind closed doors.

'My brother-in-law's birthday. We're having a party,' she said. She smelled of cigarettes and perfume.

Their bags almost filled the floor of the room. There were flowers, everywhere; on the wallpaper, the bedspread, in small oval paintings and on the corners of the towels. And a bunch of miniature fabric roses in a china vase.

They got onto the bed, on top of the bedspread, staring straight ahead and numb. They didn't even shower, they just crawled onto the strange, deep bed together, and slept.

30

The next morning they sat in the dining room and had croissants, coffee and fruit. It was just as she'd imagined. There
were strangers at the other tables, sunshine coming in through
the windows, and the young girl helping was friendly, with a
clean white apron. The tiny dog wandered about between the
tables looking for crumbs and at the reception desk a couple
with a baby were checking in. The baby, ignored in a car seat at
their feet, gazed with myopic wonder at the chair leg and her
mother's jeans.

'Let's go and look at the town,' said Dan.

They locked their room, and walked beneath the medieval
arch into the centre. They took leaflets from the display in the
hotel, then forgot them in the first cafe they went to. Bea had
an ice cream. They shared it on a bench in the courtyard of
the Hospice de Beaune. It was a suntrap. The ice cream melted
down her hand while they looked at the multicoloured patterns
in the tiles of the roof. They both licked ice cream from her
fingers and wrists and Dan dabbed at her with a paper napkin,
squashed into a tiny ball.

'Messy girl,' he said.

Detective Dufour rang to update them. The permission to seize the money would come through from the *juge* very shortly. Once the paperwork was in order they would collect it as soon as possible.

'*We'll see you at Paligny at four o'clock,*' he said.

Bea thanked him and hung up. 'We're meeting Du*four* at *four*,' she told Dan.

'He's the knob,' said Dan.

'The racist knob?' said Bea. 'The other one was a knob, too.'

'The hairy one?'

'He perved on me.'

'Cops the world over,' said Dan. 'Pervy racist knobs.'

'Look at us, police interview veterans. We're so street.'

They walked to the Basilique Notre-Dame de Beaune.

'I've seen better,' said Dan. 'But not in real life.'

There was nobody there but them. It was very quiet, and they felt quieter too, now they were inside. They let their eyes rest on the arches and carvings, and looked at the stories in the stained glass without trying to decipher them.

Bea went to an altar by a side table, and Dan walked around the perimeter. She put a two-euro coin in the box, and lit a candle for Alex. Pain shouldn't define his life and death. It wasn't fair it would be his memorial. Murder. And a garden full of people thinking about his trust fund. She stared into the small flame until it seemed almost solid, and was the only thing she could see. He wasn't marked for a violent end. And he had been a baby once.

She closed her eyes and determinedly tried to build a good, real picture of him, but the bad things crowded it out. The smashed car, imagined blood, her mother touching him. Bea opposed them carefully. *His wit*, her memory answered, *cleverness*. But the good things were feeble. *Addiction*, her grief fought back, *loneliness*. She kept her eyes closed, and kept her focus on bringing him to mind. She forgot the fight. A sense of him came to her. She felt the intangible sweetness, unworldly and untouched, that was his soul. The rest was just covering. She didn't open her eyes until there was only that, like sunlight, filling her head, nothing else.

Dan finished walking around the church and came back to her side. He had become used to seeing her battling, and pinkness creeping up her neck, as she fought with herself. He had grown accustomed to a sharp look in her, switching languages, managing grief, managing him. Now, as she opened her eyes, she smiled.

'Better?' he said.

'Yes.'

'Come see this —'

He led her round the church.

'Dan, I've been thinking,' said Bea. 'I've been doing this all wrong.'

'All what?'

'My life. Money.'

'How?'

'I've been running away.'

'From what?'

'That money at Paligny is nothing.'

'Bea, it isn't *nothing*.'

'To people like my father it's nothing. The big money is just beamed around the world, like light. It's only us normal people paying our taxes and wondering why there aren't any hospital beds.'

'Yeah, I *know* –'

'Except I'm not normal, Dan. I am *people like him*, I have that money. Real money. You know how you said, when my father dies, I'll have millions.'

'I'm sorry.'

'No, you're right.'

'He won't be feeling so generous now, will he?'

'He'll be angry. He might get investigated. He won't be ruined. He won't cut me out of his will.'

It was strange to be talking like that in church, but it didn't feel wrong. It wasn't she who was greedy. She hadn't done anything bad.

'Anyway, I'm not sure he can break my trust. The money is mine, he's always said so.'

'And?'

'I want to act like it's mine. I want to do good with it.'

'What do you mean?'

Two people came into the church behind them. She took a step closer, to whisper.

'I want to keep doing my job, obviously. I love it. But I've realised. I can help.'

'Charity?'

'I don't know yet. But it's not a curse. It's a privilege.'

He looked into her eyes. 'That's what I keep telling you.'

They walked outside, and back towards the town and car.

'Have you got the ticket thing?' he asked.

'Yes.'

'D'you want anything else, before we go?'

'No.'

He took her face in his hands and kissed her, gently, on the mouth. The kiss was short, and very light, but behind it there was hunger. She felt precious beneath his hands, as if she were made of pure gold. She pulled away.

'We'll be late,' she said.

There was no police car outside the hotel when they got to Paligny at ten to four. They sat down on the steps to wait.

'Remember when Alex wasn't in, when we got here?' said Bea.

'Can't believe it was two weeks ago.'

'Two weeks exactly.'

'Where's Dufour?' said Dan, swinging the car keys on his finger and looking at the empty gates.

'I hope he's not going to be Dufive.'

It was hot and birds were singing.

'Even if Russ Bannam was a friend of Alex's, he was still weird,' said Dan. 'Where did he get that car?'

'Alex had a lot of rich friends.'

'He didn't look rich. I didn't believe a word that came out of his mouth, did you?'

'No.'

They heard an engine, but the car passed by quickly, in a flash of yellow.

'Shall we leave tomorrow?' said Dan. 'If they'll let us.'

'Spain?'

'Yeah.'

She looked at the empty driveway and the tall trees above them. She wanted structure. She wanted work, and to face the reality of herself, and the two of them.

'Or we could just go home,' she said.

'Home? D'you want to?'

'I don't know. I don't know what we should do,' she said. 'I don't get any of it. I wish none of it had ever happened.

I wish Alex was alive. I wish we could go back to how we were.'

'Except how we were before wasn't real,' said Dan.

'I know you think that. But it was real to *me*.'

'It wasn't honest.'

'Do you think I haven't been honest with you?'

'You didn't tell me the whole truth.'

'There isn't a whole truth.'

He looked away. 'OK,' he said.

'I'm going up to Alex's room for a minute,' she said.

'Do you want me to come with you?'

'No. I want to be on my own.'

She let herself into the hotel and closed the door behind her.

The vines over the door at the back had grown over the glass. She looked at the keys hanging silently on the varnished board. Hubris. Greed. Lust. Envy. Gluttony. Wrath. Sloth. She went up the stairs. The door to Alex's bedroom was ajar. She looked all around, at the bed, and shelves, the wardrobe, and his guitar still leaning against the wall. She thrummed the strings, just to hear them in the quiet. It was easy this time. She went straight to the desk and picked up the Simone Weil anthology.

'I'll take this, if that's OK,' she said to the room.

She opened it, anywhere, flicking through pages. Circled and underlined, she read:

'*If someone does me injury I must desire that this injury shall not degrade me. I must desire this out of love for him who inflicts it, in order that he may not really have done evil.*'

Alex had circled it three times, in different pens. He had added '*S*' onto '*he*', and '*her*', diagonally, over '*him*'. In the margin he had written, vertically —

'*I must desire this injury shall not degrade me. I must desire this out of love for <u>her</u>, in order that <u>she</u> may <u>not</u> really have done <u>evil</u>.*'

Green ink, blue and black. Like all his different imaginary hotel visitors, as if each of them were himself, returning, in a different skin. His life had been an extended struggle to absolve his mother. He hadn't managed anything else, only that good fight. He had conceived of forgiving his abuser. It was cruel it was always left to the victims to be the bigger person, the better person, and no real punishment for the ones who hurt them, who carried on unchanged and unpunished. His pain was nothing to his mother, she made it her pain. She took everything from him, even his death. And he had forgiven her. To love the person who had broken you. That was brave. Then she thought Alex couldn't help but love Liv. Maybe he had tried, but couldn't, because she was his mother.

She could not find it in herself to forgive, but Alex had. She, who prided herself on her truth and honesty, had kept her truths and hatred secret. She took the letter from her pocket. She did not intend to send it to Liv, to whom everything was fuel. But she should tell Dan. He had to know. She was frightened he wouldn't love her, if he knew the sickness she lived with, but she was a coward. He should know. The latch on the sash window stuck, and she bruised her thumb, pushing at it, but at last it gave. She dropped the folded letter, holding it out, so it wouldn't get caught in the vines. Then she took the snakeskin, gently, from the wall.

Outside, Dan checked his phone; five past four. He got up and stretched, and walked down the driveway towards the gate, slowly, vaguely, waiting, as his mind wandered. The sun was very hot, the day was still. Bea didn't trust him. He didn't think just going home would solve it. It would be better to be separate from everything they knew. The two of them, away from family, and grief, just themselves, in emptiness. She wasn't like herself. There was need in her now, and fear. She hadn't been like that before. He had done it to her, as much as Alex dying.

The afternoon was at peace. The trees lived. He was beginning to grow accustomed to the many greens and blues and browns. The sounds and silences of it were only as oppressive or as restful as he felt looking at them. It wasn't a good place or a bad place, it was just a place. He thought of home. He pictured their little flat in Holloway; the sofa, and each of the four mismatched wooden chairs at the pine table. In his mind's eye, he saw their bedroom, and the laundry basket, spilling clothes; their bed as they left it every morning, with the imprints of the way they had slept, like a map of their night together. He felt a longing for the grey city comfort of the lives they had run away from. They had been doing all right. They didn't need to travel for months. They could go home if she wanted. The Cushion was plenty for two or three weeks, and some left over, while he found himself a job. She didn't want to call Arun, and get involved with bank transfers and sums, and nor did he. They weren't lost. They just needed a holiday. Holiday. The word had felt so conventional and so restrictive. Now it sang with pleasure and fun. He stopped going towards the gate and the empty road. His body felt light and easy. It was a perfect idea. He had to tell Bea. They could work on everything else. It was simpler than they thought. He wondered if she really meant it, about using all her money for good. He couldn't tell if it would be too big a change for her. He didn't want her to be changed. He began to turn back towards the hotel. Then he heard a car, and paused. He checked his phone. Almost quarter past four.

The sound of the car got louder, and then it came through the gates towards him. For a second he stared at it, thinking slowly that maybe he had it wrong, and it wasn't the same bright blue BMW, but it got closer, and he saw Russ behind the wheel, and he knew that Russ had seen him.

'BEA!' he shouted, over his shoulder.

He started for the hotel. He couldn't see her at the window. He didn't know if she'd heard. The car was crawling behind him, slowly, and he turned to face it. He didn't want to shout for her again, or look like he was panicking. He reached for his phone. Russ was looking through the windscreen at him. But then he stopped, and reversed, slowly, out again, and went. Dan couldn't see the car. He hesitated, undecided, and looked behind, towards the first-floor window, then back again, to the empty gateway.

He walked towards the gate. As he walked, he rang Bea, but it cut off. Two beeps, and off. He dialled again. He reached the road. There were bushes and nettles at eye level, swelling from the hedge, and he couldn't see around them. He took a tentative step, trying to look. Dufour would come from that direction. He kept expecting to see the police car. He thought he heard it. They were on their way. He looked round the bulge of green, and saw one headlight and a corner of gleaming blue. He straightened up and squared his shoulders. He made his walk purposeful and aggressive, and stepped out. The BMW was tucked in on the other side of the recycling bins.

'Hey! What are you doing here?' he said.

The car was empty. There was a slowing of every moving thing around him, and every detail came into focus. It felt like a very long time; the moment between seeing the car had nobody inside, and hearing the sound behind him. In the slowness, he saw the brightness of the day, amplified and sharp. The sunlight throbbed. He felt the warm air on his skin, and wished with every part of himself that he could go back. He wanted not to have walked out of the gate, and not to have looked for the car. He should have gone back. He needed to warn Bea. He was afraid. The moment ended. He glimpsed movement in the corner of his eye and sensed the rush of air behind him, and in a hair's breadth of that broken second, felt dreadful sadness.

Her phone rang. It was Dufour. She turned and paced the room as they talked. He said he was on his way, and apologised. She thought she heard Dan call her name, and picked up the book and snakeskin. Dufour was telling her he'd have at least one other man with him. He was talking about the paperwork for the money, and saying they had passed Russ Bannam's description to the Police Nationale. The line beeped over his voice.

'*What did you say?*' she asked Dufour.

She finished the call, put the phone on the ledge, and looked down from the window. She couldn't see Dan, just the empty driveway, and the Golf, parked below. She leaned out. She saw the folded letter, on the ground. Her phone rang again, jumping on the painted sill. It fell, and lay crooked on the floor. Griff. She picked it up – rejected the call and saw she'd missed Dan.

She went down to the hall, holding Alex's book, and letting the snakeskin flutter, looking at it. The front door was open a few inches. Dan wasn't there. He wasn't in the car. The letter lay on the gravel. She looked out, down the drive.

'Dan?'

She stood on the steps in the sun, wondering where he could be, then went back inside. She heard a car start up, out on the road, but when she turned, saw nothing.

'Dan!'

She left the door open and the book and snakeskin on the desk, and went through to look out into the garden. She rang him. She couldn't hear ringing. She should have been able to hear it, if he was nearby. She tried again, holding her phone against her leg, to muffle it, but there was only silence. The sun was beating into the dining room through the closed window. There were dead flies on the floor.

'Dan?' she said to his voicemail. 'Where are you?'

She reached up to struggle with the stiff bolts on the garden door, bending, with her back to the room, not knowing why she felt such urgency. The door opened, and she went out into the garden and called again, her voice strange in the quiet.

The garden lay in the heavy heat, the birds were resting or had gone. The chestnut garden furniture looked sticky in the sun. Bea felt the silence thicken around her, and, in the silence, danger. It pressed and quivered. She looked behind her.

'Dan!' she called, but quietly.

She sensed somebody who wasn't Dan had heard. She went back into the house. Russ was standing in the hall. The front door was wide open. He had a grey T-shirt with a big shape on the front, like a dark sun. He was carrying a tyre iron. It was long, and had a blue curved handle. He looked taller.

'Hey,' he said, smiling, as if they were friends. 'Car broke down.'

They stood looking at one another. He waited for her to speak. The only difference from the night before was a certain hurry in him, a slight sweat. He was just a little out of breath.

'Really?' she said, her own voice distant in her ear. 'Where's Dan?'

'Could I use your phone?'

Her eyes flickered, trying to take in the periphery. They were alone. He was nearer the desk than she was.

'Sure. It's there. On the desk.'

'No,' said Russ. 'I mean *your* phone.'

Her heart began to race, unevenly, as if it were starting up; it hurt her chest.

'Why do you need mine?'

He could see her phone in her hand. It was too late to put it behind her back.

'Use that one,' she said, the breath in her voice making it small. 'The one on the desk? It's better.'

Her mouth around the words was clumsy, like a foreign language, like being anaesthetised.

He smiled again. 'Nah, I'd like to use yours.'

He started towards her. If she ran, it would be the end. She held her phone out to him, trying not to flinch when his fingers touched her palm. He took it.

'See?' he said.

He was closer. The tyre iron loose in his right hand.

'Where's Dan?'

She looked from his face to his chest. The shape on his T-shirt was shining. She had thought it was a design, but it wasn't. It was wet. She knew what it was.

'Will you come with me?' said Russ, relaxed, as though they were both in on something.

She looked back to his face. There was only his face, nothing else around it, just him.

'No. I'm waiting here, for the police.'

'They coming here?'

'They'll be here in a minute. They're coming now. Where's Dan?'

She looked at the open door. She saw her car. Dan had the keys in his pocket. There was another one in the glove compartment. But the glove compartment was locked, with the small key on Dan's key ring, in his pocket.

'Where is he?'

'Where's the money Alex told me about?' said Russ.

'In the attic.'

'Yeah?' He said it as if she'd lie about it.

'It's up in the attic. You can have it.'

Russ sighed. 'Shit. We'd better be quick.'

He turned off her phone and put it in his pocket, taking his eyes off her for a second, but not long enough.

'What about your car?' she said.

'What?'

'You said it broke down.'

He sort of laughed. 'Yeah,' he said, like she was stupid.

'You first.' He gestured, gentlemanly, towards the stairs.

She couldn't move.

'No.' Her voice was weak. 'Where's Dan?'

'C'mon. Let's go.'

She shook her head. 'You go up,' she said. 'I'll tell you where it is.'

He suddenly jumped at her, arms out, the tyre iron flying up towards her head. She ducked and yelped. He stepped back again, smiling. Her eyes were hot with tears, she felt urine, leaking from her. There wasn't very much of it. He wouldn't know.

He hadn't touched her. She closed her mouth and breathed through her nose.

'All right. I'll take you up and show you,' she said. 'Then tell me where Dan is.'

'OK, sure,' he said.

He kicked the front door closed. She waited for the sound of the police car turning into the driveway. They'd see his car, she thought. Russ ran the tyre iron along the banisters as they went up. They passed the bedroom doors.

'I've got to say,' he said, like a tourist, 'it's not much of a hotel. I mean, what the fuck? It's not like he described at all. When I came the first time, I thought I had the wrong place.'

She pointed to the trapdoor, and the ladder.

'Up there,' she said.

'There? I didn't even see that. I've been looking in the basement. And all over. You didn't know I've been in and out of this place, did you? Couldn't find a fucking thing.' He tested the ladder against the wall, keeping an eye on her. 'You sure it's up there?'

She nodded.

'The money Alex told me about?' he said. 'You know about the money?'

She nodded again. 'Yes, it's there.'

'You get it.'

She didn't move because her body wouldn't obey, but he thought she was waiting, and he stepped back to give her space. She climbed the ladder as he watched. Her skirt swung out, she was scared he was looking.

'What's up there?' he said.

She unbolted the trapdoor. The trap was right there, resting on the joists. He didn't know that. She climbed up into the roof on hands and knees. It felt like escaping, just to be up there, that it would be possible to get free now. Her fear went, and she felt quick, and sharp. She looked down at him, staring up from the corridor, naked skin and eyes, the tender skull beneath his hair. She moved sideways, out of his eye line, into the dark.

'What are you doing?'

She looked around, in the airless heat. No windows, no gaps or holes, no roof light or access panel, no chimney, no way of getting out.

'You got it?' he said.

'Yes.'

'What are you doing?'

She looked for a weapon, but there was nothing. Forensically, she remembered the empty, weightless snake traps, the rubbish bags, carpet, nothing. No fire extinguisher. No tools. Nothing.

'Come on!'

'One second.'

He was just below but he couldn't see her. She was still on her own. She felt a sort of bliss.

'I'm coming up,' he said.

'No. It's here.'

She picked up the money in its box. It was heavy. She held it above the open hatch to show him. His vulnerable face looked up at her. She could throw it at his head. She could throw it hard down onto his face. But she couldn't find it in herself to do it. He hadn't hurt her. She didn't dare to start a fight with him. She imagined him holding up his hands to protect himself, as it glanced off, and then the impossibility of being quick enough, or wounding him badly enough, to save herself. She handed it to him. She was giving him what he wanted.

'Jesus, it's heavy,' he said, halfway up the ladder.

His bony hands reached in. He took it. The second he was clear she closed the trapdoor and knelt on it. She heard him below her.

'Hey –'

'You can go now. The police are coming.'

Kneeling, she pushed it down as if she could make herself heavier. There wasn't a bolt on the inside. She reached over her head and braced her arms against the slanting beam above her. The only light was from the small gash in the plasterboard, where Alex said he'd put his foot.

She waited. She heard the clicks of the catches on the snake trap. She listened, in the heat, straining her ears over the viscous silence. She heard an engine on the road. But it faded. Then his fist thumped the trapdoor, two loud bangs, shaking the wood, like a child's game. She braced herself against the rafter.

'I won't tell anyone,' she said.

The ladder squeaked, the trapdoor heaved. She heard him grunt. Light came in around the hatch. She was lifted, tilting, and she flung herself off, squashing herself between the joists, splinters and dry rough wood. He grabbed her ankle and she pulled away, but then he was up there with her. He grabbed her arm. She pulled. More strength than she knew she had. She felt his nails break her skin. She thought he'd rip her bicep from the bone. He had another hand on her. He grabbed her hair. He gripped her neck. She clawed, swiping at the empty air. Suddenly he stopped, and let her go. She fell and pressed herself down between the joists.

'Get up,' he said.

He bent over her. He had to dig and wriggle and force his hands underneath her body. He couldn't get a grip. Her skirt tore at the waist, buttons ripped. She gripped the joists with raw fingers, eyes screwed shut, but he got her by the leg and lifted. Her hip was wrenched and the terror of her legs opening wide in front of him made her struggle. Once she was fighting, he could bend her. He flipped her over and grabbed her shoulders. She tried to kick. She could knock him down with a hard kick to his groin, she could fell him, he'd be breathless. She could cause him pain and wound him. She kicked, hard, wildly, but he got down with her and knelt on her and she couldn't get her hands to his face.

He was calm. He had a good hold of her now. He hoisted her up. Unbalanced by her writhing, he staggered in the dark. At the open trapdoor, without bending, he dropped her from a height, head first to the floor below. She fell haphazardly, like a corpse, on her shoulder and her head. Blind and bright, the pain struck. She couldn't breathe. The floor was nothing, nor the air. She seemed to float. Then he was standing over her.

'What are you doing?' he said.

He bent down, took her by the top of her arm, backed off a little, and punched her. She felt his knuckles split her mouth. He held her up by the wrist. The agony of hanging from her shoulder spread. He punched her again, and that punch was black and distant, brief and soft. She couldn't see. He dropped her. Her vision cleared. She saw a flash of red as he picked up the plastic box, in and out of focus. She didn't see it hit her, she heard breaking, tasted metal. Her mouth wasn't like her mouth, but pulpy, floating. He picked her up by the arm she had fallen on. With one eye she saw his boots, and blood falling on them, glossy and dark, like dripping marbles, one after the other, perfect circles, flattening as they fell.

'Jesus,' he said. He didn't sound angry. 'We need to move.'

He dragged her along the corridor, down the stairs, and she saw the banisters go by like watching a film.

'Walk,' he said.

Her feet couldn't find the stairs. Her shoulder was out of the socket, like a chicken leg from the joint. He reached the hall, and hoisted her up alongside him, round the waist, as though he were saving her, and dragged her backwards to the kitchen door, clumsily, the tyre iron in his fist across her face. Through her hair, she saw the front door at an angle, and a sliver, bloodied, of daylight and the driveway through the window. Sky. A car. The bonnet of a white car. A white car. She saw it, but before there was time, before any time at all, he pulled her backwards through the fire door, and she saw it close. His breath rasped. Past the empty counters, no knives, no boards, no metal pans, just wiped down surfaces she and Dan had tidied, all going away from her, and her own legs dragging on the ground. The annexe. The fridges.

He whispered, 'Wait.'

He wrapped his arm round her head and face. She hung in the sweat-muscle vice of his arm. She heard him turn the key, the door. She writhed. She heard the doorbell ring, loud and long. He closed his hand around her neck. Her eyeballs swelled. Her veins, constricted, burned. Then she fell, gently as a leaf, down, drifting, in enormous space. And quietness. She had no sense of herself, no thoughts at all. Then light burst onto her, and pain came back. They were outside. He was dragging her across the ground. The world was like a broken mirror, smell and taste and splintered vision, seeing pain, breathing bubbling blood between her nose and throat.

Her feet were on grass and stones, tangling in weeds. Her arm, flailing, grasped live twigs, tore a leaf. Very clearly, in a

417

second that was a normal second, she realised they were just a few feet from the drive. She saw the nettles and brambles. She saw the white police car, the clean sight of it through the gaps, like zebra stripes.

Unbalanced, Russ tripped, and his hand slipped from her mouth. She screamed on the in-breath, and sank her teeth into his wrist. He threw her down, backwards, and himself on top, tyre iron and snake trap falling with them, and as her head hit the ground, clamped his hand across her mouth and nose. His chest pressed stickily to her cheek. His breast-bone and ribs were hard. It felt like an axe cutting into her shoulder. She couldn't breathe. She tried to move her head. She couldn't move. No air. And then she heard men's voices. Russ's body grew very soft, heavier, burying her. She writhed beneath the weight. She fought. Barely shifting, still blocking her mouth and nose, he hit her. No smacking sound to draw attention, just the heel of his hand on her soft temple, heavy as a punch, dazzling. Darkness, like an inky wave, swelled, fell back, then swelled again. She was under-water, deep, deep, in a soundless night-time sea. No air. No air at all. The sea fell back. His chest was a dead weight. Reliably, her ribs heaved, but there was nothing to draw in. Her lungs burned. She heard footsteps – boots on gravel. Her eyes opened. She hadn't known they were closed. All she could see was Russ. An inch away, blue tooth marks filled with dark red blood. She saw each bristle in each pore; the flakes on his lips, the tiny lines. A drop of sweat fell from his face into the corner of her eye. She couldn't breathe. Her vision fluttered and feathered and blurred. Then footsteps, and the slam of a car door.

'Monsieur? Madame?'

She recognised Dufour. They weren't coming nearer, they were walking away. Still, no air. No air. The sound of walking, unhurried conversation.

'Monsieur Durrant? Madame?' Not Dufour. Another man, distant.

His hand moved from her face. Pure air. Just air. Breathing. Breathing. Light. Alive. She was lying on the steady ground. She was breathing. She rolled, but felt his hands on her again. He pulled her up. He dragged her along the path. She tried to use her feet against the pulling, but had no strength. She heard a shout, but she couldn't hear the words. It sounded small. Too far away. His hand pulled back her head.

'See?' he whispered. 'Cool car.'

The BMW was in front of her, the back of it, wedged into the narrow path. He dragged her through grass and bushes, along the side of it. She heard a car horn behind them, beeping twice. But no more voices. She was too far to hear their voices. He had to drop the snake trap to get the key from his pocket. He only had one hand on her. He pulled the door open, squashing branches. Still holding her, he put the trap and the tyre iron into the back, and toppling, they fell into the driver's seat together. Getting up on his knees, he threw her across the front of the car, not onto the passenger seat, just mindlessly, on her back, her head hitting the dashboard, limbs chaotic, not fitting. He was in the driver's seat. He slammed the door and he started the car.

They bumped from the lay-by to the tarmac. They were on the road. They were pulling away. She couldn't right herself. She couldn't move, lying half on the seat and half in the foot-well. Like troops falling-back, the no man's land of her body was abandoned, and she withdrew from it. From far inside the flesh cage of herself, she looked out, a small, live thing, peering through bars. He drove. And even when she was able to move, she didn't. She waited for her spark to grow brighter. *The only way into truth is through one's own annihilation.* She did not want to die, she would not be annihilated.

31

Bea took an inventory of her injuries. Her right shoulder was hanging; she couldn't move the arm and the three middle fingers of the hand were numb. That pain had masked the others before, but now she checked herself from feet to head. She had a twisted ankle. A lot of pain there. Blood and bruises on her legs. Her chest hurt from being crushed, but not sharp pain, she didn't think her ribs were broken. Both her breasts hurt a lot, and she couldn't work out why, until she realised they were bruised too. Her left arm was fine, apart from shallow holes where his fingers had dug into her and torn the skin in shreds. It hurt to swallow. Her mouth was split and swollen, and the drying blood burned, and felt like ripping when she parted her lips. Her teeth had cut into her gum inside. One tooth was broken. The roots hurt, and her jaw and face, into the deep bruising. Her cheekbone throbbed, tender, like it had no skin, and her left eye hurt to move it. It could see, but blurrily. They weren't on the autoroute, they were on small roads. Her head ached badly, much worse on the right side, ebbing and flowing when the car bumped, and she was nauseous. Her stomach was a rising ball of acid. She was scared of vomiting, and breathed, carefully, and swallowed. Very slowly, not to get his attention, she reached up and felt the back of her head with her fingertips. No blood.

'Do they know this car?' said Russ. 'Do they know it?'

She didn't answer, she wasn't sure she could speak.

'I'm pretty sure it stands out,' he said.

He turned off that road and onto another, and her shoulder seemed to scream as the car leaned. Then he turned again.

'No problem,' she heard him say, through waves of pain. 'We're good.'

She was injured enough to be protected from him. The pain was a world of its own, it gave her distance. Quietly, she went through the parts of her body that did not hurt. Her abdomen felt fine. Her right eye was clear. Her nose didn't hurt at all, and both ears were as undetectable as they had ever been. Not quite true. One burned a little, at the top. She welcomed it, letting her know it was there, but nothing serious. Comforted, she went back through her body again, piece by careful piece. It was familiar. It was her friend.

Consciousness brought perspective. She began to watch Russ as he drove. She kept herself very, very still and tried to read his mind. She knew how she looked; not like herself, crumpled in the footwell with her clothes ripped, like an ultra-violent fantasy. But she was not that. She wasn't his. Modesty was shame made palatable. She had a quick memory of how she'd covered her breasts when the boy spied on her at the river; she saw the sunlight on the ice-cold water and his strange eyes, and imagined instead that she had stood up and walked out, instead of hiding. She was her own. She was her secret mind that nobody saw, her work and the things she loved. She concentrated on the precious places inside herself, untouched, and only hers. She focused on her body's future and pictured herself well and strong. She would be. She was the mother of babies yet conceived. But thinking that cut her open, not knowing where Dan was, and awful terror for him. She mustn't cry or show what she felt. She had to keep herself secret. She concentrated on her pain, and then on forgetting the pain, and then the pain again. First things first, she thought. First things first.

She remembered seeing Russ in the hall, and being up in the roof space, but after that, her memory was faulty, like a film with pieces missing, jumping. She remembered Dufour's voice, from behind the trees. The police had Russ's registration. But they hadn't seen his car. If they had, Dufour would have sounded urgent. She didn't know how hidden the BMW had been, if the police could have just gone by it, as they turned into the hotel, and not seen it. There was a chance they were being followed. But he wasn't driving as if they were. She didn't know if she was clear enough in her mind to be aware of how long they had been driving. Maybe an hour. Maybe two. There was a chance nobody knew anything, and she was completely alone. First things first, she thought.

Through the tinted windows signs flashed by. She tried to read the place names but she couldn't. They were driving south and east, the sun swung from the right of the car to behind, but never in front. The air conditioning was cool and the car was quiet, and muted, like a hospital room.

From her place on the floor, she examined him, driving fast but not recklessly. He seemed rational. He didn't act in rage, even when he was violent. He seemed to operate within a narrow margin, from enthusiasm to irritation; the variations in his moods were small. From last night, until now, from punching her to rolling cigarettes, he seemed dissociated from the world. It was how he had seemed so harmless, he didn't see the difference in himself, everything was normal.

'I'm going to get onto the seat,' she said.

'What did you say?'

Her voice was scratchy and unclear. 'I'm going to get onto the seat.'

'Go ahead.'

Inch by inch, testing him and herself, she moved, forcing herself not to make any noise when her right arm shifted. She tried to hold it still with her other hand. He put the radio on as she eased herself upright. She shifted her position, and he changed stations, jumping through disjointed songs.

'I haven't set the system up yet,' he said. 'New car.'

She was sitting now, facing front. It felt better to be sitting. She wasn't sure how much fear she felt. Her mind was taking care of her. First things first, she thought again, repeating it. First things first.

'All good?' he said.

'Thirsty.'

He handed her a small bottle of Vittel, swimming-pool blue. The red top was still sealed, so he couldn't have drugged it. Like he must have drugged Alex. She blocked out the thought. She took the bottle. Her lips hurt against the plastic rim. She drank it all.

'Just throw it in the back when you're done,' he said. 'I'm not one of those assholes obsessed with keeping a clean car. I mean, whatever, right? I won't smoke in the car, though. I'd smoke in my old car, but not in this car.'

She wondered if it was more dangerous to talk to him or not to talk to him, whether forming a relationship was good or bad. Her instinct said it made no difference. He was impervious. But maybe she should keep him comfortable in his version of things.

'What was your old car?' she asked.

'Peugeot.'

'We had a Peugeot.'

'Oh yeah?' he said. 'Mine was shit.'

'So was ours.'

As clearly as the day they'd bought it she remembered standing on the pavement, in Tottenham, with Dan, as the guy fetched the keys from his flat, and how Dan had been so stubborn. She'd given in to him as if he knew something about cars. *It's kind of cool,* he'd said. *I like it.*

'Where's Dan?' she said. 'Tell me.'

There was no answer. She realised her eyes were closed. She made herself open them. Russ was smiling, but not at her. She wasn't sure now if she'd asked out loud, or how long ago. She shut her eyes again to keep from crying. The one he'd punched felt like a fist grinding into the socket. He was talking again. His voice came in and out like a broken signal.

'You like this car?' he was saying. 'This is the shit. Got it a couple of weeks ago. In Switzerland.'

He looked across and smiled, knowingly.

'I paid cash,' he said. 'In Switzerland?'

He wanted her to be curious and ask him about Alex. She wouldn't. She didn't need to know. She didn't want to be the one to invite him to relive it. She wouldn't give him that. She looked out of the window.

'So guess how much I paid,' he said. 'Guess.'

'I don't know,' said Bea.

'C'mon, guess.'

That's got to be sixty grand's worth of car, Dan had said, looking out at the BMW from the window of the hall. She shifted to make her collarbone grate, so the stabbing pain would take her feelings.

'C'mon,' he said. 'Ballpark.'

'About sixty?' she answered from her pain, anaesthetised.

'Nice guess,' said his distant voice. 'I'm impressed.'

'Was I right?'

'Almost! It was sixty-four three-fifty. It's a very high-spec vehicle. Alex had a hundred with him.'

She imagined Alex, freed up by alcohol, telling Russ all about his hotel in the bar – she couldn't remember the name of the bar. She couldn't remember where the police had said it was. Oyonnax. The Bar Jeanne. In Oyonnax. Or Justine. Alex would talk, trying to impress Russ with his hotel, and how Griff had sent him on a secret mission. She shifted her feet on the carpet. She felt the lightness of the empty plastic bottle in her hand. She went back to her pain.

Cars passed with faces in the windows. They could not see her behind the tinted glass.

'You know we can't relax yet, right?' he said.

'What?'

'We've got to get clear first.'

He examined the satnav on his phone, held down beside the seat, so she couldn't see. It seemed pathetic to her, as if she had any way to stop him. He must feel very weak.

'Almost there,' he said.

She drifted. She saw the BMW on the road from high above, one car, zigzagging on the network of roads, and then all the other thousands and millions of cars, ants in a maze, blind and intent. She saw Alex, driving back from Switzerland. She saw herself and Dan, waiting to meet the police outside the Hotel Paligny. Sitting on the steps.

The sun was low in the sky behind the car. It cast golden light onto the rising slopes. The road climbed and curved ahead into the Jura.

'I'd like to see more of the Alps,' Russ said.

On either side of the road, tidy houses like children's models were dotted over the foothills of the mountains, and thick pine forests crowded the ridges, and poured in swathes down the empty slopes. The grass was very short, everywhere, like AstroTurf. The land grew wider and bigger. Mist gathered on the high ground to their left and the narrow roads wound on and climbed up into the mountains. Bea had begun to shiver, her joints stiffened around their damage. She felt sleepy.

'Your brother told me about you,' he said. 'He said his sister was *amazing*. And a shrink. I said, that's hard to believe, a good shrink.'

'I'm not one,' she said with her eyes closed.

'Good to know. Shrinks are assholes.'

That's true, Bea thought, she'd never met a psychiatrist she liked.

'Be cool to be one, though, right?' he said. 'Right? Sticking those labels on you. Schizophrenia. Psycho-affective disorder. Psychosis. Dissociative disorder. Narcissistic personality disorder. Borderline personality disorder.'

She opened her eyes and tested the nerveless fingers of her right hand,

'– on the border,' he was saying. '*You've got one foot in Mexico. You could still make it home.* Want to know my personal favourite?'

He waited.

'Want to know?' he asked again, taking his eyes from the road. '*Dysfunctional*. This is a *dysfunctional* relationship. You have a *dysfunctional* family.' He looked at her.

'So?' she said.

'So? Functioning is a *basic*, Beatrice. Functioning is the bottom fucking line. Even the toilet at your brother's fake hotel over there *functions* –'

He laughed. He was on a roll. He was free-falling, loving the sound of himself. She didn't listen. She let her head fall against the door frame. She watched the reflections on the glass. She pictured Dan, lying beaten on the grass, by the hotel. She imagined the police finding him. The car swerved and lurched, in a rhythm.

'It *borderline* functions, anyhow. Assholes –'

He stopped talking. Or else she couldn't hear him. Her swelling eye was closing. She heard a rattle. It was a familiar sound, but she couldn't place it. She opened her eyes and saw his hand in front of her, holding a plastic pill bottle.

'You want something?' He rattled it again. 'I said, you want something?'

'No.'

'Make it easier on you.'

'No.'

'It's your call. Your brother *loved* his pills, didn't he?' He whistled. 'Said he wasn't drinking then he drank. Said he wasn't taking pills then he took them. You know I didn't meet him in Paris, right? I lied, I'm sorry. I've never been to Paris. I met him in a bar. Not far from here, in fact –'

'What are you going to do?' she asked, to stop him talking about that. She didn't want to know.

'After this? Move on. New car. I'll be sorry to lose this one,' he said. 'But hey, get another, right?'

428

He laughed out loud with the sudden realisation of his good fortune.

'My *God*,' he said, 'I don't even want to *look*. How much is in there? It's like a fucking *dream*. A *dream*! It's like it was *meant*, running into Alex. Real out-of-the-way place, too. It was just totally random.'

The pieces she had seen were fragments. She saw them now. The components of the instrument of her brother's destruction, the guilty acts and sins that had brought Alex to that place, on that night, she saw them. Her mother's years and years of sin, her weak hands holding on to him. The way her father risked and denigrated him. Drugs. His own helpless, guileless faith. And that he had no space to live beyond survival. None of these had been the thing to kill him, but they played their part. She saw her own cowardice, her awkward, respectful efforts. The picture shifted and dissolved. Pieces revealed themselves and receded, and then came back to nothing. London. France. Her father's lies and bank accounts, the names in the notebooks and provincial policemen, sifting through logical truths and family quarrels; bureaucracy, rules, established procedure, evaporated, at the whim of one man's anarchy. Roaming, mindless, seeking power, he'd seen his little chance and taken it, and all established evil, all efforts at good, were nothing. She saw the pieces. Each one had its share of blame. The whole had been unknowable.

'I'm blessed,' he was saying. 'Blessed. I mean, I didn't even know the guy. What are the chances?'

She couldn't answer, or try to please him. She refused to try. He sighed. He tapped the steering wheel. Then without warning, he pulled the car over, and stopped, abruptly, in a lay-by.

It was more frightening, now the car had stopped. She tried not to flinch from him, but he seemed to have forgotten her. He sat with the engine idling, ignoring her. She rested her head on the window as he, totally concentrated, set up the sound system, and scrolled through music. He found some country rock, a thin voice singing something about the flag and coming home.

'Yeah, it's cheesy, but it's good to drive to. Maybe I do miss the States, you know? Greatest country in the world. The *greatest*. Can't go back now. Nope. Maybe never. I could tell you about *that*.'

He pulled out and started off again, onto the narrow ribbon of a road.

She couldn't see any other cars now. Her mind dipped in and out, like lying down in snow. The pulse throbbed in her bruises. She imagined her blood crowding in, her cells, rallying to heal. She closed her eyes.

She opened them. And then it was twilight, and the pine forests were closer to the car. She licked her lips and dislodged a scab. She could see a gorge to one side, and ribbed, streaky rock dropping away to invisible ravines.

'Almost there,' he said. 'Almost. Jesus. Another campsite. Every place in the whole of this goddamn country. OK, this is good, this is good, right here.'

They turned. The car bumped, slowly, up a hill. She pictured the metal tyre iron, lying on the back seat. She imagined herself reaching into the back, and the feel of holding it in her hand. She couldn't reach it with her broken arm. She couldn't turn to look. And she had no rage. She didn't think she'd do it even if she could. She was wounded enough for both of them.

'Into the wilderness,' he said.

The pine trees thinned, and she could see long slopes going downwards, and no houses, not one, and no lights. She was far from help. She couldn't fight. She had to not think about it, that he was taking her somewhere nobody would see him. All she could do was not give way. All she had was that. She needed to be able to think. But she couldn't think, her mind kept failing her, and knowing that it was failing was desperate, and made her want to cry.

'Just up here?' he said, like looking for a picnic spot.

The car crawled then surged and crawled again, on rocks and into potholes. Nausea hit her like a punch, and waves of pain, and sudden sweat. She closed her eyes and dreamed of seabirds, soaring and white above a choppy sea. She heard kindly voices, talking, in another room. Up here, they said, just look, it's beautiful. She heard him whoop. A crass sound. A cowboy sound. She opened her eyes.

'Fuckin' yeah,' he said. 'This. Is. Perfect.'

The car stopped. He turned the music off. In the sudden quiet her blood rushed, and she felt terror, and a sad longing to be safe.

'Where's Dan?' she asked. She whispered it.

He turned the engine off.

'Let me help you.'

He got out of the car. The fresh chill of altitude blew over her, and the smell of the pine trees. He opened her door.

'Careful,' he said, standing above her. 'You look like shit. No offence.'

He watched her haul herself up, holding on to the door. Her head fell forward.

'Over here,' he said, snapping his fingers at her.

She leaned on the car. She looked around. It was almost night. There was nothing, just the line of pines across the short grass, which was almost invisible now, and rocks, and the smell of the mountains. Below them, she could just see the track they had driven up, curving out of sight. On the other side of the track was big, dark forest.

'Look at that,' he said, surprised. 'Your shoulder. Your bone. Shit. When did you do that?'

'When I fell.'

'Huh. OK. It's good you're here.' He went to the back of the car and opened the boot. 'Must've dropped it. Damn.'

She didn't know what he meant. His words fell out, incontinent, his only company. He shut the boot and rubbed his hands back and forth over his skull, and laughed ruefully.

'Rookie move.'

Bea rested, taking in the space around it, and how far it was to the trees. The pain in the right side of her head was louder. It was cacophonous, and hard to connect to anything beyond it. Russ leaned into the car, and pulled the snake trap from the back seat. He tested the weight of it, pleased.

'Hell yeah,' he said, then took it to the back of the car and tried to cram it into the boot, but it wouldn't fit.

Seeming to remember something, he put the trap onto the ground, carefully, and rested his foot on it, as if it would run away. He reached into the boot, groping.

'Got it.' His hand emerged with a black spotlight torch.

He switched it on and put it down next to the trap. The beam shone haphazardly onto the car wheel. In the almost-dark, he leaned into the shadow of the boot, and began to haul and pull at something.

She knew what he was doing. She couldn't see, but she knew – from the way his arms moved, and the way he was bending to see inside. It was intimate.

The ground was cloudlike as she began to walk, and there was a noise like water rushing. He leaned into the boot of the car, straining and tugging. She saw Dan's hand, loosely hanging, then his arm, over the rim of the boot. Russ bent his knees, out of sight for a second, then straightened, with an effort. He had his arms around Dan's torso, and Dan's arm hung near the parking light, his hand illuminated by the red glow.

'Dan?' she said.

Russ strained, and took a half-step back. He dragged Dan out, clumsily, over the sill, and dumped him on the ground, heavy, curled up, like an embryo, facing away from her. His T-shirt had ridden up to show the skin at the small of his back. Russ stepped away.

Dan didn't move. His knees were bent. His feet, in their trainers, lay one on top of the other, quite neatly.

'Dan?'

It was three steps to reach him, then she knelt. His hand lay palm upwards, the arm bent back awkwardly. His head was in darkness, facing away. She couldn't see his face. She touched the crease of his palm with the tip of her finger. His fingers didn't move.

'Dan?' she whispered.

She heard Russ start talking, somewhere. She touched Dan's shoulder. He didn't respond. She tugged, one-handed, and his upper body rolled. His head fell towards her, and his cheek hit the ground. His eyes were open but not looking. She touched his cheek. It was warm. She touched his mouth. Her fingers rested on his lips but she felt no breath, and his eyes stayed open, shining. She touched his neck, no rise or fall, no pulse, no flicker on the skin. His fixed eyes didn't blink.

'Dan?'

She couldn't look at his eyes. Slowly, she moved her hand, along his cheek, under his ear, to the back of his neck. Her hand knew the feeling of his dense, soft skin, and the shaved-close touch of his hair, and how the gradual fade went softer over the base of his skull, and the roundness of his head. Her fingers felt their way, but there was no smooth dome. She felt the bone give way to breakage, pulp, then nothing, touching the ground where the ground shouldn't be, and wetness. She felt the jagged splinter of his skull and pulled her hand away. Her breath was quick, then panting, her body jerking at each breath, and she couldn't stop. Without wanting it, she looked back to Dan's blind eyes. Then there was no sound, not even pain, just silence.

Slowly, she straightened up. Unaware of herself, she travelled him. The dip above his collarbones, the ribbed neck of his T-shirt, the rest of it, hoisted up, his bare stomach, his belt buckle, the denim of his jeans, and a big, blackish stain, which must be blood. His legs looked uncomfortable, knees bent and feet side by side, neat. She could see the soles of his trainers, the rubber treads on them, impossibly exposed. She looked down, at his hand again, and how still it was. She wiped her fingers on the grass and pulled his T-shirt down over his stomach as well as she could. She put her hand over his eyes. She had the idea she could hide the horror from him. He didn't seem to have left his body, but his body was dead. It was him and not him. Terrible. Horror. She could not take her eyes off him. His corpse. She could not take her eyes off his corpse. She smelled cigarette smoke, drifting.

'OK, now,' said Russ. 'Get over.'

He pushed her and she fell onto her side. From the ground, her eyes stared at Dan's dead eyes, a foot away. Then his head jerked. She watched it slide, in increments, away, out of her eyeline, as Russ dragged his body. She stayed staring at the empty place. This was their end. Like a marriage, like a birth, this was their end. This. There wasn't more. Russ was pulling him away from her, into the dark. She lay and stared at the ground where his body had lain.

The greys and browns of the earth and trees were vague and fuzzy in the night. She heard the rustling cracking sound of twigs and Russ's steps and the corpse, dragged up the hill towards the treeline. The sound grew quieter. She tried to get up to crawl, but she couldn't use her broken arm to take her weight. Slowly, she got to her feet, and stumbling, walked to the car.

The doors were closed. The car looked dark and uninhabited. Her body began shaking, uncontrollably. She was freezing cold, juddering. She stood trying to control her shaking body, knowing Russ was coming back. It was as if he were still next to her, talking. But he wasn't. She was alone. She tried the car door but it was locked. Her body stopped shaking and she turned her head. Her interrupted vision drifted slowly, adjusting to the distance, towards the place that he had gone. Night had almost fallen, and it was dark towards the trees. She could see the beam of his torch, uneven, and his silhouette.

She was alone and free. Her pain had gone. Quickly, she looked around. The cold air moved across her face, her body faded into insignificance in the open night. Without hesitating, she turned down the hill, and started towards the track she knew was just ahead. Beyond it was the forest. She began to run, feeling nothing. She focused on staying upright, holding her right arm across her body, to keep it as still as she could.

She was running. She thought she was. Quickly. Across the grass, the track, the dried earth. Her foot hit a rock and she stumbled badly. Halted, she listened for him behind her, but could only hear her breath. She ran on, painless, disconnected, all she knew was running. The trees were very black in the spaces in between. They looked like refuge. She fixed her eyes on the black spaces, imagining hiding in them, hearing her feet patter on the ground. She ran on, warm and weightless. She would hide. He would not find her in the dark. Her mouth was open, dripping blood or saliva. She observed it from far away, going on, running, thinking she was running. It occurred to her she might be dreaming because she had no pain. She might still be in the car or kneeling on the ground. She heard nothing. She felt nothing, just the air on her face.

And then she reached the trees. She stopped, because she was too out of breath to go any further. Her vision blackened, opening and closing like shutters banging in her head. The woods and the horizon and the sky tipped and tilted and spun. She put her hand out to break her fall, but it wasn't the ground under her hand, it was the trunk of a tree. She held on to it. Getting her balance, she walked into the woods.

She walked through the trees, and their presence was like company. She was among them, like stepping into a crowded cave; no, higher than that, a huge hall, filled with silent guardians, waiting for her. She heard a wind, like whispering voices, far above her, and slippery pine needles beneath her feet. She couldn't see. She held her arms out, to feel her way, groping, blind. Her breath rattled and the pain came back, and awful terror. She summoned all her courage, and held it tight, imagining the thousands and thousands of trees around her, solemn in the dark. She felt bark under her hands. She felt her way along, and around a massive trunk, and then there was a space, just nothing, and then another tree, under her fingers, and she put the flat of her hand on it, and went to it. The branches creaked. She took a step, and then one more, sensing them allowing her through, still and watching. After each step she asked her body to take one more, but the steps got smaller and her mind failed. She tried to fall slowly but it was a long way.

Her face rested on the ground. She thought it was the ground. She felt the resin-smelling pine needles and the sandy earth. She heard an owl, and for a moment remembered the bedroom at Paligny, and listening to the owls outside in the night, hunting for mice. It seemed so long ago. She would try to crawl. She stretched her hand out into the darkness and felt roots going into the ground. Her fingers moved over them, like raised letters she couldn't decipher, but it was only her hand that moved, her body was still. Her hair lay on the pine needles. She knew that there were snakes nearby. She could sense them in the dark. The owls were high above her in the sky, gliding as they hunted. They were hanging in the air, and looking down on the sandy ground and the hard roots, on the pine needles, and the snakes in curls, and small flowers studding the dark earth. They saw the gentle mice and the blameless snakes, and they saw her.

She thought of the white folded paper, left on the ground, unread, and all her rage, forgotten. She thought that when she saw Dan again and they were travelling together she'd tell him that she didn't need to be worth more than gold. She would tell him all her truths and trust him to hear her. Then she remembered she would not see Dan again, and that he'd gone. And there would be no baby. It was not for her.

She couldn't feel anything under her fingers now. Her hand slipped and rested. She turned her head, weightlessly, and looked up to the invisible sky. She was smaller and smaller, she was diminished, dissolving, quiet. She was only her eyes, and her eyes saw moonlight, shining high above her, the furthest, smallest gleam of it, touching the tallest of the trees. Acutely, cleanly, perfectly, she felt the kindness of the night surround her. She had nothing. She was nothing and content to be.

She didn't hear Russ coming for her, so she wasn't frightened. And she didn't know how easily he found her, across the track, on the empty ground before the edge of the forest, just a short walk from the car. But she saw the sweeping torchlight, silvery and bright. Inside her head were worlds as big as oceans. She gave herself up to them, and her death was nothing to her, because she was not there.

Acknowledgements

There is the very long time alone with a story, and then there are the people who turn it from private to public. Thank you to Clara Farmer, whose unique talent makes books more themselves. Thanks to Caroline Wood, who is both reader and champion, and to Rachel Cugnoni and Richard Cable. Many thanks to Suzanne Dean and Lily Richards, for the cover design, and to Harriet Dobson, Fran Owen and Sophie Mitchell – not least for their patience.

I am lucky to have Terry Karten's insight and faith, and many thanks also to Stephanie Cabot and Jonathan Burnham.

Dr Charlotte Harris helped me enormously with the research into French criminal procedure. Any inaccuracies were made either in error, for which I apologise, or to suit my story, for which I can't.